# IRIS WILDTHYME
# OF MARS

## Edited by Philip Purser-Hallard

Obverse Books
Cover Art © Paul Hanley
Cover Design © Cody Quijano-Schell
First published October 2014

**THE CHANGING FACE OF IRIS WILDTHYME**
The cover illustration and others contained within this book portray the
fourth IRIS WILDTHYME, whose physical appearance was later altered by
the Clockwork canons after they caught her flogging fake exercise videos.

*To Ma[g]rs...*

# More Iris Wildthyme
# from Obverse Books

# CONTENTS

# WANDERING STARS
## Ian Potter

*In the beginning something very definitely happened and it set the Universe we know now in motion. It had something to do with Chaos. Unfortunately, no one was taking notes at the time so accounts are a bit muddled. Still, that's Chaos for you. Whatever it was that happened may well have involved Tethys, the daughter of Gaia. No one's too sure anymore. It might have been Tethys' daughter Eurynome who did it, or maybe even grandma Gaia herself. Even the great Olympian gods themselves are hazy about those earliest, unordered days before great Zeus did whatever he did to Kronos that made time run wild and free. Their family trees are particularly knotty in those first times, and they have a nagging suspicion they've forgotten some of the more tangled bits with good reason.*

*Whoever was responsible it happened and Order emerged from the darkness, more or less. The Cosmos somehow gathered itself together, hooked itself onto rules and pulled itself out of the whirling, inchoate primal maelstrom. It arranged itself into the harmonious, regulated form we know now, in which we all play our roles, wheeling in stately dance about our neighbours, and only very occasionally bumping into each other disastrously.*

Somewhere barely imaginable, a red double-decker bus was falling, spiralling implausibly through one of those suitcase dimensions we keep tightly pressed together to avoid seeing such things.

Inside the bus were a statuesque woman made of meat and attitude and a tiny toy panda made of stuffing and thwarted ambitions. They were both far too drunk to be in charge of a dimension-smashing Routemaster.

"I found a corkscrew, Iris!" the panda cried out triumphantly, brandishing a bottle-opener in a remarkably flexible paw.

"So, did I, I'm afraid!" the woman called back from the driver's cab. She was wrestling with the vehicle's controls to no avail, her long purple rubber gloves squeaking against the spinning steering wheel.

"Why 'afraid'?" the panda asked.

"Because it's a corkscrew in reality, Panda," the woman said grimly, pulling her ringlets from her eyes.

Panda stared her through glassy eyes. "Well, so's this," he sighed. "There's not a lot of point in an unreal corkscrew, is there?"

The bus shuddered and shook as an unexpected shockwave of consequences smashed into it. The impact flipped Panda off his feet and sent him flying under the stairs.

"Brace yourself!" Iris hollered, slightly later than might have helped.

Panda extricated himself carefully from the mess he'd landed in – a tangle of over-complicated underwear and cables that might come in handy one day.

"Your corkscrew's different to mine, isn't it?" he said, pulling SCART leads from around his neck and wisps of satin from his limbs.

Iris nodded. "It's a helical breach in the Thingummy, Panda."

"Oh, another?" said Panda as nonchalantly as he could while he examined his seams for tearing.

A negated cause slammed hard against the side of the bus and set all the lampshades swinging madly.

Iris squealed as the bus lurched and creaked. "We're at a bottleneck of realities... and I think we're about to be decanted!" she yelled.

With a bone-rattling vibration the bus unpeeled. A swirling gap in geometry opened up inside everything and wrenched it in unexpected directions. Space bubbled and twisted. Scatter cushions went everywhere.

Iris howled. "Hold on, Panda! We're going in!"

Panda caught sight of her face in the driver's mirror as reality churned and the world bent around him. She was grinning from ear to ear.

The travellers spaghettified, flipped into and through themselves and then with a terrible crunch popped back into something approaching their old forms and normal Space.

They'd hardly time to express their relief before the bus smashed hard into something even bigger and redder than it was. A huge ball of fire filled the windscreen and the bus slammed straight into it. It skidded and careened over the surface of the sphere, tyres smoking until Iris finally gave up trying to steer and it came to a halt, surrounded by tall red flames. The bus' request stop bell chimed and a moment later the windscreen wipers kicked in.

"All change," said Iris groggily.

Panda checked himself over for damage. Surprised to find everything intact, he checked the arm he'd been checking with too. He wanted to be sure it wasn't just a phantom limb spectrally reassuring him about other equally lost bits of him. It appeared to be as present as the rest of him. He was either wholly there or wholly ghost.

He decided to seek a second opinion. "Are we alright?" he asked.

Iris scanned a series of diagnostic displays on the dashboard.

"I'm not sure, we are," she answered. "I think we may have done something to causality. Unpicked it a bit. We've lost FM radio."

Panda didn't like the sound of that at all. "Do you think anyone will mind?" he said. "About the causality, not the wireless."

"Well, no one living inside causality should, should they? They'll just assume everything was always the way it is now, I expect."

The windscreen wipers clicked off and the bus lights flickered and dimmed. Iris flipped a series of switches to no noticeable effect.

"We're losing power, Panda. Electrics failing. I think we've ended up in one of those realities where things work differently. Possibly a pre-Galvanic parallel." One by one the lights all went out. The bus was now only illuminated by the glow of the fireball outside.

"What are we going to do?"

Iris turned to face her companion as soberly as she could manage. "I think we'll have to drink what's left in the fridge before it overheats," she said.

They shared a bottle of white wine quietly, watching the flames lick around the bus exterior.

"It looks like a rosé in this light, doesn't it?" said Panda.

Iris nodded and Panda loosened his cravat. For some reason Iris didn't seem to be feeling the heat as much as he did. Admittedly, he was covered in fur but she was sweating a lot less than you'd expect for someone clad in impractical clingy rubber.

Panda surveyed the world beyond the bus windows. There was nothing but a curtain of red flame all around. Up on the top deck of the bus, he could just make out a dark sky above the fire and a slightly curved horizon that he suspected might lead boffins to class this ball of flame as planetoid rather than a planet, but heat haze made it impossible to pick out anything more than that.

An idle thought occurred. "Iris? You don't think we're in one of those realities where vehicles suddenly explode for no good reason?" Panda had recently been watching a lot of old Glen A Larson TV shows for medical reasons.

"That's a point. We might be. We should probably look at not being on the bus if we are." She put down her wine glass. "I'll pop out – see if there's anywhere less explodey nearby."

"Is there even air out there?" said Panda. "I'm not sure we have spacesuits handy."

"There's flame isn't there?" Iris tutted. "No flame without an atmosphere."

Panda was an arts specialist, which was sometimes quite useful in curious adventures across Space and Time, but often meant Iris had to explain any science bits they accidentally got involved with.

Iris flipped off her driving stilettoes and searched around for something more impractical. She strapped herself into a pair of towering platform boots, teetered to the door and stepped out into the flames. She hopped back a second later, the ends of her lacquered hair crispy.

"We're in trouble, Panda. Even my tallest asbestos soles can't handle that fire. There's only one way out."

Iris dived into the mound of discarded pants and wiring beneath the stairs.

Panda looked on, bemused. "What are you doing?"

"Improvising, Panda. Improvising."

A short while later, Iris and Panda stood on the hot metal roof of the bus, their arms full of copper cable and sleek fabrics. Iris had fashioned them a pair of matching parachutes out of lashed-together leads and old lingerie.

Panda hopped from foot to foot to keep cool.

"Stop prancing around and open up your pantychute!" Iris scolded. "If you fill it with hot air the thermals will lift you up and clear." She paused for a moment, then added, "You know, I don't normally have any thermals in my underwear."

Panda looked around to see who Iris thought she was wisecracking to. There was no one else there. He sighed and unrolled his bundled patchwork parachute over the side of the bus. Slowly, the stitched together masses of nylon, satin and silk bloomed. Panda briefly considered doing a "bloomers" joke but stopped himself when he recalled how odd Iris' quip to had seemed.

The wires in the travellers' hands slowly tightened as their exotic parachutes filled and rose, then Panda felt a tug at his shoulder joints as he skipped from foot to foot to avoid scalding. His left leg missed the roof, then his right, he felt his foot pads cool slightly. He was airborne! He and Iris were floating up above the bus and away from the fireball that surrounded it.

As they flew higher, away from the heat haze and the glow of the flames, they began to make out the stars.

"Iris," Panda called out, as he swung from under her pants, "I recognise the constellations."

"Yes," Iris shouted back. "So do I!"

The familiar shape of Orion loomed up above them, but, for the first time Panda could recall, it didn't just like a bunch of dots in the sky. It looked exactly a mighty hunter with a very flashy belt as well. Even the most creative arts specialists tended to struggle to see that.

"I think I know where we are," said Iris, swinging closer to Panda on a web of corset lacing and din leads. "We've entered into Greek Space."

This time Panda couldn't resist the gag. "Not for the first time either," he said tartly.

"I don't know what you mean!" Iris replied, with the kind of indignation that strongly implied she did.

"You do too!" Panda protested. "The walls were paper thin in that hotel. I could hear that matelot's every grunt."

Iris tutted. "You're a very rude Panda who should learn how to block his fluffy ears. That's not what Greek Space means at all, and you know it. Greek Space is the dimension where travelling and metaphor are one and the same thing. Travelling is a metaphor for metaphor and metaphor is the same thing as travelling here."

"Oh, we're always ruddy going there," said Panda as he swung away on his elasticated swing.

Panda took in the sweep of the heavens. He'd never seen the stars so bright and so very like the things they were meant to look like in mythology. It was an odd super-imposition, science and folklore co-existing without quibble. It was, he imagined, something clever to do with metaphor.

"Yes, but here it's all Greek, you see," said Iris. "All around us are the fixed stars of the firmament – simultaneously celestial bodies stuck to the outer shell of the Cosmos and a bunch of heroes and so forth made into dot-to-dot puzzles. Been a while since I was last here."

As Iris spoke, Panda noticed something odd happening to Orion. A vast curved shadow was beginning to creep up his legs, obscuring his starry calves, and blunting the end of his great sword. Iris kept talking.

"We're in the one of the inner aetheric spheres, I think. That red fire ball we crashed into will have been Pyroeis. It's one of the Planetoi, one of the wandering stars that don't behave properly and swing around all over the shop."

"Pyroeis?" Panda, rolled the word around his mouth as if it were gum disease.

"Yes. It's Mars, as was, well, as is here. Or, more properly, Ares. It's his wandering star."

"So that's Mars below us?"

"In a very Greek and metaphorical sense, yes."

"So, if that's Mars there, what's that up there above us?" Panda pointed to the darkness that was increasingly obscuring Orion. It was disc shaped and expanding all the time.

Iris squinted. The disc grew. Soon details began to appear in the dark, glowing dimly like dying coals in the reflected red light of Pyroeis. It had a texture to it, a landscape, the glint of water. Finally, Iris recognised it.

"That? It's the Earth. Look – there's the Gulf of Salonika where we got that Ouzo that time, and that's Thessaly where we had that funny pie with that witch lady."

Panda shifted uneasily in his cradle of lingerie. "It's a bit bloody big, isn't it?"

The disc of the Earth now filled much of the sky.

"No," said Iris blithely, "it's pretty much always this size. It's more a question of proximity, really..." She trailed off. "You know, it really shouldn't be that close, Panda. I know these wandering stars wander, but not usually this far."

A sickening crunch filled the air, then a tinkling like thousands of tiny bells. The sky ahead of them cracked like ice on a pond, stress lines coursing through it. Then suddenly it was falling in tiny pieces. There was a hole in the space between the fireball and the Earth, which suddenly stood out more clearly in the darkness. Wild roaring winds rushed through the gap, buffeting the travellers' parachutes. Panda and Iris shielded their eyes as shards of crystal slashed into the silks that supported them.

"We've broken our aetheric shell. This is ruining my scanties!" Iris shouted, her parachute swirling madly in the maelstrom. "This star's out of control! We're falling into the Sublunary sphere!"

"Oh. I imagine that's quite bad," Panda called back as his parachute flipped over.

The Earth filled the whole sky now. Glowing red in the reflected light of the rogue star, a mountain pinnacle loomed forwards through the gap in the aether.

"We're going to hit that, aren't we?" Panda yelled.

"Very probably!" Iris called back. "Time for a change, I think!" Iris called. She untangled herself from the knot of suspender straps and jack leads that attached her to her 'chute and let herself drop, falling into the arms of Earth's gravity.

Panda sighed then followed suit. He felt a wave of fabric-singeing heat as he dropped and the huge flaming mass of Pyroeis roared past above them. The star snatched up their discarded parachutes in its wake, igniting them in an eye-blink.

Panda counted his blessings. He found he had fewer than he'd hoped. He'd avoided being incinerated by a colossal ball of fire, but he was now falling towards the hard, cruel rocks of a rugged mountainside at what he dimly recalled was called terminal velocity, with a colossal ball of fire close behind him.

A sound like thunder filled the air as Pyroeis smashed into the mountain, sending huge rocks cascading down its slopes and skimming over the peak like a pebble shot across a lake. The rogue star spun off back into the aether, smashing another hole in the sky as it sped away.

The world slowly darkened as the fireball sailed away and, as he dropped through the air, Panda decided a recount of blessings was in order. He was still quite low on them. On the plus side, he was no longer being pursued by a huge fireball as he fell towards the rocks below, but on the minus side he was still falling towards them.

As Pyroeis span off, the glow it had cast on the mountain-side faded away, plunging it into darkness. Panda decided that could charitably be classed as a second blessing. He could no longer see the ground racing to meet him. All he could rely on now was sound. He let the roar of the wind and the rumble of debris rolling down the mountainside wash over him as he plummeted unstoppably through the darkness towards oblivion, and tried and failed to look on the bright side.

Panda awoke to find himself bathed in white light. He felt numb, cold and weightless. All he could see was blinding white.

"Are you there, Iris?" he called out. His voice didn't seem to carry properly. "Is there even a there, here?" he added. The sound felt like it was more in his head than outside it.

"Yes, and of course there is!" a familiar voice replied. "How would I be in it, if it wasn't?"

It was Iris! Her voice was strangely muffled and it was hard to discern where precisely it had come from. Panda tried turning to look for her, but found something was stopping him from moving.

"Where are we?" he asked.

"We're on Olympos – the home of the gods."

"Oh. Are we dead?"

"No more than usual, I don't think."

"But I can't see anything! Is the gods' palace beyond the perception of mere mortal eyes?"

"I wouldn't know. It's a bit chintzy, as I recall," said Iris dismissively. "I think you not being able to see has more to do with us being buried in snow. Pyroeis caused quite an avalanche when it knocked into the mountain last night. Probably saved our lives."

Panda thought for a moment. "Do you have any ideas for getting out, Iris?"

"No, but it's daytime now," she said brightly. "I'm hoping this might melt if we wait long enough."

As she spoke, a shadow fell across the whiteness. A moment later, with a hiss like an espresso machine, rosy fingers cut through the snow above Panda's head, reached down and pulled him up into daylight.

Panda's eyes struggled to adjust. Under the bluest sky he had ever seen stood a young woman in a saffron-yellow dress with a very daft hat and quite impressive wings.

"Are you still there, Panda?" said a voice somewhere beneath them.

The woman in yellow crouched down, and started digging, her pink fingers slicing at the ground, carving a furrow in the snow. As Panda watched she burrowed down at incredible speed, her downy white feathers moving like huge windscreen wipers mounding the snow behind her.

Within seconds she'd hit a layer of impractical, polyvinyl clothing and exposed the woman they barely covered. Iris looked up at her and smiled.

"Is that you, our Dawn?"

The winged woman beamed sunnily back.

"Thought so! I'd recognise those cuticles, anywhere."

Panda was confused. "Are you two related?"

"Metaphorically, at the very least," said Iris. "It's complicated. This is Eos, goddess of the dawn."

Awkward greetings were exchanged. Panda never quite knew what to say to gods.

"So, what's going on with Pyroeis, Eos?" said Iris, enjoying bouncing her lips around the vowels. "it's completely out of control."

"It's Ares," sighed Eos. "He's got himself in a bit of a tizz over his sister.

"He's inflamed by lust again, and that's sent his star even more off kilter than normal. It's breaking out of its usual sphere, chasing after her star all the time. It's smashing great holes in everything, bashing into Olympos and raining fire down on the Earth. It's terrible. We've all tried to reason with him but we can't get past his hangers-on."

"Hangers-on?" said Iris, instinctively addressing the least interesting aspect of the situation.

"Yes – Phobos and Deimos, they're always at his shoulder whispering, making him suspicious. You know how he gets."

Iris smiled "Oh, yes!"

Panda raised a paw. "Hang on... Ares is inflamed by lust for his sister?"

Iris rolled her eyes. "She's Aphrodite, goddess of love, Panda. You've seen the paintings. She's quite a looker."

"I know, but..."

"Gods get it on together. They always have. That's how we get to have more gods. You live forever under the same roof as the perfect embodiment of desire, and these things happen."

"And when you're a god it's hard to meet people you feel are on your level," added Eos sadly. "Poor Zeus has to dress up as animals to get any spice out of interacting with lesser beings, these days."

"I imagine it puts people at ease too," said Iris. "Meeting the father of the gods is a big thing. You're probably a bit more relaxed if you think he's just a friendly bull."

Panda opened his mouth to express disproval, then stopped himself. He was a soft toy animal who'd been known to fall for human beings; his moral high ground was shaky.

"So," Iris mused. "We need to get Ares back in balance, don't we?"

"Do we?"

""Course we do, Panda. All the wandering stars live inside crystal spheres, you see. Saturn, Jupiter, Mars, the Sun, Venus, Mercury and the Moon – each sphere inside the other, floating in the aether, with the Earth at the centre."

Eos looked on, bemused, as Iris rattled off this list of unfamiliar names.

"They clatter around in their spheres, twirl about and converge and so forth but they shouldn't be breaking out of them. If we don't get Pyroeis back in its proper sphere it could destroy the very fabric of reality."

"And we've not even got any wear out of this one, yet," Panda added.

"Yes. We do seem to get through them."

"So, how are we going to get back to Pyroeis?"

Eos raised a wing tip. "You're only small," she began. "I wonder if we could persuade someone to throw you into the heavens, like Heracles did with those other two b..."

"No," said Iris firmly. "I think that only works for bears, and, as you can see, that's something neither of us are." She stared pointedly at Eos, hoping she'd not argue the point. She'd seen too many barroom brawls triggered by taxonomical disagreements, and a bloodied professor of zoology repeatedly screaming that ailuropodae were a subfamily of ursids haunted many of her worst dreams.

"Oh," said Eos, "I could try to fly you, I suppose." She flapped her wings slightly, as if to suggest she absolutely would have a go, but thought it unlikely she'd succeed.

"I don't know if that'll be necessary," said Iris. "We're in Greek Space, after all. Travel is the same as metaphor here. Pyroeis is just Ares writ big, really – 'as above, so below', and all that. If we want to influence his star, we just need to pop in on him here at home."

"And do what?" asked Panda.

"Have a chat – set him right on a thing or two."

16

"I suppose that might work," said Eos. "It's not a very godly way to do it, mind."

"I'm not an entirely godly woman," said Iris.

Eos led Iris and Panda up a secret, winding path that seemed to appear in the snow as she flapped her away above it. They trudged on behind her, noticing the path vanish behind them as they walked, until finally they turned a corner and saw the great palace of the gods nestling on the mountain peak ahead.

It was gaudier than Panda expected. The dimensions were pleasingly classical, all pillars and steps and porticos and symmetry and golden sections as you'd imagine. It was the building every Greek acropolis was a ghostly echo of. The only problem was the colour scheme – screaming reds, greens and blues all fought for your attention.

Panda nudged Iris' arm. "Who painted that?" he sneered. "The goddess of the rainbow?"

Iris didn't answer.

Eos flapped them up towards a side entrance. "Minor deities, demigods and heroes," she said apologetically. "Mind the rubble."

They stepped into a high vaulted chamber, as artfully and mysteriously lit as an ageing film star, carefully avoiding the scaffolding and safety tape around the gateway. It seemed Pyroeis had given the masonry quite a knock the night before.

Far above them, a brawny god with a hammer in his tunic belt was making good the plaster on the ceiling. Floating nearby was his supervisor, a bored-looking goddess in an extravagant safety helmet that seemed to be covered in bird droppings. She glanced down as the newcomers entered.

"Hi Iris," she said.

Iris gave a half-hearted wave back. "Athena. Hephaistos."

Panda found the familiarity uncomfortable. "You have history with these people?"

"I do now, yes. We're sort of family."

"Sort of?"

"It's a bit complicated. We have more than one history, like Batman, Western Europe and the Land of Oz. We're definitely here in the present, just as we are, but there's more than one true way we could have ended up like this."

"This way," said Eos, as if to illustrate the point. "There are a few ways to Ares' rooms but this is the quickest." They headed down a purpled marbled staircase onto a corridor lined with torches. As Eos passed by, they flared into life in turn.

Panda mused on his friend's new past. "Is it a bit like how I can almost remember a history where we haven't met yet as well as the one where we have?"

"A bit," said Iris. "I didn't know you knew about that."

Panda remembered more negated histories with Iris than she imagined, ones he fervently wished were still real.

"I think it's a bit more pronounced here with all the metaphors and such, and the cosmology and theology all sandwiched up. Easier to be more than one thing at once," said Iris.

"We'll be in such trouble if the Clockwork canons ever catch us. They hate that kind of thing," said Panda. He wasn't sure if he'd ever spoken of them before.

Iris snorted. "Pfft. What's the worst that lot can do?"

"They could exile us, I suppose – send us to a place where the dates don't make sense and force us put everything that happens there in an order they like."

Iris shuddered.

Eos suddenly stopped in front of a tall wooden door. She hovered awkwardly, like a hawk at an uncle's drinks party.

"Ares will be through there," she said. "I won't linger, if that's OK. One of my histories with him is a bit awkward, you see." Her face flushed as pink as her rosy fingers and with an embarrassed wave she flew off down the corridor.

"Does no one have a straightforward history, anymore?" sighed Panda.

"Not in Greek Space, no. And not if you were around at the beginning of time either," Iris replied.

"I don't think I can keep up with the past, these days," Panda grumbled. "If it's not new historiographic theories based on re-interpretation of existing data, it's all of reality cheating and hedging its bets."

Perhaps keen to avoid debating the issue further, Iris pushed open the great wooden door.

A booming roar of a voice thundered from the darkness. "Who dares disturb Ares, god of war?" it echoed up and down the corridor.

"It's me, Iris."

There was a moment's pause.

"Iris?" the huge voice rumbled.

"Yes, you know – Transtemporal Adventuress, goddess of the rainbow, possibly mother of Eros."

Panda felt such a fool.

"Oh, those Irises!" said the voice, warmer for a heartbeat. "You may enter," the warmth vanished, "but be warned – my wrath is great!"

"Right-oh," said Iris chirpily. "Oh, and I've brought a friend."

She stepped through the door dragging Panda behind her.

Ares was shorter than Panda had expected, and hardly anything like his statues. He was scrawny, ruddy-featured and clothed, which meant it was difficult to ascertain if his genitals were as tiny but well-groomed as they always seemed to be in museums. He also appeared to be no more than fifteen years of age. He looked more like the kind of god you'd expect to see running a Dungeons and Dragons campaign than personifying war.

The black-and-red-painted chamber he occupied was a tip. Partially-unravelled tapestries hung askew on the walls. Toppled amphora tripods and smashed chairs littered the floor. In one corner lay a bent and twisted lyre, a top a heap of scrolls. Panda suspected they were musical scores, and that they weren't being filed in strict alphabetical order.

Ares was slumped across what would once have been a well-upholstered and opulent throne, now ragged and threadbare and troublingly stained. Behind him, at either shoulder, crouched two frightful-looking young men with wild hair and awful posture. Their eyes roamed constantly and they moved in twitchy starts, clutching at their grubby tunics nervously. With a bit of grooming and a decent osteopath they might have looked presentable, but in their current state of anxiety no one would ever get close enough to prove it.

"Be careful," one whispered into Ares' ear, as Iris approached the throne.

"Watch out," hissed the other.

Iris shot them pitying looks. "It's true what they're saying about you two, then?"

The young men froze and looked uncertainly at each other.

"It's your own fault for spreading rumours about each other," added Iris.

19

Phobos and Deimos leaped at each other, fighting like cats, rolling across the throne room. Iris stepped over them and walked up to Ares.

"I hear you're having one of your tantrums," she said. "Throwing everything into disarray again. Honestly, you're as bad as your sister, Eris."

Ares pushed away Iris' hand. "Leave me alone!" he yelled.

"Why? What's upset you this time, poppet?"

"I'm in love and nobody understands!" Ares screamed. His voice was a high reedy wine. In his fury, he'd forgotten to affect his godly one.

"Ah," Iris nodded. "Ensnared by Eros! Your own son!"

"Possibly," said Ares petulantly. "He's not necessarily mine, though. Isn't he yours, sometimes?"

"I lose track," said Iris. "It's one of those early, blurry bits I don't poke at. Frankly, I'm just pleased he's never ours together." She smiled. "You get ensnared quite a lot don't you, Ares?"

Panda began to see why the Olympian gods might struggle with their family relationships. This boy here, Ares, brother of Eris, may have been a father to Eros, daughter of Iris. It'd be hard enough calling that lot into dinner, let alone working out who sat where at the table.

Iris continued. "You do know, this carrying on, chasing your sister will come to no good, don't you, Ares, lamb? It's unsettling cosmic order, you letting Pyroeis gad about like that. Love and War – It's not a good match. Look at that pair you had last time you conjoined, Fear and Loathing." She pointed to Phobos and Deimos, wrestling on the floor. "You need to calm down a bit, poppet – hold yourself in."

"But I exist to stir things up. I'm War!" protested Ares, stamping his foot less dramatically than he might have wished. "I bring change! I make things happen!"

Iris shook her head. "No, you don't. You move a few borders, make lots of people unhappy and make good soil out of young men and barren land. It's not all that, really, is it?"

Ares puffed out his cheeks indignantly.

"You're just attention seeking, really, aren't you, dear?" said Iris. She perched herself on Ares' lap. "You see, the thing is, I know there's two sides to war. It's not all victory marches and heroic deeds, is it?" She gave Ares a little wink. "I think you might be one of those gods who likes losing."

Ares' face turned purple. Panda braced himself, expecting a furious response, but for some reason the god did nothing.

"You know how we all end up with legends attached to us?" Iris cooed, curling a lock of Ares' hair between gloved fingers. "Well, the ones I remember about you are those ones where you end up being powerless and imprisoned – the ones where you get chained up in a brass jar, or get caught up in a metal net when you're making love." She giggled suddenly. "Ooh! Has this chair just changed shape, Ares? It's suddenly got a bit lumpy."

Ares didn't answer, just watched intently as Iris peeled off a long shiny rubber glove. She slid it down her arm like she'd been born watching Rita Hayworth, and held the god's gaze as she ran it up and down his face.

"I think you like the 'being defeated and enslaved' bit of war best, Ares. I think it might be your thing."

Ares jaw dropped open and as it did, Iris scrunched up her glove and popped it into his mouth.

"Consider this a treaty," she said. Ares just nodded. "This is what I'm going to do – I'm going to ensnare you with law, and you're going to enjoy not liking it. You can play kiss-chase with your sister all round the heavens for all I care, as long as you obey certain rules."

Ares moaned as Iris started to trace symbols on his chest with a fingernail.

"I'm going to make you do sums," she said. "Hard ones. From now on, your star's motions have rules that'll stop you smashing everything up. From now on, you and Aphrodite will spin about missing each other, hardly ever aligning. You'll have your moments – brief snatched occultations you'll long for for hundreds of years – but nothing more. I think, if I were an immortal who liked being thwarted and bossed about a bit, I might just enjoy that. Don't you?"

"Amd, ib I dibobeyed debe bules?" said Ares, through a mouthful of rubber.

"I know a thing or three, young man," said Iris sweetly. "I taught your sister one or two of them. There's a sweet pain I can give you and there's an unbearable one too."

"Trust me," said Panda, "she really can be an unbearable pain."

And that was how the Cosmos came not to be ripped apart.

"I wish I were immortal," said Panda a few hours later.

"Why?" asked Iris.

"No particular reason. I just think I'd enjoy all the life-and-death situations we end up in a bit more, that way."

"I think they might end up a bit duller, myself."

"It's an absence of risk I'd be prepared to accept."

They were back on the old faithful bus, waiting for a miracle.

Zeus had come to them in the form of a polecat after they'd dealt with Ares and granted them a boon for their labours. Iris had asked to be set free from the curse of metaphor and to be allowed to travel on, and Panda had asked for the same and an amphora of decent nectar. Zeus had promised to honour both wishes.

"Very well," he'd squeaked. "It doesn't travel well, though." It was, Panda presumed, some kind of metaphor.

A divine lightning bolt arced into the bus and its engine came to life.

Jump-started by the gods, the bus ripped its way back into a less-layered reality. Its wheels smoked and span as it flipped through a kaleidoscope of oily potentialities, and out into a Space where you'd struggle to see heroes mapped out in the skies.

The Great Bear raised a paw in farewell as it faded to points of light. Panda pretended not to see.

As the bus sped across the asteroid belt and between the icy rings of Saturn the FM radio kicked in. It was playing Pat Benatar's "Love is a Battlefield".

"You know," said Iris eventually, "it's a much worse song without all the dialogue bits from the promo film."

Panda agreed.

"Iris, if everything was a metaphor in Greek Space...," Panda began.

"Then some of the things that happened there were more about us than about where we were, yes."

"Both of us knowing," Pat Benatar sang.

In that one hanging, perfect moment Panda wanted to grab hold of Iris, kiss her and tell her just how very, very fond of her he was underneath everything. He didn't. In his little toy heart he knew he mustn't. It would be breaking the rules.

"Both of us know it," Iris sang along incorrectly.

They listened to the rest of the song in silence. Paul McCartney and Wings came on the radio next. They were singing about how Venus and Mars were alright tonight.

"I'm sorry about being noisy in that hotel, that time, Panda," said Iris, eyes ahead, steering the bus to new adventures. "It wasn't very kind."

"Think nothing of it," said Panda. "All's fair in love and war."

# LIEUT. GULLIVAR JONES: HIS BAD WEEKEND

**Daniel Tessier**

Dare I say it? Dare I admit that I, a married man, one who should have been content to live a life with his beloved, had returned to the distant world of Mars? I feel that I must, for I have a new story to tell. A second chapter of my adventure on the Red Planet, if indeed you believed the first.

I confess that, as much as I adore my dear wife Polly, I had grown restless in my life of domesticity. An extended sabbatical from the navy had left me feeling ill-utilised. I craved stimulation! I could not help but think back to my time in the world of Mars, among the fair folk I knew as Hithers. Perhaps I was romanticising my own recollections, for I recalled my time there as a great adventure, even as I was beset by difficulties at every step. But what is a life without difficulties? It is a life without excitement! And what is a life without beauty? I had seen a preponderance of beauty in the land of the Hithers.

"Alas!" I cried to myself as I sat alone on my porch, my wife away in town on her usual errands. I had only voyaged to Mars through the most unlikely and unexpected contrivance; a magical carpet that had dropped from the sky. The threadbare item had somehow heard my whimsical desire to journey to Mars, and had swept me up in its folds and taken me there!

"Alas!" again, "How I wish I had that carpet once more!" The rug was gone, I know not where, and I was grounded, rooted to this Earth as any other man. Perhaps, some day, this fine nation would voyage to the other worlds of the solar system, and our brave men would plant the Stars and Stripes in otherworldly soil, but for me, such a voyage was an impossibility.

It was with surprise and delight, then, that I saw a dark, oblong object fall from the sky at my feet. By Jove, it was the impossible rug, returned to me! Had it sensed my longing, in whatever far-off clime it had been hiding? Did this mere stretch of fabric somehow know that I required it? Such questions crossed my mind, but I quickly dismissed them. I wasted little time. I hastily packed a few essential items, wishing to be better prepared than on my previous trip, and was soon ready. I grabbed the rug by its frayed corners, I repeated my original request:

"I wish I were in the planet Mars!"

And thus it was that I came to be, once more, in Seth, the city of the fair and gentle Hithers. I lay there, after several days of sheer unadulterated pleasure and relaxation. Yellow-robed servants brought refreshments to those of higher birth, and we lounged comfortably in the faint warmth of the Martian summer. I lay, unfettered by care or chore, among the lithe bodies of Hither maidens.

I was gripped by a terrible boredom. Why, this was worse than the vacation time in New York! I had hoped for stimulation, and all I had was leisure, and what use is leisure when there is no work with which to contrast it?

I lay, disconsolate, until, at the edge of my hearing, I noticed the most singular sound. It was an engine. An engine! The first of its kind I had heard in the world of Mars. Who could possibly be working such a mechanism? The unexpected, at last! I pushed myself to my feet and hurried out of the city's southern gate in the direction of the sound. There I was greeted by the sight wholly unforeseen – a carriage!

The vehicle was, evidently, some manner of automobile, yet gross in capacity and stature. As long as a carriage and its horses taken together, its chassis was lined with windowpanes. It supported a full second storey upon its main body. Whoever had fashioned the contraption had decided to paint it the boldest shade of red, as red as the distant sandy hills that gave this planet its unmistakeable hue in the Earth's night sky. I figured that it could only be intended for mass transit of some kind, perhaps for taking troops into battle or to ferry workers, yet there was no evidence of the bustling of multiple passengers one might expect.

With a start, I noticed what, at first, I had ignored due to overfamiliarity. Upon the great vehicle's front was a sign, upon which was printed the phrase "No. 22. Putney Common." The precise details of the phrase are not the important matter – this was a sign in America's own language! A sign in English, here upon Martian soil. The only possibility was that this mighty vehicle had been constructed by someone from my own home sphere.

I cannot say how I truly felt at the prospect of another Earthman having set foot on the world I had come to think of, I confess, as my playground. My Earthly complexion and build had made me something of a novelty amongst the Hither-folk and Thither-folk alike. Still, I welcomed the promise of discourse with another of my race – of the race of Man, I speak, for an African, a Chinese, even a Frenchman would be noble company on this savage planet. And yet I confess to a little trepidation, for what if the creator of this vehicle was merely one of many Earthmen now camped on Mars? What if this were but the first of a phalanx of Earthly pioneers, each great vehicle carrying a cohort of men come to settle this world? What would become of Mars then? And what of Lieut. Gullivar Jones?

As curious Hithers clustered around the vehicle, I strode forward, beckoning them to step aside and allow me to investigate this intruder. It was as I approached the vehicle that finally, an occupant was made apparent. From the doorway strode, not an Earthman, but a human woman! And such a woman. A vision, no pale, vapid ghost but an example of true, female vitality. Beauty that put even the Hither girls to shame, honey-coloured locks spilling forth, atop a face both noble and gentle. She wore clothing that, while practical, accentuated her feminine form and gave me pause to stop and simply admire. For a brief moment, the promise of my love back home on Earth was quite gone from my mind.

The woman caught sight of me, and smiled. She spoke, in rich, strident yet feminine tones:

"Put your tongue away, love. Now, where's my bloody carpet?"

"Carpet?" I queried, as the Hither-folk began to gather round this sudden, unexpected newcomer. The young lady did her best to ignore them as they cooed and pawed at her strange, glossy garment. It was a brief moment before I realised what she could be referring to, so dumbfounded was I at her appearance here. Of course, the carpet – that very object that had led to my being in this foreign world in the first place!

"Madame," I ventured, "would you be referring to an oriental rug, about so big," – I opened my arms to indicate a rough guess at the rug's breadth – "rather tattered, depicting a chart of the heavens in its faded design?"

"That's the one, love," she replied. "I've tracked that carpet through the Very Fabric of Time and Space, to right here, right now. That carpet is my property, bought and paid for, and I want it back!"

I realised too late that I should have kept quiet about my knowledge of the thing. Clearly, I had spent too long among these Martian folk. Too many days lying in a state of sweet repose had left my wits as soft as theirs. This woman, whoever she might be, had come to claim my rug, and I had immediately spoken true my knowledge of it!

I stepped forward, extending a hand by which I took that of the young lady. Her delicate fingers were pale as snow, and soft as I pressed them to my lips.

"Madame, if I may introduce myself. I am Lieut. Gullivar Jones of the United States navy, currently on leave, and your humble servant."

"The navy?" came a plummy voice, such as that I imagined to belong to an English lord or aristocrat. "The navy are here? Don't let Iris know that, she'll be all over them, and not just for the rum."

I confess myself bemused at this point, for I knew not from where this voice originated.

"Is there another with you, my dear lady?" I ventured.

"Oh, come out of there, Panda," said the vision in yellow, directing her order to, of all things, the large bag slung over her shoulder. There was a commotion within the bag, and by all the saints, what should emerge but the black-and-white head of an oriental bear!

"Good Lord!" I cried. "It truly is a panda!"

"And what of it?" snapped the unlikely creature. "A panda has as much right to be on Mars as a human being, you know."

"Oh, give over, Panda," scolded the young woman. She returned her attention to me. "It's a pleasure to meet you, Lieutenant," she said, pronouncing it, I noticed, in the British fashion, which helped isolate her peculiar accent. Clearly she was from the same fair isle as the panda bear. "I'm Iris Wildthyme, adventuress in space and time, voyager between the dimensions, and this is Panda."

Such a sight is so incredible that I dare not ask you to believe. Yet such a sight it was, a woman and a panda bear, on the surface of the planet Mars. Indeed, I could scarcely believe it myself, but after all I had witnessed on this world, was such a thing so incredible? There is no such thing as the impossible in this universe!

"Honestly, Iris, do what do we need that grotty old carpet for anyway?" said the panda bear, clambering out from within Iris' bag and dropping softly to the ground. "It's just a bit of old tat."

"That carpet offers us a unique tactical advantage. It's a Zalbreckian travelling mat, one of only half a dozen ever woven. You have no idea how lucky we were to find one in the Hyspero market! They're extremely rare. And it was a bargain."

"Really though, Iris, an escape rug? Whatever next?" The panda bear steadied himself on the ground, whereupon he seemed to suddenly notice the lithe forms of the Hither girls who had gathered around. "I say!" he cried. "Totty!" He did not protest as he allowed himself to be picked up by two of the nimble creatures, who had by now lost all interest in the canary-clad woman in front of me.

Iris watched her chuckling companion be carried away into the crowd.

"Don't mind him, he'll have a whale of a time with that lot," she smiled. "Now, you know what my carpet looks like, so you should know where it is, too. So where is it, chuck?"

"The name is Gullivar, madame," I corrected her, "and I admit, I do know the whereabouts of your carpet. Or rather, should I say my carpet, considering that it came into my possession some time ago through perfectly fair and reasonable means."

"Really," she pouted, looking me square in the eye, not a difficult task, for this statuesque beauty easily matched me in height. "You see, after I bought that carpet at no small expense, some greasy little Hysperon snuck up and nicked it right off me. The little toad, stealing from a defenceless woman while she's sampling the local spirits."

"This thief," I asked, "was he a shabby old fellow in ragged clothes? A grey-bearded old Turk with pent-roof eyebrows?"

"That sounds like him, the little sod. Took right off with it, he did, vanishing into the aether. I saw he had dirty hands, he'd better not have marked it."

"You shall be perhaps pleased to know that the miscreant did not survive his trip. He arrived in New York State, falling near-dead at my feet. I took him to the local hospital, but there was no helping him, and I came into possession of that carpet when no one else was present to claim it."

"And how does that count as 'fair and reasonable means,' eh? Sounds like you nicked it just as much as him!"

"Because after my initial journey to this strange world, the accursed rug took me home and then vanished into thin air! It was only some time later, after I had married and recounted my tale to a publisher, that the rug showed up again upon my doorstep. Wretched thing has a mind of its own."

"It very likely does, love, knowing some of the arcane arts that went into creating it. Never mind, I'll take it off your hands and we'll say no more about it."

"You most certainly will not, madame!" I cried, and not without reason, I should think. "That carpet that you claim to own is my only means of returning to that blue-green orb we call home, and I shall not let it fall into the hand of another, no matter how fair she may be!"

"Good grief, someone likes the sound of his own voice," came a familiar, English tone. I glanced down to see the panda bear approaching.

"You can talk, Panda," snorted Iris, in a rather unladylike fashion. "Where are your fancy girls?"

"They got bored and wandered off," said he, with an ill-disguised air of disappointment.

"Already?" scoffed Iris. "Flighty lot!"

Indeed, the small crowd of Hither-folk who had previously congregated at the site of Iris' remarkable entrance had drifted back into the city during the short time she and I had been discussing the carpet's rights of ownership. This singular lack of commitment was something I was altogether too familiar with amongst the Martian folk.

"I cannot express surprise at this, madame. The Hither people are an indolent and childlike race, capable of little in the way of focussed thought or deed. The females with which your... associate has been cavorting will no doubt have found something else to distract themselves, if they have not lapsed into inactivity altogether."

"A whole culture suffering from ADHD," suggested the panda bear, but I cannot say I understood his meaning. I came to find this a common problem over the subsequent days.

Iris turned her attention back to myself, her golden locks swaying as she turned her comely head.

"Listen, Gullivar, is it? You don't have to worry. We're not going to leave you stranded on Mars for the rest of your natural. Once we've got the rug safely secured on the bus, we can give you a lift home, no problem."

"A lift home?" I repeated, not quite comprehending. "Do you mean to tell me that you can transport yourself between the worlds, in that... contraption?"

"Too right I can!" replied the young woman, a broad smile spreading across her pretty face. "That's no ordinary omnibus, you know! I can get you back to the US of A in two shakes of a rattlesnake's tail, or whatever it is you Yanks say. How about? It'll be fun!"

I confess I was tempted by the offer. The opportunity to spend more time in the company of this delectable creature was a desirable one, but nonetheless, I baulked at the thought of giving up the rug which had brought me here.

"Madame –" I began, but she cut in with a retort.

"Now, stop calling me madame. You make me sound ancient!"

"I should coco!" exclaimed the panda bear, only to be silenced by a scathing look from his mistress.

"Call me Iris," she instructed me.

"Iris," I continued, "perhaps you and I could discuss this back in the city. The Hithers, in spite of their indolence, have crafted a multitude of methods of relaxation and leisure. Why, the food and drink alone –"

"Drink?" This time it was the panda bear who interrupted. "He knows you well enough, old girl!"

I ignored the creature, although I made sure to recall this particular detail of Miss Wildthyme's predilections later.

"Iris, perhaps we should adjourn to a more comfortable location, and come to a more suitable agreement regarding the use of the rug. Surely, the conveyance of a mere ribald colonial such as myself could not be of use to a woman of such sophisticated means?"

I could see from her expression that Iris was softening to me, and considered that I might yet secure the use of my valued carpet. However, my good work was interrupted by a sudden, monstrous howl.

"Thithers!" I cried, and swung round to face the city. Three of the fair Hither-folk fled from its streets, pursued by the dark, bestial shapes of two monstrous Thithers. They had returned for another invasion! It seemed that my vacation was once more to be disrupted by the onslaught of these brutes.

"The whatters?" asked Iris, looking on at the scene.

"Thithers," I repeated. "It is the name I know them by. The Hither city has been attacked by them before. Their vicious king desires the sweet folk of this place as his own possessions. He sends raids to take all the goods and people he can carry. I battled these brutes myself on my previous visit here."

"Well, come on then!" rallied Iris, stooping to pick up her panda bear, whom she slipped back into her shoulder-bag. "Let's get in there! We can't have these buggers raiding your friends, can we?"

"Indeed not, fair lady!" I cried, recalling that, with my carpet stowed away in the city, I had no choice but to enter again should I wish to make my escape. "They must have come through the north entrance. I fear much damage may already been done!"

We raced into the city, but as I feared, we were too late. The scene around us was one of chaos. Thithers were already storming out of the north gate, their arms loaded with colourful foodstuffs and bottles. Others were manhandling Hithers, the largest of the brutes carrying a struggling waif under each arm.

To my shock, Iris whipped a pistol from her capacious carry-all. While it was unlike any I had ever seen, bulbous-ended and smooth, it was unmistakeably a firearm. She knew how to handle it, as well; a military man can always tell a skilled marksman.

"Oi, you with the hairy back!" cried this remarkable woman. "Put them down or I'll blast you to kingdom come!"

The beast ignored her, and thus Iris let loose with a volley of pink fire. What a weapon! I thought to myself. Why, if I could bring that design back to America, both the army and navy would pay handsomely for its secrets!

The flaming energy struck the brute square in the back, felling him. He dropped the two stunned Hithers upon the ground. It was too late an intervention, however. With the sudden appearance of this weapon, the invaders increased their pace, fleeing the city with great haste amongst Iris' blasts.

"What the blithering hell was all that about?" came the muffled voice of the panda bear, ensconced as he was within Iris' shoulder bag. "Who were those appalling people?"

"The Thither-folk exist in the forests of this world," I explained, more for Iris' benefit than for her pet's. "When I was here last, they invaded this peaceful kingdom and had the gall to abduct the fair princess Heru for their king's own harem. The Hithers' own ruler was as lacking in fortitude and impetus as his subjects, and it was up to me to rescue the helpless maiden from that brute's calloused hands."

31

"And quite right, too," said Iris. "Eh, I bet the princess was grateful, though, eh? Eh?" She gave me a bawdy wink quite unsuited to a young lady.

"Alas, the delicate Heru was soon married to the president-king. I stayed for only a short time after that. A second assault by the Thithers soon put paid to any notion of staying longer. As I understand it, these assaults have become a periodic horror, but the Hithers have little stomach for conflict. They merely allow these scoundrels to raid their city, and soon become distracted by their leisurely lives once they've gone."

"I don't like it," ventured Iris. "They don't seem like much more than a bunch of kids, this lot. Looks like they can hardly take care of themselves."

"The Hither lifestyle has its attractions," I confessed, "but it soon becomes tiresome. One longs for a more vital existence."

With the assistance of Iris and her diminutive companion, I assisted the frightened and wounded Hithers where I could. As I expected, however, they had soon forgotten their plight and were more concerned with their usual lethargy and merrymaking. I took the opportunity to return to my own temporary accommodation, to take stock of my own meagre possessions. It was with horror and a sinking heart that I discovered they had found my humble pile.

"Miss Wildthyme," I began, before catching myself, and continued with the more familiar, "Iris. I have heart-rending news for the both of us. The carpet is gone. The Thither band must have sequestered it and taken it with them on their retreat."

"Either that or it's wandered off again," she suggested.

"I'm afraid not, dear lady. I took precautions against such an occurrence. The carpet was affixed securely to the floor by means of some sturdy carpet-tacks. I did not wish to run the risk of being stranded on this world."

"Well, there's only one thing for it!" she cried. "We've got to get after them! You've been here before, you know the terrain, and I've got the transport and the means to track them. We can rescue those poor Hither fellas, and get my carpet back in the process."

"Your carpet?" I began, but upon seeing the look on Iris' face, deigned not to continue. I had learned, through much experience, not to argue with that look upon a woman's face.

"Very well," I agreed, "We shall follow these Martian monsters and recover what they stole. I must caution you, however, that they are known to move their bases frequently, and that they know the dense forests well. It may take some considerable time to locate them."

"Not to worry," said Iris, "we can make a road trip of it!"

"And perhaps we should take some provisions with us," interjected the panda bear, "if there are any left after that attack."

"It'll be an adventure!" cried Iris.

And I confess, my heart swelled with the thought of it.

Iris' omnibus was revealed to be quite a vehicle. Its interior was bedecked with rich fittings and luxurious upholstery, including a well-stocked drinks cabinet. The cabin was decked out with surprising equipment, sophisticated in its design and notion. I made no lie of how impressive I found the carriage – and its owner.

"Oh, give over," said Iris, her fair features rosy with the lightest of blushes.

"Oh, dear lord," interjected the panda bear, who had chosen to perch himself in the omnibus' cabin. "I'd tell you both to get a room, but this bus only has the one." He tinkered with the complex mechanisms of the vehicle in a manner that I could not fathom. Suddenly, without warning, raucous music began to play. It seemed somehow to emanate from all around us, suffusing the vehicle with its mysterious, unearthly tones.

"Ooh, Tammy Wynette! Good choice, Panda!" cooed Iris.

I knew not who this Tammy Wynette was, nor how she could be responsible for such remarkable sounds. I was more intrigued by the mechanism of the music.

"Friend Panda," I called, "how do you create such music? I see no instruments or phonograph."

"It's a cassette player," answered the ursine character. "Quite beyond your comprehension, I'm afraid." He waved a small rectangular object in my direction. "The tape's a limited edition though. Rennigan's Records, 1999 memorial compilation. So keep your mitts off it!"

Iris joined her pet in the cabin, although she took an altogether more practical course of action.

"I can locate the carpet using the same methods of transtemporal triangulation I used to track it here," she explained, and I nodded enthusiastically. It does not do to give the impression of ignorance, even when somewhat out of one's depth.

"Then wait no longer, fair Iris," said I. "Let us make haste, into the dense jungles of Mars!"

The journey was not easy. The steel bulkheads of the vehicle offered us considerable protection from the elements and the strange fauna of the Martian jungle, but it was not suited to the uneven terrain, nor the dense foliage and low-hanging extremities of the canopy. There were several points at which Iris and I had to step outside into the naked jungle, to clear the thickets, I with my knife, she with her fiery pistol. My impression of Iris improved all the while, so taken was I with her fortitude and grace.

"Oh, bloody hell!" she cried eventually, exasperated at our lack of progress. "We should've done this on foot. The sun's setting now, too. We'd best get back to the bus for the night, carry on in the morning."

"Will there be room for all of us to rest?" I asked, uncertain as to where her panda bear was kept.

"I'm sure we can think of some kind of arrangement," she replied, winking at me once more.

Iris and I retired to the omnibus, her panda bear tutting all the while. I reasoned I knew how to mollify the disapproving creature – and perhaps ingratiate myself further with the ravishing Iris. I reached into the hastily packed bundle of supplies I had made back at the Hither city. Iris' eyes fair lit up at the sight of what I produced.

"Blue Oblivion!" I declared, brandishing the ornate bottle. "Truly the finest of the Martian spirits, a fortified brew capable of transporting the drinker to lands of sodden contentment."

"Good work, that man!" cried Panda. "Perhaps it wasn't such a bad idea bringing you along after all!"

A pleasant few hours were spent engaged in the imbibing of the Blue Oblivion, as the sun finally set and hard darkness enveloped the land. The omnibus, in its great modernity, was equipped with electric lighting throughout, thus we were able to continue our enjoyment into the small hours. Iris spent much of her time working on her journal, which I understood was a pastime of some importance to her.

"How do you spell Gullivar?" she asked. "With an 'A-R' or an 'E-R'?"

"Either is acceptable," I replied, not in the mood to care. "My dear Iris," I murmured, as the panda bear snored quietly beside us, his glass eyes disconcertingly open. "My dear Iris, tell me more about yourself. How did you come to be here, on Mars of all places, in this miraculous vehicle? Are such things common in England?"

Iris laughed, then sipped upon her drink. "Not just yet, love, no. I'm not originally from England, you see, although I have spent an awful lot of time there, in one shape or another. No, I'm a traveller, you see, from beyond the farthest reaches of time and space. I do like to pop back to the old neighbourhood now and again, though, keep an eye on Mars and Earth, and some other favourite planets of mine."

"By Jupiter!" I cried, "So you're from another world as well? Tell me, do all the worlds of the heavens hold their own wonders and cultures?"

"Most of them do, I'd say, although not always and not at all times. You've got to pick your moment, you know. Turn up when the party's starting, not when it's been over for thousands of years, or before it's even begun."

"And what of the men of your world? Or are there only females there, adventuresses such as yourself, careening about the grand cosmos in contraptions such as this?"

"Oh, there are men back home, but they're a pretty boring lot. And I'm the only one with a bus. I'm unique!"

"Such a universe of wonders!" I sighed. "And to think, dear Polly scarcely believed I'd set foot on Mars."

Iris' expression hardened, and in my jolly inebriation I saw I'd let slip too much.

"Polly?" she demanded. "Who's Polly when she's at home?"

I considered a fanciful lie, but, in truth, my mind was too addled by the soporific effects of the Blue Oblivion. I confessed that Polly was, indeed, my lady wife.

"Your wife!" cried Iris. "And where's she then, back on Earth? So that's how it is, eh? She stays at home while you nip off to Mars at weekends for a bit of Hither's-your-father?"

I attempted to protest my innocence, but it was too late.

"Good night, Loo-tenant Jones," she fumed, rising unsteadily to her feet. "I'm going to bed. There's a beanbag in the corner if you want something to sleep on."

And with that, she retreated to the vehicle's upper deck, leaving me in the darkness with only the stertorous sound of the panda bear as company.

The following morning began slowly and with not inconsiderable grumbling and discomfort. The spirits and wines of the Hithers are best taken with an antidote potion to mitigate their more harmful effects. To my great satisfaction and relief, the terrestrial form is more capable than the Martial in shaking off the stuporous aftereffects. Nonetheless, Iris, the panda bear and I were all suffering somewhat in the harsh light of the Martian day.

"Good grief!" complained the panda bear. "What in the name of Gene Wilder was in that stuff? I can barely stand up straight."

"Oh, stop your griping, Panda," commented Iris, although she herself was looking somewhat paler than she had the night before.

"You know when you've drunk so much it feels like your head is full of cotton wool?" said the panda bear. "Well, imagine how bad it feels when you've drunk too much and your head *is* stuffed with cotton wool."

There was none of the strange music of Tammy Wynette that day.

In time, we drove through to a large clearing, trampling and cutting our way through the undergrowth as we went. Scratched by thorns and bristles, bitten by verminous flying motes, and thoroughly disheartened by it all, we had finally reached our destination. It was not quite the adventure I had been hoping to have with the lovely Iris Wildthyme.

The clearing was surrounded a dark, rocky formation, sprouting from the ground like a monstrous carbuncle, its surface punctured by a large cave mouth. Iris took one final reading from the omnibus' devices.

"It's down there," she sighed. "We'll have to go the rest of the way on foot."

"You are joking, Iris," complained the panda bear. "Into the cave, with nothing but your flimsy little pen-torch? Who knows what's in there!"

"Your companion is right, Iris," I ventured. "Who can say what horrors dwell in the gulf? Perhaps we should do better to admit defeat on this occasion." Though I consider myself something of an adventurer, I am also a practical man, who knows when to let go of a venture.

"It's Miss Wildthyme to you," Iris admonished me. "And we've got to go in there. Those poor people are being held by that horrible lot, and in case you've forgotten, so's your ticket out of here."

36

I could not fault her argument. Without the carpet to guarantee me passage home, one way or another, I would be stranded in this alien world. Unhappily, we pressed on.

The dank, tepid environment of the cavern was accompanied by an unpleasantly foetid smell, compost-like in its flavour. With only the minor illumination of Iris' astonishingly compact flashlight to light our way, we fondled the stone walls to keep from tripping or knocking our heads. It was not long, however, before we approached our quarry.

"I can hear something!" hissed Iris. "Voices, up ahead! Chanting!"

I could hear it too, a low, sonorous tone.

"We must be careful," I declared, "lest we alert them to our –"

I was silenced by a set of hairy knuckles to the back of the head.

Foolishly, we had not considered the possibility that Thithers might enter the cavern from behind us. With only the briefest of struggles – Thitherine eyes, it seems, being better adapted to the dark than our own – we were captured. Our weapons were removed from us, and the two brutes who held us forced along the stone passageway. In short order, we entered a larger cavern, illuminated somewhat by feebly burning torches.

"Iris, your gun!" I exclaimed. "What if they –?"

"Don't panic," she replied, "it's set to isomorphic. They won't be able to use it."

The cavern held further Thithers – one a guard, it would seem, like our two captors, barely clothed and well-stocked with muscle, the other a priest or holy man of some order, judging by his low chanting and the colourful robes in which he was clad. In the centre stood an emerald crystal atop a wooden stand, and around that were five Hithers, bent in supplication.

"Follow my words," ordered the Thither priest, continuing his chants with renewed vigour.

The superfluous guard smacked his great paw against the back of the nearest Hither.

"Ai! Hai!" he squealed, and then began to chant in fear of another beating. His fellows joined him.

The hirsute brutes bore down on our shoulders, their gnarled hands forcing us to our knees. My shins hit the black stone with a painful slap. Iris, struggling gainlessly within the Thither's grip, turned to me.

"Now what do we do, Loo-tenant?" she snapped.

37

"You're the adventuress," I retorted, "perhaps you have some ingenious plan!"

"I should just have had that bloody carpet off you in the first place. We never would have ended up here, being manhandled by these hairy sods!"

"I was perfectly content before you arrived in your omnibus! I could have been off in my rug and safe before they even penetrated the city!"

"Oh, shut up the pair of you!" shouted the panda bear, wriggling in the grasp of another monstrous guard. "A fine pair of adventurers you both make! I don't know why I even came along! I should have stayed in the city with those nice young ladies."

"Quiet!" bellowed the Thither priest, his filthy robes quivering in time with his jowls. "You will be silent in the presence of the Great God of Yet-to-Come!"

"Yet-to-Come?" whispered Iris, and I too found the phrase peculiar. My attention was taken, however, by the activity in the centre of the cavern. In front of our disbelieving eyes, the green crystal began to glow. A sickly yellow-green emanation, its intensity increased with slow but inexorable progress. In little time, a distinct mass had formed. Shapeless incandescence, a cloud of viridian vapour in which there were suspended tiny particulates. They hovered, barely visible but for how they caught the sickly light. The glistening cloud manifested with an unearthly smell, overpowering even the stench of the sweating Thither guards that grasped us. It was truly nauseating, I must say.

The glowing ball of vapour had soon expanded to the height of a man, and of a comparable breadth. Yet, this was not the last of it. You may think that, after all the uncanny adventures I have recounted to you, I could no longer feel surprise or disbelief. I say, however, I most certainly could, for what happened next took me quite aback. The glowing mass spoke! A hissing, tinny sibilance, just barely audible, yet at the same time close, as if some creature were whispering into my very ears.

"Explain the presence of these creatures," spoke the voice. "How do such terrestrial forms come to be on this planet?"

It was the Thither priest who spoke next, addressing his master.

"These heathens profaned your temple, my master. We bring them forth to be judged by you."

"These are Earth creatures!" hissed the voice. "How can this be possible?"

"Who are you calling an Earth creature?" cried Iris, earning an extra shove forward for her trouble. "How are you even speaking to us, anyway? That's never telepathy, I don't have the tingly feeling I usually get. What is it, modulated sound waves? Very clever, must have taken you ages to get the hang of that."

"What do you know of us?" demanded the voice.

"Only what I can work out. Vaporous, are you? Little droplets of biomatter linked together in a swarm? I've met things like you before. There's nowt new under the sun, believe you me. What are you up to then, eh? Where have you come from? This isn't your world, is it? Not right for you at all."

"This creature is from the Earth?" came the voice, and I ventured it was referring to me.

"I am an Earthman, that is true," I replied, feeling not a little absurd, addressing what was little more than a cloud of greenish steam. "And what of it? What do you know of *us*, hey?"

"The Earthmen should not be here," came the voice, its anger evident even through its spirant monotone. I felt it was growing deeper, stronger, as the cloud grew in intensity. "It is too early. We calculated that it is too early!"

"Too early?" I questioned. "You were expecting us?"

"Silence, invader! You people of Earth came to Mars and destroyed us. You annihilated us, and took our planet for yourselves! We of Mars have travelled back through millions of orbits to prevent that!"

Finally, I understood what this unearthly creature spoke of. This horror was not only from another world, but another time! Could such things be possible? Even after all I had seen, I could not quite believe it true.

"So you've come back, have you?" interjected Iris. "Travelled back millions of years, and to do what? What are you going to do now that you're here, eh?"

"We shall make our home here, in this time, before Mars enters its final phase of existence. While it is still verdant. We shall grow in number, and with our fellow Martians, take the Earth before the hated terrestrials can strike us!"

"And what gives you the right to come storming into an earlier era and remake it? You'll bugger up the very history of your world, if you're not careful."

39

"The Earthmen destroyed us! We are but few. Millennia of war have left our people near extinction. We have every right!"

But Iris was in full flow now, and even the ghastly voice of the Martian cloud could not quell her ire.

"Oh, don't give me that! I know your lot, oh yes! I've been to your Mars! I've travelled up and down the history of the solar system. Who started the war, eh? Who started it? You picked a fight you couldn't win, didn't you? And now you've been beaten, you're fighting dirty!"

"We have to defend ourselves!"

"Ah, you're just another bunch of Martian invaders, same as all the rest! It doesn't matter if they go ak-ak or ulla or yip-yip-yip, you're all as bad as each other!"

"Silence!" hissed the voice, vibrating in my ears, almost deafening. The cloud pulsed violently, and in the sudden onslaught of sound and fury, Iris made her move.

Iris broke free of the Thither guard's grip. She swung her shapely leg round and tripped him, knocking him violently in the neck with a flat-handed chop. The Thithers were larger than us, of course, but we had light-footedness and agility on our side, not to mention a disproportionate strength in the Martian gravity. The guard who held me was more prepared, but Iris still had him off balance enough for me to swing him over my shoulder. The bestial malefactor would have pinned one of us down, but he was unable to hold us both back. With quick-footed ease we put the blighter onto the ground. There was a strangulated yell from our right – we turned to see the panda bear drop to the ground, his own captor holding his broad hands to his hideous face. Blood trickled through his fingers.

"Aha!" said the diminutive being. "Bit him right on the hooter!" He then proceeded to spit on the cavern floor. "Disgusting!" he complained, and I imagined that indeed it was.

The high priest looked on in rage as the fight continued, and moved to guard the Hither-folk.

"You lot!" cried Iris, as she and I shielded ourselves from the blows of our terrible captors. "Get out of here, now!" She grabbed her pistol, dropped by her captor in the struggle, pointing it at the Thithers to prevent them from stopping the fleeing prisoners. I moved to block the priest, tackling him and sending him plunging towards the green crystal. It shook uneasily upon its pedestal, eliciting a look of terror upon the unholy holy man's grotesque face.

It was then that I registered that the very thing I had come for: the miraculous travelling rug lay unguarded, the priest having abandoned it in his attempt to prevent the Hithers' escape. I moved for it, grasping it tightly. I knew if I but thought of home, it should take me there. Indeed, my mind was full of the thoughts of home, more than ever. My humble house, my familiar bed, the comely face of my patient wife, all were in my mind's eye. Why then did I not leave this place?

I knew why, of course. After our adventure together, I could not abandon Iris Wildthyme to the horrors of the Thither cult. No, nor her little panda bear!

"Stop this!" demanded the cloud entity. It had continued to grow in intensity and size as we fought, and with a blazing flourish, split itself in two. The twin globules moved for us, one after Iris, the other after me, while a Thither brute bound in my direction also.

"The crystal!" cried Iris, as the panda bear hurried the enslaved Hithers out of the cavern opening. "Gullivar, smash the bloody thing!"

I wasted no time. I kicked myself forward out of the grasp of the struggling guard, and with a hefty shove, sent the veridian rock tumbling from its perch. It shattered upon the dusty floor, showering the cavern with tiny fragments, their glittering green particles reflecting the nature of the beings which they supported.

The priest howled, vainly trying to gather up the crystalline shards. It was too late, however. The guardsmen fell to their knees, prostrate in the face of their god's wrath, as the hissing, inhuman voice screamed in our ears. The two clouds dissipated before our very eyes, rapidly fading until there was little of them left but two faint circles of greenish light upon the stone floor.

The voice came again – deeper, this time, louder too, full of such rage and hatred I care not to think on it. A voice we could feel in our very souls.

"We will return!" promised the voice. "We shall return for the Earth! This... is... the..."

But with that, they were gone, silenced as they ceased to be, the faint circles fading finally to nothingness.

"Good heavens, man!" cried the panda bear. "Let's get out of here!"

We ran, with all the speed we could muster, back the way we had came. Of the Hithers, there was no sign. I reassured Iris that they would have already begun their journey back to their city on foot. They would no doubt take their happy time about it, their mistreatment at the hands of the Thither cult already forgotten. Such is the childlike mind of the Hither.

"Those things," I asked Iris. "Were they really beings from the distant future?"

"Sure were, love. A gestalt entity, formed from millions of tiny spores, creating one huge, malevolent mind. Don't you worry about it, though. They've been scattered into the Maelstrom. Even if enough of them survive to reform, it'll be centuries before they try again. By then, the Earth will be ready for them. Trust me, in centuries to come, they'll be facing a united Earth. The whole spectrum of humanity will be there to stop them!"

I noticed that I was still clutching the carpet to my breast. The rough fabric felt strangely comforting against my fingers.

"You know what?" said Iris. "I don't really like that carpet much anymore. It's in a right state, isn't it? Maybe you should keep it."

"After all that?" said the panda bear, aghast. "Honestly Iris, have you gone soft? Or have you just got a thing for Captain America here?"

"Oh, be quiet, Panda." She turned back to me. "Just promise me that you'll get straight back to your lovely wife, alright?"

"Absolutely," I answered. "I've had my fill of Martian adventure. I know where my heart belongs." And I truly did. What a time I'd had – but what a waste of the time I could have had in the arms of my dear Polly.

"And I'm keeping the rest of that Blue Oblivion," she added.

"Of course, dear lady. Have it with my compliments." I bowed to her, Miss Iris Wildthyme, the adventuress. To my delight, she gave me the softest of kisses on the cheek, and then she, and her panda bear, boarded her miraculous vehicle. Before my very eyes, it disappeared – slowly, trumpeting like a herd of pachyderms, before it finally faded from sight, as the terrible cloud had before.

I held the carpet in my grasp, its worn edges rough against my skin. I wondered... was it quite necessary that I return home immediately?

# IRIS: CHESS-MISTRESS OF MARS
**Simon Bucher-Jones**

*"When the skimmer-pawns advance in lines across the burning sands,*
*And crab-knights make their sidle dance, with fiery claws for hands*
*While the pillars hymn their threnodies, and all the air is light,*
*A canny Martian holds its knees and wishes it were night.*
*Extending poly-silicon cells on its photovoltaic feet*
*It shades itself from solar storms, from radiation sleet.*
*The Hob-tree Towers cast shadows long, and threaten many a pawn*
*The visitors from Other Powers bet wrong, and soon are shorn,*
*As the Martian skies revolving, as the Moons go gallop by,*
*Chess is the sport evolving, beneath the Martian sky,*
*So place your bets my alien Lords, beneath my spreading feet,*
*For Martians always keep their words, no Martian stoops to cheat.*
*Place a Wockle Shell upon the board, and bet upon each piece*
*And may the Gods of Martian Chess bless you with its increase."*
*So cry the Martians, upside-down, their noses in the dirt,*
*But do not think a Martian knows nothing of words that hurt.*
*To all who come, we make ourselves all they would wish and more,*
*And still they think us bestial things whose only wish is war.*
*Few are the souls who come to Mars, who know to be polite,*
*And those are the souls we nod to, when we stand erect at night.*

> Translation of the Wulfvic Scrolls
> Minf Dynasty, Old Martian
> Canto X, "The Chess Match".

During the preceding night, the Martian Chess-Machines had been marking out the course across the dried river-bottoms of the K'tmf Delta, patterning the sands with the grids and devices necessary to this exacting sport.

The glittering spread of the forty-eight boards of Holy Battle, that ages ago had replaced ancestral war as the "game" of choice, shone with an intense lustre, and from another world could easily have been mistaken for a skein of watercourses.

43

To say Martians love chess is to say fish love water. Whole ages can pass without a grand tournament, and yet – one suspects – if a tournament were not being planned in the background all other activity would simply wither away. Even in the expansionist Imperial period of the Anti-Chess Tyrannies, when the words "pawn", "castle" and – nearly disastrously – "mate" were stricken from the Middle Martian language on pain of tarmacking of the feet, the secret hierophants of the great game carried boards tattooed on their inner stomachs for safety, and illicit chess-easys and chess-masters' holes could be found in every Martian city or Hob-Tree tower.

The aged Martian groundskeeper peered along the delta valley floor with its true eyes, observing the preparations with quiet pride, but its other eye, the articulated organic radio telescope formed by the parabolic centre of its underfeet, couldn't help but gaze skyward with trepidation. There was really only one thing that could spoil a grand tournament. While the dust swirls of the Martian upper atmosphere were no certain predictor of the problem he feared, they were all he had to offer him any guidance. Despite the hopeful prognostications offered by *Old Mars' Almanack*, no intelligence of the Red Planet had yet come up with a genuinely valid way of predicting the random appearances of chess-disrupting pests.

Panda, who fancied himself as something of an armchair chess-master, had been dropping hints for some time to Iris that a visit to one of the Martian Great Chess Games would be a slightly more intellectual day out than the ones they usually ended up having. Iris, despite a ruthless competitive streak that came out particularly in respect of drinking and Scrabble, had a blind spot for chess and ping pong (at least since she went blonde). How did the little horsey pieces get over the net anyway? Nevertheless, she was perfectly willing to indulge Panda for once, and soon had the bus rattling down the space-ways in the general direction of Mars. Consultation, by Panda, of Dermick Wulfvic's translations of Old Middle Martian poetry suggested the Minf Dynasty period as having a particularly thrusting and exciting set of games, in which the subtlety and drama of the click of the giant carved spider-cuttlefish-bone-ivory and polished liftwood pieces (shod with meteor-iron for counterweights) on the multiplex boards of fused silica, sang like music.

As the faithful bus spun its wheels in the Martian dust with a whirling, moaning noise, the Martian groundskeeper's attention was focussed elsewhere. "Bloody time-travelling tourists," he muttered.

Ten subjective minutes earlier in another world entirely, Dan Flambeau, method actor and heart-throb, ex-star of Canadian TV romantic flop *Toronto Nights*, hard drinker, sword-fighter and lover of women, had held his head in his hands and felt profoundly sorry for himself. He wasn't any longer drunk, but his head ached and the costume he was required to wear, basically a gem-studded metallic harness padded to give the impression of naked muscle where it covered, and show it where it didn't, was riding up under his arms and even more painfully elsewhere. He'd come a long way for this part and it wasn't paying that much, and he had an almost certain feeling that he'd backed the wrong SF series. It had come down to a coin-toss. *Battleship Anathema* remake, heads, *Farley Farrier: Warrior of Mars*, tails. He'd thrown tails. Now, giant two-handed Martian sword slung across his back, Dan shuffled towards the exit of his trailer, ready for his call, Mr DeMille. It was going, he thought, to be a long day. He little realised how long.

Still, he had to admit as the trailer door swung open, they'd done a damned fine job on the scenery. The desert stretched out forever under an unearthly salmon pink sky (the fabled sky that the Voyager probes had shown Mars didn't have). In the distance the false mountains looked profoundly real. How did they do that? In the foreground the shining canals gleamed. Except they didn't really look like canals now he thought about it. That was a pity.

He recalled the Director telling him about them. "It's retro, Dan, it's like, you know, the past's idea of Mars. It'll be a romantic science fantasy epic, not the militaristic bullpucky of some SF shows I could name." The set designers had got that wrong though. The shining waters – if they were water – weren't wide enough to be canals, they were more like grids or ribbons of metal, woven or painted onto the horizon. There had to be some sort of forced-perspective effect involved, something the camera would see that would look right to the audience. He jumped down from the trailer steps, and felt light and right and dizzy with possibilities and the thought that may be this was all coming up roses for once, for him.

Then he turned to stick his thumb up to the Director, and there was no Director and no trailer and no cars and no cameras and no Los Angeles in the smoggy distance, and no people, and nothing but more desert. Well, nothing but more desert and a giant metal crab machine weaving metal strands out of its guts and patterning them into the sand in deliberately alien ways. A mechanism in whose design no wheel had ever featured, and which he instinctively knew hadn't been built on Earth.

"Oh fudge!" he swore with the instinctive self-editing of someone who'd come up via children's television, and, before he knew what he was doing, jumped thirty feet into the air from shock.

The groundskeeper watched, hearts sinking as the pinkish, yellow-haired figure in its ridiculous harness bounded into a sky with the force of its higher-gravity-planet muscles and started waving a sword about in one hand.

The Martian just *knew* the wretched pest was going to attack his Chess-Machines. It was one of *those* lone time-lost humans. They were far worse than the explorers. You could patronise explorers, pander to them a bit. You could be quaint, or strange, or insist they were mad until they went away. If you were lucky they could be tricked into being afraid, and scared away, but even if they absolutely demanded an exploration with such psychic persistence that no Martian would be able to do anything other than politely fall in with their desires, eventually they'd get in their clockwork rocket ship, cerulean tempus cabinet, or Ares One Lander and go. They overstayed their welcomes but they had at least some idea that there was such a thing as a welcome, which could be overstayed. Occasionally you could have a moral conversation with one.

The self-centred sort of humans who fell alone out of time-voids, however, invariably possessed bulging thews and small foreheads and had absolutely nothing better to do than to hang around expecting to run the place. They spent months, jumping like pink mars-hoppers, overthrowing perfectly peaceful kingdoms, brawling and looking futilely for Martian women to steal, but mainly brawling. Sword-wielding barbarians liked to fight something, it seemed, and if one thing got in the way of chess it was fighting. *Old Mars' Almanack* predictions, bah! "Little fear of humans stopping play." The chances of anything coming from Earth was a million to one, they said. Million to one indeed! He would have words with the editors about this.

Clanking and shouting from the Chess-Machine reached him through the thin Martian atmosphere. The human was hitting it, and it was trying to get him to stand still on a board-spot, having mistaken him for a piece.

Something or someone was going to get broken. Besides that, he could feel the hot, sweaty force of the human's belief sweeping across the sands. Sheer instinctual Martian politeness gripped his body with a desire to conform to the human's cultural expectations. This was going to be gross.

Iris and Panda had been waving for some time trying to attract the attention of the Martian they were walking towards, but it was clearly focusing on something in the distance, further west. The crystal and brass breathing mouthpieces they were using to augment the thin Martian air prevented them talking easily or shouting, and besides Iris wasn't sure if this particular sort of Martian had ears. The question, Panda knew, had simply never come up in their archeologically recovered poetry. They had a language – a fine and expressive one – which it its written form had been partly translated, but it might be conveyed by mime or gamma rays for all the human scientists had been able to discover. They were getting close enough to have a proper look at the fellow, though.

The Martian looked, Panda thought, like a medieval depiction of a skiapod. It had two big glittery feet held over its head, but they locked together into one mirrored block. Not so much a foot perhaps as a combination sun-shade and organic solar energy converter, and its body was an armoured collection of mandibles and scuttling limbs close to the sand. They couldn't see its head from this side, but if it was one of the "chess-players' of Mars depicted in the artwork of the Seabottom Strata, and hymned in the scrolls, then its everyday eyes would be at ground level, and its astronomical eye would be in the sole of its umbrella foot. In the searing Martian day it lived "upside-down", only standing on its then separated "feet" in the Martian night. Panda was thoroughly confident he knew everything that fifty-ninth-century archaeology had discovered about the Martians, so he was rather taken aback when, just as they got close to it, it changed.

Groundkeeper Vrilli shook and trembled under the psychic intensity of the barbarian human's exultation. His copper-coloured skin turned to verdigris, he flipped upright, photosensitive feet crusting over. From his bulky, pear-shaped midsection extra arms budded. A searing, angry, boiling rage burned through his chess-master's calm. Oh, oh here it came! Running along the edge of one of the completed boards, he wrenched with his five hands (three of them new) a variety of ceremonial weapons from the life-size grasp of the chess pieces. A tri-bladed sword that could shoot its blades like spears. A razor-edged triskelion that could be thrown. A thing like a giant lead-weighted cotton-bud. A black-bladed sword that whistled a shrill and ancient song as its fluted edge cut the Martian air. A spear that could change size from a toothpick to a massive javelin. An armoured gauntlet with nine weird gems on its alien fingers. Wait, some sane part of his mind concluded, wasn't that six things? He tried to count his hands again.

Panda and Iris watched as the now martial Martian fumbled, threw down the gauntlet, gripped the other weapons fiercely, grunted a fearful antique oath from the years when Mars had seas, and, weighted beyond its capacity, stumbled and fell forward on its face. This wasn't what they'd been expecting at all.

Iris pulled her breathing mask to one side and shouted, "Give me a hand Panda chuck, the poor lad's fainted."

Panda lifted one of the long, rangy, new green arms and discovered that he couldn't pry the weapon from its fingers. He let it slip back into the receiving sand. "Did you see that? He suddenly changed into quite another sort of Martian."

"A very dangerous sort, I'd say. It's what, 2014? This type of Martian shouldn't be here."

Panda nodded. "Quite, the Minf Chess-Dynasty was aeons ago. If this is 2014 then this is an anachronism. I thought the bus was going to take us back in time."

"I just set it for the Martian Chessianic Era, but that's not what I meant dear, although it's another worry. I meant that this is a fictional Martian and one firmly trademarked. What's it doing here and why did it start out as a perfectly reasonably-extrapolated, possible 'real' Martian, if you like that kind of thing, and suddenly shift into a brawling, tusked, green Martian of the 1930s pulp style?"

Panda was shading his eyes with a carefully-placed paw, so he could gaze into the brilliant west. "I don't know, but I think he might." Black against the glowing sky a figure fell towards them like a hawk in flight.

Dan Flambeau – or, as he reckoned he must now call himself, FLAMBEAU OF MARS – bounced and spun as he leaped off the glittering carapace of the giant death machine. He was alive with adrenaline and the exuberance of his muscles. He could do gymnastics he couldn't even have managed as a child. This was so great!

He could almost change his centre of gravity in mid-leap, by a cunning contortion of his lithe form. From the uppermost bound of his jump, he could see across the metal-lined plains of Mars, which were decorated by a multitude of armed statues in black and red armour, poised with a hideous array of alien weapons which managed to be both prehistorically barbarous, and futuristically aesthetic. Cripes, if the SFX people on *FFWOM* had been able to pull off a fiftieth of this grandeur, they'd have knocked grey-military SF into a cocked hat.

He could see now three figures on the sands ahead of him roughly where the arc of his leap would bring him lightly to rest, his momentum being absorbed by powerful legs bred and exercised in Earth's mightier gravity.

One was a typical multi-armed Martian warrior, weapons clutched in all its hands, temporarily downed in battle no doubt, but likely to be dangerous at any moment. The others were wildly different. One was a small Martian animal which if he wasn't seeing things bore a slight resemblance to a terrestrial panda bear. An example of parallel evolution, possibly. It was probably viciousness incarnate. THE GROWLEYBEAR OF DOOM! he thought to himself, in CAPITALS. Hey that was good! He really should do some scriptwriting and directing for the show if he ever got back to Earth.

The third figure numerically, but by no means the last in terms of interest, was the only sort of character Dan had been missing so far from this astonishing adventure, and yet it was absolutely the single character guaranteed by the books to be on Mars, from the first in the series onwards.

Clad in tight-fitting flexible metal that clung in bands around her shapely limbs, and which served only to accentuate and bring to their firmest state her legs, arms, and well-formed breasts, her blonde hair falling in medusa-waves in the slow Martian gravity, was a woman who was simply fully set to stun. A Princess of Mars! A warrior woman! She must have downed the Martian and now stood at bay to the fierce Growleybear which was holding her back until its Martian master could recover and enter combat anew!

He clearly had only one option. Deftly controlling his landing, he gathered the beautiful woman in his arms, and let the strength in his legs lift them both up into the iron-dust-red sky. "Don't worry ma'am, I've got you. No darn Growleybear nor Martian's going to hurt you while I'm around."

Panda groaned, "Oh for crying out loud, come back!" but the bounding, er, bounder had already sprung away. Next to him, the five-armed – or was it six now? – Martian levered itself from the sands, clanking with assorted edged pig-stickers. They watched Iris and her captor vanish into the distance.

Then the Martian spoke. "Excuse me, but is he with you? Because frankly we're getting sick of this." He coughed, and added, "I mean, by the Twin Jewelled Moons of Mars, our warlike blood is fired for vengeance against this fierce pirate of the third planet!" He stopped, and Panda couldn't help feeling he was waiting for a round of applause.

"That's as may be," Panda said, noting the differences in the Martian's dialogue style and wondering what it indicated, "but I'm afraid I can't exactly leap after him, not with my legs." He hopped experimentally but even in Martian gravity the absence of any real working knees prevented him managing more than a human high-jump.

"Young man," shouted Iris forcefully through the thin air, "I do not approve of non-consensual abduction!"

She'd acclimatised as quickly as she normally did and didn't need the breathing gear any longer, but she was slightly surprised to see that her Martian masher didn't either. Perhaps it was the vast expanse of his muscled chest which had to house lungs of quite startling capacity. Perhaps, if his appearance here was one of the kind of phenomena she suspected it might be, he'd arrived pre-adapted by the strange forces that quite often had snatched single, muscular, male humans to the Red Planet. He started to say something in reply, but the air – thin or otherwise – was whisked away as they landed, his knees bent, her body held in his brawny arms, atop one of the Martian mesas.

"Do you think," the Martian asked plaintively, "that we should go after them? Or we could just wait here and, um, perhaps play some chess, if you'd like."

Panda looked around. The Martian's war-fever seemed to have abated, and it was carefully fitting the assorted weapons back into their slots in the nearest Giant Chess Pieces of the Grand Tournament. He'd probably never have another chance to play chess with a genuine Minf dynasty Martian – even if it did seem to be a couple of aeons late if this really was the early part of the twenty-first century. It wasn't as if Iris wasn't perfectly capable of rescuing herself.

Then again, she'd certainly be cross if she discovered he hadn't exerted himself fully, and immediately in her pursuit. And he didn't want anything to happen to her. Well nothing too serious. She could get a jolly sight too certain of herself sometimes. Then again, if you looked on chess as a kind of mano-a-mano struggle – Pandao-a-Martiano, that is – he could be said to be striving to beat this Martian psychologically. He could even learn from it, subtly, what it knew about the jumping human, and possibly where Iris had been taken.

"Best of three games?" he said, before he could think himself out of it.

"Now that's handsome," the Martian replied, positioning its nose comfortably at the edge of one of the massive boards. "You're on."

"And that," Dan explained, "is how I found myself here. One minute I was in my trailer preparing for episode one, scene three, 'Captain Farley Farrier arrives on Mars', and then, one small step for an actor and there I was, shim-shalla-bim, on what I presume is Mars, or at least a functionally equivalent alien planet or dimension. Wow!"

"Tell me, dear," Iris went on, seemingly oblivious to the effect her recent onset of bodaciousness was having on the virile male actor, "were you thinking hard about your role? Trying to cast your mind into the shape it would have to be to inhabit it, as it were?"

"Exactly," he positively gushed. "You're so right – so few non-actors really appreciate the efforts we go to, to live a role. I'd got the original pulp novels and was imagining the sights and sounds of Mars, so that I'd display the right expressions and body language as the character."

"I thought as much. Bah, I knew it would cause trouble. I told Constantin Stanislavski, 'Stanislavski', I said, 'perhaps dear sir, they could try acting', but would he listen to me, oh no, it was all 'mastering the magic *if*,' putting yourself in someone else's position, 'drawing on the deep emotional wellsprings'. Well you've done it now. You've well sprung yourself right off Earth. You've got what space doctors of the future call *Martis volens lacu*. You've thought so hard about bloody Mars, you've sent yourself there psychically and you've given yourself an ego-stroking imaginary muscleman's body too. It's not the first time this sort of thing's happened. That's how the books got written in the first place."

"But this is my body. I really do look like this."

Iris felt a trifle weak at the knees. "Really? You've looked after it well. Mineral water and egg-whites, I suppose? Lots and lots of... sweaty... vigorous exercise..."

His arm was still around her waist. She supposed that, possibly, there wasn't really any hurry. Panda was probably rustling up a rescue but he might be ages yet. With any luck.

Martian Chess is played on an unfolded tesseractic board or "course", which is to say a grid equivalent to forty-eight human chess boards, linked at the edges by folding rules which permit pieces to move between them, as if the regular octachoron which the shape would form in four-dimensional space actually existed. As well as the "normal" pieces which exist in the frankly much simplified game of "Earth chess", there are twenty-three variant pieces which replace the knights on each of the other boards. Two of these are the Priest, which moves like a Bishop but only a maximum of three diagonal spaces, except when it is moving to be next to a Bishop of the same player when it can move a full Bishop's move (a move known as "toadying"), and the Damsel, which moves two spaces in any direction until it is promoted by "marriage" (a complex move involving a Damsel, a Bishop or Priest, and one of the male sub-King-caste pieces) after which it moves as a She-Knight. Panda was having the time of his life at it.

He was two Marauders up, and he had eleven of his opponent's Kings in check.

Iris wasn't enjoying things quite so much. Oh, it had been developing very promisingly, right up to the moment when the top of the Mesa had swivelled open, and the Sirens of Mars had come out. There were seven of them, they wore very little, and were quite firmly mammalian at least up to the neck, with no trace of radio telescopes in their dainty feet. It was true that from the delightfully delicate throats up, their faces were bleached skeletons and their massive transparent skulls fairly pulsed with visible multiple-lobed and densely-furrowed brain-matter. But they also had nice eyes and giggled. They'd made Dan a rather embarrassing offer, and to Iris' annoyance he was apparently considering it.

"Well why shouldn't I help them repopulate this part of Mars?" he asked disingenuously. "I'm unmarried, I don't have any commitments. They've admitted they've been pulling humans through space-time, whenever they could find one thinking hard enough about Mars for them to latch on to his thoughts. If I actually help, they'll stop kidnapping people, at least for a generation."

"Yes, yes," Iris said crossly, "I know all that. We've heard quite enough about them pulling Earthmen, and how until now they've only got malnourished Confederate soldiers, or bleary-eyed professors, who despite 'presenting' in their psychic forms as he-men have been quite unable to follow through. You needn't flatter yourself that anyone's impressed by your actually having biceps, you know. I don't see why it matters, anyway, if you're not really here. Your actual biceps are probably actually just as actually asleep as the rest of you, actually on Earth."

"We are ourselves a psychoplasmic species," one of the Sirens explained. "We wear the forms created for us by expectation, as do our fleshy male counterparts upon the plains. Long ages since, female and male divided in this part of Mars into two long-lived forms, one solely of the mind, the other..." She sniffed, presumably mentally. "Too obsessed with bloody Chess to abandon their bodies. We'll not see any action in that quarter until they finally finish their daft tournament."

"Provided the human's psychoplasm is a true expression of his form," a slightly – if possible – more voluptuous Siren interjected, "we can take from it the diffraction patterns that will engender in our wavefronts a new Martian generation, which given our lifespans will outlast Mankind, and yet preserve the best of both our species."

"Our charm," one of the other Sirens added, "his muscles."

"Our mental abilities," a fourth chimed in.

"His actually having a face," Iris muttered. Then a thought struck her and she brightened. "Psychowaveform diffraction? Mmm. So he'd just be being scanned by some sort of giant ancestral machine then. I doubt he'd like that, great big fella like him. Probably wouldn't fit. Maybe we should just be going."

"Oh no, our methods of diffracting psychoplasm are far more pleasurable."

"For all of us," one of the other Sirens added. She leaned forward and ran her hand through the substance, seemingly, of Dan's skull, down through his throat and sternum, towards his groin.

"Oh... Wow!" Dan said, and sat down suddenly, with what – even for Martian gravity – was a substantial thump. Where her hand had moved through him, streamers of dancing light were spilling forth, joining him by strands of effervescent ectoplasm to her fingertips that now showed ghostly and gleaming. She licked her fingers suggestively.

"Don't mind me, I'm sure," Iris said snappishly. "I'll just go look at these interesting rock formations then."

One game each, and Vrilli had slyly suggested the ancient Martian concept of "making it more interesting" with a series of small wagers. Panda won a Martian flyer of liftwood and Old Sea pearls, with sails woven of stabilised gravity; but then his Berserker was jailed by a pack of Lawyers acting in unison, his fourth-to-last King was beheaded by a Regicide, and he lost his key to the bus!

Iris had her fingers in her ears and she was whistling, loudly. If Panda got to hear about this she'd never live it down.

Panda frantically castled, and offered a triple Queen swap with a side bet of his Martian flyer for the bus key. If Iris found out he'd lost it gambling he'd never live it down.

Flambeau of Mars gasped. Although his body, harness, and weapon were exact replicas of the genuine articles back on Earth, he nevertheless found the attentions of the Sirens to be almost beyond pleasurable, almost vampiric, as if part of his psychoplasm was being leached away forever.

He gulped. If he went back with it that size, he'd never live it down.

Panda was just about to start up the Martian flying ship that Vrilli had cheerfully loaned him back from his winnings, so that he could go and look for Iris. Panda had only won one game out of three, which was still a staggering success for a non-Martian, but he'd won the bus key back on a side bet about whether he could marry the last of his Damsels to opposing Lords before the end of the game, and that was victory enough.

He had struck a commanding pose in front of the great iron steering wheel which was poised at the ship's centre of gravitylessness, when a whirling wind on the horizon swept down suddenly from the distant Mesas. Swirling and then dissipating it deposited firstly a grumpy Iris, and then a blushing human whose harness was very badly buckled, and whose massive two-handed sword had shrivelled to barely a dagger.

Iris gave Panda a "don't ask" look. "Freudian psychoplasmic confusion," she said. "He'll be all right when he's had a rest, and he's going to be too sleepy to start anything in the way of fighting for a while. Now what's been happening your end?"

Panda quickly explained the problems the pathologically helpful plains Martians had been having, with humans imposing their expectations about them all over the place. The barbarian warrior types were the worst, but even a small party of Victorian steampunk space explorers could muck up any chance of chess for a month, with their demands for secret Martian caverns, gigantic jewels, and interplanetary intrigues. He felt considerable compassion for the long-lived but often thwarted Martians, who only wanted enough peace and quiet to get on with their national sport.

Iris listened thoughtfully, occasionally nodding and making the "Mmm" noises which suggested to Panda that she might well have an idea.

"So what can we do?" Panda asked, after Iris had filled him in a little more about her adventure. "Now that the Sirens of Mars have been placated, there probably won't be any more human daydreamers popping through psychic portals all pumped up like God's gift to Martian Women, at least for a while. But that still leaves these poor chess-loving psychoplasmic fellows at the mercy of any passing exploring party. How can they just be left to get on with their lives in peace? We can't really blockade Mars, and it's only going to get visited more often from this time onwards."

"Well now," Iris said, "I think I have an idea, if I can get the bus to co-operate. It's all a matter of relativity. If you don't care how long something takes, and you have a time machine, there are ways to share a planet. Time machines can do more than move in time you know. They can change how other things move in time, too."

All through the human encroachment upon Mars, through its highs and lows, its terraforming and its climatic disasters, its "back to basics' aeon, and its Martian Heritage restorative, the Martians lived their quiet, slow, slow, slow, chess- and joy-filled lives. Humanity frothed around them like a hot desert breeze that they felt only as a minor note in their own long symphony. No human ever noticed the strange-shaped long weathered rocks in the desert, very gradually shifted in their aeon-long chess matches by Martians living at a time-rate of about one (Earth) second for every (Earth) eleven and a half thousand years.

"And that," Iris said triumphantly to Panda, "is why I always say, 'A time for everything and everything in its time'. The male Martians get their world in their own time-phase, and by shifting the start of their tournament back into the deep past, the humans also still get to keep their lovely dreams of the high flowering of Martian culture. Everybody's happy. The Minf Dynasty's back where the fifty-ninth century archaeologists will find it. Only no-one knows that it's still ever so quietly going on. Tah dah!"

"And you get to be insufferably smug for a week. You do know you say no such thing, by the way. I've never heard you say that."

"Well, I will from now on. All the time."

"That I'm sure of."

Scooped up in Iris' arms, Panda was lifted back aboard the bus. He had to admit this had been one of their more successful holidays. The diamond badge of "Chess Excellence" glittered against his black and white fur.

"Best three-billion-year-long long weekend ever," he mused. Iris and Dan were still outside. He waved at them from the step.

"It was quite something," Dan said, and he reached out to touch Iris' elbow. "So do I have to go home right away? Martians are all very well, but I'm a sucker for a pretty face, when it comes right down to it."

Sometime round about 5811 CE, Professor Dermick Wulfvic passed by Old Mars and excavated the tessellated hills of the Chantry Bore and marvelled at the ingrained images embedded in the silica strata. As his translation of the poetry scrolls suggested, here were pictures of the great chess games of prehistory: stained-glass pictograms of the grand embassies and balls of a long vanished Mars. It would have been marvellous to have lived in those long lost aeons when life on Earth was only a thin oxygenating smear, and to have walked with the prehistoric peoples who apparently had flocked here from other solar systems, now also long extinct, to pit their wits against the Chess Masters of Ancient Mars. The prismatic glare of the Martian symbols strained his eyes something more than somewhat, and he almost thought for a moment that part of the tessellation showed two humanoid figures, heads pressed together in a stylised kiss, while, a smaller black-and-white shape waved before a larger shape that, if he squinted, curiously resembled a double-decker bus. Odd how the human mind can make patterns out of the lost art of a long-vanished race. If you sat and watched the images for a long time, they almost seemed to breathe.

*"When the pieces of the game have swept their patterns in the sands,*
*And the Final Queen has said the Name that honours all our lands,*
*No alien guest stands unimpressed, by the moves both strong and light,*
*When the bets are paid to the unafraid, to the Martians who stand right.*
*Our feet they glitter on the sands like ruby slippers neat,*
*Under Moons that twirl like burning brands, o'er the Graves of Old Defeat,*
*No Martian born can be long forlorn, when the dark defies the dawn,*
*And each Hob-Tower closes its white flower, round the tattered and the torn.*
*We heal our wounds in the mulchsome dark, and we raise a loving cry!*
*And none shall mourn for the Martian-born, who only live to die.*
*So raise your crests my lovely lads, my ghostly lassies neat!*
*We rear up on our ruby pads, our burning sizzling feet,*
*And the sand may fuse, with the heats' decrease,*
*Be it win, or lose, we will find surcease."*
*So cry the Martians, right side up, by gestures now they flirt,*
*They flutter arms in semaphore, and their eyes glim through the dirt,*
*In the glimmering dress of après Chess they twirl across the floor*
*Be it little or black, or a strapless back, when the polka plays full score.*
*Few are the soles that come to Mars, that can dance on sand alight,*
*But those are the soles we dance with, when we dance into the night.*

Translation of the Wulfvic Scrolls
Minf Dynasty, Old Martian, Canto XIII, "Après Chess".

57

# DEATH ON THE EUPHRATES
**Selina Lock**

Panda was woken by a jolt. He opened his eyes and wondered whether the bleary view was due to the excesses of the night before, or the wave of water hitting the windows of the bus.

He saw Iris jump down from behind the steering wheel, her pink platform-heeled boots hitting the floor with a thud.

"Abandon ship! Abandon ship!" she shouted as she came careening down the aisle towards him.

Panda grunted and heaved himself upright in the armchair he had fallen asleep in as they were leaving the imaginatively-named Galactic Spaceport 475 the previous night. Or had it been yesterday morning? Time got a little confused aboard the celestial omnibus.

"Come on lovey, abandon ship before we got down with her," Iris said. She grinned at him, grabbed her pink blaster off the coffee table and slotted it into her thigh holster. Then she made for the stairs to the upper deck.

Panda shook his head and peered through the window. Water still dribbled down it, but the wave had been replaced by a solid band of murky grey liquid. Panda had a sinking feeling, literally, as rising water surrounded the lower level of the bus. He grabbed a randomly-chosen glass of liqueur from the table and downed it in one. He pulled a face at the rank taste of slightly curdled Irish cream and hopped down from the chair.

"Iris, wait for me."

As Panda reached the top deck of the bus, Iris reached over the railing and hoisted him up by his short, hairy arm. He saw a swirl of brightly patterned catsuits lying on the floor, as Iris whirled him over her head and plonked him down on the unmade bed. He gulped to stop the hastily imbibed liqueur from making a reappearance and steadied himself against the headboard.

"Think the emergency exit is still broken – we'll have to go through the window," Iris said. "I'll give you a leg-up."

She cupped her hands and offered them to Panda. He gave her a look.

"This is most undignified."

Iris raised her shapely blonde eyebrows and proffered her hands again. Panda sighed and let her lift him upwards. He grabbed the window lock, clicked it to the side and the top half of the window swung down. Panda scrambled on to it and met a watery embrace.

"I am not designed to get wet. Do not tumble-dry!" He shouted as the current pulled him away. The water tossed him around, but he got a final glimpse of Iris. Her blaster was caught on the window ledge, and she was dragged down as the bus sank from view.

Iris tried to groan. Her whole body ached. She didn't remember tying one on the night before, but then everything felt a little unfocused, so perhaps she had. She tried to groan again and realised she couldn't, because some idiot had shoved a tube down her throat. She scrabbled at the apparatus attached to her face and yanked the whole thing off. The tube scraped free of her throat, causing a coughing fit. She sat up and dry-heaved for a few seconds with the whiff of antiseptic filled her nostrils.

Once she got her breath back she glanced down and realised that someone had cut the top of her catsuit off. Cheeky things! At least they'd covered her up with some kind of gown and her bottom half was still tightly clad in pink lycra. The green-grey colour of the top did not complement her complexion, but it confirmed she was in a hospital. It didn't matter what planet she found herself on, hospitals always seemed to boast institutional colour schemes and the same smell. This one also felt like it was swaying slightly.

She was sitting on a narrow cot in a small curtained cubicle made of material that matched her gown. The mask she'd pulled off earlier dangled from an indignantly beeping machine. No doubt someone would be by to check on that shortly. She wondered where Panda was. He should be by her bedside, wringing his hands with concern or supplying grapes. Preferably in fermented, liquid form.

She swung her legs off the side of the bed and managed the groan she'd tried earlier. She needed a couple of painkillers and a nice cup of tea to wash them down. She wouldn't say no to a bag of chips either. Hospital canteens did chips, right?

She re-arranged the gown into a knotted bra top, fluffed her hair up and patted her hip holster to find it empty. She went through the drawers next to the bed and was relieved to find her blaster untouched. Raised voices floated through the curtain. She peeked through a gap into the next cubicle. It was empty, but she could see figures facing off behind the next curtain.

"Put that thing away, you don't frighten me," a male voice said.

Iris saw one of the figures raise something and plunge it into the other's chest. Like a gross parody of shadow theatre.

She ran forward and threw the curtain aside. As she did so the injured person fell backward, grabbing the material and entangling them both. Iris staggered as the material flicked her in the face. She swept it aside and saw the injured person was a man in a white tunic. He had a very large hypodermic needle sticking out of him and was struggling to breathe. She bobbed down, wondering if she should remove the needle. He tried to speak, but only managed to say "Hhhee..." before his whole body shuddered and he stopped breathing.

"Help!" Iris shouted, looking around for medical staff. She saw a figure fleeing towards the end of the ward. She drew her blaster and got off a few shots before the attacker disappeared through a door. The rays went wide, taking out an empty vase and a chunk of door frame. It only dawned on Iris as she set off in pursuit that the figure seemed to be dressed in bright red nun's habit.

Panda prodded his sodden stomach and a more few drops of water oozed over his fur. He really was not built for unexpected dips in what he had now discovered was a very large canal. He'd lost track of Iris once the bus went down and had been ignominiously scooped out of the canal with a fishing net. I mean, Art Critic Panda being poked and prodded like an experimental specimen by a load of off-duty ship's engineers! Admittedly, being used in mad scientific experiments did seem to be a common side-effect of travelling the cosmos with Iris.

Once he'd loosed a stream of invective at the would-be fishermen, they soon decided to free him from the net. He now found himself perched on top of a warm air vent in the engine room of the hospital ship the *Healing Embrace of Her Lady of the Shining Sun*, known colloquially as *Warm Hugs*.

Panda noted the presence of a convoluted structure of glass tubes half-hidden behind a makeshift curtain, and a pack of cards on a packing case. These looked like his kind of people.

He squeezed a bit more moisture from his fur and jumped down from the vent. Several sets of dark-green eyes followed him as he sauntered over and picked up the brightly-coloured cards.

"So, do you play poker on Mars?" he asked, waving the pack around.

Iris burst through the door after the nun with violent tendencies and was confronted with a choice of three corridors. Each one was populated with at least one person in bright red flowing robes and yellow wimples. Several were assisting patients, judging by the gowns they were wearing. All of them turned their heads towards her as she waved her blaster around and shouted for help. None of them looked like they had just fled a crime scene. The nearest nun, a short woman with dark green eyes and a lived-in face, hustled towards her.

"Are you hurt?"

"Not me," Iris replied, "But there's a chap in there with a great big needle in his chest."

Iris followed the nun as she rushed into the ward and crouched over the injured man. The nun checked for vital signs. She closed the man's eyes and touched the man gently on the forehead, chin and each cheek. She then repeated the gesture on her own face and murmured, "May you find peace with the Lady of the Shining Sun."

She started to struggle to her feet and Iris lent her a hand to rise. The nun's calm dark eyes studied Iris for a second.

"You're the woman we rescued from the strange sinking vessel. I didn't expect you to survive, let alone be running around this soon."

"I'm quite hard to kill."

"Obviously," the nun replied.

"I'm Iris."

"And I'm Mother Healer by Her Grace We Live, or Mother Grace for short. Head of this branch of our order and Captain of the *Healing Embrace of Her Lady of the Shining Sun*."

Mother Grace indicated they should both enter Iris' original cubicle. The nun sank wearily onto a wooden chair while Iris leaned against the bed.

"Tell me what happened," Mother Grace said. She didn't seem particularly surprised that someone had murdered one of her staff.

Panda won the first hand of Martian poker, his prize a glass of pungent hooch from the apparatus he had identified as a home-made still. He downed the shot, to the appreciation of his audience and then convinced the assistant engineer to go in search of news of Iris. He turned back to his main opponents in the card game, the Chief Engineer and her Second Assistant. Mother and son he would guess. They both had the same build, stocky but not fat, muscles developed from maintaining the ship. The same dark brown hair, both wearing it long and pulled back in a ponytail. The Chief Engineer had laughter lines around her eyes and mouth, and a mottled patch of skin on her right temple. Her son wore the intense look of youth but sported the same birthmark on his forehead.

The Chief tried to stare him out and then grinned when she realised he didn't actually blink. Panda dipped his head and raised his glass in appreciation of her efforts. They played a few more hands before they were interrupted.

"There's been a murder!" the assistant engineer exclaimed. He looked disappointed by their lack of reaction. Panda studied the crew. By their sighs and resigned looks he deduced none of them was the murderer. Otherwise, the culprit would have to be a better actor than he had ever had the pleasure of watching.

"Who's dead then?" the Chief asked.

"Doctor Rangan. No one knows how. Mother Grace has appointed someone to investigate the matter."

Panda groaned and helped himself to another glass of hooch.

"Bet I can guess who that is," he muttered, downed the drink and jumped down from the card table.

"There'll be no shortage of suspects," the Chief said. "Rangan was a womanising, drunken, no good sonofabitch. Mother Grace only kept him around because doctors are in short supply these days."

"He wasn't that bad," her son replied, grinning. "You're just upset 'cause he never propositioned you."

Panda bowed to the group.

"I bid you adieu, my friends. I hate to imagine what trouble Iris could get into trying to find a murderer without me to assist her."

He heard the Chief giving her son a clip round the ear as he exited the boiler room.

Iris surveyed the crime scene. The large needle that was still hanging out of Doctor Rangan's extremely still chest. She probably ought to be doing something clever with powders and brushes and fingerprints, but that seemed like a lot of hard work. She backed away from the body and nearly tripped over the flowing red robes she now wore, at the insistence of Mother Grace. Her previous outfit had been deemed unsuitable. At least she'd managed to strap her blaster to her thigh underneath the robe. Best not to leave that lying around with a murderer on the loose.

"Iris Wildthyme, MBI, Martian Bureau of Investigation," Iris intoned as she mimed holding out a badge and swung round to face an imaginary suspect. She let out a squeal of delight as she found Panda staring up at her, one eyebrow raised.

"Panda lovey, am I pleased to see you! Glad you haven't floated off to who-knows-where."

"The last I heard you were unconscious. I see that didn't last long."

"You know me, it never does. Apart from that time with the spiked cocktails and the lizard men... or was it spiked lizards and giant cockroaches? Never mind, we have a murder to solve!"

She strode towards the door, adjusting her wimple as she went.

After several circuits of identikit corridors, Panda was relieved to finally arrive at Doctor Rangan's cabin. Though 'cabin' was putting it generously: it was more like a bunk or a cell. There was a narrow bed suspended halfway up the wall, with a cramped desk and chair beneath it. The only other furnishings were a thin cupboard and a small set of drawers.

The deceased doctor had not been the tidiest of people. There were heaps of papers on the desk and a pile of dirty undergarments on the floor, which Panda carefully skirted.

"Where shall we start?" Iris asked.

"I'll take the desk. You take everything else," Panda suggested.

Iris grabbed him under his arms and deposited him on top of the desk. Panda wished she would not take quite so much pleasure in manhandling him.

He started rifling through the papers as Iris tossed clothes from the closet. He soon discarded most of the items, leaving him with a set of patient notes for one Arne Duran and a bundle of gambling slips.

"Aha!" Iris exclaimed.

Panda glanced up to find her brandishing a bottle of dark spirits in one hand and some strongly perfumed letters in the other. The bottle disappeared beneath the folds of her habit. For medicinal emergencies, Panda guessed. The letters were scattered over the table.

Panda noticed a variety of handwriting styles and the aroma of spicy aftershave mingled with floral scents.

"Our clues so far, my dear Panda. A multitude of lovers, a gambling habit, accompanied no doubt by a drinking habit. Plus medical notes indicating a dispute over a patient," Iris said.

"It appears the doctor had a surfeit of vices." Panda agreed. "Pity we didn't meet him when he was alive."

"Two birds with one stone to start with," Iris suggested.

"The fractious patient and rival doctor?"

"Yes. You play good cop and I'll play bad cop," she said.

Panda smiled at the idea of Iris playing hardball. She could be a tough old bird, but she trapped more flies with honey.

Talking of flying things, Panda suddenly found himself nose to nose with one as he followed Iris into Arne Duran's room. The creature looked like a small ochre-coloured lizard attached to oversize iridescent insect wings. It cocked its head to one side and eyeballed Panda, then flew over to a small man huddled in the far corner of the ward.

"What is that?" Panda asked. "And is it likely to develop a taste for panda?"

"It's a bizzard. Her name is Blinky and I don't know why she would develop a taste for anything other than bryophyte roots," a soft voice responded from the side of the room.

"Panda's just a little leery of reptiles. We've not always had the best of luck with them," Iris replied, looking at the short nun who had just spoken. "And you are?"

"Sister Brings Healing to the Body and Mind – or Sister Headshrinker."

Panda noticed she had a more pronounced version of the mottled birthmarks the Chief Engineer and her son shared. The man in the corner started crooning to the bizzard. Panda thought he looked pretty harmless for a dangerous mental patient.

Blinky fluttered into the air before settling down as Panda sat on the floor next to the odd pair.

"Arne?" he asked quietly.

The man looked up at Panda. His eyes widened, he nodded and went back to petting the flying lizard. Arne was bald, with a spider-web of scars over the right side of his head and face. Panda wondered what kind of weapon would cause such injuries. The pattern was too even to be accidental. In the background he could hear Iris questioning the nun, but he ignored them. He let his gaze wander over the patched clothing Arne wore.

He realised he was being sized up in return. The wariness in Arne's expression relaxed. Panda realised he had been categorised as non-threatening.

"I need to talk to you about Doctor Rangan," Panda said.

"Heard someone offed him. Wasn't me," Arne replied, looking Panda straight in the eye. "I've killed when I had to, but I don't take no pleasure in it."

"We'd heard...," Panda started to say, but Arne interrupted him.

"You heard the psycho had a beef with him. I do... I *did*, but only when he tried to take Blinky away and shoot me full of drugs. If he'd tried again, I might've hurt him, but everyone would've known it was me. I don't like to leave my room."

Arne gave Panda another hard stare and then started feeding Blinky some kind of pale vegetation. The flying lizard flicked her tongue in and out in delight. Panda got the impression their conversation was at an end.

Iris sauntered over to Sister Headshrinker. The sister watched her carefully. Iris could tell from her posture that her quarry might flee at any minute. This was not a woman in the secure and serene grip of faith. Iris stopped a couple of feet away.

"I assume you've heard about Doctor Rangan?" Iris asked.

"Yes."

"Did you get on with the deceased?"

"No."

"Where were you when he was killed?"

"Here."

"You're a woman of very few words aren't you?" Iris asked, exasperation tingeing her words.

The sister looked at Iris. Her dark eyes betrayed little.

"Do you mean you were in this room? Don't just say yes! Exactly what were you doing."

"Yes, in this room. I was helping Arne with his guided meditation therapy."

"Why didn't you get on with Doctor Rangan?"

"He was from a very traditional school of medicine. He saw patients as a puzzle to be solved with medication and intervention. I come from a holistic healing background. He felt I was not qualified to be treating patients."

"I'm sure that made you very angry."

"Sometimes. Now, if you'll excuse me, I have other patients to attend to."

With that, the sister left. Iris poked her head round the door to watch her walk quickly down the corridor. She sighed. It was always so difficult to tell the evil nuns from the good ones.

Panda and Iris got into a rhythm over the next couple of days of pouncing on suspects and interviewing them. Though Panda felt it was probably unnecessary for Iris to yell, "Nobody expects Iris Wildthyme!" every time they stopped someone to talk to them. They made themselves at home in the engine room when not wandering the ship. Panda felt he thought better with a full glass in hand. The Chief was happy enough to accommodate them while she tried to win back her reputation as the sharpest card player on *Warm Hugs*. Meanwhile, the boat wended its way along the Euphrates towards North Point, the floating city that marked the crossroads of several of the major Martian waterways.

Panda sat playing Patience as he mulled over the possible suspects. It had taken several days to work their way through Doctor Rangan's roster of lovers. The Doc certainly had wide-ranging tastes, and prodigious stamina, judging by the procession of skinny, rounded, freckled, pasty, well-endowed, loud, tall and short men and women he'd been doing the horizontal tango with. One of the older nuns had been very embarrassed to find her passionate love-notes had been discovered, but none of them were obvious suspects.

The Chief's son, affectionately known as Chief Junior, or CJ, plonked himself on the stool next to Panda.

"Figured out who done it?" he asked.

Panda threw his hands up theatrically.

"It could be any of them."

"None of his bits on the side did it then? I was dead sure it might be one of them. He did seem to be trying to work through most of the staff and patients before he got off at North Point."

"Rangan was leaving at North Point?"

"Yeah, he was a refugee from South Point. Decided to get out when the local government lost control to the Scorched Dirt Brigade. Mother Grace agreed to let him work for safe passage. Her Ladyship's order is neutral, see. Gives medical aid to anyone, so most people leave us be. They might need us someday."

"Umm...," Panda pondered. "Perhaps somebody didn't want the Doc to get where he was going?"

He turned towards the cot at the back of the room that Iris had taken to napping on. All that greeted him was a rumpled blanket. Where had the woman got to now? CJ followed his gaze.

"She went haring off when she saw Sister Headshrinker going past the starboard porthole."

Iris was attempting to creep down a ladder onto the lowest deck of the ship. Sister Headshrinker had disappeared down it a few seconds before. Iris stepped carefully off the lowest rung and into a narrow dark corridor. She saw the sister go through a door further down.

Iris contemplated the thick steel door and put her ear to it experimentally. All she could hear were muffled sounds. Only one thing for it, she decided. Burst through the door and surprise them. She gripped her blaster in her right hand, pushed on the handle with her left and fell against the door as it refused to budge. Iris decided to make a tactical retreat.

She noticed an identical door on the opposite side of the corridor and hurried through it. Inside was a large, dimly-lit storeroom, filled with spare beds, equipment, blankets and other medical supplies. Unlike the rest of the ship, it was a mess. Things were piled high and deep, as if in a hurry. She grabbed a chair from a stack. While she was waiting she decided to make a few alterations to her borrowed habit and started hacking off the bottom of the robe with a pair of surgical scissors from a nearby box.

She'd just finished hemming her new mini-robe when she heard a creak from the corridor outside. She moved over to the door and eased it open. Peering outside she saw Sister Headshrinker heading back up the ladder.

Iris waited until she was out of sight and then slipped through the door. She quietly padded up and down the adjacent corridors until she was satisfied that the locked room was a mirror to the storeroom she had been in. The question was – what did the sister have hidden in that room, and had Doctor Rangan found out?

Panda and Iris reconvened on the upper deck, making themselves comfortable in the chairs usually occupied by convalescing patients. It was late and deserted. Panda studied the twin moons rising in the sky. Familiar, yet always looking down on a different Mars.

*Warm Hugs* had been making her way to one side of the gigantic canal over the last few days and Panda could now see the way the landscape dropped suddenly away on the left horizon. It was easy to forget that the canals criss-crossed the planet several miles above the surface, suspended on giant pillars. A feat of amazing engineering by a long-dead race.

Iris sat forward in her chair, deep in thought. Panda thought she looked surprisingly elegant in her short-skirted, sleeveless red robe. The wimple had been reduced to a headband, holding back her long blonde locks. He occasionally had trouble reconciling this version of Iris with the older, shorter, more bohemian version he had also travelled with. Adventures all over time with multiple incarnations of the same person could play havoc with one's synapses. He rubbed the bridge of his nose.

Iris surfaced from her reverie and grinned at him. She had that look of mischief in her eyes that Panda recognised, no matter which face she was wearing.

"Tomorrow we track down our last suspect," she said, waving the gambling slips around. "But first a nightcap and some beauty sleep."

They started out by questioning their new friends among the crew. The engineers obviously liked a bit of a wager. Mother Grace did not approve of gambling, so they kept their card games strictly between themselves. Iris noticed CJ looking a little squirrelly and cornered him afterwards.

She smiled at him and trailed a finger down his cheek.

"A strapping lad like you must have gone looking for a little excitement outside the engineering room?"

CJ blushed. Growing up aboard a ship run by nuns had not equipped him to deal with Iris in fullblown charm mode. He nodded.

"Tell me more...," Iris whispered.

"You...," He croaked and cleared his throat. "You want to see Nobby, he's an orderly. Has his fingers in all the pies."

Iris gave CJ a peck on the cheek, and smiled inwardly as his entire face coloured.

There was always someone around who was wheeling and dealing.

"Come on Panda, let's go and see if we can find some trouble."

Panda sighed. Finding trouble was never much of a problem for them.

They cornered Nobby in a supply closet near the two hospital wards on the main deck. As expected, he was a weaselly-looking man, with short tufts of hair sticking up at all angles and several large moles on his face. There was a similarity between all Nobbys in the universe, Panda thought. They all had darting eyes and talked ten to the dozen. Panda idly wondered if they were a hitherto unknown parasitic race, inserting themselves into communities to fulfil the function of slightly dodgy geezer.

Nobby looked at them in surprise and then adopted a cunning expression.

"'Allo lady and furry gent. I'd 'eard we had strangers aboard. I knew sooner or later you'd come to see old Nobby. Everyone does, 'cause Nobby 'ere can cater to all sorts of needs."

Panda felt his fur flatten in distaste. He waved Doctor Rangan's gambling slips at the man, while Iris leaned against the door to ensure Nobby could not do a runner.

"We wanted a piece of the action, old man," Panda said.

Nobby grinned and nodded vigorously.

"A man after me own heart. What's your game? We have a different one every night." Nobby flicked the papers in Panda's hand. "Normally you'd 'ave to provide a stake to come in on the action, but you could take Rangan's place... and his debts."

"Left a bit of a hole did he?" Iris asked.

"He 'as, he 'as. Regular player, was the Doc. Of course if you don't fancy taking on his debts then we could work something else out." Nobby said, leching towards Iris.

Panda slapped the gambling strips against the palm of one hand, making Nobby jump.

"Big debts. How were you going to get him to pay?" Panda asked.

69

"I 'ave me methods. Look, I gotta get on."

Nobby slipped past Panda and pinched Iris on the bum, causing her to leap away from him, giving him a clear exit.

"Cheeky little bugger," Iris said, rubbing her behind.

"A most revolting man. I believe he could commit murder, but would have preferred Rangan alive to pay his debts." Panda was getting fed up with their investigation.

Iris must have been feeling the same way as she declared that enough was enough. They would gather all the suspects together that afternoon and get the whole thing sorted out.

Panda looked at her in surprise.

"You know who did it?"

"No idea lovey, but I'm sure a bit of theatrics will flush them out."

Panda groaned to himself. Iris and theatrics could be a very explosive combination.

Iris fluffed her hair out and applied a little lipstick, which she had stolen from a nurse's' room. She smoothed down the mini-dress she had fashioned from a nun's habit and took a deep breath. Showtime. She pushed the open the double doors to the ward where the murder had happened. Heads turned towards her. All interested parties were there, perched on stools, chairs or beds. Some leaned against the walls. She clocked the presence of the engineering crew and a couple of no-nonsense nurses that Panda had recruited in case of trouble.

This was fun. She could see why her chum Aggie loved a good dénouement scene. Now to unmask the killer.

She pointed at each suspect in turn.

"One! Of you! Is a murderer! This afternoon we will discover who plunged that gigantic needle into Doctor Rangan's chest," Iris said, miming the stabbing for emphasis. She noticed Panda rolling his eyes at her and grinned.

She walked over to Sister Headshrinker. The sister leaned against the bed that held Arne and his flying pet. Arne was as far back on the bed as he could get, with his knees pulled up in front of him. The sister was trying to shield him from the rest of the room.

"How dare you drag my patient here and subject him to accusations?" the sister demanded, her eyes scrunched up angrily.

"Because he attacked the Doctor before, so why not again?" Iris asked. This elicited a slight gasp from those unaware of Arne's history.

"He had no reason to attack him again. His new treatment regime was working," the sister argued.

Iris nodded, surprising the sister by her agreement.

"No he didn't, but you did, Sister. Doctor Rangan called you a witch doctor. Said you shouldn't be let loose on patients. Tried to stop you treating Arne."

"The man was prejudiced, but he was also a talented surgeon. We needed him to treat people."

"Maybe," Iris said. She leaned forward and whispered in the nun's ear. "Perhaps he found out what you're hiding on the lower deck."

Fear rippled across the sister's face. Iris winked and turned her attention to the next suspect.

Panda saw the sister's reaction to whatever Iris had whispered and indicated to the Chief to keep an eye on the nun. Iris strolled casually over to Nobby, who was jangling something metal in his right hand and tapping one foot against the floor. He was the epitome of guilt, but just what was he guilty of?

Iris leaned against the wall beside Nobby. Panda nonchalantly placed himself on Nobby's other side. Nobby jiggled from foot to foot, looking from one to the other. Iris gave him a wide smile. Panda looked up at him with wide, dark and unblinking eyes.

"Nobby. You also have a motive to kill Doctor Rangan. He did owe you a rather large amount of money," Iris said.

Nobby looked from her to Panda. He had developed something of a perspiration problem.

"It weren't that much really."

Iris produced the wad of gambling slips from her pocket and bopped Nobby on the nose with them.

"Not much? He was an avid, if rather unsuccessful gambler."

There was a loud tut from Mother Grace.

"Couldn't pay it back if he were dead, could he?" Nobby said. "Dead players ain't good for business."

There was an even louder tut and Nobby shot a glance at Mother's Grace disappointed face.

"Unpaid debts are also bad for business," Panda pointed out. He saw the muscles on Nobby's legs start to bunch. Panda gripped Nobby's arm and motioned for CJ to cover the doors to the ward in case he jackrabbited.

Nobby gave him a disgruntled look, but left Panda's paw where it was.

Iris wandered over to the largest crowd of suspects in the room. The many and varied lovers of the dead Doctor.

"So, we have the unstable patient, the maligned nun with secrets and the wheeler-dealer who proclaims death is bad for business. But we also have the rest of you," Iris pontificated, pointing at the crowd of exes.

"I think...," she paused for a second. "It was all of you!"

She was pleased with effect her statement had. Several men and women surged to their feet and gesticulated wildly in protest. She concluded that the Doctor obviously had a taste for overly dramatic people. She could make out calls of "Don't be ridiculous!", "How could we all do it?" and other protestations.

From the corner of her eye, she saw Nobby wrench his arm from Panda's grip, dodge past CJ and flee. Sister Headshrinker was also heading for the exit in a serene but deceptively fast glide.

Iris performed a theatrical bow.

"You've been a great crowd. If you'll excuse me?"

She ran towards the door, shouting at Panda as she went.

"You and CJ take the weasel. The Chief and I will take the nun on the run!"

Panda was puffing slightly as he dragged himself up the final steps to the upper deck. CJ and a burly nurse had trapped Nobby on the starboard prow. The little man had climbed up the side of the boat. Nobby balanced precariously, his arms windmilling as he tried to avoid plunging into the murky depths of the Euphrates.

CJ and the nurse waited for Nobby to return to the deck. After a few more minutes of arm-waving and eye-rolling, Nobby rejoined the party on deck, his face white with fear.

"It was me or 'im you know. They were gonna kill me if I didn't get the money."

Nobby's shoulders sank as he made his confession. He lowered himself down to sit on the side of the boat. He looked down at his dangling feet.

"You killed Doctor Rangan?" Panda asked.

"Me or 'im. The bosses wanted the money or an example setting. Said people needed to know you couldn't mess with them."

"The bosses?"

"The North Point Syndicate."

Panda heard CJ's sharp intake of breath and looked at him questioningly.

"They run North Point – mainly through fear – but *Warm Hugs* is neutral. All the gangs pledged not to operate on board."

"Yeah, well. They lied."

CJ closed in on Nobby and grabbed him.

"Mother Grace saved your life. She offered you a job, a life away from the Syndicate. This is how you repay her."

CJ yanked Nobby down from the side of the boat and the man fell to his knees on the deck.

"I should throw you overboard right now," CJ threatened.

Nobby did not react. He seemed like a rag doll with the stuffing knocked out.

"We better let Mother Grace decide what to do with him," Panda said.

Iris headed for the bowels of the ship. Taking a shortcut through the Chapel, and leaving ruffled nuns in her wake, she arrived at the storeroom just as Sister Headshrinker was unlocking the door. Iris skidded to a halt and drew her blaster. The sister looked at her calmly.

"Put your weapon away. You don't need it," the sister said. She opened the door and ushered Iris inside.

Iris motioned with her gun. "After you."

The sister stepped through the door. Iris heard her say, "Don't be afraid." She assumed the sister was talking to her until she moved inside. She saw rows of wasted bodies lying in cots. A few healthier individuals were moving among the sick, giving them sips of water or spoons of gruel. Iris recognised the ravages of starvation in the paper-thin skin stretched across prominent bones. The distinctive mottled birth marks on all the faces standing out brighter than their hollow eyes. Most of them were too ill to react, but some put themselves between their families and Iris. She realised she was still brandishing her blaster. She blushed and holstered the gun.

73

"Sorry, I..."

The sister walked among her people, soothing them with a smile or a touch. She looked back at Iris.

"None of this is connected to Doctor Rangan's death. He didn't know about any of this."

"What happened?" Iris asked quietly.

"Resources are dwindling. The weakest suffer." The sister gave a small, sad smile. "Our tribe relies on water from the Euphrates. Our supply disappeared."

The sister moved to back towards Iris.

"The North Point Syndicate blocked the tributary that fed our settlement in the desert below." The expression in her eyes grew flinty. "I was part of a diplomatic group sent to plead with the Syndicate. The others were killed, but I escaped. Mother Grace took me in and started helping us."

Iris knew desert life was hard. The elements would soon reclaim the settlement. Distant memories of dehydration and helplessness surfaced, prodding her into action. She leaned toward the sister.

"Tell me more about this tributary and the North Point Syndicate."

Within twelve hours, Iris had put a volunteer strike team together. Panda sometimes forget Iris had been an agent of MIAOW. That she knew how to plan a mission if needed. He followed her down to the crew cabin where they were keeping Nobby.

"We need intel on the Syndicate defences of the tributary, Panda. And we've got just the murderer to provide it."

"What if he doesn't co-operate?" Panda asked.

Iris smiled back at him. One of her jaunty, "don't worry, I've got a plan" smiles that generally led to trouble. Often accompanied by running away from something dangerous.

"He'll co-operate. Mother Grace has given me permission to offer him a deal."

They arrived at Nobby's cell and nodded at the orderly guarding him. He unlocked the door and they squeezed inside. Panda found himself face-to-face with the desk beneath the bunk and no sign of Nobby. He cleared his throat several times until Iris glanced down at him.

"Sorry lovey," Iris said and lifted Panda up so he could perch on the edge of the bunk. Nobby was lying on his side with his wrists tied together in front of him. Panda wiggled to the far end of the bunk, making sure he was out of kicking range. Nobby stared at them sullenly.

"What d'ya want?"

"Your help," Iris replied.

"Huh?"

Panda saw Iris' face harden.

"You will tell us everything you know about how the North Point Syndicate controls the water system. If not, Mother Grace will hand you over to them with a declaration that the sisterhood will no longer treat Syndicate members."

"But – they'll kill me!" Nobby wailed.

"You're dead one way or another," Iris replied. "Help us and we'll see you get looked after."

"Take the deal, old chap." Panda added. Playing good cop to a tee, even if he did say so himself.

Panda was more than ready for a drink by the time they finished grilling Nobby a few hours later.

Shortly after sundown, Panda found himself in a small rowing-boat. They were gliding along a tiny waterway between the floating brothels and casinos of North Point. Panda watched the oars dipping smoothly in and out of the water, accompanied by small grunts of efforts from CJ. The young man carefully steered them around the other boats moored along the sides of the passageway.

Panda could make out the small boat in front of them with the Chief at the oars. Iris was silhouetted against the moonlight as she sat in the lead boat, her head bent over the map Nobby had scrawled for them earlier. Panda clutched a copy of the map in his paw. He saw Iris lift a hand above her head and pump her fist. Panda repeated the gesture. Signal received and understood.

"Next left," he whispered to CJ.

CJ grunted in return and concentrated his effort on the left-hand oar. The boat swung slowly around a slight bend as the waterway split in two. Panda waved to Iris as they floated out of sight.

Panda was acutely aware of the home-made explosive nestled in a sling against his furry belly. His stomach gurgled with nerves and the Dutch courage he had consumed before leaving *Warm Hugs*.

Panda and CJ flinched every time they spotted another boat or a voice floated from a balcony above. At one point, Panda had to duck as a bottle came flying through the air from a particularly rowdy bar. He felt it brush his ear and land with a plop in the water beside the boat.

Finally CJ eased the oars from the water and let their momentum nudge them into a nearby pontoon. He jumped from the boat, taking a guide rope with him and quickly tied them off.

"Come on," he said and offered a hand to Panda.

Panda stood up. His legs turned to jelly as the boat rocked. He inched forward and grabbed CJ's hand. The lad lifted him cleanly from the boat, so all Panda needed to do was plant his feet firmly on the floating decking.

Panda re-arranged the sling, ensuring the explosives Iris had concocted with the Chief were unlikely to bounce around. He examined the map and trotted off down a narrow alley. CJ drew a large knife from a sheath on his waistband and followed the little bear.

Iris lowered her fist and saw Panda's boat disappear from sight. Their boat ploughed on towards a busier area of the city. Iris checked that her bag of explosives was still safe and dry in the bottom of the boat. She was still dressed in her modified nun's-habit-slash-mini-dress. The Chief remained in her usual trousers, and a slightly prettier than normal shirt. The sister had shed her habit and borrowed a similar outfit to the Chief's. Their route would be busy, so they aiming to look like crew on shore leave. Or at least the other two were. Iris had argued that if she were on shore leave, she would want to look like she was going to a damn good party.

They floated out of the quiet channel they had been following and entered a busier fairway. Fairy lights and lanterns adorned the gaudy entrances to bars, brothels and gaming houses. Taxi boats puttered past them with drunken passengers. Iris merrily waved at them, brandishing a half-empty bottle of hooch which she had been swigging from.

"Cheers!" she shouted to a particularly rowdy group of lads.

"Don't draw attention to us," Sister Headshrinker hissed.

"Your long face will draw more attention," Iris shot back. "Smile! Look like you're having a good time."

The sister smiled thinly. Iris sighed. Obviously brooding looked much better on her. The Chief cut through the tension by exchanging a bit of banter with some fishermen who invited the ladies to join them for a bit of fun.

The channel suddenly widened into a basin area and the fairy lights faded as the Chief heaved on the oars. One side of the basin was a straight line, where the Syndicate had built a dam across the tributary that normally provided water to the desert tribes below. Iris could see lanterns hanging at either end of the dam. Solitary guards stood in the twin pools of light. Panda and CJ should be taking care of the nearest guard. Iris and her group needed to take out the other guard and there was no way to sneak up on him.

The Chief continued to steer the boat towards the far side of the dam. Iris saw the guard straighten up as he noticed their approach.

"You need to turn around and go back!" he called.

"I hope this ridiculous ruse of yours works," the sister said as Iris stood up.

Iris swayed unsteadily. Just one too many nips from that bottle, she thought as she started singing loudly. Some piratical ditty that had popped into her head. She had some of the words wrong, but the natives would hardly notice. Especially as she was slurring most of them.

The guard continued to shout, but Iris' singing just grew louder in reply. The boat bumped against the side and the guard grabbed their mooring rope. He looked annoyed but not suspicious.

"Sorry about our friend," the Chief called. "She's new to the city, wanted to see the view from over here."

Iris tottered toward the dock, causing the boat to rock wildly again. The guard steadied her before Iris tipped them all in. She simpered at him in thanks, and got him to help her out of the boat. She pretended to stumble as she stepped on to the bank and threw her full weight against him. He toppled to the ground with Iris landing on top of him. She apologised, drew her blaster and stunned him before he had time to react. She twirled round to face the boat triumphantly.

"What did I tell you girls? Iris knows a trick or two."

Panda and CJ peered around the edge of a wooden warehouse that stood next to the dam. They could see the guard propped against a lamppost, looking bored. Panda grinned as the sound of Iris' very bad singing carried over the water towards them. The guard also noticed the noise. He stood up and wandered to the edge of the water, straining to see what was happening at the far end of the dam.

Panda and CJ crept quickly from their hiding place. Panda motioned CJ forward. The lad carried a knife, whereas Panda could only swipe at the guy's legs while juggling his load of unstable explosives. Iris had sworn blind the explosives were safe but Panda knew better than to take any chances.

CJ got behind the guard and brandished his knife. But then Panda saw him hesitate, reverse the knife and give the guard a good whack on the head with the hilt. The guard crumpled to the ground, raising a bit of noise and dust. CJ and Panda looked around worriedly, but luckily no-one was near enough to hear. They dragged the guard behind the warehouse and CJ made quick work of tying him up.

They ran back towards the dam and saw the guard on the far side had also been incapacitated. Iris and Panda made their way onto the narrow dam wall from their respective ends. About a third of the way in, they each stopped and got to work with their explosives.

Iris set the explosive as far down the dam wall as she could reach. The dam had been hastily constructed and water bubbled out of little fissures in the cement. The twin explosions should be enough to breach the wall. She carefully fed out the fuse wire behind her as she started to make her way towards Panda's end of the dam.

She stopped to rest and to check that the Chief and the sister were rowing back to the city side of the basin as planned. She carried on across the dam while trying very hard not to look down at the deep drop to her side. It was agonisingly slow progress, having to make sure the fuse wire did not snag or break. She finally made it to the far end where the others were now waiting.

"About bloody time," Panda grumbled affectionately as he helped her down from the dam wall.

"Okay, fingers crossed everyone," Iris said.

"Why would we cross our fingers?" Sister Headshrinker asked.

"Pray or something then," Iris replied as she bent to light the fuse wires.

The wire ignited and they watched silently as the little flame made its way across the dam. The nearest explosive blew with a booming noise which echoed around the basin. A minute later, just as people were starting to run towards the dam, the second bomb went off. They all felt the dock tremble beneath their feet. There was a tremendous roar as the force of the water forced its way through the holes they had made. The dam structure tumbled to the desert below, accompanied by a foaming waterfall.

"We did it!" Sister Headshrinker said, her eyes shining with tears.

"They'll rebuild it, you know," the Chief commented.

"I know, but it gives us a few months."

Iris looked around at the chaos they had wrought and smiled down at Panda.

"Our work here is done."

"Indeed," he agreed. "Time to get back to the bus."

"Do you think anyone around here would have any scuba gear, or a diving bell?" Iris mused.

"Don't know, but it's definitely time to go. In fact, run!" he replied as he spotted a group of angry-looking men heading towards them.

They ran.

# AND A DOG TO WALK
Dale Smith

The overall effect was like being trapped inside a rubber pyramid. The walls sloped down until they became a floor. There were two small portholes at the apex, and on one side a small hatchway led out into darkness. Iris squeezed out of it, wearing silver hot-pants that made the most of her long legs, but didn't sit well with the floral tea-tray she pushed ahead of her. She didn't have much room to sashay, and the four steaming mugs clinked against each other ominously.

Sue gave Phil a look.

"By rights," he said, "we should tip it straight down the toilet."

"You've tasted Iris' tea before, then?" Panda said archly.

Iris tossed her head back dismissively, but by then Sue had already reached up for one of the mugs, and Phil quickly followed suit. They both drank at the same time, making identical slurping noises as they discovered how hot the tea still was. They caught each other's eyes and giggled nervously. Then Phil started to cry.

"I'm sorry," Phil said with a fierce sniff.

"No, you're right," Sue said softly. "This is the saddest cup of tea I've ever tasted."

"Oh loves," Iris sighed. "You wait until you try the hobnobs."

Their friends said that empty-nest syndrome had driven them mad, but they would snap out of it. This was Phil and Sue, after all: they'd been together since university, raised two kids, shrunk one mortgage. They both worked with computers but it was by no means rocket science. But they were middle-aged, relatively fit and very definitely in love... not just with each other, but the dream of manned spaceflight. They had met when Sue had spotted Phil reading up on the Mercury 13, and at their wedding he arranged for Dr Helen Sharman to send a card warning Sue it wasn't too late to change her mind. They talked it over with their children, and volunteered the next day. As they had climbed into a bunker in Los Angeles for a thirty-day trial run, the mission psychologist had warned there was still a significant chance the training might kill them before they even got off the ground. Phil had asked whether the team would learn something that would help the next couple reach Mars. Now here they were: sitting in their underwear in a tin can travelling at 32,000 mph.

"Eight, nine, ten, Jack, Queen, King, Ace," Sue said, triumphantly throwing her cards down. "Boxer shorts please, Philip."

Phi grabbed protectively at his underwear.

"You cheated! I only suggested strip rummy because you're no good at it!"

"More fool you: I practised."

Phil looked cautiously around the habitat: it was smaller than his shed at home, and that had trouble fitting the lawn mower and Danny's old bike in it. This had machines and computers and flashing lights covering nearly every available space, and despite the training Phil still couldn't remember exactly what each of them was doing.

"You're sure there aren't any cameras?" he asked, not for the first time.

"Nope," Sue said. "But there are more beautiful sights out there than your scrawny little arse."

"Careful, woman!" Phil growled. "I will fart. You know I will. It will take the charcoal filters days to get rid of the smell."

"You," said Sue matter-of-factly, "are disgusting. Boxers: now!"

There was a tinny crackle in the air.

"Inspiration habitat, this is ground control," came the distorted, slightly mumsy voice. "When you receive this, it will be time."

They leapt up as one. Outside the portholes, as big as the moon in the night sky back home, was a milky white planet, its surface swirling and writhing under their gaze. Phil's hand found Sue's, and they both squeezed tight.

"Inspiration habitat, this is Ground Control," the distorted voice echoed again. "Your fly-by is on schedule. Congratulations: you have just become the first human beings to see the clouds of Venus with the naked eye."

They could hear the dull echo of the cheering back at Ground Control, and the instruments embedded all around them sprang into life. They knew that there was important cataloguing and diarising that they were expected to do. But just for that moment, they held each other tight and enjoyed it.

It hadn't even been the plan to fly-by Venus.

There were two windows of opportunity to fly to Mars every fifteen years, a magical alignment of the heavens that meant a rocket with the right kind of kick could coast there and back almost on gravity alone. If they had launched on the fifth of January 2018, in 501 days they would have seen Mars and been back telling the tale. But the politicians got involved, and so of course that deadline went whooshing by.

The problem was – as it always was – getting into space.

Or, more specifically, staying there.

It was easy to get up – but once you were in orbit you needed to move fast, otherwise you'd very quickly be a large crater in whatever desert you lifted off from. That took fuel, which added weight, which took more fuel, and pretty soon you were too big to go anywhere. To get something the size of the Inspiration into space needed a pretty serious push, and the Foundation just didn't have the time or the money to put it together.

NASA did. In fact, they were already building it.

It wouldn't be finished until 2017, but the Space Launch System would be big enough to get all the individual parts of the Inspiration into space. Then it would be relatively simply to fit them together and shoot Phil and Sue up there in a more traditional rocket, ready to climb aboard and head off into infinity. But convincing NASA meant convincing Congress, which meant the backup plan of a 2021 launch came into effect: a secondary alignment that would take them slipstreaming around Venus. It would take eighty days longer, but it would get them to Mars.

"So what do you want to do now?"

Phil sat with his back hunched against the wall, curled up almost into a ball. He looked around the tiny habitat again, but still nothing new had randomly materialised. Sue stood over by the "Waste and Hygiene Compartment", with the nozzle of the pee tube pushed firmly into her groin and her back turned to him. He couldn't see the point in the pretence of privacy, but it was more than his life was worth to admit that he could see what she was doing.

"Phil," Sue said exasperated, "I'm not your carer."

Phil didn't answer. He took the child's shape sorter out of the toy cupboard again and diligently dropped the square peg into the correct hole. They had to use the toy every couple of hours, as a backup check that the oxygen and the pressure were at normal: if they weren't, Phil would start trying to push the triangle through the circle and wouldn't be able to tell you why. He half-suspected it was just a ploy to give them something to do: 589 days took some filling.

"I want it to rain," Phil said sadly.

Sue just tutted loudly to herself.

"I know it *won't* rain," Phil retorted sharply. "But they could play us the sound or something. We could pretend."

Sue spun around, teeth tightly clenched and the pee tube still poking out of her waistband. It looked a little like somebody was trying to inflate her, but the look on her face told Phil that he'd better not laugh.

"Can you not," she growled, enunciating each of the words crisply, "just be quiet for one fucking minute?"

The radio crackled into life.

"Inspiration habitat, this is –"

Sue exploded.

"Christ!" she shouted into the ether, completely drowning out the radio. "Will you keep out of it too, Control!"

"Brilliant," snapped Phil. "It'll take three minutes for them to find out they've got to say that again!"

Sue folded her arms.

"Say another word before they do, Philip," she hissed dangerously. "I dare you."

One of the many computers that fed data out into the habitat suddenly woke up, spitting out a number of figures that Sue recognised as 3D co-ordinates and Phil called gobbledegook. She automatically looked at the gyroscopes that told them which way was up, because otherwise it would be impossible for her to tell that the rocket had just changed direction. But it had.

"That looked like a big one," Sue said, her anger boiling away.

Still, for the next six minutes, Phil said nothing.

A few hours later, the gyroscope twitched again without warning. Phil and Sue both glanced to each other, and then to the speaker that was their only connection with home. It remained silent, which meant that this latest course correction had been so urgent that Control didn't have the three spare minutes they needed to warn the habitat. Course corrections were inevitable on a flight like this – the only maps that existed for this journey effectively said that here be dragons – and they had been a pretty much daily fact of life since the launch. All the same, Phil and Sue found each other's' hands.

"Inspiration habitat," the voice came eventually: a different one from usual, sounding only a little less on edge than they were. "This is Ground Control. The onboard guidance correction system has notified us of a course correction. We just wanted to check in and tell you that everything is still looking good from down here."

"Onboard system?" Phil echoed.

"Control," Sue spoke clearly for the benefit of the microphones. "We understood that the onboard system was a failsafe. Please confirm current status."

They sat together in a tense silence while the radio signal made its slow progress back to Earth. It was almost a full ten minutes before the response came:

"Please hold for response," Control said.

"Sue?" Phil said. His grip on her hand tightened.

"They'll be checking with the PR people," Sue said, her eyes still on the speaker. "Anything they tell us will probably be on the front page of the *Sun* before it gets to us."

"So there's something they don't want everyone to know," he said flatly.

A few minutes later the speaker crackled into life again.

"Inspiration habitat, this is Ground Control. Current status is good. All systems are performing within parameters," the new voice said, with earnest sincerity. Then there was a slight pause. "The onboard guidance correction system was activated at 6:47am GMT: that's three hours ago in case you're not looking at a clock. The exit from the Venus slingshot was not as clean as we would have liked, but still within parameters. We have a new trajectory plotted and are using onboard systems so that radio delays don't stop you from getting back on track as soon as possible. But I have to reiterate: this is within the stretch we allowed when we planned this journey, and there is no need to worry."

"Is he reading from the press release?" Phil asked Sue.

She didn't answer. There was a crackle of static.

"Inspiration habitat: please await further assistance."

"Was that the same voice?" Phil asked.

"Further assistance?" Sue asked, struggling to keep her voice calm. "Control: please clarify further assistance."

"I think they mean me," said a deep voice behind them.

Phil and Sue turned. Floating in the air was a toy panda.

"Surprise!" it said.

"The Inspiration is crashing," Panda said, running his paws through the innards of one of the habitat's computers. There was a smell of singed polyester as he tapped two wires together and made a spark. "One of your backup propulsion units has failed, and Ground Control are a little worried about the signals they're getting from the tertiary unit. So at the moment, you're going to crash straight into Phobos."

Panda paused and pressed his paw to his ear.

"Yes," he said irritatedly to someone Phil and Sue couldn't hear. "I *am* breaking it gently. Would you like to take over?"

He gave them both a "what can you do" shrug and smiled.

"Yes, yes I'm doing it now. Hold on," Panda looked to Sue, who had her hand in the air and a look of confusion on her face. "Yes?"

"Crash?" was all she managed to say.

"Well, yes," Panda said with a slight tut. "But that's why I'm here."

"You can fix it?"

Panda paused.

"I wouldn't go so far..."

He winced and clapped his hand over his ear. When he spoke again, it was very much through gritted teeth.

"I was sent because there was some concern about the negative effect additional mass might have on your course. Whilst I am low on mass, I am not exactly high on experience of rocketry. But I am in contact with an —" Panda winced and cut off for a second again. "An expert! I was going to say expert. An expert with many years experience. *Many* years."

Somehow, neither Phil nor Sue were filled with confidence.

"But they can get us out?" Phil asked. He looked at Sue for reassurance, but she was still trying to come to terms with the talking stuffed toy. "I mean, if they got you here, they can get us out. Can't they?"

Panda snorted.

"Oh, yes. That would be pretty wouldn't it?" he giggled. "Two people with all of your DNA, on a jury-rigged transmat beam and no moonbase relay station. Oh we'd definitely want to give *that* a try."

Panda's paw clamped on his ear again.

"But it won't come to that," he said through gritted teeth. "You'll be perfectly all right."

Phil and Sue found each other's' hands again.

The panda floated into the middle of the tiny room and pulled something from a pocket. Phil could see it looked like a small silver ball. The panda twisted it once or twice in its paws, and then stopped: Phil had started to recognise when the panda was listening to the voice in its ear. He glanced over at Sue, but she didn't seem to have any more idea what to do. With all the training, all the preparing, all the planning, no-one had ever mentioned stuffed toy pandas to them.

The panda nodded, and twisted the ball again.

A wave of purple light flashed through the habitat and out through the walls. It struck Phil and Sue at chest height and passed through them with an electric tingle. The panda just looked at the surface of the globe intently.

"The scan will tell us what's wrong with the rocket," the panda said. It paused, and looked up at Phil. "Oh: and you'll be infertile for the next forty-eight years."

"I'll be *what*?"

The panda's paw clamped to its ear again.

"Hours!" it spat angrily. "For goodness sake will you enunciate, woman!"

Sue took a step forward, and grabbed the panda by its little furry neck. She pulled it up until they were nose to plastic nose.

"Listen," she said. "I'm starting to think that you could maybe be a little more helpful."

The silver globe pinged and turned blue.

"Shall I read you the results?" choked the panda hesitantly.

"That would be lovely," snarled Sue.

The panda was released with such force that it started to float away from them, spinning slowly top to toe as it went. It barely seemed to notice, staring deep inside the ball in its hands. It looked for all the world like a fortune teller at the fairground, and the furrowing of its brow suggested that the future didn't look good. It looked up at Phil and Sue as its backside bumped slowly against the wall.

"What?" Phil asked slowly.

"Two of your rockets have failed," the panda said.

"You told us that," Sue snapped.

"It seems you had a minor collision with some debris. It was always a possibility. That's why you have multiple fallbacks. But the tertiary backup has suffered damage as well, and a fuel pipe is blocked. The pressure has been building. I'm afraid it's at a critical stage."

"We're going to blow up?" Phil asked.

"It's a possibility," the panda admitted.

"Can we get your data to Ground Control?" Sue asked.

"I can turn the guidance correction off from here," the panda said, moving back to the Inspiration's computers. It was listening to its earpiece again. "But we'll be unable to manoeuvre –"

"That's great," Sue interrupted. "But if we get the data to them, they can fix the *next* spaceship."

The panda put its paw to its ear.

"We're sending the telemetry through to Ground Control now," the panda said, sounding only a little surprised.

"Okay. So now we have to go out and fix it," Sue said flatly. "Don't we?"

The habitat did have an airlock – they had gotten inside after all. They had even been trained in the procedure for getting outside for an EVA, but everyone had been at pains to stress that they wouldn't actually be expected to leave the habitat before splashdown unless something had gone horribly, terribly wrong. And now they were going to have to leave the habitat. Something had gone horribly, terribly wrong.

"I'll do it," Sue said. "If he's infertile, there's nothing to keep me here now."

But the panda was staring into its globe, shaking its head.

"Going outside won't help," it said, clearly receiving guidance from the unseen voice again. "There aren't enough pieces of the two rockets left to repair the third. But what we can..."

The panda's voice trailed off.

"Iris?" it said, tapping its paw against its ear. "Iris? I can't... Where are you going, you stupid woman? Iris!"

There was a squeal of static so loud that even Phil and Sue could hear it. The panda let out a shrill cry and pulled a small buzzing insect from its ear, throwing it across the habit: the insect hissed like dead air and crawled away up the first wall it landed on. The panda watched it, dumbstruck.

"I've lost her," it said. "She's gone."

"But you know what to do?" Phil asked the panda. "You can fix this?"

It didn't answer.

"Inspiration habitat, this is Ground Control. We are in receipt of data from..." The voice from the speaker paused: it clearly had no idea where the data had originated. "We are in receipt of data. Please confirm your current status."

"We have spoken —" Sue glanced across at Panda, and he shook his head violently. Sue took a breath and started again. "We are aware of the data you have received. We are awaiting further guidance."

Another long wait, and then:

"Please await further guidance."

The radio clicked off.

"They don't know you're here?" Sue asked.

Panda shook his head.

"Did you do this?"

"No!" he exclaimed, offended all the way down to his little feet.

Sue nodded, satisfied.

"Ok," she said. "So what do we do now?"

"Await further guidance," Panda said.

"The primary propulsion unit is gone," Ground Control told them. Phil and Sue sat at opposite ends of the habitat, staring at the speaker. They didn't look at each other. "Secondary too. We think... excuse me... we think they suffered a stress fracture some time during the Venus slingshot and had been falling apart a little more every time your course was corrected since then. There's nothing there now that we can use. Our people here are still going over this, but we haven't managed to come up with more than two options. Neither of them is going to bring you back to us. Mr and Mrs Yarrow, I want to assure you we will not stop looking for a third option here. But time is against us."

Phil wanted to scream at them to just get on with it.

"We can alter your course a little. You will still crash, but we can get you past the moons. You'll go right down to Mars in ten days time. We can follow the same drill we had for splashdown on Earth, but you'll come down hard without an ocean to land in. The Orion module we are using to get you down will not be able to get you back up again. We do not anticipate being able to maintain radio contact with you on the surface. Once you are down there, you will be staying. That is your option one."

Phil glanced across at Sue, but she was still staring intently at the speaker. The panda caught Phil's eye, but the glass beads were unreadable. Its face didn't move.

"We can overload what remains of the tertiary propulsion unit on your starboard side. We won't have any fine control of it, but we are pretty certain we can get it to make a pretty big bang. Big enough to push you out of your current trajectory and past the Mars slingshot. You would be free floating until one of the other bodies up there pulled you in, but we would have a little more time to try and come up with a follow-up plan. You would go into radio blackout in eighteen days. That is your option two. I'm sorry we don't have anything better for you. I'll give you some time to make your decision."

Sue stood up and rested a palm against the habitat wall. She could feel it throb gently underneath her skin, like a heart beating.

"My mother warned me this would happen if I married you," Phil said softly.

Sue smiled wanly.

"We should do the second one," the panda said urgently. "Anything that gives Iris more time to rescue us. Or there's always a chance that NASA might think of something, I suppose."

Phil looked across at Sue.

"You know what I think," Sue said, and he nodded. "What about you?"

Phil closed his eyes.

"Ground Control, this is Inspiration habitat," he said, his voice cracking a little. He rested his hand against Sue's, still pressed to the skin of the habitat, still pulsing with its strange chemical life. "We came here to see Mars. No-one promised us that we'd come back."

Seven minutes later, they had their reply:

"God bless you both."

It was the slowest crash in history.

The first thing they had checked was the toilet. Not for hygienic reasons: it was an essential part of their life-support, a similar design to the one in the main habitat. It did its best to recycle water that went into it in any form, and send what it managed to claw back either to be split into its component hydrogen and oxygen for breathing, or straight back into the water cycle. The solid waste was dried and stored in the walls as part of their radiation shielding. They were lugging as much of their physical supplies of water and air into the Orion as they could as well, but if the toilets weren't working it almost wasn't even worth it.

Life in the habitat had never been easy. It was a space that two people who loved each other couldn't sit in without wanting to kill each other. But it had been designed with the idea that they would spend 589 days in it, and everybody had done their best. The Orion module was half the size, and the longest anyone had ever expected to stay in it was twenty-one days. Its main purpose was to get them through the short journey from orbit to the Pacific Ocean without shaking them completely to pieces on the way. Now it was going to be their home for the rest of their lives.

Stop that thought. File it away.

Of course there were the food supplies to move too: they had to be left until last though, as most of the desiccated meals were packed into the walls as more radiation shielding. With stricter rationing, there was enough for the two of them for perhaps another 300 days. It was a ridiculously short amount of time, but it was still long enough for them to know about it if they got a good dose of radiation.

Phil looked up, and saw Sue dragging her spacesuit into the Orion. There were still two days before they needed to move in. The look on her face said that she was thinking the same thing. But their choices were limited: the panda was convinced that its Iris would come for it, but it had been nine days since it had lost contact with her, and no sign that she was on her way. Sue had started to wonder if she wasn't an invention, just the strange little creature's way of trying to give them hope.

Every one of those days, they had been crashing to their likely deaths.

Slowly.

When it came to it, they were alone. They entered radio blackout in the morning, after saying their goodbyes to friends and family and the space

90

enthusiast billionaire whose dream the Inspiration had been. Sue had wanted to leave everything to the last minute, enjoy the relative luxury of the habitat while they could. Phil had overruled her, not wanting to get stuck if anything went wrong. So they sat in the Orion, and then the panda told them it was time. Sue had sealed the outer hatch, and Phil had read the countdown aloud.

The separation was automatic, and they all felt the kick as they pushed away from the rest of the module. It would enter the thin Martian atmosphere just after they did, but several miles away. It would burn and disintegrate, falling onto the planet like a shower of meteorites. Sue knew that Phil was wondering if they might have been better staying aboard it. The Orion was designed for re-entry, but only through the relatively buoyant atmosphere of Earth and with a nice soft ocean to aim for. They were aiming for the north pole, but there was still a good chance that they might just spread themselves across the surface like a very expensive jam.

If they made it safely down, no-one would ever know. There was little hope of re-establishing radio communications from the surface. There was little hope of anything.

"Come on," Sue said to Panda.

She was just about to lift her helmet on, but motioned for the little stuffed toy to squeeze inside with her. He looked for a moment as if he might refuse, but anything might happen in the next few hours. Even if it turned out to be something that the suit couldn't help protect him from, he might be grateful of the simple human contact. He squeezed inside, and Sue and Phil checked and double-checked the seals on each other's' suits. Then they strapped themselves into the two seats provided. They were just too far apart to reach for each other, but that was probably for the best: once the descent began, their arms would snap clean in two if they tried to lift them.

"I always loved you," Phil said.

"Always?" Sue echoed. "You used to fancy my best friend."

"Yeah," Phil agreed. "But she never took me anywhere exciting."

And then they entered the atmosphere.

They didn't talk about the landing. They had all known how many different ways it could go wrong. One of the last messages they had received from Earth was Ground Control reminding them how to manually take control of the Orion if the corrections that had been sent to the landing software got overwritten: apparently there was a chance that the capsule could've forgotten it was landing on Mars and opened the parachutes at the wrong time. As it was, they were working off data that had been collected decades ago by the Viking probe. They had managed to survive: that was enough.

The first thing they found was each other, and hugged so tight that they could both feel the panda struggling inside Sue's suit. The next thing was to check the local atmosphere inside the capsule. Everything looked good, so the helmets came off and they kissed like they hadn't kissed since they were at university. The only thing that tore them apart was the panda struggling out of Sue's suit, gasping for air and weak at the knees. It waved their lack of concern away affectedly.

"Please, don't worry about me," it panted weakly. "I'm sure one day I'll be able to forget the horrors I experienced in there."

"Come on!" Sue said excitedly, pulling at Phil's hand.

They had come down in a narrow valley, icy slopes rising a few metres on either side of them. The sky was a mass of swirling clouds – $CO_2$ sublimating its way back into the Martian atmosphere. All around them was a landscape of ice and mist, looking more like it was made from cottage cheese than the red sand that Mars was famous for.

But somehow, it was completely, impossibly alien.

"We're here," Sue breathed softly.

"Congratulations," the panda said grandly behind them. "You two are the first human beings on Mars. Whatever else happens, history will never forget your names. Now *please* tell me they provided you with champagne for some moment similar to this."

Phil and Sue just enjoyed the view.

They hadn't even been there a day when the argument started. Perhaps they might have expected more of a honeymoon period, but time was short. It was minus 150 degrees, and the downed capsule was being buffeted by carbon dioxide winds so fierce that they could feel it shifting on the ice. The Orion had been built and tested to withstand the rigours of spaceflight. It could probably survive perfectly fine on unknown alien ice fields... but no-one had ever expected it to need to, so no-one could say for certain. It almost didn't matter: it was an absolute certainty that one day –

one day sooner rather than later – they *would* be the first humans to die on Mars.

Which was what caused the argument.

"Whatever we do here is pointless if no-one ever finds out about it," Sue said, in that quiet and calm voice that Phil had long ago learned to dread. "We have to re-establish radio contact."

"There's no airlock, Sue," Phil cried again, exasperated. He knew she wouldn't listen. "The only way out is to depressurise the whole place. Even if we *can* repressurise, how many days will that knock off our lives?"

"And what will they mean if no-one can study what happened here?"

"Oh, *thanks*!"

"You know exactly what I mean, Philip Gordon Yarrow. No-one has ever been here before. This ship is collecting information every second that could help somebody else do this and make it back alive. This whole bloody thing is pointless if we don't try to get every scrap of data we can back to someone who can use it."

The panda coughed politely.

"I hope you don't mind me interrupting..." They both turned and glared at it. It shrugged and laughed a little nervously. "I know I haven't known you long. It doesn't matter... It's just that you usually seem to lose these arguments. I thought it might save time if you just did what she wanted? If you're concerned about how much you have left, I mean."

Phil glared. Bugger if it wasn't right though.

They checked the equipment once, twice, three times. But there was no way to test the repressurisation of the Orion that didn't involve just doing it. What if it took more time than there was oxygen in their spacesuits? What if it just didn't work? The panda assured Phil there was no reason for concern about that, but how convincing could a stuffed panda be? Even after all this time, Phil wasn't entirely convinced that it wasn't a product of some kind of deficiency or other. But he had agreed that they were going out there, so at some point they were going to have to open the door.

They both suited up. Roles had been agreed and assigned. Phil was going to set up the external transmitter. Sue was going to try and dig out as much ice as she could: the Martian poles were mostly water ice, and water meant life – whether they drank it or turned it into air. If anything happened to Phil, Sue was going to take over – working as best she could with the panda nestling inside her suit again. The transmitter was the priority: they were both dead anyway, but what they had learned still had a chance of living on.

Sue opened the hatch to the outside world and dropped through.

The scream echoed in Phil's ears.

"Sue!"

He was out of the hatch far faster than he intended, and when the wind caught him it nearly flung him halfway across the planet. Sue was there, clinging on to the safety line and pressed flat against the skin of the capsule. She was looking up at the horizon, the cottage-cheese ice and $CO_2$ clouds that sped by. She was still screaming in exhilaration, but tried her best to control herself.

"I'm sorry," he heard her pant over the radio. "The wind, and then... Mars, Phil. We're standing on the surface of Mars!"

"I know," he said.

For a moment, neither of them moved.

But the wind tore at their suits, and Phil started to worry just how tough the various layers of fabric and metal might actually be. Or what might be picked up and hurled at them. Or how far it would take them, if the safety line failed. He closed his eyes and gave himself a mental slap.

"We can't stay in this for long," he found himself shouting, even though he could hear nothing of the wind outside his helmet. "We'll have to stay as close to the capsule as we can. OK?"

"You work underneath," Sue suggested, untying a makeshift spade from the safety line. "I don't want to risk cutting the ice out from under us."

Phil nodded, even though he realised Sue wouldn't see. He found himself a little space where the bottom of the capsule had melted itself into the ice and set to work. The device was only really a relay for the transmitter inside the capsule, boosting the signal that was meant to let the pickup crew find their splashdown site. For now it was a bit hit and miss, but the computing power they had inside the capsule could probably target the radio waves a little better given time... and maybe even track down a returning signal. It would be good to get some confirmation before they died.

"How are you doing?" Phil asked.

"Terribly," the panda replied.

"I'm barely even chipping it," Sue admitted.

"Get what you can. It's not important."

"Phil," Sue said. He glanced at her: she had stopped hacking at the ice. "Look."

He looked.

Down the tunnel of the valley, he could see the sky darkening. There was a red haze there now, as if the sky was burning. The winds brought the stain ever closer – it had almost doubled in size whilst they stopped and stared. It was... He was going to die on this planet, millions of miles from almost everybody else who loved him. He was never going to get drunk again, or eat proper food, or lie out on the grass and feel warm summer rain gently soak into his skin.

Seeing that storm coming towards them made it seem worth it.

"It's big," he said. "Do you think it's planetwide?"

"We could just stay here," Sue said softly. "Let it take us."

Phil hesitated for a moment.

"Only one of us could," he said. "The other would have to hook the suits back up to the mainframe. Get the data home."

"Oh Jesus," Sue said. "That's how it's going to have to be, isn't it?"

Phil didn't answer.

"Ahem," the panda coughed. "I would like to go back inside now please."

Phil made a last adjustment to the transmitter.

They squeezed through the hatch long before the storm reached them, but the wind was still trying to dismember them. Perhaps there were ghosts on Mars after all, jealous of any still living thing. Sue went to slam the hatch closed so they could start the process of recycling the atmosphere... but there was a loud hollow clang and everything outside suddenly went dark. She glanced up at Phil in surprise, but he clearly had no idea either.

"Wait," Panda said. "Leave it."

Sue saw something through the hatch. A flash of silver, a glint of golden sunlight. She jumped back in surprise.

"Sue?"

Someone was coming through the hatchway.

"And where the bloody hell have you been?" Panda yelled in shrill annoyance.

A woman with blonde hair and silver hot pants appeared in the room, her legs and her arms bare. She wasn't even wearing any breathing equipment, which meant that she should be rolling around the floor asphyxiating by now. But instead wagged a petulant finger at Panda and apparently sucked good, clean air into her lungs.

"No," the stranger said waspishly. "You do *not* want to know where I've been. Let's just say that it's a bloody good job for all of us that you got that radio working and I could home in on you at last."

"Iris?" Phil said.

"Yes, loves. You can take your helmets off: the bus has replenished your local atmosphere."

"Bus?" Sue echoed.

As she peered through the dark hatch, she thought she could just make out a line of hideously upholstered seats.

"Now," said Iris, clapping her hands together. "Shall we get you home, or would you like a cuppa first?"

Phil laughed a little too hollowly. Panda gave him an arch look.

"No, seriously. Now Iris is here, you can go home."

There was a crackle on the radio.

"Orion capsule, this is Ground Control," said a voice fading in an out of existence. "We don't know what kind of state you are in out there. But we have received a radio transmission. Repeat: we have received your data. If you can, please respond."

The voice cut out again.

Sue was already on her feet and shouting into the radio.

"Control! This is Orion. We are here. We are both here!"

"Give them a chance, Sue!"

They caught each other's' eye and giggled. Neither of them really knew exactly how long it would take the signal to make it home and back, but it felt something like a hundred years.

"We can *be* there in a matter of minutes —" Panda started to say, but was silenced sullenly by a frantic shush. He looked like he wanted to tut, but then he caught the look on Iris' face.

The radio crackled again, broadcasting a very surprised sounding profanity across the length of the solar system.

"Excuse me!" the operator corrected himself. "Orion capsule. We are all very glad to hear that you are both ok. Please confirm your current status.

Are you really... oh Lord: please confirm your current location and status for the history books, Orion."

Phil put his arms around Sue's waist.

"Control, this is the Orion capsule," he said.

"You're lucky you caught us," Sue said breezily. "We've only just got back from a little stroll on the northern pole of Mars."

"Give us one minute and we'll send you the onboard data."

Even as he spoke, he was digging into his suit to pull out the fibre optic cable that connected the onboard computer back to the Orion's mainframe. It was the apple falling from Isaac Newton's tree. It was the telephone wire that first connected two computers in different cities. Once the information their suits had collected while they were on the surface of an alien world was in humanity's hands, there was simply no predicting what would come of it.

"You can wait, can't you?" Sue asked Iris.

She smiled sadly.

"Of course we can, love. You just say the word."

"We'll need to set something up to send them what we've recorded since then," Phil said, hurriedly pressing buttons and flicking switches. "Every second we have, anything we can give them could be the difference between..."

He stopped. His smile suddenly froze, and he looked at Sue. It took her a moment, but suddenly it hit her too. She glanced at Iris and Panda.

"All of it?" Sue asked quietly. "Will they really need it all?"

Phil took her hand.

"It doesn't need both of us," he said.

"Don't be silly," Sue chided, sadly.

For a moment, there was silence.

"Come on, Panda," Iris breathed. "It's time we were off."

The panda just looked confused.

"But... but..."

"We can't do it, can we?" Phil said flatly. "We're the first people ever to come here. Anything we can tell them is going to make it easier next time. Not just the data – they can shoot a million probes for that. What it actually feels like, what we can actually see. The things that mean the next people here might even be able to stay a while longer."

"But you'll *die*," Panda objected quietly.

97

"And they'll learn something from that, too," Phil said.

"Eighteen people have died because they tried to go into space," Sue told him gently. "We'll be in good company."

"Don't forget the monkeys," Phil interjected with false joviality. "And Laika."

Sue smiled thinly.

"Yeah," she said. "Eighteen people for company, and a dog to walk. What more could you ask for?"

The radio crackled into life again.

"Orion capsule," Ground Control said. They could barely hide the excitement in their voices. "We are receiving more... ah, hell: tell us everything!"

"Come on, Panda," Iris said again, pulling him gently.

"But... but," Panda stuttered. "We could save one of them, then. Couldn't we?"

Iris looked across at them.

"Do you think they want to be apart?" Iris asked.

Begrudgingly, Panda let himself be led away.

"Wait!" Sue said.

Panda and Iris stopped, and Sue leant into the radio for a moment.

"Please hold, Control," she said. Then she gave Panda an awkward smile. "Perhaps we could have just one last cup of tea before you go?"

Iris smiled warmly.

"I think I might even dig out some biscuits," she said.

# TALKING WITH SPORES
Juliet Kemp

Kathryn walked swiftly along the dome's main corridor, mentally running over her plan for the rest of the morning. To the left and right, office doors, open or shut as their inhabitants preferred, gave or concealed glimpses of her colleagues. Some of them were hunched over keyboards or scribbling on data pads, their faces intent and anxious. Others were already packing equipment and notes into boxes in two piles: go or stay. Kathryn hated the thought of leaving their rubbish, however carefully sealed, behind to litter Mars. She hated even more the thought of leaving Mars, of leaving Mars *now*, without finishing her experiment, with so much still to do.

They'd all been elated, if surprised, by the first discovery of the blue-yellow fungus. Just a tiny patch, climbing out of a crater vent near the dome. Head of expedition Billy had worried about how the exploratory missions had missed it, but then Billy was a worrier. Kathryn, as the mission's microbiologist, took the lead in carefully investigating it. But when the fungus started to spread, quicker and quicker, towards the dome, Billy's worry had spread to the rest of the team. Then yesterday, Robin, in charge of maintenance, reported finding it growing onto the dome's skin. Billy had called an emergency meeting, and they'd decided: they had to leave. Now. Kathryn had been the only dissenting voice, and they already all thought she was crazy anyway.

Kathryn patted her pocket to feel the lump of the bio-translator. An optimistic title for something neither she nor sysadmin and all-round techie Sunil were at all sure would do what Kathryn hoped. She still had a couple of days. She'd check over the overnight generations, and hook the bio-translator up again to her test setup.

Her lab was on the left at the back, facing the bubble of the emergency exit airlock, its green lights flashing rhythmically and just slightly off-beat with one another. As always, she paused as she unlocked the door, gazing out through the airlock's clear skin. When they got here, there had been only red dust, and boulders. And, it turned out, that one tiny patch of blue-yellow fungus. Kathryn had been excited enough by that, by the chance to

99

explore alien life, however microscopic. Then she'd found the changes in mineral concentration across its surface. Her colleagues hadn't grasped the importance, despite her best and ongoing efforts to explain. Kathryn had to admit that at this point, it was looking increasingly unlikely that she'd get authorisation for her crucial next experiment. To her mind, the fungus creeping up to the dome just backed up her claim that it was trying to communicate. The others just thought she was dreaming.

She chewed her lip as she stepped over the lab's threshold – then halted in horror. The nearest of her transparent mini cleanrooms didn't contain its usual neat stacks of petri dishes, or its gently bubbling flasks of the older colonies. Instead Kathryn could see the shelving thrown down, smears of yeast spread across the glass plates, and piles of broken glass puddling on the floor. She could hear the blood pounding in her ears. Dimly, she noticed that the other cleanrooms, containing other projects, were intact. *Just* the yeast? Just *that* project? But who on earth – on Mars – could have done such a thing?

"Oh dear," someone said from just behind her. "That doesn't look good at all."

Kathryn spun round, opening her mouth to say something scathing to whichever of her idiot colleagues was there, then stopped dead. Behind her, in the corridor, stood a woman in a dark green catsuit and knee high black boots, her golden hair caught back in a loose ponytail. A very practical-looking wide belt with a couple of pockets offset the deeply impractical shoulder tassels. But most notable about her was the fact that she was not any of the other nine members of the science team.

"I'm Iris," the woman said chattily. "Pleasure to meet you, I'm sure. The famous Kathryn Serras, am I right? Nice place you have here. Well, other than..."

Recalled to the situation, Kathryn swung back round again.

"Dear me," Iris said. "That is a mess." She tutted sympathetically.

"You!" Kathryn shrieked, barely able to hear herself over the thumping in her ears. "It must have been you, you're the only one..."

She turned and made a grab for Iris, which Iris held off without seeming to exert herself in any way at all.

"Now, calm down a little, dear..."

"But why, why would anyone... My poor yeast!"

"Not me, dear," Iris said. "Remember, you just unlocked the door? And here I am outside it."

Kathryn looked down at her fingers, remembered punching the code in, and let go of Iris. She stumbled towards the cleanroom to peer into it. All mixed together, all drying up... She couldn't begin to think how long it would take to fix this. More than two days, that was for certain. She clenched her teeth against baffled fury and a searing, devastating sense of loss.

Iris, who had followed her in, patted Kathryn soothingly on the shoulder, and decided not to mention the *first* time she'd been in there, an hour or so previously, when the lock on the door had yielded to a deftly applied hatpin. After all, she'd only taken a little bit, and she hadn't smashed anything. But when Panda had just found a box full of home-brew kit in the back of the bus, well, she needed to find some yeast from somewhere, didn't she? She'd been halfway back to the bus when something prickling at the back of her neck told her to return to the humans' dome. Iris always paid attention to the prickle at the back of her neck.

"So, dear," she asked. "What exactly was it you were doing here?"

Scientists always like talking about their work. "Yeast," Kathryn answered, sniffing a little and trying to pretend that she wasn't. Iris handed her a handkerchief. "Well – it started out as yeast. When we found that fungus, I'm the microbiologist, so I studied it, right? And I found concentrations of certain trace elements travelling across the network. Mycorrhizal networks on Earth do the same thing, like a form of communication, transferring information between trees. Except this was so much faster."

She stopped and looked expectantly at Iris. Iris looked back.

"*Communicating*," Kathryn said, as if Iris had missed an obvious cue. "What if it was communicating? Then I started thinking: isn't that a bit like electrical impulses being transmitted across a human brain? Okay, fine, it sounds crazy, and everyone else here thinks it is, but I couldn't stop thinking about it. And I had the supplies, and a little space, so I've been trying – well, it's a bit complicated, but I've been trying to engineer a yeast that can do something similar. I want to see if I can connect with them, communicate with them."

Iris nodded with enthusiastic interest, but she had to admit: it did sound a little crazy. Unless you already knew about Kathryn Serras, and the Ancient Martian Fungal Empire, and the Human-Martian Treaty of 2118.

Kathryn bit her lip, and took a shaky breath. "I thought, I really thought that I was nearly there... We just got the bio-translator working, too."

Slowly, she pulled on her cleanroom kit. Iris watched her, looking a little guilty. There hadn't been anything to *say* it was supposed to be sterile.

"It's all dried out, though, I can tell from here, none of it will have survived..."

"Mycorrhizae, eh? Maybe you can start again?" Iris suggested.

Kathryn shook her head. "We're leaving. Two days." Her shoulders sagged. "And I can't get the others to agree to authorise my experiment anyway. They say it's too risky, interfering like that. But I'm *sure* I'm right! I'm sure we can communicate! I was supposed to present to the others again tomorrow, I was going to be so convincing this time, but... What's the point, now? When I've got nothing."

Iris tch'ed sympathetically and patted her pockets a little guiltily.

Thoughtfully, Iris leaned against a convenient lab bench, watching Kathryn clearing up, and tried to remember what she knew about the Human-Martian treaty. Had someone else been involved? Who, other than Iris herself (and of course good old Panda, currently back at the bus having a little siesta), might be wandering around Martian space and dropping in unannounced on poor unfortunate human scientists?

"I was hoping that there might be some left, somewhere, that wasn't all mixed up..."

Kathryn, who had been piling up broken glassware, sat back despairingly on her heels.

"Oh dear, surely there must be something," Iris said, wandering over to the far corner of the lab. "I mean, all this broken stuff, of course it's going to take you a while to look through it properly..."

She poked at one of Kathryn's piles, with her back turned.

"Look!" she said triumphantly. "Here you are. Isn't this what you were looking for?"

She swung round with half a petri dish in her hand, pointing at the tiny piece of grey-blue substance it contained.

"My yeast!" Kathryn cried, leaping to her feet and grabbing it from Iris. "But I – didn't I already look through that pile? I'm sure..."

"Well, you're upset. It's easy to miss things when you're upset," Iris said, waving an airy hand.

Surreptitiously, with the other hand, she shoved a plastic bag back into her pocket. There was still a bit left for her to take back to the bus. Kathryn paid no attention, crooning to her tiny snippet of yeast and looking around for more unbroken glassware.

"So you're going to breed it all up again?" Iris asked. "With just two days?"

"I need to find out which generation this is first," Kathryn said absently, as she tenderly took a bare shaving off the yeast and applied it to a microscope slide. "But it looks like one of the later generations, and I increased the breeding speed really early on, and there's the incubator..." She trailed off, peering through the microscope, then let out a soft noise of satisfaction.

"Well, that's good," Iris said vaguely, beginning to sidle towards the exit. "I'll just take myself off out of your hair and leave you to get on with it, then, will I?" She had her hand on the door handle. "Bye now!"

Kathryn just grunted in response, busy focussing her microscope.

Outside the lab, Iris popped a small package out of one of her ballooning sleeves, shook it out, and threw it neatly over her head. It settled down around her body, and for a moment she looked like someone playing ghost dressup. Then it adjusted itself around her body and disappeared to the casual eye. Iris wriggled a little to help it settle, and screwed up her nose. Membrane envelope suits were more convenient than the cumbersome full-body things the humans of this era had, for certain, but she still could never quite shake off the sensation that she wasn't getting enough oxygen. Still. It did the job. Actually, now she came to think about it, she had a vague suspicion that membrane envelopes had originated from a Martian Empire technology.

The emergency airlock was conveniently next to Kathryn's lab, with a nice, obvious, alarm net around it. In theory, then, if anyone came in from outside to damage Kathryn's research, they should have set off alarms.

Iris poked around at the settings for a moment before stepping into it, and conscientiously put the alarms back again before stepping outside, just like the last time. Resetting this stuff was child's play; only a truly incompetent saboteur would have struggled. Which did at least rule out a few of the possible candidates.

She had a little wander round the outside of the bio-dome, poking at the dusty Martin soil from time to time. A thin network of yellow-blue fuzz formed a path running away from the dome towards a distant crater. Questing tendrils were spreading away from its path. Iris cautiously avoided it. She couldn't remember offhand how robust the Martians of the Empire were. Nor what had happened to them to reduce them to this. It would come to her soon, she was sure.

She ducked under each of the dome's windows as she passed them, although, nosy as ever, she took the opportunity to peer over the odd windowsill in case there was anything of interest. There wasn't. Just anxious humans busy packing. Finally, near another emergency airlock, she found a few traces of movement on the dusty soil. Whoever it was had been making some effort to conceal themselves, but it was careless and half-hearted at best. In a hurry, perhaps?

Iris sucked on her teeth gently. If someone had come to finish off Kathryn's project, then there must be a reason for it. And if there was a reason for it, then when they realised they hadn't succeeded, they'd be back. Which in turn meant that if Iris just parked herself down for a little while and waited patiently, she might find out a little more about the matter.

She sat herself down on an outcrop of rock that was bare of the blue-yellow fuzz, and wished that you could smoke a cigarette either through a membrane suit, or indeed on Mars at all.

Time passed. More time passed. The sun got to zenith, and began to sink. Iris hummed to herself, then drummed her fingers on the rock for a bit and tried to remember what else she could about the Martian-Human Treaty of 2118. She looked thoughtfully at the yellow-blue fungus extending slow tendrils up the outside of the bio-dome. Sentient mushrooms. Honestly, there wasn't anything the galaxy didn't throw up sooner or later.

She snapped her fingers. That was it. The Ancient Martian Fungal Empire had been sentient mushrooms that had made their way out into the galaxy and done quite well for themselves. But they needed their partnership with native vegetation to survive. And eventually, careless of their long-term future and seeking to expand ever faster, they had eaten straight through their resources. The Empire crumbled, and for eons, only a tiny colony of starving fungi hung on, nursing the knowledge of their race and hoping for a miracle. Which, eventually, appeared in the form of some visiting humans. These visiting humans, and Kathryn Serras as the lead on the Martian-Human Treaty. The humans provided resources (Iris eyed the opportunist fungus on the dome disapprovingly) and the Martians provided their spacefaring knowledge. And off they went, out into the universe. So if Kathryn didn't get to try this out, and the timeline changed...

Her musings were interrupted by a not-so-delicate prod in the ribs. Cursing herself for totally failing to pay any attention, she turned round. Behind her was a large, squat being that was reminiscent of nothing so much as a slug with legs. Six of them, indeed, and an overlarge head at one end. It was the head end that was closest to Iris, and one of the top, tentacle-like legs held the laser pistol that had just prodded Iris in the ribs. The whole thing was encased in a suit of space armour that served to increase its already impressive bulk.

"You lot?" she exclaimed. "I thought you were banned from this sector for at least, ooh, another few hundred years."

The Zeffn were renowned for dealing in anything that would fetch a profit, considerations of ethics and legality (inasmuch as any legal system had much power in the vast empty swathes of space) very much secondary. Their only apparent moral qualm was that they refused to deal in living beings, although that might have been less of a moral issue and more that living beings were untidy and didn't pack well for travel.

The particular Zeffn in front of Iris rippled a shrug inside its bulky space armour. So much more awkward than Iris' membrane suit. So much more impervious to most weapons. Iris sighed.

"Nobody round to see us," the Zeffn said. "None of their business anyway. None of your business either," it added, prodding her again.

"But what business could you have here?" Iris asked, ignoring the laser pistol. "I can't see anything much round here to deal in." Yet, she added silently. "Unless you have some clients that really like rocks."

"Earthers," it condescended to explain. "Barbarian pre-galactic artefacts, very rare. Very expensive."

"But there's only about a dozen Earthers here," Iris said. "Why not bog off to Earth and do your collecting there? Generate a few more UFO stories, that kind of thing."

Iris wasn't keen on the Zeffn, but she wasn't that bothered by them scaring a few farmers. As long as they put them down again carefully afterwards. Then enlightenment struck.

"Oh. Of course. The Treaty kicked off human expansion into the rest of the galaxy, didn't it? Humans everywhere, rarity value down the toilet, money-spinner gone. So what, you're trying to hijack the Treaty? By wrecking poor Kathryn's research?"

Worryingly, Iris had a suspicion that this meant that the Zeffn had access to some sort of time device, but she filed that away to worry about later.

"No need to hijack," the Zeffn shrugged. "Just to delay until the humans go back home. Transmissions say, soon." It sounded smug.

This was all very not good. But not nearly as not-good as the laser pistol that had now moved from her ribs to her head.

"Bored now," the Zeffn announced.

Iris, cursing herself again for not coming armed, screwed up her eyes. A long moment passed, then instead of the expected laser pistol burn, she heard a meaty, drawn-out, thump. She opened her eyes again to see the Zeffn agent on the floor. A dull metal bunsen burner lay beside it.

Panda stumped out from behind a rock.

"Just as well I got bored and came looking for you," he said, picking up the bunsen burner.

"What use is that through space armour?" Iris said. "Did you *cook* it?"

Panda shook his head. "There's a spot on that model of armour, in the helmet. Catch it just right and you get a nice shockwave through the whole thing. Knocks out most compatible species."

"And you knew that it would work on the Zeffn," Iris marvelled.

"No," Panda replied, "I just didn't know of anything else that might."

"All's well and all that, then," Iris concluded, standing up and dusting herself off. "Right, well then."

She updated Panda on her current understanding of the situation.

"So, we need to find Kathryn and warn her, I suppose. And see if we can persuade her to try out her experiments. She was all worried about getting permission." Iris shook her head. The idea of asking for permission was a little alien to her.

She scowled down at the still-unconscious Zeffn for a moment, then bent to relieve it of its laser pistol, and dismissed it with a wave of the hand.

"Can't be bothered worrying about that one," she announced, and marched off back towards the base, Panda trailing behind her.

"But when they got there, the cupboard was bare?" Panda asked.

Iris, looking at an empty lab and an equally empty cleanroom, swore colourfully and inventively for a few moments.

"I'd think maybe she'd just gone for a coffee," Iris said. "Or gin." She got a faraway look for a moment, then snapped back to concentration. "But there's none of her yeastie stuff left here either."

"Maybe she's started carrying it around in her pocket," Panda said. "Safety first."

Iris shook her head. "I could believe it of her, but she didn't have big enough pockets. No, she'd have camped out here instead and done without her coffee. And gin. So where is she?"

She was poking around cupboards again as she spoke, and stopped suddenly.

"Now, the last time I was here –"

"Poking around," Panda added helpfully, and Iris shot him a baleful look.

"The last time I *just happened* to see this cupboard," she said, "it had an environment suit in. One of those nasty bulky twenty-first century ones."

Panda grimaced, adjusting his own membrane. Iris was never entirely sure what a stuffed panda needed with a membrane suit, but it had always seemed impolite to ask.

The cupboard was conspicuously empty.

"Oh dear," Iris sighed. "Did you notice any footprints by that door we came in?"

"Only yours," Panda said. "And I was looking."

"Another exit, then," Iris said.

Leaving the lab and turning the other way along the corridor, they soon discovered an emergency exit with its alarm circuitry yanked out. Iris sighed. Humans were so *unsubtle* sometimes. Delicacy only took a little more time. The airlock still worked, though, and once back outside, the big, clunky, atmosphere suit footprints leading off into the distance were unmistakable.

"Well, then she's off to talk to the Martians, and we can stop worrying, right?" Panda said, already starting back in the direction of the bus.

"Mission accomplished. The brewing stuff is all set up and waiting, Iris. Come on, let's go."

Iris wavered for a moment, then firmly shook her head.

"You're forgetting, my duck. Those Zeffn are still out there. I don't believe for a second that that enthusiastic individual you knocked out was the only one on planet. And Kathryn doesn't know about them."

"She knows someone's here," Panda objected, half-heartedly. "Unless she still blames you, I suppose."

"We need to go after her," Iris declared, and set off following the footprints, then stopped dead. Panda cannoned into the back of her.

"No we don't," she said.

"We don't?" Panda said.

"What's the point in three of us dancing around out there, you and me in flimsy membranes? We need to find the Zeffn, not Kathryn. Which means, back to the bus, and let's do a bit of a recce."

She about-turned, and headed back in the direction of the bus, Panda once again trailing after her.

"So what are we going to do?" Panda asked over the roar of the engines as Iris fired them up.

Iris peered at the scope to one side of the bus' complicated console. It looked rather like a traditional radar scope, but on further examination, the surrounding landscape was shown in surprising detail. A little cluster of light-green pulsing dots over to one side of the scope were surrounded by a faint image of the bio-dome, and a trail of pink ones led from the dome to a crater and a searingly intense patch of pink. Iris made a pinching gesture in front of it and the dome image shrank as the scope zoomed out. She scowled at the screen. Still no other dots. The bus engine revved again as she tapped her foot with irritation.

"Get her in the air and try a few low-level buzzes, I thought," she shouted to Panda, crunching into gear.

The bus juddered and rose a little into the air, then a little more as Iris shoved the accelerator down.

"Keep your eyes peeled, they must be around here somewhere."

The bus' engine ground a bit more as it rose further skywards. Iris had another look in the scope, zoomed out again, then walloped it on its side.

"Come on, you ridiculous piece of machinery. Alien life signatures, non-human, non-Martian, there can't be that many else of them round here. Aha, there we go."

Iris swung the bus in the direction of the three clustered mustard-yellow blips on the scope's screen.

The Zeffn spaceship, when Panda caught sight of it, nestled just below the edge of a canyon. It was an unprepossessing thing, faintly bullet-shaped, and showing the pocks and dents of a long life spent jaunting around in space and in and out of atmospheres. With a whoop, Iris swooped the bus over the edge of the canyon and downwards, coming within a couple of metres of the spaceship's roof.

"Iris," Panda yelled. "It's a spaceship. It can withstand vacuum and asteroids. They're hardly going to be alarmed by a Number 22 coming a bit too close."

"Ah, but they won't want to come *out*, will they now?" Iris said, hauling the bus around for another go.

In the back, a series of clangs and bangs suggested that quite a lot of things had fallen to the floor. Panda, looking anxious, hurried back, hanging onto the rail, to check for breakages.

"You'd better not have cracked that demijohn..."

Iris cackled and did another handbrake turn, preparing for a third run.

There was a whistling bang and the windscreen shattered. By the time Iris had registered the red of a laser-pistol beam shooting past inches above her forehead, she was already locked in wrestling against the bus' plummet to the ground.

Dust stirred up by the passage of the bus was pouring in through the broken windscreen, and Iris' eyes were streaming as she tried to pull up. They hit the ground on two wheels with a huge bump, banged down onto the other two, and rocketed towards the edge of the canyon. Iris slammed the brake to the floor, swearing.

With a screech and a lot more bumps, the bus slowed and stopped with its nose just over the canyon's edge. Iris sat back, wiped the dust out of her eyes, and turned the engine off.

"All OK?" she called, and relaxed at Panda's grumpy but affirmative response.

She turned round to inspect the char mark in the back of the driver's seat, just above her head.

"And the windscreen," she mourned, "that's going to take a bit of fixing."

"Iris!" Panda said urgently, pointing through the hole where the windscreen had been.

A couple of hundred metres away, what was presumably another Zeffn, also wearing a bulky atmosphere suit, was making six-legged tracks away from the ship.

"Kathryn went that way, didn't she?" Iris said. "Well then."

She opened the glove compartment and grabbed her own blaster, tucking it into her boots. She wasn't about to be caught napping a second (third) time.

"Panda, you stay here and get going on repairs. Never mind the blinking Martians, I'm not putting up with those rotten Zeffn doing something like that to *my bus*."

She was out of the door and setting off at speed after the lumbering Zeffn before Panda could draw breath to answer.

Kathryn's fingers shook with nerves inside her gloves. She took a deep breath to calm them, then knelt, the articulated joints of the bulky atmosphere suit feeling awkward despite the practice sessions she'd religiously done twice a week. She began to lay out her petri dishes. She'd hoped to use more of the next forty-eight hours, to breed another few generations and get that bit closer to the vision she had of the Martian-Earth hybrid mycorrhizal.

Just after Iris had left earlier, and she'd put the tiny saved fragment, with a couple more adjustments, into the incubator, Billy had come by. To give him some credit, he'd been shocked by the destruction. But he refused to take it seriously in terms of actually investigating her colleagues, given that they were leaving anyway. When she'd made the mistake of mentioning Iris, his eyebrows had shot to his hairline. Kathryn could see him wondering if she might have lost it to the extent of destroying her *own* work.

"At least it'll be quicker to clear up, now, hey?" he's said, attempting good cheer.

Then he'd made it clear: no more meetings, no authorising of one last experiment. Shut down and ship out.

Kathryn had stared unseeing at the humming incubator and the chaos of her lab for a long while before deciding that she had to at least *try*. Her plan had been a carefully controlled test, at least at first, with a sample in the lab. Contamination free, circumscribed, reasonable, and might not work even if a full-scale trial did. A piece of the network wasn't the same as the full network. Releasing her hybrid into the Martian biosphere was unethical, she knew that. But every time she glanced out of the window and saw the fungus path to the dome, seeming almost to pulse as she looked at it, the compulsion just to *do* it increased. Eventually, it was just too strong.

Thank goodness that tiny survivor colony had been the most recent one; and four hours in the incubator had bred just enough of it to make the experiment with. If she got anything, anything at all, then she would have proved the point. Then maybe they could stay, or come back, or...

She had to try.

At least she and Sunil had been working on the translator when the destruction had happened. She wouldn't have had a hope of rebuilding that in time. Translating mineral and chemical composition changes into an electrical signal was the easy part. Doing it in reverse, and to affect Kathryn's yeast, had taken her and Sunil weeks. She didn't entirely understand what Sunil had done in the end, but all she actually had to do was to tap on a microphone. At the last moment he'd added a hookup to her suit radio for input as well as output. He thought she was just as nuts as everyone else did, but he liked her, and he liked a technical challenge.

She trailed the delicate filigree of wires that "spoke" to the yeast into the petri dish. This close to the fungus, every time she looked at it, her head rang slightly. For a moment, she was reminded of spring back on earth, of walking between the trees in deep forest, the air humming around her...

Maybe they were all right and she had lost it. She sighed deeply, sat back on her heels, and took a deep breath. It was time.

She tapped once – pause – twice – pause – three times on the microphone, and waited.

She imagined that she could see the vibrations turning into chemicals and transferring themselves to her yeast; the yeast making its own chemicals (she would have brought the detectors with her, but they were in pieces like everything else). The chemicals travelling through to the edge of her fungus, to where its tendrils met the Martian fungus. To where she was breaking every rule, every guideline, in the book. She felt sick, and the ringing in her head was getting worse. The smell of trees was in her nose.

The moments ticked by. Kathryn tried not to panic.

Then the speaker hooked into her suit radio began to hum, very gently. Kathryn's heart jumped. She reached out her hand to try the signal again, but the hum was already changing in pitch and volume, going up and down, and she paused.

Knock – pause – knock knock – pause – knock knock knock.

Kathryn nearly fell over in shock.

Just the reaction, just the changing hum, would have been enough, nearly enough. Could they really be echoing back? She tried it again, and this time it came back faster. Again, increasing the series by one, and the echo was there almost before she had lifted her hand from the mike. She was shaking now, the excitement almost unbearable. This was enough, this really was enough. She should go back straight away, tell them, bring them all out here.

She wasn't sure what made her try hooking in the final plug that connected the translator to her suit communicator microphone.

"Hello?" she said.

There was a pause again this time, and she was starting to laugh at herself. Of course not...

"*Hlllll,*" echoed back.

Kathryn, giggling slightly hysterically, gathered her scattered wits, and settled down to communicate.

Iris saw Kathryn from quite a distance – her bulky Earth-issue suit made her an easy target. About as easy, in fact, as the Zeffn in its nearly-as-bulky suit, stopped between Iris and Kathryn, raising its pistol for a leisurely shot.

Kathryn, kneeling down, deeply focussed, was clearly oblivious. Iris, leaping sideways in a move she feared her knees might regret later, got her own blaster out of her boot and up just in time. For a moment she thought she'd missed; then the Zeffn's pistol went cartwheeling across the Martian plains, and it was clutching its tentacle in shock, turning towards Iris. Iris kept running.

"Ow," she heard as she got closer. "What was that in aid of?"

"Your friend tried to shoot me," Iris said crisply. "Count yourself lucky I only aimed for the pistol. Now – you're too late. Look at her there. Only one reason for someone to pay that little attention to their surroundings. Humans and Martians are talking, and you've missed the boat. Now, I suggest you clear off sharpish, pick up your friend, and get off home."

112

She waved the blaster at it to underline her point. They stared at each other for a tense moment. Iris did her best eye-narrowing look. Finally, eyeing her malevolently, the Zeffn backed away, then took off at a run back towards its ship.

"And don't try anything," Iris shouted after it. "*My* friend Panda has his eye on you, and so do I! Straight off with you, or next time I'll aim a bit closer to home!"

She turned back to see Kathryn still oblivious to what was going on, and rolled her eyes. Perhaps best not to explain. But – she hesitated – perhaps she should check that Kathryn really had got her yeastie whatsits going.

At that moment, Kathryn sat back again, and started disconnecting things.

"Kathryn," Iris said cheerfully, and bounced forwards to tap her on the shoulder.

Kathryn jumped enough that it looked like she'd hit her head on the inside of the atmosphere suit helmet. Obviously those Earth issue ones didn't allow for outside sound transmission, which would at least explain why she hadn't noticed any of the laser-pistol business. Sighing, Iris rooted around in her pockets till she found a tiny radio, and spoke into it.

"Is this reaching you? Good. What's going on then, ducks?"

"The Martian," Kathryn said. Despite the tinny radio link, the awe in her voice was apparent. "The fungus *is* the Martians. Or it's what's left of them. I think they were saying they were bigger once, a mightier race, but..." She shook her head. "I didn't quite understand, but we'll need to get some xeno folk in, some kind of cultural experts, I suppose. Martians, though. Martians!"

"That's good," Iris said encouragingly. "The human and the Martian should be friends, that's what I say."

"We have to stay. They say they'll keep away from the dome, that they need something though... We have to stay, I have to tell the others."

She was already moving back towards the dome, and Iris jogged alongside her for a moment.

"Well, that all sounds great," Iris said cheerfully. "You go off to take care of that. I'll see you around, I'm sure."

Kathryn's forehead creased, and she stopped suddenly, seeming to see Iris for the first time.

"But... Who are you, anyway? How are you out here without a suit? What..."

"I told you, ducks, I'm Iris. And I do have a suit on, just... Well. It's all a long story, is what it is, and didn't you ought to be getting on with things and not worrying about me?"

Behind her, Iris spotted a sudden blast trail in the sky, with a bullet-shaped outline at the top of it, and swallowed her sigh of relief. She really hadn't wanted to have to chase them down. Firefights were always a bit boring, and she had enough bus repair work on her hands already.

Kathryn blinked at Iris for a moment, then, some protective part of her brain obviously deciding to stick with one improbability at a time, dismissed the whole thing and started again to lumber back towards the dome. Iris stood and watched her go.

"Well, that's that sorted, then," she said, putting the radio back in her pocket "Human-Martian Treaty of 2118, back on track. Back to the bus for Iris, and onto the next adventure."

She tapped her pocket to check on the little baggie that was still secreted there. It would take a while to fix that windscreen, after all. More than enough time to get the brewing going.

# DOOMED
## Richard Wright

*"You're one of* them, *aren't you. A cosmic thingy. I can't stand you lot. I don't want to play."*

*"Alas Miss Wildthyme, there is no such option on the table. You are trapped. If you wish to go free you will play to the end."*

*"You're all the bloody same. Standing outside the Universe, fiddling with it and chuckling. You treat it like it's a massive chess board."*

*"And you waltz in and out of it as though it were an open bar. We all have our defects."*

*"I'll escape."*

*"No. That is not a thing that will happen. Your only route to freedom is the game. Play, win, and walk away. I have already put events in motion. If you do not accede, a great doom will befall your favourite little world."*

*"The one with the Bacardi Breezers?"*

*"Indeed."*

*"Arse. Fine. What do I have to do?"*

*"You've seen the pieces. Choose one and begin."*

Hot blood whips into your eyes, and you flinch back against the plasteel corridor wall as Barty's scream turns to a limp gargle. A crazed scientist bends over the limp comms officer and bites deeper into the wound, shaking him back and forth like a dog with a bone. Barty twitches once more, a dismal resistance, then stills.

You remember your pistol. Wiping your eyes on your sleeve, you take a step forward and jam your weapon against the back of the scientist's head. The shot punches through his brain. Whatever has happened to the researchers on the Mars base, head shots are the only sure way to put them down.

It feels like a weary lifetime since Sergeant Campbell led you all into the lab complex, twelve tooled-up soldiers ready for whatever might be thrown at you. The Mars assignment was supposed to be the dullest in the corps, a tiresome courtesy extended by the military to the Corporation who had set up there. After weeks of boredom, pacing the barracks on the moon of

Phobos, you weren't the only one to experience a guilty relief when alarms sounded and a call came through from the red planet below. In the seconds before the operator was cut off he gabbled about being overrun, of legions unleashed and a portal opening... the details made no sense to any of you.

Hucker checked instruments to confirm that no ships had approached the besieged base, while the sarge swore at the madness of being based on the moon Phobos instead of the planet's surface. You remembered old stories about the creatures that once lived on Mars who were said to have dug deep when catastrophe struck the planet, but you didn't say anything. The sarge has little patience for flights of fancy. His decision was fast and decisive. Get down. Get in. Shoot stuff until it's sorted.

Less than an hour later you were on the surface of Mars, kicking up burned sands as you and the team followed Campbell into the modular building complex of laboratories and storerooms. The first scientist you saw was an old lady with a tight bun of grey hair, half-rim glasses, and strange mottle of something mould-like on her face and hands. She tore out Kramer's eye before anybody knew what was happening, and you joined the others in unleashing a frantic hail of gunfire that shredded her in seconds.

That must have been... what? Five minutes ago?

A lifetime.

You and the sarge are the only soldiers left alive. Your friends are piled around you in the dark, gore-streaked corridor. The gunfire wasted on the old lady had brought hordes of transformed personnel down on you, and soldiers began to die.

The air is filled with the moans of your attackers, though you can barely hear them over the crash of your own heartbeat. Lit by a cracked and flickering bulb, the sarge bellows with senseless rage. A skinny scientist clings to his leg, biting into the thigh. The officer holds another at arm's length, and you wonder when the big marine lost his gun. Your vision is streaked with red and your eyes sting, making you blink frantically while you brace yourself and aim at the mould-covered personnel stumbling towards you from the rear. You fire, and a plumber in grey coveralls splashes back into the crowd. Holding your stance you aim again, at a snarling lady in a form-hugging business suit.

The lights go out. You fire repeatedly into the absolute dark. Between shots you hear a whimper from behind you. The sarge is down.

The tide of biting, tearing bodies smashes you to the ground. As they rip at you, your thoughts fly to warm sheets and a lover's limbs. Mars was supposed to be safe, a last posting to shore up your savings before you made the biggest commitment.

No marriage now. No future at all.

The blackness swallows you whole.

*"Would you care for a jammy dodger?"*

*"Shhh. I'm concentrating."*

*"There's always time for a jammy dodger. The sugar will assist your concentration."*

*"I've got to watch the... was that..."*

*"I understand. So many options. So many details you could change. What will make the difference?"*

*"There... that's it. That'll do."*

*"Are you certain? There are countless things that can go wrong."*

*"I know. This isn't remotely my style."*

*"How would you normally proceed?"*

*"Strut in there myself. Cock my hips, pout, probably sink a gin. Make things up until everything's more or less fixed."*

*"You cannot go in. It is sealed."*

*"Wouldn't you have more fun playing with somebody else? Somebody better?"*

*"No."*

*"Bugger."*

The shuttle jerks as it touches down on the rocky surface of Mars. Standing in the bay with the rest of the team, you get ready to sprint across to the laboratory. Nobody has any idea what you are facing, but after weeks of boredom the action and uncertainty are welcome. Barty glances over his shoulder, winking through the toughened glass of his helmet.

"Listen up scumballs!" Sergeant Campbell's voice in your earpiece, almost jolly with anticipation. You check your weapon as he gives a sitrep. "Surface is clear. No landers, no perimeter security that we can see. Whoever these amateurs are, they're inside. We go single file, Barty in the lead. Hard and fast, ladies." Barty squeezes forward, ready to be first down the ramp. You slide down your helmet's polarised facemask with gloved hands. The daylight isn't a problem outside, but the mask will protect you from the unfiltered radiation beating the planet.

The lights turn green, and the landing ramp slams down, puffing rust dust into up from the rocks. Air rushes from the shuttle into the thin planetary atmosphere, tugging at you as it passes. Barty bounces down the metal platform, taking a few slower steps to get the feel of the weaker gravity, then dashing away with the unit in tow. There is no sound, despite the weight of the guns and the armour. You can hear breathing through your earpiece, and that is all.

You have been assigned a recon role, and so have only a pistol in order to stay fast and light. Until otherwise instructed you will remain at the rear, with the sarge offering cover if it all goes to hell. You step forward, trailing Whiteley, then freeze. The sarge walks into your back. "What the hell? Get a move on soldier!"

You try to apologise, but your mouth is not your own. "You're going to die," you tell him. You want to apologise as soon as you say it, but you cannot force the words out. Instead you lick your lips, which feel too soft and full. "There's blood in there, Mister Campbell. Blood and teeth. Death and darkness." Even though you do not know why you are saying this, the words slap their truth into you. Your face is clammy and cold.

The sarge grabs your arm and turns you around. "What? Get a hold of yourself! We are *live*, soldier!"

"Five minutes, love. Then you'll all be dead. You have to call them back."

If he could he would spit in your face. Instead he pushes you aside. "Stay here. Guard the shuttle. I can't take you into combat like this." He jogs after the rest of the team, but stops at the top of the ramp. "Full psych test when we're done here. If you pass it, if you're fine, then I will bury you. Understand?"

You watch him go. The threat is hollow, because he isn't coming back. With a sigh, you shake your head. "Well, at least *you're* still here." There is nobody left in the shuttle but you. Are you talking to yourself now? "Sit tight. Listen. Learn. Get it done."

You slump, entirely yourself again. Horrified at your own behaviour, you collapse onto a bench. If the sarge wants to, he can court martial you for the level of insubordination you have demonstrated.

Five minutes later you stop wondering what the sarge might or might not do, because you hear them over the helmet comms. Gunfire. Shrieks. Death.

You are alone.

It takes three people to pilot the shuttle. You cannot run away.

You're trapped.

*"A splendid strategy. Separate the avatar before disaster strikes."*

*"Wish they'd all stayed, but it buys a bit of time. Can't you fast forward this bit?"*

*"Alas, the story must unfold in real time."*

*"Could be here a bit, then. Any jammy dodgers left?"*

Four hours later the shuttle's diminishing oxygen supply forces you to follow them. The base has atmosphere generators, and if you don't find somewhere inside to hole up you're going to suffocate long before help can arrive.

The iron oxide sands shift beneath your boots as you approach the airlock. There are heavy tracks to follow, made by men and women you have shared meals and card games with for what has felt like endless days.

All dead now.

As the airlock door rolls back on darkness you switch your flashlight on. The chamber is clear. As one door closes and artificial atmosphere fills the room, you raise your face plate. The air is good.

Crossing the airlock threshold into the base proper, you almost collapse as your legs buckle under your own weight. The gravity shift to Earth-normal. It takes a few moments for your muscles to settle and adjust after your tramp over the planet's surface, so you sweep the flashlight back and forth across the corridor. It's clear, save for the offal on the walls. The team made it further than this, so that must have come from base personnel. Some of the streaks look almost like words, written in a language that hurts your eyes.

Holding your light at your shoulder and your pistol extended, you scuttle to the door at the far end of the corridor. Silence is important. Noise will draw them down on you in impossible numbers. That's what went wrong last time.

For the team. It went wrong for the team when they opened fire on... on... a woman?

Somebody must have said that over the comms, in the middle of the battle. How else would you know?

The first few rooms and corridors are clear. Your skittering heart counts down the inevitable minutes until you encounter one of the scientists who...

Who you're there to save, if you can. Why are you scared of the scientists? It makes no sense, but you are. You're terrified that they'll find you.

Kramer's body is on the floor, exactly where you expected it. You kneel, rolling him onto his back. The left side of his face has been ripped away, the eye scooped out. Somehow his condition does not surprise you.

An ancient shotgun, his weapon of choice, lies at his feet. You picture enemies in lab coats wearing snarls on mottled faces, and snatch the shotgun up before hurrying deeper into the base.

*"Oh, this is a splendid bit. The proof of the pudding. Did you make the difference, or is it all going to end the same way?"*

*"You're not helping."*

*"Forgive me, I get so lost in the story."*

*"What story? There's barely a narrative. Walk down here. Hide from that. Don't get your head blown off."*

*"The story is the possibilities. It is lived in moments of action and reaction. You are the story, Miss Wildthyme, just as much as the avatar."*

*"Bollocks. You just like watching things die."*

*"A foible I confess to. Speaking of which..."*

Most of your unit are an unrecognisable pile of chewed meat. You have to press yourself to the wall to ease past them. They did not fall like that. They have been arranged. A light flickers above you. The iron smell of cooling blood is on the air, along with the bitter, fading taste of gunfire.

A thick trail of wet crimson is streaked along the corridor, and you try to count the bodies. It is difficult to tell without disturbing them – something you are not willing to do – but there may be one missing. Following the trail, you come to a pair of swing doors. Could somebody have survived? The lights were out during the fight, and you only assumed the sarge had been taken down. Perhaps, in the darkness, he crawled away?

A wave of dizziness staggers you, and you throw out an arm to catch yourself on the wall. You weren't *there*. You *don't* know that they died in the dark. You *didn't* hear Sergeant Campbell whimper behind you as you emptied your pistol.

Something is wrong.

The thought almost makes you laugh out loud, because *everything* is wrong.

Crouching at the doors, you push one open with a shoulder. There are no lights inside, and you run the flashlight over chairs and tables. A recreation room of some sort? There are broken plates on the floor, and a mug on its side next to a dark stain on the carpet. Coffee, not blood.

There are men and women in blood spattered white coats, crouched over a big carcass in your unit's colours. They pull handfuls of flesh free with their fingers, shoving your friend into their mouths. In places he has already been eaten to the bone.

They see your light and their heads snap around. Their eyes shine yellow in the beam. The mould is thick on their faces, and you realise it is some manner of organic weapon that makes men mindless and frenzied.

Shock freezes you, and they caper forwards. You try to bring the shotgun up, but with the flashlight in one hand you are clumsy and slow. Before you can get a single shot off they bear you back into the corridor, pinning you down.

As they begin to tear you up your thoughts fly to warm sheets and a lover's limbs. Mars was supposed to be safe, a last posting to shore up your savings before you made the biggest commitment.

No marriage now. No future at all.

The flickering light goes out, and blackness swallows you whole.

*"Ow! What the hell?"*

*"Ah, did I fail to mention? How awfully remiss. For every failure there is a consequence, not only for the avatar but for the player too. They worsen with each reset."*

*"But... that's not fair."*

*"No. It isn't."*

*"Look, how about this? Let me go, and I'll raid my little black book for contacts. I'll come back with allies. I won't run. What you've started on Mars has to be stopped. It will make things more interesting. I've got powerful friends."*

*"Really?"*

*"Well... I've got colourful friends. There's one with all these masks, and when he puts them on..."*

*"No. You will fix this alone. If you do not, slaughter comes to Earth."*

*"You're not making any friends here."*

*"The last checkpoint has loaded. You must proceed."*

121

They see your light and their heads snap around. Their eyes shine yellow in the beam. The mould is thick on their faces. A weapon, you realise. Something to make men mindless and frenzied.

You don't remember when you taped the flashlight to the barrel of the shotgun, but you're grateful for it now. Striding into the room, you pump the handgrip with one hand and hold the trigger down with the other. The noise is deafening, but the slamfire tears through their upper bodies like they are rotten fruit. None of them get up again.

Turning on the spot, you scan for any more movement. It won't be long before the racket brings more of them down on you, a lesson you learned well when...

A lesson the rest of the unit learned when Kramer was attacked.

Examining the body – definitely the sarge – you almost weep with joy when you realise that he had a deathgrip on his own weapon. The shotgun is almost empty, and even if it were full you would trade up.

You break his fingers to make him release it. A BFG. Vast, heavy and boxy, with several modes of fire and ammunition choices. A small army can be held off with one of these. All you need is a defensible position. You strip the flashlight off the shotgun, bind it to the BFG, and empty the corpse's pockets of spare ammo packs before putting some distance between yourself and the scene of the crime.

*"You don't look very well. How many times now? More than the avatar would guess. Fifteen? Twenty?"*

*"I... just bugger off, will you?"*

*"Was it the gas? I confess, I had no idea what it might do to somebody with your biological makeup. Would you care to describe the sensations?"*

*"No."*

*"Please reconsider. It would make a fascinating entry for my blog."*

*"You're going to pay for this. I'm going to make you pay."*

*"Perhaps, but not yet. For now, the game goes on."*

It is half an hour later, but you are starting to wonder if instead it has been many years. Each new confrontation or challenge you overcome feels somehow familiar, as though you are remembering the sense of it from another life. Familiarity does little to quell your fear, for it is the oddest moments of instinct – small choices that could easily have gone another way – that have seen you through the labyrinthine station.

You are underground now, working through a maze of smeared corridors and laboratories, hunting as much as you are hunted. The crazed scientists are fewer, but there are new things in the dark, child-sized creatures with mad red eyes made of tears and desperate hate. They are armed, these grubby, capering, naked things, with metal tubes that spit balls of hot plasma at you. Your left ear is a weeping mess from one that flew too close.

There are larger Martians too, if Martians they are. They are hulking brutes with the same eyes and scaly green skin. When your bullets puncture their flesh, clouds of dry spores fill the air, and you now know the source of the infection that ran through the base personnel. As gargantuan as these brutes are though, you prefer them to their smaller kin. Armed only with their vast swords, they must get close to do any damage. The BFG has prevented that so far.

You step carefully through the remains of the two that had burst through the doors of a large room, and take a fast look inside. A large technical laboratory of some kind, full of strange red glow coming from the right. Nothing moves, so you step inside. The terminals flicker with spiralling graphics and formulae way beyond your limited scientific knowledge, so you ignore them and turn towards the light.

The far wall is covered in heavy, interlocking machinery, wound round with dull industrial piping. At its heart there is a hole, once filled with a huge and heavy metal door that lies on its side against the wall. A strange semi-solid light seals the gap now, like the sort of forcefield you have seen only in poorly researched sci-fi holos. Fondling patterns of nauseating green swirl through the violent red.

Noises from the corridor behind you. You run back to the doors, slamming them just as something shoves hard from the other side. Jamming a chair beneath the door handles buys you enough time to drag the nearest desk across, and you load that with computer terminals to add weight. It will only hold for a short while. You scan the walls. The grim stoicism you clung to during your explorations falls apart as you realise that there is no other exit.

Movement catches the corner of your eye, and when you turn and raise the BFG you see a huge shadow approaching the forcefield from the far side.

There is time to fling another desk onto its side and crouch behind it, and then a Martian twice the size of a man steps out into the room. Its armour is a vile and shining red-brown, with twisted horns on the helm. It grins, showing you wicked teeth. Foul effluent drips from muscled arms that twist and bulge beneath the weight of some sort of bazooka. It brings the weapon up one-handed. The missile poking from the barrel eyes your position.

You raise the BFG and blast at its head, which makes it flinch and not much more. It squeezes on the trigger.

As the explosion tears you to pieces your thoughts fly to warm sheets and a lover's limbs. Mars was supposed to be safe, a last posting to shore up your savings before you made the biggest commitment.

No marriage now. No future at all.

Blackness swallows you whole.

You raise the BFG and aim at its head, knowing somehow that you don't have the firepower to make a scratch. Instead of firing you scan the room, hoping for another option. There are tables and shadows, a mirror in the corner, computer terminals and bloodstains. The moment in which you could have taken a desperate shot vanishes, and the Martian squeezes the trigger.

As the explosion tears you to pieces your thoughts fly to warm sheets and a lover's limbs. Mars was supposed to be safe, a last posting to shore up your savings before you made the biggest commitment.

Blackness swallows you whole.

You drop the BFG and race for the door, knowing you don't have the firepower to hurt this thing. The aliens are still on the other side of your barricade, but at least you can hurt them.

Time is not your friend. You barely have your hands on the desk before you hear the whoosh of the rocket launching.

Warm sheets and a lover's limbs.

Blackness swallows you whole.

Tears pour down your cheeks, and you drop the BFG. You remember now. You have been here so many times, trying so many things that do not work. Dropping to your knees, you let the gun clatter to the floor and wait. The Martian cocks its head, confused, and squeezes on the trigger.

Warm and welcome blackness swallows you whole. You wish you could stay in it, but know that you will not be allowed to.

As the explosion tears you to pieces your thoughts fly to...
Your thoughts fly to...
You cannot remember. It has been too long.
Despair strikes you down, and then blackness swallows you whole.

*"...aaaaa..."*
*"You can lie on the floor moaning all you like, but it isn't going to get you anywhere. I thought you people were tough."*
*"...hurts..."*
*"That's rather the point."*
*"The avatar... can't see the bloody solution. Keeps..."*
*"Yes indeed. You could be here for a very long time, relying on that one. Forever, in point of fact. Torment upon torment. A new one every time they surrender. Unless..."*
*"What?"*
*"Perhaps a more direct intervention?"*
*"I can... do that?"*
*"Only twice. It's an option to be reserved for the very direst circumstances. Which this may be. You should have some water. You've lost a lot of fluid."*
*"Should have said..."*
*"Well, you know now. It's the green button. Have fun."*

You reach out to yank another desk over for cover, but your body is lighter than you are used to, and you fall against it instead. Your hands splay across its surface, your soft, fine fingers more delicate than they were before. Somehow, you have long fingernails. The gloom makes it difficult to be certain, but they might be electric blue. You try to lift them up for closer inspection, but they don't respond. Nothing does.

"Don't fight me," your unfamiliar lips tell yourself in a feminine purr. "This is hard enough as it is."

As before, the shock of hearing words from your mouth that you did not put there is like a slap across the mind. As you recoil from yourself, somebody else steps in.

Your body turns, an elegant pirouette that you are not responsible for. Your arm raises your gun single-handed, and the weapon is no longer the BFG. Instead you clasp a stupid neon pink pistol unlike anything you've seen before. Your finger fires the shot without you, aiming not at the huge alien standing before the force field, but at the tip of the missile itself. A laser streaks across the room before the beast can squeeze its own trigger, and your body hurls itself behind the desk.

The explosion that slams against your barricade, sliding it and you several feet back across the room, tells you that the shot was true. The heat sucks the oxygen away, but the room's atmosensors replenish it before more than a breathless moment passes. The woman in your mind uses you to peer over the top of the desk, and gives a satisfied nod. Your view is framed by long eyelashes.

"Job done," she says. "Now listen. I haven't long. You've got to keep going, honey. No giving up. No dying. Everything's at stake." As your body stands you catch a glimpse of your reflection on a dead computer screen. A curvaceous woman in figure-hugging leather, with flowing blonde hair and a devil-may-care stance. You are wearing heels. "Ah, ah, no peeking. Focus on the forcefield. It's a Martian bio-filter, to cleanse the lurgis off their warriors when they pass to and fro. You can walk through. It'll fry the bacteria in your gut, and you'll be making water for days, but there's nothing long term to worry about." You want to nod, confused though you are, but still have no control of your body. "I've got to go. Remember, the only way out is through, for both of us. I'll be watching. You're not alone."

She leaves, and you are yourself again, in military uniform with the BFG in hand. You stare at the forcefield.

Go through to get out. You are not alone. That makes you want to cry with relief, but the hammering at the blocked doors behind you redoubles and you hold it in.

Hours (*decades*) have passed, and still you fight through the red rock tunnels beneath the Mars base. You have slain your way through passages lined with crimson weed, past statues of monsters from another age, and beneath caverns of blue ice that made you weep at their beauty. You have torn apart

126

vicious bat things, carnivorous slugs the size of a two man flyer, and Martians in a thousand sickening guises.

At some point you found papers or records, so you think. The Martians were sleeping when the scientists dug down and began to tinker with their technologies. Something woke them. You do not know what, and you do not care. Most things are beyond your concern. You are nothing but rage and terror. Killing is all you know.

Now you are trapped. Crouched at an open door, you stare with feral eyes into a cave that has killed you over and over again. Every rending is seared into your memory. It is a vast storeroom, a warren of plastic crates and barrels brought down by the Corporation to supply whatever experiments they were conducting, and it only *appears* deserted. As soon as you step in the first aliens will fall on you. Around every corner you will find more. Eventually they will overpower you. No matter how long you wait at the door, none of them will present themselves to be taken out from the safety of cover. Somehow you know all this, because somehow you have tried it.

You remember a female voice urging you on, a long, long time ago. *The only way out is through.*

There is a control panel on the wall next to you, a curious manmade addition to the environment, but it is not a threat so you do not examine it. With maiming on your mind, you ready yourself to spring into action.

Pressure builds in your head, as though there is a vacuum at the base of your skull. Your eyes cross and the strength leaves your knees.

Warm sheets drape you as you wake. There is somebody on the bed beside you. This is all so familiar, yet you cannot grasp why. Something... limbs... something.

Your face twists into its customary snarl, and you scan the bedroom for a weapon. Nothing suggests itself, but your bare hands have torn things stronger than a human body apart, many times.

A naked woman has her back to you. She has strong shoulders, elegantly muscled. Long blonde hair splays over the pillow. A single twist of that pretty head will snap her neck. You reach out.

The woman gasps and tenses, one arm pulling the sheet up to her throat. "*Bloody hell!* Don't you have any *pre*-coital memories you could have dragged me into?"

The shock of a human voice blows holes in the creature you have become. "I..." It is a struggle to speak. "What?"

"Well it's not *my* memory, sunshine. At least, I don't think it is. Sheets are synthetic. I'm an Egyptian cotton kind of girl."

"Memory," you say. Warm sheets and a lover's limbs. "What's happening to me?"

"*There* you are. I thought we'd lost you. Can't have that. Whole planet on the line, et cetera, and so on."

"I died. I keep dying."

She does not turn around, perhaps due to some sense of modesty, but her shoulders relax a little. "My fault chuck. I'm sorry. *I'm so, so sorry.*" She doesn't sound at all sincere.

"I don't believe you."

"Yeah, bollocks isn't it? Meaningless. No point telling *him* that, of course. He'd only agree with you, and probably apologise again."

"Who?"

"Doesn't matter. A friend. He does things like this all the time. Sets people up to be in the right place at the right moment. Makes them heroes." With a sad puff of sigh, she whispers, "He's really good at it. Makes it look easy, but I don't think I've got the same knack. Don't you dare tell him I said so."

"Why... what?"

"Cliff Notes version. I'm playing a cosmic game, for the sake of the Earth. Bloody thing keeps getting destroyed and put back together again, but nobody ever checks the edges. There are cracks and holes all over. Things slip through. Beings. A mad old god woke the Martians while the Corporation's pet scientists were messing around with their old teleportation kit. I got to choose one man to make a difference and save the Earth from what happens next. Your number came up."

"Earth?" You can barely remember what your homeworld looks like.

"Martians used to 'port there all the time, thousands of years ago, but there wasn't much to see back then. Big lizards, mainly. It's much more interesting now. There are people to conquer."

"They want to go through?"

"Reckon they might as well, once they get the portal powered up. Listen, these things will wipe you lot from history if they get through. You've got to get to it before it's active. Blow it up or something. Whatever

128

soldier boys do. If you win, Earth will be saved. If you lose... the game never ends. Every time you die you get kicked back a few minutes into your own history and we have to start over."

"I remember them. All my deaths." There is a dull pressure under your ribs. Grief and frustration. You want to kill her again.

She smells of flowers and something sweet and alcoholic. "They build up. The more you fail, the more you remember. You've failed quite a lot more than I thought you would. Sorry."

"Somebody can take my place. Somebody better."

"Sorry, tried that. Nothing can breach the recursion cycle for more than a few moments. This conversation's happening in one of the few memories of your life I could still find, but less than a second's passed in the real world. I can maybe come through one more time physically, but not for long. After that you'd be on your own."

Sharp pains shoot from your palms, and you realise your fists are tightly balled. You do not unclench them. "If I win..."

"Earth is saved. History resumes. I get to walk free from the prison I sleepwalked into. Until then we're both trapped, and so is everything else. The whole of everything is stuck in this moment. Time can't squeeze past the recursion loop he wrapped you in. On a billion worlds, everybody is being struck by the most intense déjà vu of their lives. There's a man in Spain having a small octopus surgically removed from his bottom after the strangest fishing accident ever recorded, and even *he's* got a weird feeling that it's happened to him before."

"I... don't remember octopus."

"Cling to who you are. You'll win, in the end. Don't lose yourself on the way. I wish I had more time to explain. Check the panel. Good luck."

The vast storeroom on the other side of the door has killed you dozens of times, so you ignore it and examine the control panel on the wall. It is a human-installed security system for the warren of toxic chemicals and expensive parts in all those crates and barrels. There are only three settings – *Off*, *Non-Lethal*, and *Lethal*. It is switched off.

With a twist of a dial, you reset it to *Lethal* and stand back with the BFG aimed at the door.

From inside the room comes the whirr of ceiling mounted weapon systems finding targets. Then the shooting starts. During the automated bloodshed only three Martians make it to your door, and they are easy pickings for the BFG.

Your throat feels ragged and torn, but you cannot stop howling. The sound frightens you, for it is joyous and insane. Your slaughters are a majestic dance.

The low-slung metal tripod is most monstrous of them all, and rears over you on creaking legs. You discard the BFG, having emptied it into the vast underbelly of the mechanical beast, exposing wire and tendrils. Now it is you and the knife. Torches blaze on the cavern walls, but you are the shadows between the light, the thing that makes the monsters run and cry.

Standing, you thrust the blade with two hands and pierce the innards. A surge of electricity zaps through you, but you disregard the twitching pain and heave through gears made of rock. Hot fluids shower you.

Rolling free, you're back on your feet in time to see it shudder and crash to the ground. Your victory cry bends you double, and you whirl in search of more prey.

There is nothing.

The cavern is empty. You and the shattered war machine are alone with the strange machinery against the wall. Light swirls there.

A portal.

You are at the portal. The caverns of Mars are behind you. The tripod is the last obstacle. You can go home now.

Strength drains from your limbs as you stumble the device, certain that it is a trick. There are tears on your face.

It can't be over.

You don't want it to be over.

There can't be nothing left to kill.

The console is complex, made of flesh and circuits. You do not know how it works. You can't go home after all. There is nothing left to do but return the way you came, back into slaughterhouse.

There's a push at the back of your mind. You push back. She is not welcome.

She bats you aside like a gnat, and between blinks you can feel yourself shrink and adjust.

"Enough of that, sunshine," she says. "You're going home whether you like it or not." Her hands whiz across the console, flicking switches and tying off small grey tentacles. "I can't leave you here. We're walking free."

The portal flashes. "One in, two out. Should work. You ready?"

You cannot answer, because she has your mouth.

You cannot answer, because you don't know whether you'll ever be ready.

She walks you to the portal, and slinks you through.

Earth is burning. Buildings crumble all around. The sky is made of fire and poison. A weird, musical howl fills the air from somewhere nearby. Bodies are strewn everywhere, some of them Martian, most of them human. You turn and see the woman for the first time. It is possible that she is beautiful, but you cannot remember what other people look like, so there is no point of comparison.

She is staring at a stick thrust into the ash, upon which somebody has placed the charred head of a stuffed panda. Her look of horror would hollow you out, if you were not already a numb void.

When she turns to you she cannot meet your eyes. "You were too late," she mumbles. "They got the portal working and came through. You didn't win."

You hold your breath, needing to hear the words before you can contemplate what she is forcing on you.

"You weren't fast enough." She raises a gentle hand to your cheek, and wipes away tears you did not realise you were crying. There is something hard in her eyes. "I'm sorry."

You don't believe her.

*"I am an insufferable cosmic bastard of my word. You are free to go."*

*"Is there a way to win. Can this be won?"*

*"If you play again? Of course! It would be poor sport otherwise. Do you really wish to stay? Will you really bleed more for that place? Once we begin, we cannot stop until we reach the end once more."*

*"I can do it. I can beat it."*

*"Even with the difficulty dialled up? It gets harder each iteration. So do the penalties. Many do not survive a second effort. Nobody survives a third. This is your last chance to walk away."*

*"Shut up and bring me a gin. I'm going in."*

You blink, and you're on the shuttle. A fierce black joy fills your heart. You scream it free, not minding the frightened looks that Barty and the sarge give you.

There is hot blood waiting to be spilled.

# THE LAST MARTIAN
## Rachel Churcher

*Something was screaming in the Maelstrom. The screams distorted the flows of the time winds, crying out for someone – anyone – to help. They rang with the colour of loss and shimmered with the sound of pain. They were everywhere, and nowhere. They were a beacon, snatching help and drawing it into the dark...*

*Out in the Maelstrom, something responded.*

When Iris opened her eyes, it was the absence of windscreen that she noticed first. That, and the intrusion into her driving cab of the branch of a large apple tree, complete with ripe, rosy apples. From behind her in the bus came a clattering sound, and a groan. She tried to sit up, but found her seat occupied by a mess of apples and leaves. Her head was pounding.

She twisted out of her seat, under the apple branch, and emerged unsteadily into the aisle of the bus. The light was bright after the green, leafy darkness of the cab. Panda was picking his way out from under a pile of chairs, books and crockery. The bus looked as if something had turned it upside down and shaken it – which, she reflected, is probably exactly what had happened. She remembered a sound like a scream or a moan, a warning light flashing on the dashboard, and then blackness. And the apple tree.

She focussed on the scene outside the bus. It was a bright, sunny day. On a tidy lawn, in front of a neat clapboard house, stood a garden table. Around the table, seated on matching wooden garden chairs, three women were staring at the bus in alarm. Their iced drinks lay forgotten on the table, their conversation abandoned. Iris moved towards the doors.

One of the women stood up, and ran to the bus. She reached the doors just as Iris found the emergency release handle, and tumbled out onto the grass. The woman caught her and helped her to her feet. Her companions hurried over and helped Iris to a chair, where she sat, dumbstruck, staring at her new surroundings and trying to piece together what had happened. She was dimly aware that the women were busying themselves with finding another chair, a glass and a first aid box.

Someone was wrapping a blanket round her shoulders and asking her a question. She pulled her attention back to the garden.

"Are you OK? Are you hurt?"

Another voice – "How many fingers am I holding up? What's your name? Can you tell me the date today?"

Iris laughed.

"Three fingers, Iris, and I have absolutely no idea!"

Ten minutes later, Iris was feeling better. The women had introduced themselves, poured her a tall glass of iced tea, and applied antiseptic and plasters to the minor grazes on her face and hands. She was huddled in the blanket, cradling her drink and enjoying the warmth of the afternoon sun. Panda had freed himself from the chaos in the bus, and after brief introductions (the women had thought he was a simply darling robot), he had returned to the Number 22 to begin the clean-up. Judging by the clattering and grumbling audible over the birdsong in the garden, he had not entirely appreciated the robot comments.

Iris and Panda had, it turned out, crashed (literally) the afternoon tea party of Anna, her niece Dot, and her best friend Joy. Anna's apple tree had suffered the most from their arrival, and no one had yet mentioned the state of Anna's formerly beautiful lawn. The date, it transpired, was September first, 2005. An offer of gin, misheard and enthusiastically accepted by Iris, had in fact been an offer of ginger ale. They had settled, awkwardly, on iced tea as a suitable substitute.

Iris watched her rescuers laughing and reliving the events of the last half hour. Anna, a tall, elegant woman in her forties, projected an aura of calm control. She had been the one to rescue Iris from the bus. Joy was obviously more shaken by Iris' arrival. Several ringlets of hair had escaped from her Alice band, and she sat looking hot and flustered, drinking her iced tea. Both women were dressed in beautiful, pinch-waisted summer frocks with long sleeves, high necks and calf-length skirts. Iris doubted that this was the height of fashion in 2005, and would have concluded that the women were simply dressing up for a garden party, if it hadn't been for Dot.

Dot was much younger than the other two. While clearly enjoying the company of the older women, she looked as if she had dressed for hard work rather than an afternoon of gossip and refreshments. She wore denim dungarees over a red T-shirt and work boots, and her shoulder-length hair was tied back with a red scarf. She was more Rosie the Riveter than Little House on the Prairie, and looked out of place in the manicured garden.

Iris took in the outfits, the American accents, the lawn, the iced tea and the clapboard house. "So, where are we?" she asked. "Kansas? Iowa?"

Dot laughed. Joy looked puzzled.

"Iowa?" she said, "This is Mars, Iris! Iowa is a very long way from here."

"And this bit! What does this bit do, Iris?"

Iris was on her hands and knees under the apple tree, extracting components from the engine of the bus and assessing the damage caused by the crash. Dot knelt next to her, peering closely at each piece and mechanism and indignantly demanding to know what role each one played in the propulsion of the transtemporal vehicle.

After the iced tea and conversation had been exhausted, Dot had offered to help Iris with repairs to the bus. Her outfit, Iris discovered, was explained by her profession – apprentice mechanic at Anna's husband's gas station and workshop – and she was a very enthusiastic assistant. Unfortunately, the bus was not the straightforward combustion engine-powered vehicle that she had been expecting. Iris was getting used to providing a running commentary while she extracted the damaged sections of the drive.

Panda, taking a break from fetching and carrying tools and spare parts to Iris, was sitting in the doorway of the bus, happily relating the pair's past adventures to Joy. Anna had retreated to the house to phone her husband, partly to excuse Dot's failure to return to work, and partly to request the immediate dispatch of a tow truck. Both were proving hard to explain.

Iris and Dot pieced together the surviving components with the spare parts in the afternoon sunshine. Panda was occasionally called upon to bring additional equipment from the many storage compartments on the bus, and Joy could be seen looking more fascinated and less convinced by Panda's stories as the afternoon progressed.

Eventually, Iris was ready to test the reconstructed drive. She and Dot placed it back inside the engine compartment, and with a lot of guidance, Dot reconnected the mechanism. A healthy blue-green glow brightened in the centre of the compartment, and Dot was mesmerised. Iris pushed the bright red external cover into place, and turned her attention to the windscreen.

"We still haven't replaced our spare one of those," she said, shaking her head. "You couldn't order one from your workshop, could you, Dot? We'd be very grateful."

Dot looked thoughtful, and agreed to ask her uncle.

At that moment, the sound of the tow truck's arrival in the street beyond the house interrupted all conversation in the garden. Joy stood up, a panicked look in her eyes. She looked at Panda, and at Iris.

"We can't... I mean... you... can't..."

"What?" demanded Iris.

Dot followed her gaze.

"She's right. You'd better come inside."

Joy and Dot hustled Iris and Panda into the house, just as the tow truck driver followed Anna into the garden to inspect the site of the crash.

"Would you mind explaining what's going on?" whispered Iris, once they were safely inside.

Dot and Joy stared at her, and slowly looked her up and down.

"You're not... exactly... decent!" said Joy, eventually.

Iris struck an indignant pose, hands on hips, showing off her skin-tight electric pink catsuit, neon orange utility belt and thigh-high orange stiletto boots to the full. Panda rested his head in his paws.

"I'm not *what*?" she asked.

"What Joy is trying to say, I think," said Dot, "is that skintight stretchy stuff isn't... normally... worn... on the outside. Around here."

Panda shook his head, eyes still hidden by his paws.

"I mean, it is probably absolutely OK to wear that where you come from! You probably all wear stretchy outfits, all the time! Even the men! And that's great!" Dot paused to look at her own choice of outfit. "I can see how useful it must be for fixing your bus and having adventures."

"I think I can safely say that you two have only the vaguest notion about where I come from," barked Iris, hands still on hips.

Joy looked distinctly uncomfortable with the idea of a man dressed in Iris' outfit. She shook her head.

"Iris. Let me find you something to wear. You still need to find a windscreen for the bus, and that will involve... meeting people. And some

136

of those people might be... men. And some of them might get the wrong idea..."

Panda snorted, and Iris shot a hurt look in his direction.

"It's what I do. I'm a seamstress, and I have plenty of lovely dresses at my house. Let me go and fetch some for you. You can try them on, and choose something to wear while you're here."

Reluctantly, Iris relaxed and nodded.

"I suppose. If it will make fixing the bus easier. There had better be a pocket for my laser pistol though!"

Joy grinned. "I have just the thing!"

Anna's husband, Walt, shook his head. "We don't have anything like that in stock."

"Can you make me one?" Iris asked.

He shook his head again. "That's out of our league, I'm afraid."

"Then we'll have to order one!" said Iris, brightly.

The owner and manager of the Blue Sail Automotive Company looked uncomfortable. Dot coughed nervously.

"What's the matter? Can't you order spare parts?" Iris paused, and then looked horrified. "You don't have to wait for it to arrive from *Earth*, do you? Goodness. I could be here for months!"

"Oh, no, Iris!" Dot looked relieved. "It's not that. It's just that – well – it means dealing with Creek."

"Creek." echoed Iris, looking lost.

"Creek runs all the commerce on Mars," said Walt, shaking his head. "There isn't a car or a suitcase or even a hot dog bought or sold on Mars that doesn't come through Creek. Kind of runs the show – import, export, distribution. We're pretty restricted on what we can buy, and lately it's been getting harder to get everything we want. We try to stick to our regular orders and stay out of Creek's way."

"...and this wouldn't be part of your regular order?"

"I'm afraid not, Iris. We don't have many London buses on Mars. You'll have to find a way to persuade Creek to help you."

"Couldn't we try, Uncle? Just this once?" Dot protested.

"Not unless you'd like to risk all our jobs." He turned to Iris, waving a hand to indicate the workshop around them, and bus taking up one side of the space. "I'm sorry, Iris. It's more than my business is worth to get involved with Creek."

"What do we do now?" asked Dot, despondently.

They were standing across the street from the workshop in the evening sunshine, Dot in her work clothes and Iris in an outfit provided by Joy. The khaki creation was a great deal less comfortable than the jumpsuit she had reluctantly left at Anna's house, but she had to admit that it was practical and more in keeping with local expectations. Featuring a long linen skirt and a shirt with rolled-up sleeves, the ensemble looked as if it had been designed for a Victorian safari hunter. The matching waistcoat, with its many pockets and buttons, only added to this impression. Iris had decided to not to wear the coordinating sunhat, but had insisted on keeping her boots, which showed as a flash of orange heels under her skirt.

She was furiously smoking a cigarette, produced, along with her lighter, from one of the waistcoat's pockets. She met Dot's disapproving gaze.

"We go and see Creek."

"You're going to need a boat."

"A boat?"

"For the canals. It's the easiest way to reach Creek's headquarters."

Iris, Anna, Joy and Dot were sitting round the table in Anna's dining room, speaking in hushed voices and finishing off the last of the coffee. Walt and Panda were on washing up duty in the kitchen. Panda stood on the worktop, brandishing a tea towel and taking advantage of his captive audience to relate further tall tales of his adventures with Iris. His task was to distract Walt from the after-dinner conversation, and he jumped into the role with glee, acting out dangerous encounters with the aid of dinner plates and cutlery.

"Surely *we're* going to need a boat?" said Iris in a stage whisper. "I thought you lot were coming with me!"

Anna shook her head.

"I can't, Iris. Walt would be terribly upset if I came with you. He's much too worried about the workshop."

Dot glanced at Iris, then looked down at the table and slowly shook her head.

Iris looked at Joy.

"What? Me?" Joy looked shocked. "What use would I be? I can't exactly sew you out of trouble! No, Iris. I don't think so. Sorry."

"Right then," said Iris, tightly. "Where do I find a boat?"

Dot looked up. "My brother has a little motorboat – it's tied up at the quay in town. He uses it for fishing on the canal. I'll tell him I want it for a girls-only party. He'll be okay with that."

Anna shot Dot a despairing look, then spoke to Iris.

"I think you might be better off heading out at night. That way no one will wonder who you are or where you're going, and you'd get to Creek's first thing in the morning. I'll lend you a coat and some blankets – you'll need to wrap up warm. Can you sort that, Dot? You'll need to get Iris some fuel, and a map."

Dot nodded enthusiastically.

"Go call your brother. See if you can get the boat tonight."

Dot hurried from the table to use the phone in the hall. Exciting sounds of swashbuckling and crockery-related adventure were still coming from the kitchen, and Walt was laughing at Panda's antics. Anna gathered up the coffee cups and took them to the kitchen in an effort to prolong the washing up process.

Dot rushed back into the room.

"We've got the boat! Tonight!" she said, a little too loudly. "I'm going to fetch some fuel and maps from home – I'll meet you here at midnight and take you down to the quay."

"That's wonderful! Thank you, Dot!"

Anna came back into the room as Dot's shouted goodbye echoed from the front door. "If everything is settled, I'll make up a bed for you in the spare room, Iris. Would you like to give me a hand?"

At that moment, there was a crash from the kitchen as one of Panda's re-enactments proved a little too athletic for his props. Joy jumped up to help Walt, and provide further distraction while Anna and Iris headed for the spare bedroom to pack a bag of warm clothing, and make up a bed as a cover story.

"Pssst! Iris!"

"Dot?" Iris emerged from the shadows at the side of the porch to find Dot crouching in the bushes. "Let's go, before your Uncle works out what's going on."

Dot led Iris through the sleeping town, down to the quayside and the old Martian canal. The street lamps were lit, but the houses were mostly in darkness. The streets were empty as they made their way to the mooring of a small fibreglass rowing boat, retrofitted with a motor.

"We'll need to row the boat to start with, to avoid waking anyone up. Once we are out of town, then we can use the motor." Dot slung her bag into the boat, and offered Iris a hand to help her step in.

"We?" said Panda, pulling himself up from Iris' bag. "I thought you weren't coming! Iris, did you change the plans?"

"Not me, Panda. Dot, are you sure you want to come? Your Uncle didn't sound too keen on the idea. Nor did your Aunt, come to think of it."

"I don't think her Aunt's opinion matters now," called a voice from the darkness across the quayside, "seeing as she's here to make sure everything goes according to plan."

"Auntie!" exclaimed Dot.

"Is there space for me?"

Five minutes later, they were all perching on seats and bags in the boat. Dot stowed the fuel, dug out the oars, and cast off from the quay. She was just starting to row when a figure appeared on the quayside, running towards them, hair flying.

"Wait! Wait! I'm coming too!"

"Joy!"

Dot grinned, and steered back towards the quay. Anna helped Joy down into the boat, and everyone shuffled round to make space for her. When everyone was more or less comfortable, Dot set off again.

"So what are you all doing here?" asked an incredulous Iris, when Dot had started the motor and they were moving along the canal outside town.

"Dot was always coming," said Anna. "She put on a nice act for me back at the house, but there was no way she was going to miss this."

"What gave me away?" challenged Dot.

"You said 'we'. 'We've got the boat'. I heard you when I came out of the kitchen..."

Dot slumped in her seat next to the motor.

"...so I thought I would come along and make sure that nothing too crazy happened. I've heard Panda's stories, and they don't fill me with confidence."

140

Panda looked flattered. Iris grinned. "We can't guarantee that!"

"I'm coming for me," declared Joy. "I thought about it, and I realised that I want some adventure in my life. I don't want to die an old, boring, spinster who sewed a lot. And I want to meet Creek, and find out what everyone is so afraid of. I won't get another chance like this!"

"Wait...," said Iris, looking puzzled. "Creek is a person? I was assuming Creek was an organisation. We're going to see a person?"

The others nodded. "A very powerful person," said Anna.

The boat pushed on through the night, with only the sound of the motor to break the vast Martian silence.

Panda snored. Iris stirred. She had intended to stay awake after taking her turn steering the boat, but she must have drifted off to sleep. She yawned and sat up, careful not to disturb Panda as he slept in her lap.

"Good morning, Iris," said Anna from the tiller. "We're nearly there." She pointed ahead of the boat.

In the dawn light, Iris could see an enormous complex spanning both sides of the canal. They were some way off, but the towers and pipes and slab-sided buildings already dwarfed the boat. As they drew closer, she recognised the signs of industry. Smoke and steam poured from cooling towers and stacks. Lights flashed. Conveyor belts moved piles of gravel and dirt into the building. Clanging and crunching noises filled the air.

She roused the others and handed round a flask of hot coffee. Panda made a horrified face when he tasted the coffee, but drank it anyway. The mood was subdued.

Dot unfolded a large piece of paper. "According to my map, there should be a dock area on the left hand side, just past the first building. We should try to moor up in there."

Anna nodded, and steered the boat gently towards the left bank.

They motored into the dock area without incident, and found a place to tie up the boat. The dock walls were high, and climbing out of the boat required the use of a series of metal rungs cast into the concrete. Iris climbed up first to check the dockside, but found it empty. She crouched over the ladder, reached down to lift Panda out of the boat, and froze as she heard the unmistakable sound of a gun safety being released. Several guns. Very close to her head.

Slowly, she put her hands above her head and started to turn around. She was seized roughly by the shoulders and dragged backwards, away from the dockside. She had time to register Anna's look of fury and Panda's look of panic before she lost sight of the boat.

Iris found herself sitting on the concrete dock with her back against another wall. Two men dressed in black combat gear held guns pointed at her, while their two colleagues, similarly armed, instructed the rest of the party to climb out of the boat, one at a time. Iris watched the men closely as the women emerged onto the dock. She hoped that Panda had the sense to hide under their coats and blankets.

When all four women were sitting quietly against the wall, hands on heads, one of the men began to pace up and down in front of them.

"Anyone care to tell me who you lot are? Hmmm? Or how you got here? This is a restricted area! What is it you are here to do, exactly? Sabotage? Hmmm? Anyone?"

Before anyone could answer, the man standing at the edge of the dock called out.

"Hey! There's someone else in the boat! Sir! Look!"

Two more men rushed to the dockside.

"There is, too! Smith, you get down there and drag them out."

Iris held her breath.

Smith lowered himself down the ladder and disappeared from sight. There was some grunting, and the sound of several items being thrown into the water. Eventually, Smith called up from the boat.

"Got it, sir!"

"Aaaagh! Get off me! Put me down, you hooligan!" The sounds of Panda in distress were unmistakable. Iris didn't know whether to laugh or cry.

Smith reappeared, climbing one-handed up the ladder while clasping the struggling Panda under his other arm.

"What is it?"

"Dunno. A robot?"

"I am no such thing! Put me down immediately!" commanded Panda.

By now, all the men were standing round Smith and Panda, speculating on what he might be, and poking him while Smith tried to restrain his struggles. He had their full attention.

Iris crept to her feet, pulling her laser pistol from its pocket in her waistcoat.

"PUT. HIM. DOWN."

The men turned in surprise, and were shocked to find themselves staring down the barrel of a bright pink energy weapon, wielded by a tall woman in stiletto heels who was otherwise dressed as if she should be hunting lions on an African game reserve.

"I said, *put him down.*"

Three men reached instantly for their weapons, as Iris fired at Smith. He staggered to the ground, clutching his shoulder and dropping Panda, who curled up on the dock and covered his head with his paws, groaning.

Iris ducked as one man fired at her, grazing the top of her complicated hairstyle. The other two had turned to help Smith, but pointed their weapons at her as soon as they heard the gunshot.

For a moment, everyone froze. Three guns pointed at Iris. One gun pointed back at them.

"Drop your weapon!" The men stepped closer to Iris.

Iris stood her ground. "You alright, Panda?" she called.

Panda grunted, and waved a paw in the air.

"Drop it!"

Iris glanced around at the men. She couldn't shoot them all – not before they could shoot her, and Panda, and the others. Her shoulders slumped, and she lowered her pistol.

One of the men stepped forward and snatched it from her hand.

"You lot! On your feet! Keep your hands where I can see them!"

The frightened women stood up slowly, keeping their hands over their heads. Panda clambered to his feet, dusted himself down, and began to walk towards Iris.

"Oh no you don't." Panda stopped. "You! Alice band! You pick him up." The man gestured at Joy with his gun. "And you," pointing the gun at Panda, "behave! No struggling!"

Panda nodded. Very slowly, Joy stepped forward. She glanced nervously at the men and their guns, and then bent down and gently picked Panda up.

"You. Dungarees. Why are you here?"

Dot glanced at Iris, who nodded.

"We're here to see Creek."

The man laughed. "I think Creek will be very interested to see you."

The women followed the guard into the factory complex. Another guard walked behind them, still holding his own gun and Iris' weapon. The third guard stayed behind to help Smith.

"Stop wriggling!" hissed Joy, as Panda squirmed in her arms.

"She's only gone and singed my ear!" he hissed back. "Look! She's far too dangerous when she gets carried away with that laser gun." He pulled at a mat of burned fur at the top of his ear.

"Shhh!" whispered Joy. The guard at the back was watching them carefully.

They walked across the dock area, under cranes and conveyor belts, and into the nearest building. Service tunnels and concrete corridors led them deeper into the structure, and eventually they came to a hallway with a row of grey plastic seats on one side, and a set of elevator doors on the other.

"Sit here!" commanded the guard at the front. He pressed the button to call the elevator. The women sat in a line on the chairs.

When the elevator arrived, two more armed guards stepped out and stood in silence, watching the women. The guards from the dockside stepped inside, and the doors closed.

Iris leaned across Dot to talk to Panda.

"That got a bit exciting, didn't it? You okay?"

"My ear, Iris! Look at my ear! I really don't appreciate being on the hot end of that weapon, you know!"

"Quiet!" shouted one of the guards.

Iris mouthed "sorry" and leaned back in her seat. Panda grunted.

They waited in silence.

Some time later, the doors opened again, revealing an empty elevator car. The guards ushered them inside, and the doors closed. The elevator began to drop down the shaft.

"Well! Come out, then!" called a female voice. "I haven't got all day."

Iris stepped out through the opening lift doors. The others followed her, gingerly.

They were in a vast cave in the bedrock of Mars. Spotlights illuminated the rough-hewn walls and the distant ceiling. They stood on a balcony, jutting into the space. In the centre of the balcony, bent over a block of industrial control panels and computer terminals, stood a woman. She waved at them to come closer, never lifting her eyes from the screens in front of her.

She tapped on a keyboard, checked the screens again, and finally turned to meet her guests. She was a tall, slim olive-skinned woman with a long ponytail of red hair, the colour of the Martian rock behind her. She wore the same black combat gear as her guards.

"Welcome to my headquarters. I am Creek, and I am very busy. Who might you be?"

"Iris, and these are my friends. We've come to ask for your help."

Creek laughed, coldly. "Everyone wants my help. You are only here because I caught your little performance on the dockside, Iris." She indicated a bank of screens showing security camera footage. "I was impressed by your determination, and your weaponry. I'm in need of some help myself, and I think you might be the people to give it to me."

"Come with me, Iris. I want to show you something."

After introductions and reassurances, Creek showed the women to a seating area near the elevator doors. The plush red sofas made a change from the hard plastic seats upstairs. A pitcher of water and five glasses were waiting on a side table, and Creek invited the women to make themselves comfortable, before speaking to Iris.

She walked to the edge of the balcony, and pointed into the cave.

"I know what you have heard about me. That I run Mars. That everything that happens here goes through me. That I hold up all the progress."

Iris nodded, looking out from the balcony.

"That's not quite true. Everything that happens on Mars goes through this room, certainly. But I'm not the only controlling agent. At least, I wasn't."

Iris stared, trying to make sense of what she was seeing. The floor of the cave was covered with a network of boulders and a web of cabling. Some of the cables were dull and grey, while others glowed or pulsed with a familiar blue-green light. Each boulder was connected to the boulders around it, and patterns of lights played across and between them. Iris realised that she was looking at a giant computer, built from the natural rock of the cave.

"What is this?" she breathed.

"We don't know," said Creek. "We found it. It thinks and it calculates, and it runs Mars for us. But we don't know who built it, or why, or when. It just seems to know what we need. Or it did."

"What happened?"

"I have a rival. Someone else who wants to control the markets of Mars. When we found this... machine... there was something in it. Something alive. Coyote stole it from me, and now the machine can't think clearly." She turned. "It's failing, Iris. Mars is falling apart, and there isn't much more I can do."

She pointed towards the centre of the cave.

"See, there – that burned patch?" Iris nodded. "That's where they took it from. They came with so many men, with such violence. They burned it away from its rock, and took it across Mars." She brushed a tear from her cheek. "I can feel it. I know it is in pain, but I cannot reach it. We are joined, Iris. I was the one who found it. I was the first person to enter this room, and it found me. It touched my mind, and understood us. We have run Mars together ever since."

"I heard it," whispered Iris in surprise. "It's what called us here, to Mars." She remembered the sound in the Maelstrom, the scream and the moan, and then the crash. She shook her head.

"Why are people so afraid of you?"

"It understood us, through me. It knows what we need – not what we want. It plans over years – decades, maybe even centuries. It knows how to provide for our needs, but it doesn't give in to greed. I have to say 'no' to people, and that doesn't win me any friends. I can't be bought or influenced either – the machine has the final word. That gives me power, and people are afraid of power. The people out there – they don't know about this. They assume that I am some sort of tyrant or criminal, stopping them from getting rich. That's exactly what Coyote is, but he can't use what he stole. Without me, and without the machine, it's just a creature in pain."

"And you want us to get it back for you?"

"You're my best chance. I've tried sending my guards, but they can't get near Coyote, and I need them here. I have a feeling you and your friends will be a bit more devious than my guards, now that you know what is at stake."

"And in return? Can you fix my vehicle?"

146

"I can. Your friend has told me what you need, and I will manufacture it for you. But it must be in exchange for the creature."

"I'm going to need my pistol back."

"You'll have it, once you are on your way."

The pickup purred along the empty highway. In every direction, the Martian desert stretched away to the horizon – red sand, red boulders, red hills.

When she saw the vehicle Creek was providing for them, Dot had demanded to drive it. It was a beautiful brand new red pickup of a type that every farmer, miner and prospector on Mars dreamed of owning. She couldn't wait to take it out and see what it could do.

Panda and Joy were map-reading from the front seat, while Anna and Iris went through their pockets and bags to see what they had to use against Coyote and his organisation. They were heading, Creek had explained, to Coyote's Casino in Locust City. Her men were sure that the creature was being kept in a safe at the casino while Coyote worked out how to make it work for him.

Their inventory was not promising. One laser pistol (pink), one packet of cigarettes (half empty), one lighter (likewise). Several blankets and coats, an empty coffee flask, a torch. Iris' lipstick, makeup mirror, eyeshadow and mascara. The emergency sewing kit that Joy kept with her at all times.

"What's the plan, Iris?" asked Dot, still ecstatic to be driving the pickup.

"We're not sure yet," said Iris, trying to sound cheerful. "I think we'd be best to get there and take a look around first."

"Right!" said Dot, oblivious to Iris' growing concern. She leaned over and turned the radio on. A country station was playing "The Gambler".

Iris smiled.

"What now?" whispered Dot, from the driving seat.

"Now we come up with the plan. Right, Iris?" whispered Joy.

They were sitting in the pickup in the casino parking lot. The sun was setting behind distant red cliffs, and the garish casino lights promised "Blackjack! Roulette! Girls Girls Girls!". The parking lot was beginning to fill with cars and the casino was filling with customers.

Iris and Anna had taken a brief walk round the low-rise building, past the plate glass doors to the gambling floor, the staff entrances and the

147

manager's office. They had returned to the pickup with the beginnings of a plan.

"We're going to have to make ourselves look a bit more like customers," explained Anna. "Most people in there aren't dressed quite as respectably as we are." She looked decidedly uncomfortable.

Iris was shaking her head.

"I don't think that the customer look is what we should be aiming for. If we want access to the manager's office, we are going to need to look like staff."

"So what are the staff wearing?" asked Dot.

"Go and take a look for yourself. You too, Joy – you're our dressmaking expert."

"Ouch!"

"Hold still!"

"Don't stick pins in me then!"

Dot had moved the pickup behind a nearby gas station, and the women were busy converting their outfits into costumes more suited to the advertising of "Girls Girls Girls!" Joy's sewing kit lay open on the tailgate, and she attacked their clothing with scissors, pins, needles and thread.

Iris styled Dot's hair into pig tails, and then plaited them. Dot had reluctantly taken a pair of scissors to her dungarees, and converted them into tiny denim shorts. She shortened her T-shirt and knotted the front. Her work boots stayed. Anna registered a protest, but Dot and Iris both laughed, and agreed that she looked fantastic.

Anna's neat striped daydress was next, and lost its sleeves and high neck. Joy worked on the neckline until it was scandalously low-cut, and Anna almost refused to leave the safety of the pickup. Joy used one of the thinner blankets to create a petticoat for Anna, and tied a ribbon round her neck as a choker. Iris piled Anna's hair on top of her head and used some of her own hairclips to create a messy bun with some stray curls. When Anna looked in the mirror, she wasn't sure whether to thank Joy, or hide until they could all go home.

Iris discarded her shirt, and cut the waistcoat down to a corset. Joy pinned it discreetly at the back. She gleefully put a daring slit in the skirt at one side, exposing her boots, and used some offcuts from Anna's dress to create a flash of petticoat underneath. She tied a ribbon round her neck and roughed up her hair.

Joy's outfit had to be more conservative, as the plan called for her to dress as a customer. Her dress, like Anna's, lost its sleeves and collar, but her neckline remained tasteful and her skirt remained untouched. Iris removed her Alice band, and used more of her hair clips to create a sophisticated up-do. Joy was delighted by the result.

Iris used her makeup to complete the transformations. Bright red lipstick and heavy mascara all round, with different shades of eyeshadow to suit each outfit. They took turns inspecting themselves in the tiny mirror, while Panda looked them up and down and grunted his appreciation.

"We tart up alright, don't we, Panda?" grinned Iris. Panda winked.

Joy straightened her skirt, checked her hair, and feigned confidence as she strode through the front doors. A girl dressed as a Wild West Madam held the door open for her. She walked to the nearest table and hovered at the edge of the crowd, watching the game. From the corner of her eye, she watched the bar.

Iris, Anna and Dot made their way to the staff entrance, Dot carrying Panda, who did his best to look like an inert stuffed toy.

"The secret," Iris explained, "is to act as if you own the place. March straight in and start work. You'll be amazed how few people notice you."

She paused at the door. "Does anyone know how to mix drinks?"

Anna looked shocked, and Dot looked scandalised. "Of course not, Iris! We've never been anywhere like this before!"

Panda regained his voice temporarily. "It'll have to be you, Iris. You work the bar. These two can take orders, serve drinks, and keep people happy. I'll help with the drinks!"

"I bet you will. Right – you heard him. I'll take over at the bar. You two take orders, pass them on to me and – well. You know the rest."

The women exchanged nervous glances as Iris opened the door.

A few minutes later, Iris had installed herself behind the bar, telling the bar staff to take a break. Anna and Dot were carrying trays and mingling with the customers. Panda was hidden under the bar, ready to lend a hand.

"Look at all this booze, Iris!" he wailed. "This would make for a wild night!"

"Control yourself, Panda – the night is going to be wild enough." She paused. "On the other hand, I am dying for a drink. What do you fancy?" She grinned.

"That whisky looks interesting."

"It does, doesn't it? Coming right up!"

Iris kept an eye on the gambling floor while pouring two shots. She handed one to Panda, and knocked hers back while Panda sniffed and gingerly tasted his. He made a face, and downed it in one.

"Rough?"

"A little. What about that one?"

"Can't hurt to try."

Anna carried her tray and paced around the room, watching the customers. Iris had asked her to locate Coyote, and report back on where he was, and what he was doing. She had finally made it as far as the VIP area, and was about to head back to the bar with her report.

"What's your name?"

The voice startled her, and she struggled to remember her cover story.

"My name? Krystal. Can I get you a drink?"

She turned to smile at the man who had spoken, and froze when she saw his black suit, black leather gloves and earpiece. Security. He laughed.

"You're new, aren't you?"

She nodded.

"Well. Mr Coyote, over there," he pointed into the VIP area. "He'd like to meet you."

He led the way to the red velvet rope, unclipped it and beckoned her inside. She glanced over her shoulder and caught sight of Dot at the bar, reciting a list of her orders to Iris. She took a deep breath, and stepped inside.

Dot had collected a list of orders almost too long to remember, and was busy calling them to Iris as she worked behind the bar. Panda ran along the shelf under the bar, pointing at the different drinks as Dot reeled off her list. Iris was mixing and pouring drinks as fast as she could.

"Where's Anna?" She asked, between drinks.

Dot shrugged. "Somewhere out there."

Together they loaded up Dot's tray, and she rushed back to her customers. From under the bar, a voice called out.

"Iris! I've found the gin!"

Dot delivered her last drink, and wandered towards the VIP area. Was Coyote inside?

A large man with an expensive suit and a cigar was lounging on a red sofa, surrounded by other men in suits, his arm around a woman in a striped dress. With a start, she realised that the woman was Anna.

She nearly dropped her tray, and rushed back to the bar to tell Iris.

"She's *where?*"

Dot explained. Iris looked thoughtful.

"This could be a good thing. We've got Coyote distracted. Give Joy a nudge, would you? And whatever happens, keep this lot entertained. We need all the time we can get."

Dot turned back to look for Joy. Iris produced the gin and tonic she had been hiding behind her back, and collapsed into giggles. Panda snorted, and started pouring another gin.

Dot located Joy next to the Roulette wheel, and brushed past her.

"Iris says go!"

Joy let Dot walk away, straightened her skirt, and started to scream.

"My bag! Somebody's taken my bag! Help! Thief! Help!"

The other customers were starting to stare. This was where Anna was supposed to come and take her to the manager's office. Where was Anna? Joy screamed some more.

Dot looked around at the customers. Everyone's attention was on the wailing woman. The security guards next to the VIP area were starting to look interested. They needed a distraction.

Her eyes fell on the juke box next to the bar. She had an idea.

Iris finished her gin.

"We're up, Panda," she said, lifting him down to the floor. "Can you make it to the office?"

Panda nodded, saluted, giggled a bit, and sauntered to the end of the bar. Iris stifled a laugh, and rushed out to take care of Joy.

Waving off the security staff as she approached the Roulette table, she put her arm around Joy.

"Are you alright, madam?"

Joy shook her head, and screamed again. Iris had to admit that she had a talent for the dramatic.

"Please come with me, madam. We can sort out what happened."

She led the now sobbing Joy past the bar to the manager's office, where a good-looking security guard intercepted them.

"Can I help you ladies?"

"This lady has had her bag stolen. I'm taking her into the office so she can calm down, and we can go over what happened."

The security guard looked doubtful. Iris glanced at his ID badge, scanning for his name.

"She is very distressed, Sam." Iris lowered one of her stilettos onto Joy's toe. Joy let out a loud wail. "I don't think Mr Coyote would approve if we kept her out here, disturbing the other customers."

Reluctantly, Sam nodded, and unlocked the door.

Iris and Joy stepped inside, followed by Sam. As the door closed, Panda dived through into the office and flopped onto the floor, looking like a piece of lost property. Iris kicked him gently out of sight.

Iris pulled out the manager's chair and sat Joy down.

She turned to Sam.

"Could you fetch her a glass of water? She's terribly upset."

Sam looked very uncertain. Joy managed a weak smile. "Please?" she asked. Iris watched in amazement as Joy fluttered her mascaraed eyelashes at the man.

"Certainly." He stepped over to put a consoling leather-gloved hand on Joy's shoulder, then turned and left the room. Iris jumped up and closed the door behind him, wedging the other chair under the door handle.

"Right!" she cried. "Where's the safe?"

Iris and Panda looked around the room. Apart from the desk, two chairs and a filing cabinet, there was no other furniture, and no sign of a safe in the walls.

"Where's the safe?" she shouted.

Panda hiccupped, and tried to look serious. "S'not here, Iris," he managed. "Not here." He sat down.

Joy began to wail in earnest.

Anna squirmed in her seat next to Coyote. His breath stank of whisky and cigar smoke, and his arm around her was becoming less and less appropriate. She tried to pretend that she was enjoying herself, that she had always wanted to meet Mr Coyote. She tried to ignore the man sitting opposite her, who couldn't take his eyes off her neckline. She pretended to drink the glass of bubbly that Coyote had put in her hand.

Briefly, she heard Joy begin to shout, and was painfully aware that she should be out there, playing her role. She waited to see what would happen.

Joy cried and wailed. Coyote started to look concerned, and shifted in his seat to catch a glimpse of the gaming floor. Joy's wailing died away, and Anna realised that Coyote needed a distraction. She turned to him and fluttered her eyelids.

"So how much is a man like you worth, Mr Coyote?" she asked, taking a sip of her drink.

Dot walked up to the juke box. Taking a handful of the money she had collected for her drinks, she fed it in and chose some of the loudest songs she could find. She turned back to the gaming floor and willed herself to stop shaking. Then she climbed onto a bar stool, stepped on to the bar, and started to dance.

Iris paced up and down in the office. Sam would be back any moment with Joy's drink. She stopped.

Rushing to the door, she pulled the chair away just in time for Sam to turn the key in the lock and step back into the room. He closed the door carefully behind him, then turned to put the glass down on the desk. He froze, looking down the bright pink barrel of Iris' laser pistol. He reached for his walkie-talkie.

"Don't," said Iris. She indicated the chair. "Sit down."

He sat.

"Perhaps you can help us. My associates and I," she tipped her head towards Joy and Panda, "are looking for something. Something Mr Coyote has stolen. I believe it is in the safe."

Sam looked nervous, and his eyes flicked towards the floor under the desk.

"It's under the floor!" yelled Panda. "Iris! Move the desk!"

"Joy," said Iris, keeping her gaze, and her gun, fixed on the security guard, "could you move the desk and tell me what's underneath, please?"

Joy jumped up, and pushed the desk a short distance across the floor. Panda jumped up and rushed over to take a look.

"It's here, Iris!"

Joy knelt down and pulled up a handle embedded in the floor. "It needs a key."

Holding the gun steady with one hand, Iris held out the other hand to Sam. He put on a determined expression, and shook his head.

"Don't make me shoot you. I've already had to shoot one person today. I don't really want to have to shoot another."

Panda lowered his head and pointed at his damaged ear. "It's true! Look what she did to me by mistake! I wasn't even the one she was aiming at!"

Sam stared. He reached into his jacket pocket.

"Slowly!" warned Iris.

He obeyed. With exaggerated care, he produced a bunch of keys and handed them to Iris. She held them out to Joy, who took them. "Which one?" she asked.

Sam glared at Iris, who tightened her grip on the gun. He sighed.

"The silver one."

Joy selected the right key, and turned it in the lock. The safe sprung open.

Dot was drawing a crowd. One by one the customers were abandoning the gaming tables and heading for the bar to see the dancing waitress. She'd been nervous to start with, but she had to admit that she was starting to enjoy herself.

Just as she was considering turning a cartwheel on the bar, the casino's regular bar staff reappeared after their break. They stared open-mouthed at Dot, who tried not to show her surprise. Instead, she beckoned them to join her. One of the girls jumped up and started dancing with her, while the others realised that the people at the bar would buy drinks and leave tips, if there was anyone serving them. They got to work.

Anna was starting to worry. Joy had been quiet for a long time, and she hadn't seen Iris or Dot since Joy had started screaming. Now there was some sort of disturbance at the bar, and Coyote was losing interest in her conversation skills.

"What is going on out there?" he asked, eventually. He stood up, and motioned to his guards to walk with him. Anna jumped up, and draped herself on his arm. He shot her an irritated look, but then wrapped his arm round her waist and pulled her with him to the bar.

Coyote seemed angry when he saw that his customers had abandoned his gambling tables, but his mood changed when he reached the bar. Anna couldn't believe what she was seeing. Dot was up on the bar, dancing with another girl. Several more girls were serving drinks. Even Anna could see that large amounts of money were changing hands.

Anna caught Dot's eye, and nodded towards the back door. Dot winked at her, and carried on dancing. Coyote started clapping, and wolf-whistling the dancing girls. Anna took the opportunity to slip away, and headed for the office.

Dot caught Anna's signal, and wondered how to get off the bar without breaking the spell she seemed to have cast. She continued to dance, but beckoned another of the waitresses to join them on the bar. The girl grinned, and Dot helped her up. They danced together, much to the amusement of their audience, who whooped and whistled and cheered. Slowly, Dot edged her way to the end of the bar, and stepped down onto a bar stool. She hopped to the floor, and headed round the bar, where she served a few drinks before making her way to the staff entrance, and out to the pickup.

Joy and Panda stared into the safe, transfixed by the blue-green light. Iris was losing patience.

"Have you found it?" she asked again, not looking away from Sam. Then she noticed his expression.

Stepping behind Joy, she glanced down.

The creature was beautiful. It seemed to exist as a sphere of light. Its surface flickered with calming shades of blue and green. The same colours, reflected Iris, as the Maelstrom engine in the bus.

"Pick it up," she said to Joy. "Let's get going."

155

She blinked. Sam had drawn his gun.

"Not again," she muttered, and was about to shoot when Joy screamed.

"It's in pain! It's in such awful pain!"

Sam stood up and moved closer to Iris, and the safe.

"That belongs to Coyote. Keep your hands off!" he warned.

Iris rolled her eyes.

"It belongs to no one but itself. It is a living creature, and it will never work for Coyote. It needs to return to Creek – she can help it."

"It's not yours to take!" exclaimed Sam. He pointed his gun at Joy, who was watching the creature, and sobbing.

"Touch it," said Joy. "Touch it and see whether you think it belongs here." She gave him an imploring look.

He gave her a long look in return, then lowered his gun and knelt down next to her. Slowly, he took off one of his gloves, reached out and touched the creature.

He gasped. He held his hand steady, and he began to sob. Tears ran down his cheeks. He moved his hand, dropped his gun, and looked up at Iris.

"Where does it need to go?"

There was a tap on the door. Iris looked up.

"First things first. Answer the door, and make sure no one comes in."

Sam rubbed his face, stood up and crossed to the door. He opened it a crack. The sound of loud music filtered in. He appeared to be listening to someone. He nodded twice, and closed the door.

"Someone called Anna wants you to know that the mechanic is at the back door." He frowned. "And there are people dancing on the bar."

Iris grinned.

"Well done, Dot! Now, let's get this creature home."

The country station was playing on the radio again, and Iris, Panda and Dot were singing along. Anna slumped, exhausted in the front seat, while Iris, Panda, Joy and Sam were squashed into the back. Sam held his jacket in his lap, wrapped around the creature. His other arm was round Joy's shoulder. Dot was driving like the wind.

They had locked the safe and moved the furniture back in an effort to hide the theft. Then they had escaped through the staff entrance, their exit from the office attracting no attention while there were girls dancing on the bar. Someone had pulled out a soda dispenser and started to use it in the dance in inventive ways. No one in the casino had eyes for anything else.

The sun was coming up as Dot pulled the pickup into Creek's factory compound.

Creek burst into laughter when the party emerged from the elevator.

"What happened to you?" she demanded, then shook her head and held up a hand. "No, actually, I don't want to know." She looked at Sam. "Is that it?"

Sam nodded, and held out the creature, still wrapped in his jacket.

Creek stepped forward, and pulled back the jacket. She smiled, and picked up the creature in her hands. The colours playing across its surface flickered and flared, and Creek laughed again.

"Thank you," xhe said.

"Cheers!"

Iris took a long drink from her glass. A bottle of gin and a bottle of tonic, liberated from the bar on her way out, stood on the table. Panda stood guard over them, his own drink in his paws. The women stood round the table with Sam, starting to feel a little silly in their waitress outfits. Creek stood at the edge of the balcony, watching the machine below.

Iris poured another drink for Creek, and joined her overlooking the cavern.

"It's beautiful," she commented, indicating the creature.

"It is." Creek nodded, and accepted the drink.

The machine was fully alive. All the boulders were lit with flashing colours, and all the cables glowed with maelstrom light. The creature sat on its boulder at the centre of the cavern, rippling waves of light wandering across its surface and lighting the Martian bedrock with a bright glow.

"It's not in pain any more. It's back where it needs to be. And I can feel its joy." Creek smiled and sipped her gin.

"And my bus?"

"Your bus is fixed, Iris. You can go home."

Iris shook her head. "Home? Not likely! I'm off to my next adventure."

Creek laughed. "I hope it's a good one. Don't shoot too many people, will you?"

Iris smiled. "I'll try not to," she said.

"So this is really goodbye?" demanded Dot. Iris nodded. "I can't believe it!" Dot threw herself at Iris and gave her a tight hug.

They were standing in Walt's workshop. The bus had not only been fixed, but cleaned, waxed and polished. It looked wonderful, Iris thought.

Walt and Anna stood arm in arm, Walt looking as proud of the bus as Iris felt.

Sam stood with his arm around Joy, both of them unable to stop smiling.

Dot let go of Iris, scooped Panda up from the steps of the bus and gave him a tight squeeze.

"Thank you all for your help," said Iris. "I'm very grateful that the bus is ready to go, and I hope you've all enjoyed our adventure."

Anna coughed and glared at Iris. They had agreed not to tell Walt all the details of their excursion.

"I'm not sure what to offer you in payment, Walt – other than to assure you that you won't have trouble ordering anything from Creek again."

Walt looked impressed. "That'll do." He said. "Thank you."

"And sorry about your apple tree."

Walt shrugged, and Anna stifled a smile. "It was worth it, Iris," she said. She looked at Joy and Sam. "You two – look after each other. Okay?" They both nodded enthusiastically.

Iris leaned into the bus and pulled out a plastic bag.

"For you, Dot. Open it when you get home."

Dot placed Panda on the top step and took the bag from Iris. Iris turned and stepped into the bus. Panda looked around at his fellow adventurers, and took a bow as the doors closed in front of him.

Iris sat down the in driving seat, thankfully free of apples, leaves and branches. Panda climbed up onto a chair and braced himself for the Maelstrom. Iris started the engine.

The others watched as the Number 22 to Putney Common pulled out of the Blue Sail Automotive Company workshop, drove a little way along the street, and slipped away through a gap in spacetime.

Dot returned home via her Aunt's house in order to borrow some decent clothes. She doubted that her mother would approve of the short shorts and crop top she had been wearing since their arrival at the casino.

158

Alone in her room, she gingerly opened the bag from Iris, and laughed out loud.

Inside was a bright green skin-tight catsuit, with a shocking purple utility belt and a pair of spectacular purple knee-high boots with heels that would probably lead to major ankle injury if she ever tried to wear them.

Probably not an improvement on the bartending outfit, thought Dot, smiling broadly. But you never know. Fashions may change. People here might get less stuffy. And a bright red double-decker bus might turn up again one day, and tempt her to another adventure.

She decided to try the outfit on.

*The fire had spread across the south continent of the starship. It had been a difficult decision – the Unknowable Brains had taken three whole nanoseconds to make it – but the entire section would have to be jettisoned. Bloot-V-Kinnock-0-Zero-4, swinging through the vaulted ceiling of the library, knew there would be only be time to save one volume. One book, one book from the billions shelved here. Hu alighted at what hu knew was the right bookcase. A million years of human technological progress, and there was still no better way to store a story than in a printed, bound book. Hu needed to find it, and hadn't long. Thick yottosmoke was obscuring even hur enhanced vision. No matter: even the ultrafingertips of a child would be able to read the raised letters of the printed pages – another advantage of this storage method over primitive digital systems. Dialling hur psychometric inputs down to Far-Less-Than-Typical, so as not to hear the frozen death screams of the pine and cow from which this book was constructed, hur nimble fingers ran along the first page of the first volume hu'd plucked from the shelf. It turned out to be merely* The Complete Works of Shakespeare. *The next was* The Iliad, *which Bloot-V-Kinnock-0-Zero-4 tossed dismissively over hur middle shoulder. The next was* Don Quixote. *Hur ninth brain could, of course, have scanned this book, perfectly preserving it in its solid nitrogen memory strata, but hu'd never got around to reading it. No one on the starship had. There was a windmill in it, hu knew that much. A pang of the fourth preposthuman mindstate, Regret, briefly flickered in hur mental playspace. This was quickly replaced by the third: Joy. Joy because hu had found what hu'd come here to find, the one book, the one book to be saved in the event of biblioclasm. Hur mission had been accomplished. As hu turned to leave, Bloot-V-Kinnock-0-Zero-4 took a moment to savour the words on the title page:*

# LILAC MARS
### Mark Clapham and Lance Parkin

"There's something quite lovely about Mars in the late summer," said Iris, moving her oar in a well-practised motion. She rowed at a steady, deliberate pace, the gondola drifting down the canal in a straight line.

"It's always late summer on Mars," said Panda, his voice slightly muffled by a straw hat over his face. While Iris rowed, he lay at the other end of the gondola on a pile of cushions, pointedly not taking in the view. "Artificial weather control guarantees a comfortable, warm atmosphere all year around, apart from the scheduled April showers and Christmas blizzard."

"Aren't we the little guidebook today?" said Iris with a low *harrumph* of annoyance. A gentle trip from the little quay near Santa Diana University, down the canals and ending with coffee and cake at the Cohaagen Tea Rooms seemed an idyllic way to spend an afternoon to Iris, but Panda seemed determined to affect an air of boredom about the whole enterprise.

"If I were being a guidebook," said Panda sleepily. "I would point out that the recommended way to travel the canals of Mars is to employ a robot gondolier and relax, rather than row oneself."

"Psshk," hissed Iris. "Bloody robots, you can't trust "em.""

Which was true enough, but not the whole truth. In her current incarnation, which was tall, blonde and statuesque, Iris enjoyed the occasional physical exertion, of putting her strength to practical use in between all the fags and gin, but she had a louche reputation to live up to so she wasn't going to tell Panda that. Instead she concentrated on the view and her rowing, and let the cheeky little sod drift off to sleep if that was what he wanted.

Since cessation of hostilities in the last Martian war, many decades back, the Red Planet had become a peaceful place. The pleasant environment and low gravity made it an ideal place for retirement or recuperation from long term illness, and most of the permanent population lived a relaxed life of convalescence, while similarly laidback visitors came to Mars for study, academic conferences or a lightly educational holiday among the ruins of Old Mars.

Put like that, Iris thought, she had to concede that maybe Panda was right and it was a *bit* boring. Maybe she was getting dull in her youth? Well, sod it, at least it was picturesquely boring, and a girl couldn't spend her whole life being thrown from one post-modern crisis to another.

Iris began to hum an old Native Martian showtune as she rowed, blowing raspberries for the brass section, and watching the world go by. The desert sands stretched out between pockets of suburbia, and she saw a pack of those funny pink dog things that lived on Mars frolicking and playing in the dunes.

"Look at that one, Panda," she said with a dirty chuckle. "It's got a head shaped just like a —"

It was then that a wave threw the gondola up in the air. Thankfully Iris' oar was threaded through a steel hoop on the side, so she clung on like a windsurfer as the gondola rose up, then landed back with a splash, the aftershocks carrying the gondola forward and causing it to spin.

"Aresquake!" exclaimed Panda, his beady – well, actual bead – eyes wide open, his fur wet and tangly.

"There's no need for that kind of language," said Iris, trying to get the gondola under control. "It's just a little wave."

"*Ares*-quake," said Panda grumpily, no doubt irritated at the prospect of being done over with a hairdryer later. "Like an earthquake, but on Mars. It is the only explanation for such a ruckus. The moons of Mars are not big enough to exert –"

"Oh, belt up and towel yourself off," said Iris, finally getting the gondola straight. This was harder than it looked. Maybe they should have gone for the robot after all? "At least it's all ovAAARRGGGGHHHH."

Panda's screams mixed in with hers as the gondola was thrown up again by an even bigger wave, one which threatened to capsize them altogether. They held on tightly as the gondola rose up on the wave then crashed down, spinning towards the banks of the canal. If things had been slightly different this would have been the worst possible outcome, but as it was there was a barge spinning towards the exact same stretch of bank, threatening to hit the gondola then drive it into solid Martian rock, so that was the worst possible outcome instead.

Iris swam out of the way with swift strokes, Panda spluttering in her grip, and the barge hit the bank with a crunch. Once at a safe distance from the barge, which showed no signs of further motion, Iris swam to the bank, tossed Panda over arm so he landed on dry ground with an irritable *thump*, and climbed out of the water. Standing up, she gave a little shimmy and the water fell off in a gentle rain, leaving her silver catsuit dry as if she had never been for an impromptu dip. Praise natural woollens all you like, thought Iris, there are some advantages to a good artificial fabric.

Panda was waddling towards the barge, shouting up at the unseen crew. All that was visible from his level was a railing, and a flagpole.

"Ruffians, demons of the waterways!" he ranted with a splutter. "You shouldn't be allowed behind the wheels, or the controls, or the..." He trailed off, running out of steam.

"Oh, hush," said Iris. "There's no need for that. You know they were just as taken by surprise as we were."

Panda murmured reluctant agreement. It was Iris' turn to call up to the unseen crew of the barge.

"Coo-ee!" she called. "Everyone alright up there?"

A quite extraordinary head popped over the edge of the railing. It was furry, orange-brown hair streaked with grey, and had little black eyes, a twitching nose and dear little whiskers. It was accompanied by two small paws holding the railing, and looked like nothing else than a hamster the size of a small human.

Iris was about to give a little "awww" at the creature when Panda screamed.

"Rat! Vermin! It's a plague boat," he cried. "Where did such a dreadful creature come from?"

## One Hour Earlier – Where Such a Dreadful Creature Came From

Professor Megali Scoblow, formerly of the Santa Diana University, former owner of Eros' premier escort agency, part heir to a literary fortune that was then mostly taken away in tax, veteran of the seventh great universal war, the one the Xlanthi called "Bringer of Tears and Unwelcome Feelings", bronze medallist in the Wheel Run at the 407th Space Olympics, academic, bon vivant, genius, sentient rodent and the only being ever to get a lifetime ban from the Lego Club of Earth, wondered quite how her tumultuous life, containing as it did so many unlikely career changes she could be a model one week and a journalist the next, could have brought her to a point where she was required to carry an umbrella even though there was absolutely no chance of rain.

It was the perils of a life well-lived, she supposed. Her excursions into literary management and romantic services had been successful, but had somewhat damaged her academic reputation when she returned to Mars in 2613. The academic community could be so prejudiced and judgemental, she thought, mentally brushing over the fact that her previous academic conference had ended with near-disaster, actual murder, and the collapse of one of the planet's largest corporations. The real scandal, she'd always felt, was that she'd lost tenure. Her committee stubbornly refused to accept her defence that nuclear holocaust had been *avoided*. So, she'd pointed out, increasingly shrilly, the precedent was set, was it: now any professor could be sacked for *not* starting a nuclear war. That was what they were saying, wasn't it? So much for academic freedom.

For over fifteen years now, she'd regularly had dreams of her colleagues sat in their smug little ivory towers, writing their smug little papers, reviewing each other's smug little books when suddenly the nukes went off. A flash of light, a shockwave, them seeing and hearing and smelling their skin melt away a mere instant before their eyeballs popped, their eardrums burst and their noses exploded. She woke from these dreams invigorated, strangely comforted.

Oddly, it was an old contact from those days who had found her a new job, one which capitalised on her deep knowledge of Martian history and low-level media notoriety. The latter still baffled Scoblow. Admittedly, she had been involved in an entirely separate near apocalypse on Eros, but it was hardly enough to earn her a *reputation*, surely? The people doing those nervous giggles about "patterns", again, missed what was clearly the key point, which that on Eros, as on Mars, yes, again there were missiles, but, yes, again not a single one of them left its silo.

At least this new job was educational work, of a sort. And with that comforting thought, Scoblow waved her green umbrella in the air and whistled for attention:

"Ladies, gentlemen, welcome visitors to Mars, the Makhno River Cruises Inc. historic canal tour will be departing in five minutes. If you have pre-booked tickets please gather around me, if you still require tickets please visit our ticketing robot in the booth."

Scoblow pointed her green umbrella at a dilapidated-looking blue shed with a tired-looking one-armed robot, who gave a rusty, half-hearted wave as many eyes fell upon him before turning back to Scoblow.

"If you require an audio translator they are an extra five sovs and available on the barge," added Scoblow. "Please ensure you have the correct change, as none will be given. Thank you."

As the tourists gathered around her, standing with her green umbrella raised high in the air, Scoblow's heart sank. There were a couple of off-worlders and a few students, but otherwise the tour was dominated by a group of ancient humans, many clearly veterans of the war, some of whom she thought she might dimly recognise from her academic days.

Great, she thought, just what every tour guide loved, a group who knew – or at least thought they knew – more about the sights than she did. She could expect a full three hours of being repeatedly corrected.

This was going to be boring, thought Scoblow.

And she was right. It was boring, right up until two tremors knocked the barge off course, they crashed, and a small stuffed toy accused her of being a plague rat.

If nothing else, that livened things up.

## And We're Back

"Oh, don't be so rude," Iris told Panda. "You'll frighten the little darling away." She gave a wide smile to the rodent creature looking down at them. Honestly, it was like something out of Beatrix Potter. Adorable.

"I am not a little darling," snapped the creature. "In fact, I'll bet I'm considerably your senior, young lady."

"Ten sovs says you're wrong," said Iris.

"Well I'm Panda and this is Iris," said Panda, trying to steer the conversation back on course. "Is there anything we can do to help?"

"Stand back," snapped the rodent. "I need to get my party on dry land in case another quake hits." Then she disappeared from view again.

Iris and Panda backed away a little.

"A party boat!" said Iris. "This should be fun."

"Marvellous," said Panda.

A gate opened on the deck of the barge, and a shimmering gravity slope projected from deck level to the ground. The little rodent creature appeared at the top of the slope, waving a green umbrella and floating gently down the slope like a gerbil Mary Poppins. Now Iris and Panda could see the whole figure, they saw she – it was definitely a she – wore a tweed twin-set, surprisingly adventurous high heels, and a pair of spectacles on a chain around her neck.

"Follow me," she said, and as she descended a group of tourists, some walking and others in hover chairs, began to descend behind her. A few of the older ones had cybernetic limb replacements and implants, which on Mars usually signified veterans of the last war.

"Oh yes," said Panda. "This lot look like a barrel of laughs. Two barrels even."

Iris decided to rise above it all. Besides, the rodent lady was approaching.

"Professor Megali Scoblow," said the creature, nose twitching. She held out her paw, but not very far, so Iris had to lean down to shake it. Scoblow then did the same to Panda, who had to stand on tiptoe.

This one was definitely trouble, thought Iris, warming to Professor Scoblow more and more with every passing second.

When Professor Scoblow offered Iris a cigarette from the depths of her handbag, it turned to something close to love.

Some brief introductions and a couple of crafty fags later, they needed to decide what to do. There had been no further tremors, but the barge wasn't going anywhere and Iris and Panda's rented gondola was lost for good. They'd landed near some arid shrubland, with pyramids in the distance, but that wasn't much help as getting there would involve crossing some tall dunes. It was quickly decided that following the towpath by the canal – which was split between foot and cycle paths by a painted white line – was their best bet.

So, with Scoblow waving her umbrella to direct her group – and one disgruntled barge pilot – to follow, they began walking down the towpath, hoping to find a road leading to a monorail station, or, failing that, at least some sign of civilisation.

It didn't take long for them to round one of the dunes and find something. It was a gated complex, slightly off from the canal side, lush shrubbery and palm trees behind the black iron fences and the tops of imposing Redstone buildings visible over the treeline. From within the complex came the sounds of ringing alarms, and the smell of smoke.

At the centre of the fence facing the canal they found open wrought iron gates and a sign:

KING'S VALLEY RETIREMENT COMMUNITY AND LUXURY
PRECROPOLIS

"Precropolis?" said Panda. "That's cheery."

"It'll do," said Scoblow briskly, waving her party through the gates. A wide, level path led down the trees into a gently sloped valley cut out of the Martian rock, and as they walked down Iris could see that the red buildings they'd seen from outside were indeed mausoleum-like great stone structures looming over them, but actually divided into tiny apartments with little balconies. Some of the buildings had been damaged in the quake, and they edged around a burst water main which was bubbling water on to the path, creating a little river that wound its way down to the basin of the valley.

Staff in black-and-gold uniforms were running from place to place with tool boxes and first aid kits, and Scoblow caught the elbow of one of the slower ones with the handle of her umbrella. Having made a polite enquiry and found that, in spite of all the fuss, there had only been minor injuries amongst the residents and staff, Scoblow asked if there was somewhere her party could rest.

"Of course, Madame," said the staff member, a young woman with long hair growing on one side of her head and a shaved patch along the other. "Our manager, Ms Tallyman, will be able to help you. She's down by Anubis."

The girl dashed off before she could be asked any more questions, and so Scoblow and Iris exchanged a shrug before continuing down hill. Anubis?

Anubis. He was actually hard to miss. In the very centre of the King's Valley was a courtyard. On one side was a domed building, that dome now broken by a huge crack that spread down to ground level and cut across much of the courtyard. Right in the centre of the courtyard was a water feature with gentle fountains spraying water into a central pool, and at the centre of that pool towered a great statue of Anubis, Egyptian gatekeeper to the afterlife. Part of the water feature had also been damaged by the quake, and Anubis listed to the right slightly.

It didn't take long to find Ms Tallyman, a smartly dressed woman who was happy to lead Scoblow's party to a dining hall on the opposite side of the courtyard to the cracked dome.

"He's a bit of a grim fellow," said Iris to Ms Tallyman, pointing up at Anubis.

"Here at King's Valley we treat the end of life as an important moment, well earned," said Tallyman. She was speaking very loudly, and Iris realised this sales pitch was being aimed towards Scoblow's tour group. Even in the midst of chaos, Tallyman was looking to drum up custom. "Anubis sums up our core values; that a worthwhile life will result in a worthwhile death."

With that conversation-killer delivered, Ms Tallyman organised tea and biscuits for the whole party. The older members of the tour group were pleased with this – a couple had asked for brochures – and the handful of younger tourists seemed happy enough.

"You seem to have got off lightly in all this," said Panda, munching a custard cream. He was warmed up – literally, the central heating was on high and his fur had just about dried out – and ready to unleash the small talk. "Apart from your dome over there."

"Yes, that's a strange thing," said Ms Tallyman. "Those quakes seemed to emanate from beneath the dome itself, although most of the nearby buildings are undamaged. It was as if the vibrations tried to break open the dome and then leave everything else unharmed."

"That quake was hardly harmless," said Iris, remembering her poor gondola and worrying about what the hire company were going to say.

"Of course not," said Ms Tallyman hurriedly. "I wouldn't think there was any purpose to the quake at all, if it wasn't for what it uncovered."

"Uncovered?" squeaked Scoblow, suddenly interested. "What did you uncover?"

"Well... stairs," said Ms Tallyman. "A crack opened up in the floor in the meeting hall floor, and down there we can see an old, stone staircase. We don't know quite who to call about it, to be honest."

"Call no-one," said Scoblow. throwing her umbrella aside. "I am a prominent archaeologist, formerly of the Santa Diana University, and I'll be delighted to look at your mysterious ruins."

Scoblow presented a card to Ms Tallyman, who looked unconvinced. "I'm afraid I've never heard of you."

"I'm quite famous," Scoblow noted, a little aggrieved, but adding quickly, "don't look me up, though."

Iris, meanwhile, wasn't letting Scoblow entirely take over.

"Now, steady on here, this may be an archaeological site but it also sounds like dark powers are at work, and you need a fearless adventurer," said Iris. "And it just so happens I'm one of those." She pointed a thumb towards her chest.

"Fine," said Ms Tallyman. "It's not like I can stop you both having a look, but we take no responsibility for your personal safety and so forth. I suppose you want to go now?"

Both Iris and Scoblow nodded eagerly, then tried to look a little more professional.

"Can you manage to keep my party entertained while we investigate?" Scoblow asked Panda, her nose twitching with doubt.

"Madam," said Panda, bristling defensively. "When the lead actor collapsed of the drink midway through a matinee of *Dial M for MPREG* at the Tiverton Old Vic in 'seventy-two, I improvised all the way to the interval and the audience never knew a thing was amiss. I think I can manage to keep a party of senior citizens amused while you unleash terrible horrors upon the universe."

"Just keep it clean, nothing blue," said Iris. "I've heard your cabaret set and this lot don't look like they could take that kind of sauce."

"You wound me," said Panda, producing a banjo. "I will perform some standards from the old Martian war days, provoking good cheer and nostalgia."

"That sounds wonderful," squeaked Scoblow, only to find her elbow being tugged by Iris in the direction of the door.

"What's the hurry?" she protested.

"If it's ancient horror that's being uncovered," hissed Iris. "I'd rather face that than Panda's interpretation of 'It's a Long Way to Albor Tholus', thank you very much."

"I take your point," said Scoblow, wincing as Panda launched into the first few bars of "I Didn't Raise My Hatchling to Wear Cybernetic Support Armour", and they shuffled past the gathered old folks as fast as they could.

As Iris and Scoblow walked away they passed two of the old folk, a man augmented by creaking cybernetic implants and an ancient, wrinkled woman, sitting side-by-side in hoverchairs, staring grimly forward as Panda played. Both had oxygen masks and other life-support tubes plugged into their bodies.

"I should have stabbed you and thrown you out of that 'copter when I had the chance," wheezed the old man.

"Listening to this," said the old woman, her voice papery thin and reedy. "I wish you had."

Their bitter laughter, punctuated with heavy coughing, continued until Iris was out of the door and beyond hearing range.

The interior walls of the meeting hall were painted a relaxing lilac, just like the dining hall across the courtyard, the serene effect disrupted by the giant crack in the ceiling and the chasm that had opened in the polished hardwood floor. As Ms Tallyman had promised, steps were indeed visible in the chasm, only a few feet down from the foundations of the building. It would be easy enough to drop down to the top step, even for someone of Scoblow's reduced stature.

"We'll take it from here," said Iris.

"Are you sure?" asked Ms Tallyman.

"Don't worry, I'll look after her," said Iris and Scoblow simultaneously, before exchanging a look.

"Fine," said Tallyman, and strode off to do more important things.

Once she'd gone, Iris and Scoblow relaxed a little.

"I didn't know you were an adventurer?" said Scoblow, offering Iris another cigarette in direct contravention of the No Smoking signs on the walls.

"I didn't know you were an archaeologist," said Iris.

"Oh, I thought you might have read about me," Scoblow said, bristling. "I've had several books written about me."

"About your discoveries?" asked Iris.

"Well, not quite," said Scoblow.

"Oh, my adventures have been in print too," said Iris airily. "I try to keep a low profile, but you know how it is..."

"Strange, I've never heard of them, and I was in publishing for a while," said Scoblow.

"Ah, well most of my adventures are too avant-garde for the big media companies," said Iris. "Most were published by..." Iris searched for the right words.

"Small press?" said Scoblow.

"Boutique publishing," said Iris firmly. "For a dedicated and discerning readership. Not print on demand, not that there's anything wrong with that these days, either."

Iris didn't know whether creatures like Scoblow had eyebrows, but she was sure she saw Scoblow raise one. A silence filled the air between them.

"Shall we go?" asked Iris, indicating the mysterious stairs.

"Let's!" said Scoblow eagerly. "You've got a torch?

"No. You?"

"No."

"Hmmmm. I've got a lighter."

"Cool."

Together, they began to descend the mysterious staircase.

Far, far below was a small chamber. They moved around it, could make out that every surface was daubed with figures and symbols. There were also metal goods, and dusty tapestries hung like curtains.

Scoblow's eyes were wide. "It's perfect. It's absolutely untouched. The reliquaries are still sealed. Look at this. Great heaven, this tomb must date back to the First Dynasty of the Pharaohs. How many thousands of years since the priests sealed the inner –"

"Who dares trespass here?" demanded a rasping, echoing voice.

Scoblow did not take this development well. Iris coped better, as she recognised Panda's "scary voice" from all the times he'd used it while reading *Hello!* magazine. He liked to read celebrity gossip out loud, doing a kind of Vincent Price impression. Iris realised she'd never actually asked him why he liked doing that.

"Got bored," Panda said. "The veterans started a punch-up, and that's not really my thing. What's all this? Looks kind of old. There's some writing here, look."

From his low vantage point, and because he'd thought to bring a torch, Panda had found something that looked significant: icons so tiny that the other two, even Scoblow, had to bend down and squint to see them.

"It looks like the small print," Iris said. "You should always read the small print."

"Scarab, Eye, Beetle," Panda said, "Ibis, Ankh, Beetle."

"At least it rhymes," Iris noted.

"'The sleeping place of Geb'," Scoblow read. "'Do not disturb.'"

"Wait, what?" Panda scowled. "Since when do you speak hieroglyphics?"

"'Oh father of snakes'," Scoblow continued, presumably quoting, because it was in quotation marks, "'father of Nehabkhau. Father of Osiris, Father of Sutekh, Father of Isis, Father of Nephthys, Grandfather of Horus, you (something like) possess/personify the lands, we pray you open your jaws and free the dead'."

"Terrific," Iris said.

"'Husband of the firmament, son of moisture and the void, your phallus points to the sky, your coitus with Nut interrupted by the air. Barley grows on your ribs. Your concubine is Renenutet, nursemaid of serpents'."

"All very fascinating," Iris said, "although I'm disappointed to learn the only roles for women in this little story are for men to have sex with them, or be mothers, or nursemaids. I mean it doesn't pass the Bechdel Test, does it?"

"The Bechdel Test?" Scoblow asked.

"A story passes if at any point there's a bit where two women discuss something other than a man."

"Oh, I see."

"A surprising number of stories fail."

"If our current adventure was a story, would it pass?" Scoblow idly wondered.

"Well, if it didn't before it would now," Iris conceded. "Look, skip over his phallus, who is Geb? What's going on?"

"Honestly, Iris," Panda asked, "do you not have a phone you can look this sort of thing up on, if you're really that interested?"

"That eye thing on the wall just lit up," Iris noted. "I think a hatchway is opening."

"I had a question, though, Professor," Panda noted. "How come you know hieroglyphics?"

"It's the language of my people," Scoblow replied.

"You're never Egyptian."

"No. In the days before legend, though, my ancestors visited many worlds in their star chariots. My people helped build mighty structures and handed out lifestyle advice. Rodents appear in so many religions and folk tales because of race memories of that golden age. We left our mark on the cultures of the Osirians, the Olympians, the Asgardians, the Jesussians, Yoda's people from Star Wars, the –"

"Fascinating, I'm sure," Panda yawned.

"We're one of the oldest civilisations in the universe, Panda. A bunch of other races eventually got in on the act and flooded the market, but back in the day, it was just us and Xenu."

"Darwin all the way for my lot," he replied. "Survival of the fittest."

"Pandas only eat bamboo, are too lazy to mate and when they can be bothered having cubs, half the time they roll over and accidentally squash them."

"Most of us are lapsed," Panda conceded, "but I do still think of myself as a spiritual person."

While all that had been going on, Iris had gone through the hatch that had opened, met Geb (who was in a state of eternal motionlessness), made her introductions, overcome an initial misunderstanding, fully recovered from the psychic blast, agreed to disable some relay or other, gone up and down a time tunnel that led to that relay, watched as Geb stood up for the first time in thousands of years, and had a sneaky look at the cushion he'd been sitting on to see if she could see a hand.

"What," said Panda, stepping through the hatch to see Geb on his feet and looking around, "has he come as?"

Geb was a rather scrawny man in a loincloth, with green shoots growing out of his side and a hat that was made from a live goose. Both man and goose were stretching.

Iris placed one hand on her hip and gave what she hoped would be a winning smile. "This is a god. I've never met a god before," she lied. "And you know what they always say, 'erotic is when you use a feather, kinky's when you use the whole goose'."

Iris was quite a lot taller than Geb, so he had to hold his head at an extremely odd angle to look down his nose at her. The goose was clearly used to it and kept his balance. The voice, when it came, was rather caustic. "What are you meant to be? Human body *and* a human head? Not very imaginative." He turned to Scoblow. "Now that's more like it. Va-va-voom."

"So you're an Egyptian god?" Panda guessed, a little too late in the day to impress anyone with his deductive powers.

"I am the father of the gods," Geb declared a little nasally. "But this... beauteous creature is from the race of the mothers of the gods. I desire her."

His loincloth twitched, although the three adventurers all pretended it hadn't.

"I know I was a little slow with the Egyptian god thing just now," Panda said, having to pause to collect himself because he'd started to chuckle, "but I think I can make up for that now by observing the irony that if Geb, an Egyptian god, desires the mother of –"

"Is this going to be something about him wanting his mummy?" Iris interrupted.

"And I thought those veterans were a tough crowd."

"Tell me of the fate of my people," Geb commanded.

173

Panda found his phone and handed it over. Geb scrolled and tapped and absorbed the information with the occasional scowl, laugh and snort. About forty minutes later, Panda realised Geb was playing Angry Birds, he had been for ages, and snatched the phone back.

"So you see," Scoblow said, "the Egyptian Gods have had quite an afterlife. Shown up in all sorts of places."

"And they really got Julian Glover in to play one of them? He's great."

"Do you smoke?" Iris asked, cigarette in hand. "And if you don't, do you mind if I do?"

The goose scavved a ciggie from Iris, produced a lighter and lit it, then hers.

Geb was deep in conversation with Scoblow. "What I was thinking was that I'd come out of retirement, perhaps rise up in a cataclysmic earthquake —"

"Aresquake," Panda chipped on.

"— and then begin a quick reign of death and desolation, blah blah, great flooding, blah blah blighted crops. Do that as a sort of big comeback. Put on a real show, you know? Show them I've still got it. It'll be very sort of 'Geb', you know? I'd be sure to bellow out my name a lot. There are towers here, right? Topple some of those. Pyramids can be tricky to knock over, but even they're doable, you just have to —"

"OK," Scoblow said, "I have some proficiency here, all right? I was formerly a literary agent and editor. Self-employed. That's kind of like knowing about brand management, isn't it?"

Geb shrugged.

"And take it from me that these days, even a good, kind, decent individual can see her career ruined by just a *hint* of a world-destroying cataclysm."

"It's political correctness gone mentally impaired," Iris noted.

"Would you like me to smite the blasphemer?" Geb asked Scoblow.

"No, no, that won't be necessary," Scoblow said, after a moment's weighing her options. Then, "I'm basically a lawyer. Near enough, anyway. I know all sorts of things about intellectual property law. We need to get you trademarked."

"Me?" Geb said, clearly flattered. "Oh, I don't think so. There's nothing special about me. I'm just a regular guy with plants growing out of my side with a goose on his head."

174

"Even David Beckham had to start somewhere," Panda noted.

Geb had a quick walk around his chamber, thinking about it, running his finger along the occasional surface to check for dust.

Iris and Panda wandered back up the stairs.

"I mean," said Iris, "I suppose we should be glad this is ending without a huge action-packed denouement. It's just that it didn't exactly start at a blistering pace, either. It's like a story with two authors, and both of them thought the other one was doing the story bit."

"It was a game of two halves," Panda agreed, "both of them goalless."

"The quake bit was quite good. And I liked the Bechdel Test joke."

"Do you think they're doing it?" Panda said, when they were back up in the meeting hall. "You could tell they both wanted to. I honestly think they'd have started with us in the room if we'd have stayed."

"I wouldn't have minded a go," Iris admitted. "He was a bit scrawny, but he was a god."

"Meh. Like I say, we pandas aren't impressed by celebrity."

"You have all forty-seven volumes of Jordan's autobiography on your Kindle," Iris spluttered, genuinely outraged. "You made us go into the future to get them all. *And* you've read them."

"Well, yes, but that's me being transmodern," Panda said. "Jordan arrives, as you know, already deconstructed for us, she's prepackaged postirony."

Iris and Panda found Ms Tallyman, told her, and then went home. The gondolier people didn't refund their deposit.

# CITY OF DUST
**Aditya Bidikar**

**one**

*Husna*

At night, she can hear the Roc calling out to her. Each heavy flap of its wings displaces acres of red-grey dust, leaving grooves behind to mark out its path. In the morning, posses of men will follow the tracks, a pattern of crisscrossing dunes of sand, and will spend half a day in the wild looking for the giant feathers and mountains of birdshit that they hope have been left behind.

One day she'll follow the Roc, she has decided. She'll take her lover's hand in hers, and they'll flee across the wild. Live like the Roc, not needing anyone but each other. The Roc, she knows, must envy her. The great bird wanders the deserts, looking for its lover. She, on the other hand, has found hers.

**two**

It is evening. From one end to the other, a path is being cleared through the City of Dust. The same path, always. Citizens stop their everyday business and lock themselves at home, watching through their gauze windows. The dervishes are coming.

Every ten days, the human-sized storms hit the city. Like repeating the same phrase a hundred and twenty-eight times, this is ritual meditation. Unknowing of anything around them, the whirling dervishes take the same turns, the same little circles, the same pauses at the same places. They once wrecked a warehouse built by a merchant who had decided that the dervishes could move around his building. He thought he'd call the sipahis on them. But you can't arrest the wind.

The assumption is that they were once people, transcending their state of being into wind, ice and fire. There are stories that they live in caves, surviving only on the elements, becoming them. That they no longer even understand that the city exists. To them, it might as well be an anthill they could tread on. It is not up to them to adjust to the city. So the city shifts around them.

### three
*Nuru*

The Sultan growls, as does his stomach. "In the bounds of the powers vested in me by our Lord God, who hath, in his infinite wisdom, decreed me his presence on this our world, and did plant the seed from which grew the dynasty al-Fahad, I, Sultan Tariq ibn Ala-ud-Din al-Fahad, have come to the knowledge that this man..." He turns to the Vazir, who whispers something in his ear. "... Ali ibn Hassan, on the night three nights after the last full moon, did murder the wife of Nuru Mehmood, upon her refusal to part with her gold jewellery and the goat she had bought that evening. Having decreed this, thus it being true, I sentence this man Ali to be executed at dawn tomorrow. I further decree that his family be charged the price of one hundred and twenty dinari for the rental of the cell and the block, and a further fifty towards the salary of the executioner." He turns to the Vazir once more, who whispers into his ear again. "Let the petitioner declare the price of his wife's jewellery to the recordkeeper and let the family of the scoundrel Ali be charged this amount, in addition to ten dinari for the price of the goat, which, in my knowledge, I understand was the next day caught in the trail of a dervish and was not further usable in any reasonable capacity."

He communes with the Vazir once more, and grins as he turns back to the court. "And we're done here. Let's – ahem. Having decreed this, I command that this court may break, that we may partake of our midday meals. I, for one, am starving."

### four
*Iris*

She sweeps into the city with an indomitable flourish. The ray-guns, the space utility belts, the semi-to-quasi-anomalous entity detector and sundry intergalactic knickknacks are all packed up in the red bus outside the city, and all she is carrying on her person is her impossibly well-coiffed hair.

No one in the city notices her entrance. It is night, and most sensible denizens are asleep. Before the seven cities of Mangala were built, it was decided by consensus that since the day lasts slightly longer on Mangala than on Earth, the extra length should be granted to the nights, so that people could sleep a bit more. And if, thinks Iris, it takes their fancy, they can stay out a little longer.

177

Overhead, one moon shines, full but morose and dim. It will speed to the east to join its tiny, almost stationary sibling, and the middle of the night, that eerie time, will be lit up in ghost light. Iris strolls into the centre of the city, past the giant fountain shaped like an island that is also a fish. The small, one-storeyed houses lining the square seem a little like mud huts to her. When she looks at the line they cut into the sky, she imagines a young thief making his way across the rooftops, having stolen the Vazir's shoes. Just one of those stories you hear. The square isn't entirely unoccupied, however. The hunger artist stands beside the fountain, trembling slightly as he stares into space. Iris notes that he looks more tired than he did the last time she was here. She tosses an old Earth coin into the fountain, wishing less pain for the artist. She resists the urge to caress his face, and, with a slight nod, she walks past him and heads purposefully into an alleyway.

There is a woman there, sitting on a wooden crate as if she's been posed by someone who thought of her as a puppet. The woman's eyes are cast downwards, and her lustrous hair cascades over her bare breasts, catching the moonlight as if designed to do so. Iris sees a hint of wings in the air behind the woman.

Then she notices that the woman's lower half is stone, creeping like tendrils a few inches above her navel where it reluctantly gives way to skin. The woman sighs deeply.

Iris reaches out to touch the woman on her shoulder, to ask her if she's alright, when she hears a voice behind her, "*Don't*. Don't touch her."

Iris stops. The woman hasn't looked up at the sound. Iris begins to turn, but the voice issues another command. "Don't turn around."

"Why?" Iris asks.

"Why what?"

"Why shouldn't I touch her?"

"What are you, an idiot? She's a peri."

"Which means...?"

"You mean you don't know?" The voice manages to sound both incredulous and exasperated.

"Not really," Iris says, turning around. "I'm not from around here. She's a... fairy?"

There is a girl standing at some distance from Iris. At a quick glance, she seems around eight years old, but a closer look tells Iris that she's in her early teens, at least. She's just short and pale, and, the way little girls do, she looks like she rules the world. She's dressed in desert garb – a thick robe tied around the waist with a leather belt, with an extra tunic over her torso, and a shawl wrapped around her face and neck.

"You'll turn to stone if you touch her," the girl says.

"How come?"

"She's under a curse. She spurned a sorcerer, and this was the revenge of his love."

"And when did this happen?"

"In times gone by. You ask too many questions. Don't you know who I am?" The girl begins to look annoyed.

"No, I don't. Are you somebody?"

"Yes," the girl insists, and she looks as if she might stamp her foot at any moment. "I'm the *princess*."

"Good for you," Iris says, and turns to the peri. "Now let's see about this curse."

The girl crosses her arms, as if washing her hands off Iris' fate. "You'll be turned to stone."

"No I won't," says Iris, smiling to herself. "As I said, I'm not from around here."

Iris touches the peri, who turns to look at Iris with her sad eyes, and then fades away into thin air.

Iris stands up and rubs her hands together, cleaning them of any hypothetical dirt.

"You were right," she says. "There was a curse. Now, more importantly, I'm Iris. What's your name, princess?"

"Princess Husna. Why weren't you turned to stone?"

"I'll explain sometime. Now, tell me, princess, what are you doing out at this time of night?"

"I've run away from home."

Iris flashes her a big grin. "What a coincidence," she says. "So have I!"

**five**

The Roc blots out the sun when it flies. This is not as impressive a task on Mangala as it would be on Earth, but the resulting three-minute eclipse is. The Roc could pick up a house in each of its claws, and if the Roc alighted on the Sultan's palace, it would leave a heap of bricks in its wake.

Mangala once had three moons, legend says. Each moon is an egg. One broke open, giving birth to this Roc. Fragments of the old moon still fall to the surface once in a while, but Mangala now has a thick atmosphere, and most of them burn up before they reach the ground. The fragments, if they did land, wouldn't look much like an eggshell, but that wouldn't mean much. They sometimes call the Roc the Third Moon.

The Roc's cries cause sandstorms, once in a while. It's calling to its lover, who will one day emerge from one of the moons. There will be a rain of moondust.

## six

Daylight fades behind the mountains, and Abida Karim prepares to close her shop. This week's takings won't be enough for the sipahis' protection fee, but she hopes she can convince them to wait till next week. Playing up her widow status has been working for the last few months, but she wonders how much longer people will make allowances for her. She folds the last of the summer robes and begins work on the scarves and belts.

"So young," she hears someone say. She looks up and there's an old woman standing in her shop, staring at her.

"Can I help you, madam?" Abida asks. "I'm afraid we're closing for the day, but if it's something I can —"

The woman steps forward and caresses Abida's cheek. Abida flinches, but stops herself from stepping back.

"So young, and so beautiful," says the old woman. "You've just lost him, haven't you?"

Abida nods, and, almost by reflex, slips into her sympathy-seeking posture – eyes dropped to the ground, shoulders sagging, lips trembling. "Yes. I don't know how I'll manage. He knew how to run the shop. I'm just —"

"I know," says the old woman. "I know." She wipes a non-existent tear off Abida's cheek, and offers her a weak smile. "Would you be a dear," the old woman continues, "and get me one of the scarves behind you?"

Abida turns to get it. "Oh, I was so young," she hears the woman say. Abida rolls her eyes. Again with the "so young". But... she frowns. What was —?

She turns back hurriedly, and finds the woman gone. Instead, there is a small moneysack on the counter, lying open. Abida picks it up. It's full of gold coins. On top of them is a note: "I deserve better luck than I got."

**seven**

*Roushan*

"Can you see those fields over there, weirdly geometric?" Iris asks. "It's somewhere in the middle of that."

"You mean it's *in* a field?" Roushan says. They're standing on the rooftop of Roushan's house, trying to see outside the city gates in the dull glow of sunset.

"Well, if I'd *known* the field was going to be so mushy, I would've parked outside the field. Or worn more sensible heels. Oh, who am I kidding? I would've parked outside."

"And this redbuss... it takes you all over time and space?"

"Oh, sweetheart," Iris says, causing Roushan's heart to briefly leap in his chest. "It's not a 'redbuss'. It's a red. Bus. A container you can travel in."

"Ah," Roushan says, abashed. "I'm sorry. All of this is quite... new to me. I'm finding it a little hard to believe, to be honest. All of these wonders."

"Humans are not too shabby either, you know," Iris says as they walk back to the small picnic Roushan has laid out for them. "You did manage to skip out on your planet."

"Yes, so you said. Honestly, that's going to take some digesting as well."

"You've just lost your history, kid. You'll get it back. Happens all the time. Especially around Betelgeuse, for some reason. I swear, they make such tacky computers."

"Computers." Roushan savours the way the word feels in his mouth.

"Yes, little mechanical things you tell stuff to. Good deal, but, as I said, they break down, and you're so used to not remembering things, you just sit down and forget it all."

"And people come to these computers and tell them everything? Does every city have one?"

"Hah! 'Every city.' You kill me, chuck."

"I'm sorry you were arrested."

181

"Oh, don't worry about that. Happens all the time. Once, I *swear* this is true, I was arrested on a planet of *nudists* for being indecently *dressed!* The nerve, I tell you."

"Uh," Roushan coughs and turns his eyes from Iris. "And all these things you've told me about. Spaceships, and carnivals as large as worlds, celebrities. Does everyone have those? Everyone can go wherever they like in time and space?"

"That last bit's just me. I do take on companions, though. Oh, there've been quite a few by now."

"Perhaps," Roushan says, "I might be one."

"Perhaps," Iris replies.

"In a few days, my probation ends, and I'll be moving to the palace in a permanent capacity."

"Good for you."

There is a short silence while both sip their wine. "I met a jinn once, when I was a boy. He told me my fortune in exchange for a frog. I didn't really believe him. My mother told me not to trust jinni."

"Sounds like a smart mother," Iris says, munching on a piece of spiced bread.

Roushan wraps his arms around his knees, and smiles to himself. "But now, I think there's so much I can do. I was always interested in making life better, but I needed this rush, a... a beautiful exchange of ideas. And with this *learning*, I can..."

"Mm-hmm," Iris says. "The wine's gone, lovey. Is there any more?"

"No," Roushan says. He thinks hard, afraid that if he doesn't keep her entertained, she might leave. "But I can take you to Zenith. You'll like Zenith. And I wanted your opinion on something. This man, he was hanged –"

Iris gets up. "If there's booze there," she says, "I'm your girl."

## eight

The hunger artist contemplates the woman who passed by him some time ago. He no longer feels anything he might recognise as lust, but he understands that he would consider her beautiful. He remembers that she passed by him once before, years ago. She didn't notice him then. Now, he remembers her because she saw him. Back then, he remembered her because she didn't look like anyone else.

Most hunger artists last a few months. This one realised he could last longer by letting go more of himself, so watching people have lives wouldn't cause him so much pain. Towards the beginning, he was hurt by how quickly people stopped noticing him, how quickly they forgot what he was doing for them. But he saw that was the wrong thing to do. Now, they are a blur to him, and what he does and why is a memory so old and musty that its pricking behind his eyes feels natural to him, and is as beneath his notice as having a body.

The hunger artist is allowed to speak. This one chooses not to. He lives in his mind now, and the rest of the world isn't relevant any longer, like his name, or the life he had before, or the fact that he hasn't bathed in ages. The way he perceives the world now is simple, like a baby.

The hunger artist will die before the sun rises. This will mean that the hunger he took on as his duty will need to be borne by the people. He will be replaced soon, and perhaps, in time, the sight of that man will become as natural a part of life for the city as to be taken for granted. But for the next short duration, there will be something amiss. The people will not like being hungry.

**nine**

The City of Dust is a beast of unwieldy size. In theory, governance is centralised. The Sultan holds the word of God, and in every quarter, from the opulent mansions in the centre, to the slums around the edge, and beyond, to the meagre farms and grazing meadows on which a majority of the population subsists, his sipahis enforce his power and bring any exceptional cases to his personal notice.

In practice, this does not work. The Vazir does his best to weed out anything that the Sultan might not find at least entertaining, and handles the day-to-day with the help of his army of clerks. And in every quarter, the sipahis are farmed out to the ruling merchants.

There is a quarter containing bohemians and kaafirs of all stripes. This is where outcasts gather. They call it the Zenith quarter. For everyone else, this place has no name.

## ten

*Husna*

It is the middle of the night. But in the bar in Zenith, it's still two hours to closing time. In a city with a severe lack of fun, Iris finds this comforting.

Husna isn't old enough to drink, but Iris decides she could do with a sip, and in Zenith, no one will doubt her judgement.

"Two of your finest sickly-sweet concoctions, bartender," she announces into the air. "And a plate of those small lamb things." A passing waiter mutters and shuffles away to bring her order.

"What is this place?" Husna asks, uncomfortable about the fact that Iris knows more about her city than she does.

"Zenith. I remember this planet called Zenith that I visited, oh, ages ago. Every building was a tower with a bar on top. Last I heard, they were connecting all the bars with bridges. A single unending party. A beautiful vision for the future. At least I *think* that's what the President said."

"Planet?"

"What are you running way from home for?" Iris asks. "You live in a palace, don't you? Must be nice."

"I am in love," Husna says. She's still distracted, scanning the bar. She's not happy at the fact that she doesn't know anyone here, but the idea of running into one of the palace attendants isn't a pleasant one either.

"Oh," Iris says. "That makes sense. So your father's opposed to the match, I'm guessing?"

"My father is the Sultan. In two years, when I turn sixteen, I am supposed to be betrothed to a rich merchant's son, who will become Sultan in my father's wake. My father, being the wonderful man he is, will ask me if I like the boy. I will say no. He will be rejected. This will happen till the merchants of the city run out of sons."

"And your lover?"

"It's all these new people coming through. Father's distracted. I asked him if we could arrange for each boy I reject to be executed at dawn the next day. He refused, even though I asked nicely."

Their drinks arrive, and the waiter, rubbing his hands on his greasy apron, stands and looks at them tetchily.

"Is our business done here?" Husna asks him.

He turns to Iris. "You bring your daughter to Zenith?"

Iris trains a stony glare on him. "How old do I look to you?"

184

"I'll get your snacks," he says and starts picking his nose as he leaves.

Iris pours their drinks, and Husna takes a tentative sip, ready to make a face. She swallows, and then she smiles, and looks off into the distance.

"My lover is sixteen," she says. "We will run into the wild, and declare our love under the skies. The sun god riding behind his seven horses will bear witness to our union. We will live in the deserts, free from the constraints of my father's law. The elements and the power of our love will be our sustenance. We —"

"I can see a flaw in your plan, princess."

Husna's smile disappears. Iris realises there is a difference between Husna being annoyed and her being angry. "I do not recall asking for your opinion," Husna says, and takes a big gulp of her drink. She sputters, and tries to stop herself from coughing.

"You're right," Iris says. "I'm sorry. So where does your lover live?"

"In a mansion near the palace. We grew up together, and in the innocent games of youth was our love born."

*Youth*, Iris thinks. Really now.

"Then your lover's father must be rich. Why don't you just tell your father this is the boy you want to marry?"

Husna pointedly turns her gaze to her glass, takes a contemplative sip, and leans forward.

"Oh Iris," she whispers, shaking her head. "You are so naïve. Would that it were so simple."

She leans back and draws a dramatic sigh. "You see, Iris," she continues. "My lover, she is a *woman*. Now tell me, are you not *disgusted*."

Iris stifles a smile. "My dear," she says, "I have loved stranger things. So you love a woman. Big whoop."

Husna looks at Iris agog, her mouth open. "But... it is a sin to love a woman. It's kufr!"

Iris waves it off. "Don't be overdramatic, darling. Men have been doing just fine loving women. Face it, we're eminently lovable."

Husna is about to say something when the waiter arrives with their snack. Husna waits till he leaves, which he does after turning his eyes from the girl to the woman and back a few times.

"Who *are* you?" Husna whispers agitatedly. "I mention a mortal sin and you treat it like it's nothing. Where are you from? Or are you... are you *her*?"

"Her who?"

185

"*Me*," says Husna. "But twenty years older."

Iris crosses her arms, peeved. "Do I look..." She turns away, then back. "*How* old do I look to you anyway?"

"You must be me," Husna hoists herself up a little, and touches Iris' cheek in fascination. "I'm... I'm..."

"Bloody annoyed is what *I* am," Iris says, swatting away Husna's hand. "What are you talking about?"

"The new people. From the future. For the last few months, they've been coming here, slowly. They all say they're from twenty years in the future. At first, we thought they were ifrits, or perizaad miracles. But they're all... human. Roushan says —"

"Roushan!" Iris says. "Is he still Vazir?"

"You know Roushan? You *must* be me!"

Iris rolls her eyes. "God save me from humans." Husna looks at her adoringly, with hope. "Okay, I'm you. Satisfied?" She picks up her drink and drains it. "Now let's get you to that mansion."

Husna's face lights up. "I have so many questions for you. Does Rukhsar's and my love echo into the stars? Is that my royal costume from the future, or do all women dress like harlots? Or do I get executed for — oh, if I'm still alive, I probably don't get executed. Does my dead father decree our love —"

"I can't tell you any of that, princess. For one, that could change the future. And for another, you're too gullible. Let's talk about this later. I want to have a word with Roushan."

"Is that why it happens? Do I unfairly take over and become Sultana? And then my love makes me such a degenerate that I ruin the entire city and they have to come back to fix things?" Husna's eyes sparkle, relishing the apocalyptic scenario.

"Really? That's what —" Iris takes a deep breath. "You know what? Sure." Husna sits up instantly. Iris sighs. "No, that's not true. I don't even know — *God*, you're gullible. How did you even get this far without — wait, of course. You're a *princess*."

Husna is sitting up, looking at Iris with giddy enthusiasm. Iris gets up.

"C'mon. Off we go to this mansion. Then I'd *really* like to talk to Roushan. Clearly the royal family has no idea what it's doing."

**eleven**

*Nuru*

"Are you a hoor?" Nuru asks Iris.

"*Hoor*?" Iris says indignantly. "Who are you calling a hoor?"

There is a short pause, while Nuru takes stock of what has occurred. "I mean," he says, "are you a nymph? From paradise?"

"Ah," Iris says. "I think I misheard." Iris is glad she isn't wearing a coat whose lapels she would have been theatrically clutching right now.

"The way you dress," Nuru says. "I know you aren't a native, but you must be from *somewhere*."

Iris sweeps her hair away from her face and leans back in her chair. "It doesn't really matter, dearie. All that matters is that I'm... interested in people."

Iris has brought Nuru to one of the lowkey bars in Zenith that Roushan told her about the night before. The alcohol they have been served is mild, sweet, with a minty taste that goes right up your nose. The clear liquid turns milky-white as Iris pours water into her second drink. Nuru picks at the accompanying snack – small specks of lamb, fried alongside tiny nuggets of spiced flour.

When they met, Nuru seemed reluctant to talk to her about anything but the little vegetable stall he ran, but after a half hour of subtle nudging, he told her about the death of his wife, and the subsequent judgement, which had left him uneasy.

"So you think the Sultan's judgement was wrong?"

"No, of course not." Nuru shakes his head vigorously.

Iris leans forward conspiratorially. "No one will think less of you for it, lovey. Especially not here. And particularly not me."

"The Sultan isn't wrong. His judgement is the truth. But, I..." Nuru leans forward as well, desperate for this to remain between the two of them, and regretting even that as he says it. "I know that Ali did not kill my wife. I saw him near my shop fifteen minutes before Ashna's body was found. It would have taken him an hour to make the distance."

"So you want to find the real killer and put him behind bars. I get it."

"No, that would be blasphemy. Ali was the culprit, and he was hanged for it."

"But he did not kill your wife?"

Nuru nods.

187

"How does that work?" Iris asks.

"If I blaspheme, I would be hanged."

"That seems unfair."

"What more could I expect, having defied the Sultan's word?"

"But it clearly isn't the truth, is it?"

"But of course it is!" Nuru starts circling his fingers on the rim of his glass, which, Iris notices, has barely been drunk from.

"How can it be the truth if it clearly isn't true?"

Nuru looks down for a moment, and then firmly shakes his head. "I know," he says, "that my wife was returning from Zenith. I'm afraid she was a regular here, and she liked some... substances that she could only find here."

"Dear God," Iris says. "You're being coy about this with the woman who brought you here?"

"So," Nuru says, ignoring what Iris said, "it was someone in Zenith, that much I know. And in all likelihood, it was someone who sells things to people like Ashna. Tomorrow, I think I will ask around."

"Let's do this, we come back here tomorrow, find the person who killed your wife, and we bloody well do something about it."

"No, we don't."

"What?" Iris has to lean back in her chair as far as she can to express her outrage, and one of the wicker strands pokes into her back.

"My wish is that I know who killed Ashna. I wish to find... some peace with her memory. Justice has already been done. I am not happy about the fact that I need more. It's not right. And certainly I refuse to take an accomplice in doing this."

"Because you'll be hanged? I didn't expect a *coward* from what Roushan said."

"He sent you to me?" Nuru asks.

"No."

Nuru thinks for a moment, looking at his still-barely-touched drink. "Iris, what you feel I should do, I think you do not understand enough. Please don't tell me again what I should be doing."

Iris lurches out of her chair. "Better yet, I'll just let you get on with it. Because you're clearly not interested in actually *doing* anything about your situation. You just want to feel like you've done something and then go back to your little shop and live out your days. I guess I was wrong to want to help you."

Still staring at his glass, Nuru clasps both his hands around it, and doesn't move his gaze when he speaks. "You came and talked to me. This was not your business. I did not ask for your help."

"Damn right you didn't," Iris says quietly. "That'll learn me for wanting to do something for you. This is a boring little planet anyway. And I had to walk miles to get a sodding drink. I'm off. Good luck with doing nothing."

With that, Iris leaves. She wishes she had been carrying something with her, so she could pick it up and storm out properly.

## twelve
*Roushan*

An hour before dawn, the hunger artist is discovered dead. His corpse is brought to the palace by sipahis, where the Vazir arranges to have final sacraments performed. Once he has made the arrangements, Roushan sends word that the Sultan be woken for an audience.

Unexpectedly, the Sultan weeps on hearing the news.

"This has something to do with the people of the future, doesn't it?"

"Honestly, my lord," Roushan says, "I doubt it."

*"Doesn't it?"*

Roushan smiles to himself. "As you say, my lord."

"Do you think we might find a new hunger artist soon enough?"

"It shouldn't be an issue, my lord. I have a few candidates in mind."

"Good," the Sultan says, stroking his beard. "Have the wheels set in motion."

"Yes, my lord. May I take your leave?"

"Roushan," the Sultan says, "I wanted to have a word with you regarding these... people from the future." The Sultan licks his lips, as if savouring the strange phrase that he still isn't used to.

"You are aware of my suggestion, my lord."

"Yes yes," the Sultan waves his hand, as if to banish the idea from his mind. "We are not executing them. They are human beings. We checked, didn't we? I am a fair and considerate ruler. What would my people think of me?"

"They would understand, my lord. The new people are a strain on our records, our grain storages, and there have been reports that our people are

189

not happy with their future selves berating them for choices they have not made yet."

"No matter," the Sultan declares. "We will find another way. We are not executing my citizens for the sin of existing."

"As you say, my lord."

The Sultan gazes into space for a few moments, and then realises that Roushan hasn't left yet.

"Are we done here?" he asks.

"My lord. We could... take care of the new arrivals *without* informing the larger public."

"Did you really just say that?"

"The merest suggestion, my lord."

"What happened to you, Roushan? When did you become this kind of man?"

"My lord," Roushan says, getting up to leave, "I'm simply saying that..." He tries to word this as precisely as he can, a skill he's been building for the last two years. "... while, as Sultan, you will always carry the burden of knowing all, it is perhaps not necessary that you consider every occurrence in the realm worthy of your knowledge."

"Roushan," says the Sultan, "we're done here."

"As you say, my lord." Roushan effects a deep bow. "Perhaps we shall discuss this again when people from forty years in the future begin arriving. We have to consider the likelihood that our new arrivals just might live that long."

"Perhaps," the Sultan says, and closes his eyes.

**thirteen**

The campfire crackles. The flickering flames light up two faces, one on either side. The man is named Trilok, "Owner of all three worlds", and his older self seems to have taken the weight of that very seriously.

The younger Trilok looks at the city in the distance. His eyes, moving away from the flames, flash darkness for a few moments, but then the jagged ridge of the rooftops begins to be visible against the night sky. Trilok can't trust how many of the shifting shadows he sees are real, and how many are sprites in his eyes.

"So that's why you brought me here," he says to his older self.

The older Trilok nods. "I was never caught, but I never stopped regretting it. I was a monster, for those few minutes."

"And five people died. Because of you." The younger Trilok looks at the knife he was handed at the beginning of the conversation. He is starting to see its significance.

The older Trilok has started crying. "I thought to kill myself a few times, but I could never do it. I was just... too scared."

"So you want me to kill you." A nod. "But, now that you've told me what I did, what if I decide not to do it? Shouldn't that change your history?"

"I don't know." The older man shakes his head. "You need to punish me. I need to die."

The younger Trilok picks up the knife. "If I kill you, I punish you. But five people will still be dead. But if I prevent it from ever happening, we die, and five people live."

By the time the older Trilok looks up, his younger self has already slit his own throat, and is lying on the ground, flapping his arms as he drowns in his blood. The older Trilok rushes to the young man, and cradles his head, still crying, unable to speak. The young man's quivering slows down, then stops.

The older Trilok picks up the knife, and waits to disappear. As he waits, he begins to twirl the knife between his fingers, keeping a count of moments passing.

"Trilok," he says to the young corpse in his lap. "I don't think it worked."

## fourteen
*Husna*

There is a balcony on which love is being professed. It is on the side of a mansion, which is surrounded by a small oasis likely simulated with the judicious use of water pipes and irrigation. Husna and her woman Rukhsar sit on the floor of the balcony, leaning against the ornate railings cut out of stone, while Iris stands in a corner trying to be invisible, thinking of the fact that she could be in Zenith at the moment, drinking and dancing with nubile men. Tomorrow morning she could do what she came here to, and look for Nuru.

191

"I've heard of deep dark forests encasing other cities. There will be starry nights, when we lie next to a lake in a forest, the trees whistling with the night wind, and I'll be scared, and you'll hold me in your strong arms, and tell me that anything might happen, but you'll be there to take care of me."

Iris is, once again, surprised that it is Husna who is saying this.

Rukhsar, on the other hand, is a little more earthy in her declarations, although Iris can't tell if she is, in fact, any less dewy-eyed. "I'll kill desert cats for you on days where we can't see any civilisation. The seven cities will tremble from the force of our lovemaking, the gods recoiling in horror, but people will not be able to tell why the gods are angry. Over the years, they will learn of two wild beings who, through their untamed nature, control the very world."

Iris has been rolling her eyes a lot tonight. She decides to venture an opinion, if only to put a stop to this.

"So is this all you two do, sit in a balcony and talk at each other? Do you actually do anything more?"

"I'll have you know," Rukhsar replies, "that we are simply aware of our audience."

"Trust me," Iris says, "you are not aware of this audience. Why don't you two kids pop inside for a little bit and get cosy? Auntie Iris will find something to keep herself busy."

The two girls look up at her, clearly horrified.

"Surely you're not suggesting...," Rukhsar starts.

"When do I become such a heretic?" Husna asks.

"And why am *I* not with you?" Rukhsar asks. Clearly she believes Husna's theory.

Iris sits on her haunches, balancing herself on the balls of her feet.

"Look, darlings. I know Husna –" Husna's eye twitches at her station not being appended to her name "– seems to believe I am her. I'm not, trust me. What would I get by pretending to be somebody else?"

"I like games," Husna says. "Maybe I still like them when I'm old." It's Iris' turn to twitch involuntarily.

"Am I dead?" Rukhsar asks. "Do the gods strike me down? Or does a wild animal maul me?"

"Wouldn't it be so much nicer for you two to believe that the gods *aren't* looking for every opportunity to kill you?"

"But," Husna declares firmly, "that wouldn't be *true*."

"What if I could take you somewhere in my bus? What if you two could live somewhere you aren't judged?"

"You'll take us to another city?" Rukhsar asks in wonderment.

"I could take you to other *worlds*, sweetheart. Other times. Any time and place from the beginning to the end of eternity. And...," Iris plants herself down on the floor and leans back. "...we could have some fun in the middle."

"What do you mean by 'some fun'?" Husna asks, her eyes narrowing.

"I didn't mean –"

"No," Rukhsar says firmly.

"But –" Husna says, turning to her.

"No, my love," Rukhsar says. "Tomorrow we will run away. I will leave my father a note begging him not to condemn us too badly. You will do the same for your father. And we will run. Right and wrong be damned."

Iris sighs. "I like how you keep *saying* that you don't care about right and wrong."

Husna gives Iris a steady look. "We don't care," she says in a measured tone, "about right and wrong."

Rukhsar caresses Husna's hand. "But doesn't mean," Rukhsar says, "that right and wrong don't care about us."

Iris shakes her head. "Clearly you've rehearsed this."

## fifteen

Each district of the City of Dust has a slightly different spirit. Considering that horse-drawn carts are a luxury affordable only to the very rich, who number less than a hundred, most of the city travels on foot, with cabs reserved for holidays and emergencies. This means that at times the city is like a gaggle of villages strapped together unwillingly.

Each village has its chieftain. For example, the artisanal district to the south is presided over by a family which claims to be descended from weavers, although this is far enough in the past that it cannot be confirmed. The incumbent of this family is married to a peri that he found haunting his bedroom one night thirty years ago. Given that he has never touched her, it should not be surprising to learn that he has no legitimate heirs. The ongoing spat between his bastard children has so far been surprisingly civil.

The governance of the Zenith district falls to a man named Muzaffar. Muzaffar considers himself the king of this realm. But he is careful to always couch this in more temperate words. His sustenance depends on good people who think of him as bad. He provides them with alcohol, drugs both sacred and profane, places to gamble in, and, on many occasions, desirable combinations of people to have relations with. But to enable this, his badness has to walk a fine line. He can blaspheme with his actions, but not with his words. He can murder, as long as he doesn't tell anybody about it.

Muzaffar has killed more than a hundred people by his own hand. Two years ago, one of these people was a woman who annoyed him by wearing a necklace similar to one his mistress wore and loved. Another man was hanged for the crime. Muzaffar has no position on this.

### sixteen

*Iris*

At dawn, Iris deposits Husna back at the palace. As they sneak in past the guards, who are mostly either asleep or hopped up on caffeine, Iris points out that Husna is supposed to have run away from home.

"Of course I have," Husna replies. "But as a runaway, my actual location does not in fact matter, does it?" Which is how Iris learns that Husna has been a runaway for the last month or so without her father noticing it.

Once Husna is bedded down, Iris heads to the roof. She knows that Roushan, as Vazir, will be aware of the intrusion, just as he must know that the princess has been away every night for a little while now.

From the roof, she watches the street sweepers begin their work in the city (street sweepers – Iris notes – in a city built on sand), and the sipahis start their early morning patrols, and the vegetable sellers set up their stalls. There is a cough behind her. "Hello, Iris," a vaguely familiar voice says.

She runs to Roushan and gives him a tight hug. He stiffens, as he did when she gave him a goodbye hug the last time.

"Roushan, as I live and breathe," Iris says. "Married yet?"

Roushan shakes his head, with a slight grin. "I would tell you what I have been doing as a substitute, but that wouldn't be delicate."

"And you call that *manners*," Iris says, slapping him on the arm. "Stuff and nonsense."

"What are you doing back here, Iris?"

"Oh, come on. Before you even offer me a drink?" Roushan looks to the horizon, where the seven horses of the sun are dragging it into view. Iris rolls her eyes. "See," she says. "That's the problem with thinking of the morning as something that happens before noon."

"Iris," Roushan says insistently.

"Alright, alright. I came back to check on our man Nuru. I know I should probably have come earlier, but you know how it is, with all of time and space at my feet. I get... tempted easily. I couldn't find him. Although," she scratches her head, "I probably haven't tried very hard. I did meet your princess, though. Your royal family is fascinating."

"The Sultan is a kind man," Roushan says. "But he is also a man who believes he is the word of God."

"I think some of that's been passed on to his child."

"Some." Roushan nods. "Would you like to go downstairs? I'll see if I can't conjure up a drink or two."

Iris sinks into the luxuriant deewan in Roushan's quarters. The candles arranged around the room are flickering, their flames down to the gutters. But sunlight has made its way above the mud huts, and day has properly broken. Iris stifles a yawn as Roushan pours some wine into two tea glasses, and offers one to her.

"So what's all this about people from the future coming back?" she asks.

Roushan sits next to Iris, but at a small distance. "It seems," he says, "that something happens twenty years from now. I think the people weren't made aware of the exact nature of what happens, but it's possible that resources run out, and the city simply can't afford that many people."

"Really? I thought you said the city was self-sufficient. That, let me see if I can remember this, 'the royal family, in its infinite wisdom, can take care of its own'."

Roushan looks testy at being reminded of his words with such precision. "That was two years ago. We haven't been doing quite that well recently. It's likely that the next twenty years will rid us of this illusion. There is a drought going on, if you hadn't noticed."

"I hadn't, actually. But then, I just got here last night."

Roushan licks his lips. "Let me put it this way. The hunger artist died an hour ago. And unlike the last time this happened, telling the public about it

195

is going to present a problem." He lowers his head. "I don't think the city was built to be on its own. Six others, all built at the same time, and we're so different that we can't even talk to them. A few hundred years ago, who knows what kind of technologies we had. They've all been destroyed, because at some point, the royal family thought it would be... detrimental to their rule."

"This is new information?" Iris asks, aware that the question won't come across as entirely kind.

"To me, yes." Roushan clenches his jaw. "I don't think anyone *meant* badly, though. Small satisfaction."

"Have..." Iris tries to be delicate about this. "Have *you* come back? Are you here right now?"

Roushan stands up and walks to the bar, where he places his untouched glass. "I was here, for a little while."

"And did you get anything useful from him?"

Roushan shrugs. "Shouldn't you be looking for Nuru?"

"Oh yes," Iris says. "My brain's not what it was." She pauses. "Actually, I don't think it ever was what it was. Do you know where he is?"

With his back to her, Roushan nods.

"Oh lovely," Iris says. "I hope he found –" She stops, thinking that perhaps it was better if Roushan didn't know Nuru had tried to break every decent law in the city.

"Found what? The man he was looking for? He did."

Iris feels a surge of pride. "Did he now? I hope he brought the man to justice."

The Vazir fidgets as he tries to articulate what he wishes to.

"Your man, Nuru," he says. "He didn't keep quiet."

"Oh," Iris sinks back on the deewan. "Did he try to kill him?"

"No. He *told* him."

"What?"

"Muzaffar, the man who runs Zenith. Nuru walked up to him and told him that he knew it was really Muzaffar who killed his wife. I think... He's quite noble, you know. I think he thought the knowledge that someone knew would destroy Muzaffar."

"And?" Iris says tentatively. "Muzaffar didn't...?"

"No, he didn't kill him. The assumption that Nuru made was that we didn't know who'd killed her. But more than half of Zenith's militia is in

Muzaffar's pocket. I thought talking to you might help him move on. Maybe you could even take him away in your red bus. I was... interested in seeing what an ordinary man would learn with you. As a test case for governance, so to speak. But..."

"Oh, I'm so sorry." Iris buries her head in her hands. She thinks she knows what's coming.

"After Nuru accused him, Muzaffar came to me and told me about it. By all rights, Nuru would be executed for heresy, for disbelieving in the infallibility of the Sultan. I didn't want to do that. So I found a compromise."

"Where is Nuru?"

"In the dungeon below the palace. I try to keep him comfortable, but Muzaffar and his men..."

"Oh dear God. Don't tell me."

"Would you like to see him?"

Iris nods.

Roushan claps for a servant, and then whispers something in the servant's ear.

Iris sits silently and drinks.

"Your methods don't work, Iris," Roushan says.

"My... methods?"

"You come here, with your stories of other worlds, and how beautiful life is there. And you... *seduce* people like me into believing in you."

"Don't put this on me. I never asked you to –"

"Who doesn't want to live like you? But all it got me was two years of... I have to watch a man be tortured just so he doesn't die. And what do you think twenty years of that will do to me?"

"Roushan, I only *talked* to you!"

"Hah!" Roushan says, and begins to pace, almost giddy with things he wants to say, not knowing the order in which to say them. Two years of learning how to be precise, how not to let anyone know what he's thinking, have abandoned him. "I never thought you'd be back! At least you *know* an ifrit wants to make life hell for you." Roushan sits on the floor, his shoulders sagging. "Iris, do you know what it's like to get a glimpse of what life could be, and then see it turn into a mirage every time you try to make it real? I tried to make things better, but each step I took, I stepped on people. And I steeled myself, told myself that one day it would all be worth it. But it isn't, Iris. I saw the future, and it *isn't*."

Iris stands next to him, and tries to pat him on the shoulder, but he throws off her hand. There is a knock on the door, and Roushan gets up and wipes his eyes. "In," he orders.

The servant comes inside, dragging a pale, starved prisoner with him, and a soldier following behind. The man in shackles has been beaten over a long period of time, and sightings of sun or food have probably been rare. There are red welts on his skin reflecting the use of riding crops. His eyes are wide and bleary, with the night's white goo still sticking to them.

"Nuru?" Iris says.

He looks up, and wets his lips so he can speak. "Iris?"

She nods. Nuru falls to his knees – his legs have barely been holding him up in any case.

Iris turns to Roushan. "Let him go with me. You can tell them he died or something. Let me take him away. I'll take him somewhere he can get better."

Roushan shakes his head. "That's not how it works. I can't let him go. You don't understand what he would go through. You... you'll take him along, drug him with adventures, and then you'll leave him. He'll be spent, somewhere he can't understand, somewhere that can't understand him. This is the only place he can live, Iris. He has a function here. He doesn't know how to live anywhere else. Did you ever think of that? Showing people things they can't have. Telling people they can live among the stars. Try to tell people that, and all you hear them say is, it's a lie, it's a lie!"

Iris turns away and kneels down next to Nuru, her hand on his back. He gives her a small smile. "I'll take care of this," she whispers to him. "Everything will be fine."

There's a high whisper of metal, and Iris looks up to see Roushan holding a sword pointed at her neck.

"I'm afraid I can't let you do that, Iris," he says, a stony determination in his eye. "That's not how it works."

## seventeen
*Roushan*

"I'm amazed at how quickly you figured this game out," Roushan says.

"It's basically chess, but simpler, isn't it?" Iris says. Her dice throws a two.

"What?"

"Never mind." She picks up a piece, a stone chipped down to look like a fat coin, and contemplates where she'd like to move it.

They are outside the city, sitting at one of the four chausar boards arranged near the four cardinal gates of the city. There is a table of stone with four chairs around it, two of them currently occupied. The table as well as the chairs, according to Roushan, are carved from a single piece of rock, which also makes up the floor for the arena.

"So you were telling me about..."

"Yes, here's this planet, with *two* sentient species, and Panda and I, we're shuffling back and forth between them, missing each other every bloody time. And it's *ages* before I realise that neither species knows that the other one can speak! All this while, they thought we were discussing a rebel faction of their own. So we brought the leaders together, *et voila*, war averted! Considering neither 'enemy' ever existed, I'd say that was a mercy."

"And did they all live in peace?" Roushan throws a four, and picks up a piece.

"I bloody well hope so, after I broke one of my favourite shoes running around for them."

"So you've visited them?" Roushan asks, rubbing the piece against his beard, either for luck, or just to occupy himself as he figures out his move.

"Not...," Iris pauses to think, "as such. But I'm sure they'll be fine. They were *such* nice people."

"I will miss listening to your stories, Iris. Can't you stay a little longer?"

"It's not about *could*, darling. There's nothing to do here. I need some excitement in my life, you know? Now come on, offer me a drink."

"A drink?"

"Yes please! I hate people who don't offer me drinks."

There are footprints in the sand, of the two players walking up to the board a little while in the past, and under them, like stories partly rewritten, those of former players, leading back to the city. A soft wind wafts over them, changing their shapes as they drift away, slowly losing focus as the sands shift.

# THE CALAMARI-MEN OF MARE CIMMERIUM
Blair Bidmead

*"Woooah! We're going to Electris!"*
Iris Wildthyme peered over the top of her Jackie Collins and smiled.
*"Woooah! Back to the red weed!"*
The speeding fun-barge had shattered her peace and quiet, but she held no resentment.
*"Woooah! We're gonna see the Martians!"*
The *Mars Balearicus* rocked slightly. On the table, her empty glass chinked against the jug of fruit dregs and slush. The fun-barge's captain waved a tentacle and Iris waved back.
*"Woooah! In the sunny Cimmerium Sea!"*
From the deck of the barge, high-spirited human tourists were bellowing. Sunburned shoulders draped in the blue, black and yellow of the Earth flag.

Then, the fun-barge was gone, as quickly as it had arrived. Out of sight and earshot, away along the Laestrygon Canal.

Iris folded the corner of the page she was on and set down her book. She sat up on her sun-lounger and stretched. The breeze carried the rich scent of spices from floating market stalls that lined the bank.

Where was the waiter?

Iris scanned the sundeck. Semi-naked guests in various stages of torpor sprawled themselves over sun-loungers. A sea of lethargy. Not a crew member in sight. She checked the progress of her tan and decided, on balance, that a trip to the bar was probably in order.

Slipping on her sarong and her flip-flops, she tucked her packet of cigarettes into her bikini top, pushed her aviators onto her head and sashayed across the deck towards the steps.

Below, Iris found the bar of the *Mars Balearicus* virtually empty. She perched herself on a stool and smiled at the four-armed barmaid polishing glasses. Ordering another jug of sangria, she retrieved a cigarette from her cleavage. It was only after she lodged the cigarette between her lips that she remembered that her lighter was next to her book, on the table upstairs.

Clink.

A lime-coloured hand, attached to a muscular forearm, proffered a shiny Zippo lighter. The orange flame danced nakedly before her eyes. Iris lit her cigarette, filled her lungs and exhaled a casual cloud of smoke before glancing up to the lighter's owner.

"Thank you," she said, in her laziest phrase-book Martian.

The muscular forearm was attached to a tall, equally muscular body.

"You speak our language?" he rumbled.

"A little," she sighed. It was an understatement.

He was from one of the more humanoid Martian tribes: two arms, two legs, one head and so on. Entirely hairless and dressed in a T-shirt and shorts that showed off an impressive physique; he clearly worked out and was handsome, in a pointy-eared, bug-eyed kind of a way.

"My name is Vardo," he said, holding out his hand in greeting.

"Iris," she replied, shaking his hand.

Vardo's black eyes twinkled. Iris took another puff of her cigarette.

"I have not seen you here before, Iris," he said, "Have you just arrived?"

"No, I have been on-board a few days now," she replied.

"Why have you not come to my aerobics class!" he exclaimed with mock offence.

"Oh, that sounds much too much like hard work, lovey!" she chuckled. "This cruise is strictly for relaxation, I'm afraid. The only exercise I intend to take is from turning the pages of my book!"

Vardo grinned, "Surely, Iris, if you come to all the way to Mars, you want to find a little excitement, no?"

Iris arched her eyebrows, "Oh, I've had my fair share of hair-raising exploits on the Red Planet, I can tell you. But, once in a while, you just want to book an all-inclusive and work on your suntan, don't you?"

Vardo shrugged.

The barmaid returned with the jug of Sangria. Iris thanked her, clamped the cigarette in the corner of her mouth and got up to leave. "Thanks again for the light, Vardo me duck."

"You are most welcome," he replied. "Iris, we arrive in Electris this evening. Tell me, would you allow me to show you around the town? Perhaps, I show you some places off the tourist trail?"

Iris narrowed her eyes.

Vardo held up his hands. "No pressure," he insisted. "I will be here, at the bar, around seven. If you come you come. If not, I will understand. I just like an excuse to show people the real Electris, yes?"

"Right you are," she said and with a non-committal wave, she returned to the sundeck.

After sunset, the port of Electris glittered like a hive of fireflies. Its terracotta domes and spires spread out from the edge of the canal, across the rocky incline of the desert floor and up, into the mountains. Scarlet shrubs edged every street. Crimson creepers framed every window, door and balcony.

The *Mars Balearicus* slid gently into harbour.

At the bar, Vardo nursed his bottle of Arbol. He had given himself until the end of his first beer before he gave up on Iris. While he waited, he chatted to some passing members of his aerobics class. Once the boat had docked, passengers were eager to explore Electris and soon Vardo found himself alone.

With a sigh, he finished the last of his beer and stood up to leave.

"Still here then?" said Iris.

She was dressed in a strappy, neon-green summer dress with matching handbag and sandals. "Grab a couple of bottles for the journey then, Vardo," she instructed. He smiled, nodded and did as she asked.

As they strolled onto the jetty, sipping their beer, Iris eyed her Martian escort. "I better warn you in advance, Vardo," she said, "I have my ray-gun in my handbag. So, think on, before you get any funny ideas, kapish?"

Vardo nodded sagely.

The harbour thrummed with activity.

Vardo and Iris wove between tourists and street peddlers, buskers and restaurant touts. The cobbled streets threw back the heat absorbed during the day and the cool breeze from the waterways carried music from the bars, clubs and eateries that lined the docks.

The hubbub was too overpowering for conversation. Vardo gestured for Iris to follow him.

They ducked into a secluded passageway, invisible to anyone not familiar with the locale. The passage led to a spiral of stone steps, which, in turn led to a narrow, winding street.

"This is better, no?" said Vardo.

Iris agreed, "At least I can hear what you're saying now. Where are you taking us then?"

"Hungry?" asked Vardo. "I have a friend with a fantastic restaurant, further up the mountain. Beautiful views."

Iris nodded, finished her beer and added, "We'll need to stop for more drinks on the way."

"Of course!" Vardo smiled. "Tell me; did you ever try Aelita's Tears?"

Iris winced at the memory, "There was this hen party one time. We shot a whole bottle of the stuff!"

"Cocktails en route then," said Vardo with a smile. He offered her his elbow. Iris threaded her arm through his and together they set off.

Iris was beguiled by the meandering alleyways of Electris. Locals nodded in greeting as they passed and the occasional wandering tourist shared their conspiratorial smiles; pleased to have stumbled onto the secret byways of the Martian town.

They came to a small, ramshackle piazza. In one corner was an informal-looking bar. It fact, it was less of a bar and more of a table and a couple of chairs plonked outside someone's cottage. Vardo and Iris sat and waited to be served.

"So, how long have you been teaching aerobics then?" Iris asked.

"Seven seasons now," said Vardo. "Since I have left school, I have travelled the canals in the tourist cruisers. I see much of Mars this way and earn money at the same time."

Iris decided to gloss over the fact that Vardo was even younger than she had previously assumed and rummaged for her cigarettes in her handbag.

A frog-like Martian with the head of a tapir hopped out of the house and over to their table. It snorted at Vardo, who ordered drinks in a different dialect to the one he had so far spoken. The waiter gave Iris a sideways glance, then hopped away to fetch their order.

"What's his problem?" said Iris, still struggling to locate her cigarettes.

"I think he is not so keen on tourists," said Vardo, somewhat sheepishly. "The canals are very beautiful. Tourism is only to be expected. There are people who resent change. I am not one of them."

Iris lost patience with her bag and emptied out its contents. Coins, keys, make-up and hairpins clattered onto the table, accompanied by her pink ray-gun.

Vardo's eyes widened, "I thought you were joking about the ray-gun!"

Iris, having now located her cigarettes, plucked one from the packet and lit it. "S'alright," she reassured him. "Found my ciggies now. I probably won't have to shoot you!"

The tapir-frog returned with drinks. Spying the debris on the table, the waiter snorted and tapped his webbed foot impatiently. Quickly, Iris began to stuff her things back into her bag. The creature barked angrily. Vardo attempted to placate the waiter, but it became more and more agitated.

"I think we'd better leave," whispered Vardo. "He doesn't like the ray-gun. He thinks you mean to rob him. He's threatening to call the militia!"

"Oh, honestly!" Iris harrumphed, "Look, I'm putting it away!" She made a meal out of picking up the ray-gun. But, before she had chance to stuff it back into her bag, the waiter flung the tray of drinks in the air and ran squealing inside, slamming the door behind him.

"We need to go!" Vardo hissed.

Iris rolled her eyes. They both jumped to their feet and ran.

Sprinting along the red cobbles, ducking down side-streets and side-stepping into alleyways; they giggled like mischievous children, until they finally felt enough distance had been put between them and the scene of the crime. They slowed their pace to a jog. "You are going to get me into trouble!" Vardo chuckled, catching his breath.

"Such a fuss," Iris tutted. "Like I would shoot someone who was bringing me drinks!"

They stopped running and Vardo glanced around to regain his bearings. "We are still quite far from my friend's restaurant," he sighed.

"Let's have a drink over there then?" said Iris, "It looks a bit manky, but I don't care. I'm parched."

"Where?" said Vardo.

Iris pointed to a dingy looking place, set back off the street between two ancient-looking buildings. It had dark windows and the door was open. Outside, a couple of tables were positioned around a cracked and broken fountain.

"That is not a bar," said Vardo, "That is a temple to the Dream King, L'Zorzil."

"Not the temple! Next to the temple. That bar. There."

"That is not a bar. That is a Turian church," Vardo explained. "We are in the spiritual district."

Iris was becoming exasperated, "Vardo, I can see the temple and I can see the church. Are you telling me you can't see that bar? That faux-Greek taverna. There. *In between* the church and the temple?"

Vardo blinked. He followed Iris' pointing finger. He looked directly at the bar in front of them. He shook his head.

Iris narrowed her eyes. Something very odd was happening.

She took Vardo's hand and led him towards the bar. Tentatively, she stepped onto the creaking, wooden veranda. As she did so, Vardo tensed. Iris moved closer to the entrance. Vardo snatched his hand away from her. "Whoa!" exclaimed the Martian, taking a step back and chuckling nervously. "That's... I don't..."

"Can you see it now?" asked Iris.

"Yeeeah," said Vardo, warily. "It's kind of hazy. It's becoming clearer now. How's it doing that?"

"It's generating a powerful anti-social field," Iris replied, over her shoulder. She brushed the tips of her fingers against the doorframe. "I don't think anyone is supposed to notice it."

"Then how did you see it, Iris?" Vardo asked, raising his pointy eyebrows.

Iris turned to him, smiled sweetly and said; "I'm not just anyone, Vardo." She plucked her ray-gun from her handbag, clicked off the safety and stepped through the door. Vardo opened his mouth to protest, but a wave of machismo silenced the words before they formed. He swallowed and followed her into the dark.

It was pitch black inside. Vardo's eyes widened. Iris' luminous green silhouette floated a few feet in front him. The air was rank with stale beer and smoke. Ahead, a smudge of luminescence revealed a doorway. From a concealed corner came the flicker of candlelight. Iris poked her head through, then beckoned Vardo over to see at what she had found.

There was a lone figure, slumped at bar.

The figure was human in shape and enormous: eight feet tall at least. Virtually naked, he was dressed only in a ragged, stained loincloth with gladiator sandals covering his feet. He was absurdly muscular, but it seemed that of late, he might have let himself go a little. Although, even when taking this into account, his beer-splattered pecs dwarfed Vardo's impressive chest measurements by some way. A matted mop of hair covered his eyes and an equally matted beard covered his chin. A bucket-sized, pewter tankard was clamped in his mighty paw as he swayed precariously, drifting in and out of consciousness.

Iris gently slid her ray-gun back in her handbag, then coughed theatrically.

*Clang!* The whole taverna shook as the giant slammed his tankard onto the bar. "Same again!" he burbled, glancing in all directions at once.

"Don't you think that maybe you've had enough?" suggested Iris.

The enormous drunk growled, then struggled pathetically to stand.

"I'd stay sat if I were you, lovey," Iris advised. "You're only going to fall flat on your face."

The man paused for a moment. He let go of his tankard, put both hands to his face and carefully pushed the hair from his eyes. He blinked and took a few seconds to focus on the intruders.

"...Iris?" he said, incredulously.

Iris and Vardo exchanged a glance. Iris asked, "Have we met?"

"Don't you recognise me?" wailed the giant. "It is I! Ares! The God of War!"

Iris took a sharp intake of breath. "*Ares?*" she squeaked. "Goodness... you've... *grown!*"

Iris introduced Ares to Vardo and spent a few moments trying to explain how she knew the pair of them. When they both seemed little the wiser for her explanation, she changed tack and asked Ares what her was doing here.

"Having a drink!" boomed Ares. "What does it look like?"

"On your own? In a taverna that no one can see?" said Iris. "What's going on, Ares? Look at the state of you!"

"Where's my sword?" the god shouted in panic. "My helmet! Where is it?"

Vardo located both items in the far corner of the room. The helmet was classic, Greek-style, golden with a red mane. Vardo attempted to pass it to Ares, but it was like lifting a manhole cover.

"Oh, they're over there," said Ares, relieved. "I thought he'd taken them too. He's taken everything else from me!"

"Who has?" Iris asked.

"Him!" said Ares. "You know... *him!*" He slapped his forehead several times. "Whassisface..." The god pulled his hair in frustration, then finally shouted: "Mars!"

"Yes, that's where we are," said Iris.

"Where?" boomed Ares.

"Mars," said Iris.

"No, we're not!" snapped Ares.

"We are, lovey," Iris assured him. "The planet Mars."

"Ares!" shouted Ares.

"That's you, love," Iris reminded him.

"The planet Ares!" sobbed Ares.

Iris sighed. She glanced over to Vardo and said; "Have a look and see if there's any coffee behind the bar, would you, Vardo love?"

Vardo searched, found no coffee, but discovered an old, dusty bottle of J'onnzon's Sobriety Tincture at the back of a cupboard. He dissolved a little into some ale and poured it into Ares tankard. The god sank the drink in one and winced. They paused for the tincture to take effect.

Iris and Vardo helped themselves to a beer while they sat and waited. Over the course of about ten minutes, Ares became slowly more coherent.

He wasn't exactly *sober*, but it was now possible to hold a conversation with him that made a kind of sense. Eventually, he was lucid enough for an explanation.

"I have been usurped," Ares sighed. "A pretender has claimed my title and this planet."

"Mars?" said Vardo.

"That's the blackguard's name! Mars!" Ares spat the name with contempt.

Iris was beginning to understand, "The Roman god of war!" she exclaimed.

"Spaghetti-eating twat!" snapped Ares.

"Hey! I'm not having any of that racialist talk, thank you, Ares!" Iris admonished him.

Ares grumbled sheepishly.

"So, there is another 'god of war'?" asked Vardo.

"Pah!" Ares scoffed.

"Ares here is the Greek god of war," explained Iris. "Now, after the Greek civilisation went out of fashion, the Romans came along with their own version of the god of war, called 'Mars'."

"It is he who has imprisoned me here, in this after-hours bar," moaned the god. "This world used to be known as the planet Ares. Now, it is his name that the planet shares!"

Iris was puzzled, "The planet has always been called 'Mars', Ares."

"He has rewritten reality!" hissed Ares.

"Really?" said Iris, doubtfully. "That doesn't sound very war-godly, does it? I'd have thought he'd have just stabbed you or something..."

"He has allied himself with the Calamari-Men," Ares whispered.

Vardo gasped.

"What? What are they then?" Iris asked.

"The Calamari-Men are a very old, very dark legend..." Vardo announced. He cleared his throat and rose to his feet.

"You do surprise me," said Iris with a sigh. She plucked a cigarette from her packet, lit it and listened.

Vardo explained that long ago, the Calamari-Men were said to have terrorised Mars for generations. They ravaged the peoples of the Red Planet like a plague. It was only when the tribes of Mars united themselves against the Calamari-Men that their scourge was driven from the land and trapped beneath the waves of the Mare Cimmerium. There they lived on, entombed in the darkest recesses of the deepest ocean trench, in their shadow city, Sub-Electris.

"But, the Calamari-Men are creatures of myth," Vardo concluded with a shrug.

"So are Mars and Ares," Iris reminded him. She turned to the war-god, "What you're saying, Ares m'love, is that a Roman myth has joined forces with a Martian myth to overwrite a Greek myth, yes?"

Ares thought for a moment. He winced, then nodded.

"How?" Iris asked.

"The Calamari-Queen has the power to alter reality," Ares explained.

"In the legends, the Queen produced a magical squid-ink that could rewrite the pages of history," added Vardo. "The tribes of Mars used her own ink against her. They rewrote the story so she forgot how to use it."

"Mars lured me here to this bar, he said in order for us to drink and bury our differences," Ares went on. "The rest is... hazy. Iris, you must help me escape from this place!"

"What's stopping Ares from walking out the same way we got in?" asked Vardo.

"I see no doors, only walls," mumbled Ares.

"Remember, you didn't even see the bar at all," Iris explained to Vardo, "I had to show it to you. Whoever encrypted this anti-social field wasn't expecting someone like me to be passing."

"'Someone like you'...," echoed Vardo, ponderously.

Iris gave him a sideways glance and twinkled.

"Iris! You are my only hope!" the war-god entreated her.

Iris opened her cigarette packet and sighed to find it empty.

"Vardo," she said, "we'll need to pick up some ciggies on the way."

She crushed the empty box.

"Alright, Ares: what do you want me to do?"

Sunrise.

Rachel scooped her hair out of her eyes and secured it on top of her head with a scrunchy. Peroxide and seawater had left it feeling like a bale of straw. She added hair-conditioner to her mental shopping list and padded across the galley to light the kettle. Hearing the creak of wood and footsteps on the jetty, Rachel peered out of the window to see who was paying her a visit so early.

It was Vardo and some bird.

"Oi! Oi!" Rachel whooped, hopping on deck to meet them. "Dirty stop-outs! What time do you call this, Vardo?"

"Sorry to call so early, Rachel," said Vardo.

"S'alright, I'm up," she beamed. Then, noticing she was still wearing the misshapen, grey T-shirt she wore to bed, added; "Just about up, anyway!"

"This is my friend, Iris Wildthyme," said Vardo. "We were wondering if we could ask a favour?"

"Depends what it is!" Rachel chuckled. "C'mon, climb aboard! Kettle's on. Fancy a cuppa?"

Rachel's home was a small pleasure cruiser, called the *Queen of Sydenham*, berthed on a discreet jetty in the quiet outskirts of Electris. Vardo had been sheepish about how he knew Rachel. Iris suspected their respective ships had passed-in-the-night at some point and was amused that Vardo would turn out to be so coy.

Rachel bustled around the galley, rinsing cups, locating teabags and asking if they took sugar. She was short, with the freckled, sun-browned skin of a person you would rarely find indoors. Her physique had the tone, scrapes and bruises of a thrill-seeker. She contrasted with a gym-bunny like Vardo — Rachel's physical fitness came as a side-effect of the buzz she sought, rather than in any self-conscious attempt to achieve a particular body-shape.

In fact, it seemed to Iris, that there was very little that was self-conscious about Rachel at all.

"Vardo says that you take people on diving trips, lovey," said Iris, sipping her tea.

"Yep," said Rachel. "You fancy it?"

"We need to leave immediately," Iris explained.

Rachel laughed, "You don't hang about, do you, love? Where'd you find this one, Vardo? She's not your usual sort of bimbo. I like her!"

Vardo gave a weak smile.

"Look, Iris; I'm happy to take you," Rachel continued. "But, you are going to have to tell me what this is all about, yeah?"

Iris looked at Vardo.

Vardo looked at Iris.

Then they told her.


"So," said Iris, bringing her tale of the previous evenings events to a conclusion. "We've agreed to help Ares escape by using the very thing that trapped him in the first place: the Ink of Calamari-Queen!"

"I know that you have dived to Sub-Electris before...," said Vardo.

"Well, yeah, 'coz the locals are too superstitious to go," explained Rachel. "It takes a fearless Sydenham bird like me to ferry any tourists who fancy a butcher's. I've been down there no end of times. It's pretty creepy, but nothing dangerous lives there. The Calamari-Men are just a story, yeah?"

Iris considered mentioning that, in her experience, there was nothing ever "just" about a story. Instead she smiled sweetly and said: "But you will take us, won't you, Rachel?"

"Course," Rachel shrugged. "One of you will have to cook breakfast on the way though. I'll fire up the boat!"


On first impressions, it was turquoise and beautiful. The Mare Cimmerium did not live up to its name.

The ocean was especially calm that morning. Gentle waves sparkled like liquid crystal and lapped softly against te *Queen of Sydenham*'s hull. The engine purred and the morning sun warmed the breeze that played lazily with Iris' honey tresses.

Iris had stripped down to her neon-green bikini and clipped her ray-gun to the holster on her thigh. She sat on deck and watched Vardo, now dressed only in his white underpants, limber up for the imminent dive.

As she watched the strapping Martian, she realised this impromptu workout was him expelling nervous energy and the realisation brought with it a wave of guilt.

She took situations like this in her stride. Rachel, meanwhile, didn't really believe the story they'd told her, but was going along with it anyway. She was up for the craic, whatever it might be.

But Vardo? Vardo was *scared*.

"Vardo, love," said Iris, "it might be better if you stayed with the boat."

Vardo froze. "What do you mean?" he said.

"You don't have to dive down with us," said Iris. "You've done more than enough already."

Vardo smiled. "Iris," he said, "I promised to show you things that you may not have seen before. Now instead, it seems, you are doing this for me. Of course I am coming with you!"

Iris grinned.

The engine cut. Rachel joined them on deck and dropped anchor. She was dressed in a sporty looking black swimsuit, revealing a small collection of mismatched tattoos. "We're here," she announced. "Vardo, give us a hand with the diving gear, will you?"

"We only need goggles, flippers and torches," said Iris and retrieved something from her handbag. It was a packet of chewing gum.

"What's that?" asked Vardo.

"Oxygum," said Iris, "It's effective for up to about two hours. Here, take one now and have a spare for emergencies."

Rachel looked doubtfully at the white pellets in her palm. "What's the plan once we're down there?" she asked.

"Squids tend to release their ink when they're surprised or scared," said Iris. "I reckon if we locate the Queen, we sneak up on her, get ready, then give her a fright and catch the ink."

"In what?" said Vardo.

"That's a point...," said Iris, furrowing her brow.

"Hang on," said Rachel. She disappeared below deck and reappeared carrying a washing-up liquid bottle. "It's empty. I'll give it a quick rinse," she said. "Big enough, d'y'think?"

"It'll have to be," said Iris, "Everybody ready?"

The water was close to body temperature. Once submerged, it was almost as if there was no water at all. The three of them hung in the warm, blue void, staring down toward an ominous patch of darkness, far below. Rachel (who was delighted to discover that the Oxygum worked a treat) gestured to show that the darkness was their destination. With a flick of her flippers, she led the way, down towards the shadows.

As the trio spiralled deeper, the darkness grew in scale. Slowly, shapes became more distinct, angles and edges revealed themselves. The temperature dropped as the serene blue gave way to a murky greyscale.

Then, the drowned city was all around them.

Sub-Electris.

The city spread out like an infected coral reef of sharp, unnatural geometry. It rose oppressively on all sides and dropped down, down into an impenetrably dark abyss, far below. Empty windows, like the eye-sockets of skulls, stared out. Wisps of black seaweed swayed hypnotically between bone balustrades, as ghostly currents wafted through the necropolis.

Rachel shrugged as if to say, *Told you so*.

Iris glanced around, looking for a likely-looking royal palace. Nothing made itself apparent. With no other options, Iris pointed downwards, further into the dark. She switched on her torch and began to descend. Vardo and Rachel followed suit.

The temperature dropped further as the darkness thickened.

Soon, visibility was reduced to only what could be illuminated by the beams from their torches. Three tiny flecks of light made a vain attempt to gain a sense of the surroundings, drenched in dark.

Then Iris found the statue.

It was a life-sized, humanoid figure. Partially concealed by a thick clump of black seaweed, only the head and shoulders were visible and seemed to be carved from some slate-grey rock. The head was smooth and the face entirely blank.

As Vardo and Rachel trained their torches on the statue, Iris did her best to part the seaweed, so as to get a better look. The torso was that of an athletic human male, but below the waist the shape dissolved into a coiled mass of squid-like tentacles. Similarly, the arms appeared human from shoulder to elbow. But, below the elbow, the arm separated out into a mop of swirling tendrils.

A Calamari-Man.

Instinctively, Iris recoiled. She trained her torch on the blank face.

The face peeled back with a snap.

The face was one, great eyelid. The head; a colossal eye.

214

The eye blinked under the torch beams. Its huge pupil contracted to the size of a fist.

Then, the sea was alive with movement.

Iris, Vardo and Rachel swam desperately to get away, but writhing tentacles uncoiled from every direction, barring their escape. Where every torch beam fell, more monstrous eyes opened. The dark was awash with Calamari-Men.

The lights strobed and flickered, compounding the panic and disorientation. A tentacled frenzy separated the trio. Then, one by one, their torch-lights died. They were lost. Bound in the stygian depths. Slithering, snake-like limbs dragging them deeper and deeper below. The icy chill of the water grew with their descent and was matched only by the cold horror that consumed their hearts.

Iris was conscious the whole way down. Although, when the senses are subjected to cold, dark and silence for a protracted period of time, they eventually default to "stand-by" mode.

Shortly, her captors changed course. Iris' head broke the surface of the water and her senses snapped to attention.

She took a lungful of air. It tasted of rotting lilies and leaking batteries. She was grateful for her Oxygum; it was unlikely she would have been able to breathe this atmosphere.

There was a low-level, blue light to which her eyes slowly adjusted, and the echo of dripping water suggested a high-ceilinged cave. She felt slippery, moss-covered stone beneath her feet. Her captors released their grip on her legs and she was ushered up some steps and out of the water.

Hearing coughing and swearing behind her, Iris glanced over her shoulder and caught a glimpse of both Vardo and Rachel, being dragged up the steps by their own Calamari escorts.

"Christ!" gagged Rachel. "It stinks!"

"Are you both alright?" coughed Vardo.

They all confirmed that apart from the cold, the smell and the bone-chilling fear, they were otherwise unharmed. They tried to gain a sense of their gloomy surroundings.

It was a cave and it was deep beneath the sea; so, where was the light coming from? Thin, glowing trails of pale blue ran, like veins, up the walls and across the ceiling of the cavern. At first, Iris thought that were seams

215

of some kind of luminous mineral. Then she noticed that the light trails were moving.

No, not "moving" – *slithering*.

"What... is that?" whispered Vardo.

The glowing capillaries seemed to converge at the far wall. There, they hemmed a massive circle of shadow. Iris', Vardo's and Rachel's eyes all settled on this patch of darkness and, when the noise began, they realised, with horror, what they faced.

The noise was sickening; a cacophony of tearing, sucking, creaking. The patch of darkness was rolling up, like a curtain. And beneath...

The Calamari-Men released their captives, slithered back a few feet and genuflected.

Iris, Vardo and Rachel stood in awe and dread as the Calamari-Queen peeled back her massive eyelid and scrutinised them with a phlegmatic gaze.

Even when open, the eye was largely obscured by darkness. The capillaries of blue light that haloed the great pupil delineated the monstrous sphere; like neon highways on planet of eternal night.

The Queen spoke.

"We... forget..."

It was an elephantine, subsonic rumble.

"You... rememberrrrrr..."

It was obvious to all that the Queen was addressing Iris.

"I 'remember'? What do I remember?" she asked and then hastily added, "Your... majesty?"

"The story..." moaned the Queen, "Remember... Ussssss...!"

"I only heard about you yesterday," said Iris. "Most people don't think you are real."

"You... seeeeeee..." rumbled the Queen.

"Well, yes. I have a rather unique sense of perception, your majesty," Iris admitted, in all false modesty.

"Remember... Usssssssss!" roared the Queen.

"Fair enough," said Iris. "I'll need some of your special ink though, your majesty."

The Queen considered this for a moment. Suddenly, she scooped up Vardo in her glowing tendrils and brandished him like a club.

"Remember...Usssss," she stated, "Or... this one... forgotten!"

216

"Alright! Calm down!" snapped Iris, "There's no need to hurt him!"

The Queen stared.

Her great eye became misty. A film of glowing, blue liquid formed on the surface of her eyeball. The liquid began to slide down the surface and collect in her lower lid. It pooled there, spilled over and dripped to the cave floor.

The Queen was weeping. Her tears were the ink that could rewrite reality.

217

"Rach, do the honors, love," muttered Iris.

Rachel looked puzzled for a moment, then remembered that she was carrying the empty washing-up liquid bottle. She unhooked it from her belt, popped the lid and took a tentative step forward. Crouching down by the puddle of tears, she squeezed out all the air from the bottle and used the vacuum to suck up some of the glowing fluid.

Careful not get any on her hands, she quickly passed the vessel to Iris.

Iris weighed the bottle in her hands. It felt warm. Alive with possibilities.

"Tell... story of... Ussssssss!" the Queen rumbled.

Iris brandished the washing-up liquid bottle in her left hand, pointing the nozzle at the Queen. "It's been said, your majesty, that you only really need two things for a story. First, you need a girl, then..." Iris lifted her right arm parallel with her left, she was holding something which clicked, then hummed before glowing a violent pink.

"...you need a gun!"

Iris squeezed.

She knew it were a misquote she had made,
But unbeknownst to Martian squid, who cares?
Quoth Godard, movies he thought best displayed.
Her ray-gun shoots pink laser light and flares
At slimy limb, wrapped over Vardo's frame,
Thus drops the burly hunk from evil's grasp.
The Queen doth shriek, no mortal wound, but pain,
An exit needed to skedaddle fast!
Ms Wildthyme conjures rocket-submarine,
From out thin air, with ink the queen did weep.
Thus Rachel, Vardo, Iris split the scene,
And exit swiftly from the stygian deep!
Alas! the usage does the Queen remind,
And slips the trap the Martians once did bind!

Tiny boat enmeshed,
Calamari-Men move in.
All lost to despair.

When you find yourself trapped on a submarine being invaded by monstrous, one-eyed squid people, do you:

a) Draw your ray-gun, start blasting and hope for the best?

b) Risk using the reality-warping ink again and overwrite the bit where the queen remembers how to use her power?

c) Squirt the ink randomly and wish yourself to safety?

d) All of the above?

Vardo found himself.

The sun's rays lanced through his closed eyelids, skewered both his eyes and impaled them to the desiccated remains of his frontal lobes in a shish kebab of pain.

Momentarily, he was distracted from this by a horrifying noise. Fear filled him for about a second, before he realised that the sound was his own, spontaneous groan of despair.

He could feel the breeze and the discomfort from lying flat on a bare, wooden surface for an extended period of time.

Time.

He sat up sharply and opened his eyes, shielding the worst of the sun with his hand. He was dressed only in his underpants. He was on the jetty where Rachel usually berthed her boat. But, there was no boat, no Rachel and no...?

Iris.

It came flooding back. Iris, Ares, Rachel, the dive, the Calamari-Men, the Queen. Then... something happened. Everything... *changed*.

The buzz of an engine cut through the sea breeze. Vardo squinted and spotted the *Queen of Sydenham* heading towards shore. He clambered to his feet and waved. A figure at the wheel waved back.

As the boat drew closer, he could see it was Iris at the helm. Her sunglasses were on, her hair was awry and she had a cigarette hanging from the corner of her mouth. She looked how he felt.

"Where's Rachel?" was the first thing Iris croaked as they moored the boat.

"She's not with *you*?" Vardo exclaimed.

Iris shook her head.

"I woke up here, on the jetty," he explained. "What happened!?"

"I took a risk. To escape," mumbled Iris. "I used the ink. I rewrote the world. Just a little bit. Just enough to free ourselves. But, me using the ink reminded the Calamari-Queen how to use it too."

Vardo creased his brow. Although he had been present for the events Iris described, it was difficult to visualise any of it. He only had an *impression* of what happened.

Iris changed things. The Queen changed them again. Iris changed them once more and changed *back* some of what had already been changed.

Or something.

222

The pain behind his eyes increased. "So, you woke up on the boat?" he asked.

Iris nodded, "I woke up *steering* the boat. The first thing I saw was you waving just now."

"So, where *is* Rachel?" whispered Vardo.

Iris shook her head, "And do you know what else is missing?" she added with a sigh. "The bottle of ink."

As Vardo got dressed, they thought about what to do next. They couldn't take the boat back to Sub-Electris as Rachel was the only one of them who knew the way. Neither of them were in any fit state to do battle with the Calamari-Men right now either.

The only thing they could think to do was to make a return visit to Ares. They had explained to Rachel earlier the whereabouts of the taverna. Maybe, she would make her way there to catch up with them.

It was a long shot, but it was preferable to the other possibility that neither of them wished to think about.

That maybe Rachel was gone.

Written out of existence.

The walk back to the taverna was torturous.

When they eventually arrived, they thought at first that they must have taken a wrong turn. The taverna was almost unrecognizable as the same dark, miserable place they had left. Now, it was a delightful little eatery, with local people enjoying lunch in the sun. The ornamental fountain had been repaired and now trickled gleefully, with a tiny gold statue of Ares (or was it Mars?) standing majestically in its centre.

Speechless, Iris and Vardo padded inside. The interior was light and airy, in total contrast to the dank pit where they had previously found the war-god slumped. Beautiful aromas wafted from the kitchen and twinkling ambient music filled the air.

They sat at a vacant table, the very same spot where they had originally agreed to help Ares.

"Can I get you any drinks?" asked a passing waitress.

"Can you give us a minute, please, lovey?" said Iris with a dismissive wave.

"On the house," the waitress insisted and plonked a bottle on the table in front of them.

It was a washing up liquid bottle.

"Rachel!" whooped Vardo. He leapt to his feet, lifted the waitress up and clasped her in a bear-hug of utter relief – she was alive!

"Alright! alright!" laughed Rachel, somewhere beneath Vardo's bulging biceps, "Pleased to see you too! What time do you call this, anyway?"

"We came straight here!" said Iris. "What happened to you?"

"It's a long story," Rachel replied. "I'll get us some drinks and tell you all about it."

So, she did.

After their reality-warping escape from the bottom of the sea, Rachel found herself waking up with a colossal hangover outside the taverna. It was morning. She couldn't remember how she'd got there and was starting to think that her visit to Sub-Electris had all been a dream.

"Then, I met Ares," said Rachel. "He wasn't at all like you described him. He was sound. I told him about you guys and what had happened and he was a bit shocked, to be honest. He said to give you this."

Rachel retrieved a crumpled envelope from her pocket. Iris opened it and found a card inside. On the front was a cartoon of a sheepish little-green-man holding a daisy with the word "Sorry" beneath it. Inside Ares had written:

*Dearest Iris,*

*I must apologise for the state you found me in. I am told that I can be a pretty maudlin drunk on occasion (although I rarely have any recollection of that being the case!) It seems you caught me in such a mood.*

*Now, you know how it can be with us immortal, archetypal types. When our emotions get the better of us, it can, occasionally, have an adverse effect on the mundane world around us – hence the anti-social field I had, in my intoxicated state, inadvertently generated and, rather stupidly, trapped myself in (oops!)*

*Rachel explained to me the paranoid nonsense I was spouting to you! I am so embarrassed! Another side-effect of immortality can be the difficulty in keeping track of who one is (or was) from one era to the next. Suffice to say that, when I sobered up, I felt much more like myself!*

*Sorry, I couldn't wait for your return. Important war-god business. Catch up soon!*
*Yours,*
*Ares (also known as Mars)*
*PS. Please feel free to keep the ink. I know you'll be careful with it!*

Iris tutted.

She flicked the card across the table to Vardo, who picked it up, but couldn't understand the writing.

"We've been on a wild goose chase, Vardo m'love," sighed Iris.

"What is... one of those?" asked Vardo.

"It's like 'fishing for moonbeams'," explained Rachel, exchanging the idiom for a more Martian one.

"That is the last time I do a favour for a mythical figure of any sort!" fumed Iris.

"Look on the bright side," said Rachel, "We're all back safe and sound, innit?"

"I wasn't after an adventure! Just for a change, all I wanted was a nice, relaxing evening with dishy bloke! Is that too much to ask?" pouted Iris.

"No, Iris. It totally is not!" Rachel agreed, climbing to her feet. "I think this is my cue to split! Iris, Vardo, it's been mental! I'll leave you to it now. But, before I go, I have a tiny bit of a confession to make..." She coughed and her skin rippled with light. Pale blue, glowing patterns appeared on her face, arms, shoulders. "... I got a bit bored waiting for you. So, I got some new tattoos!"

Vardo and Iris stared, slack jawed.

"Don't worry!" Rachel reassured them. "All it does is give me the ability to travel anywhere in time and space! I'll catch you later, yeah?" And with an unearthly wheezing, groaning sound, Rachel vanished before their eyes.

After a pause, Vardo whispered: "Did that really just happen?"

"Probably," said Iris.

She shrugged. "Vardo, didn't you say something about a restaurant with beautiful views?"

Vardo nodded.

"Let's go then, lovey. The holiday is back on!"

# GREEN MARS BLUES
Philip Purser-Hallard

On Sundays when she was little, Marcie Thackrall went with her mummy and daddy to St Joseph's, the church nestled in the wooded crater above their town. The Thackralls were Unifying Humanists, and would as happily have attended a mosque or temple if one had been conveniently to hand, but Remittance was a small town and what it had was St Joseph's, so they went there.

Young Marcie found the praying and reading boring, enjoyed the singing but hated the Sunday school, whose leader, an infinitely patronising woman named Ms Bexley, was fond of saying "Now, children," and asking questions expecting the answer "Jesus". What she loved, though, was the church itself, an ancient redstone building in the Rededicationist style. Its high, vaulted ceilings absorbed sound, and its tall russet pillars provided ideal cover for concealing a small child: all Marcie had to do was step behind one and the rest of the congregation would vanish, their voices muffling, so that she could believe she was alone in her own ruby palace.

Like many of their contemporaries, the earliest townsfolk of Remittance had been exhilarated by the novelty of building tall, and St Joseph's spire rose a full hundred metres above the church, dwarfing the high, slender oak and ash trees lining the crater-bowl. Sometimes, usually when Fr Craig was on a fundraising drive, tour parties would be allowed to climb the tower, and very rarely Marcie's mummy would take her up there (her daddy was afraid of heights). From the steepletop, Marcie could see the houses, shops, parks and offices of her town spread out along the river-fossa like tiny toys, like the model village her parents had taken her to see once on their holidays.

She loved to pick out her house, her school, the town hall flying its fingernail-sized tricolour of red, blue and green. Beyond Remittance, freight barges floated like bath toys on the silvery Usk, which trickled westwards between processing plants and spoil-heaps to join the Sequana, a broader torrent ambling down to Kasei South Lough and the docks at Firestar.

The other way, the treetops climbed towards the crater lip, where they stopped abruptly, giving onto the uplands of Sacrament Moor. That long, bleak view of scrubby highland, spattered with bracken and purple heather and flocks of woolly sheep, stretching more than a hundred kilometres to Kasei North Lough, was broken only by the old oxygen factory – an ancient, ugly ruin which stood just on the rim of St Joseph's crater and which Marcie and all the children of Remittance were always being warned never to enter.

Despite this, the steeple wasn't Marcie's favourite thing about the church, any more than the pillars. Her favourite was the carvings.

Protected by its sheltered bowl from the worst of the dry summer winds, St Joseph's had weathered well for a building of its antiquity. Down south in Marineris, as Marcie would learn as a grown-up, it wasn't unusual to see civic statues sculpted from the same stone whose faces had been scraped space-helmet-smooth by the dust which billowed yearly down from Pavonis and Ascraeus. In Remittance, though, the carvings of St Joseph and the Virgin Mary which flanked the old oaken doors were still quite recognisable.

Better yet, inside the church the long-dead stonemasons had allowed their imaginations a freer rein. Dotted about the building, on walls and pillars and flagstones, were half-hidden bas-reliefs of cats and birds, trees and towers, ships and spaceships, most of them in out-of-the-way, unlooked-at corners which made for an ideal treasure-hunt for the Sunday-school children on rainy days.

Marcie's favourite of them all, carved on the sill of a mullioned window which you had to climb up into a recess to see out of, was the church's Green Man. Every Sunday she'd run to say hello to him when they arrived, and kiss him goodbye after the service. She found his funny, ugly face paradoxically friendly and welcoming.

She'd later learn that many places of worship from that era – not just churches, but synagogues and even mosques – had such ornamental grotesques hidden away in unexpected places. The Green Man had been a popular motif in the old days, it seemed, for stonemasons with imaginative yearnings. They were also found in civic buildings, so it seemed unlikely that they represented the devil, as some architectural historians speculated. Indeed, it seemed unlikely that they had any religious import at all, except

227

perhaps to offer a subversive alternative to the certainties of faith, and of secular life as well.

The one in Remittance was fairly typical: the details varied widely depending on artistic interpretation, but some characteristics were common to them all. Since most were carved from the near-ubiquitous redstone, it was unclear why they'd been given the name "Green Man" at all.

The Thackralls left Remittance for Rincon in Xanthe when Marcie was four, and started attending an atheist assembly there. Six years later, when studying cultural history at Hecates Tholus University, Marcie remembered St Joseph's vividly enough to write her dissertation on "The 'Green Man' Motif in Post-Terraform Architectural Ornamentation", and to spent eight weeks touring significant examples from Tempe to Sirenum until she was sick of looking at the things.

"I'm Martia Thackrall," Marcie tells the receptionist at the Camiri Crashpad. "I made a reservation."

"Just a moment please, Ms Thackeray," the receptionist begrudges, poking at her screen.

"That's Thackrall," Marcie repeats. "T-H-A-C-K-R-A-L-L. And it's Dr, in fact." She's aware it's a touch pompous, but after all the work she put into that damn thesis, there's no way she's going to let the world forget about it.

Camiri Campus is an outpost of the University of Argyre at Smilie, and the venue for the conference Marcie's attending. Situated on the range of low hills between Podor Cove on Hooke's Basin and Camiri Bay on the Argyrean Sea, it offers excellent views of the nearer parts of the Hookwall, the semicircular ridged peninsula which almost completely separates the shallow waters of the Argyrean from the Basin's midnight-blue depths. The Hookwall itself is wholly given over to ruinously expensive seaside resorts, luxury retirement villages and holiday homes for trillionaires: there's little chance of any research institution getting a foot in the door there, but the fascinating marine ecology of the Boyle Straits, which connect the two bodies of water, means it's worth their while maintaining a presence here at Camiri – especially given the venue's cosmetic attractiveness to conference-goers.

Marcie, by contrast, is staying in Camiri town, a suburban dullsville of the kind you might find anywhere, mostly devoted to affordable housing for the tour-boat operators, diving instructors, cruise agents, caterers, bar staff, maintenance workers, security people and cleaners who the wealthy tourists and homeowners of the Hookwall need to keep their communities afloat. Its branch of the Crashpad hotel chain is austere compared with the accommodation offered at the campus conference centre, let alone the Hookwall's legendary opulence; it does, however, have the crucial advantage from Marcie's point of view of being cheap.

A secondary advantage – that it saves her from unwanted socialising with her fellow delegates – is shattered as the person standing behind her at reception asks, "Oh my God – are you Dr MV Thackrall, the folklorist? Thackrall of *The Angels of Pavonis Mons*? You must be here for the conference!"

Marcie suppresses a groan, composes her face instead into a guarded smile, then turns. "Yes, I suppose I must. And you are...?"

A tall, muscular young woman stands in front of her. Her eyes are the blue of the Basin's waters, ink-black hair bursts from her scalp in a positive mane, and her cheekbones are chiselled to a perfection which the departed stonemasons of Remittance would have admired. She wears a T-shirt and sawn-off jeans, which respectively show off a set of intricate metal bracelets and extremely good legs. She carries a bulky leather holdall.

"Oh – sorry," the woman says, extending her hand. "I'm Jenna Farris." Her voice is warm and slightly husky. Marcie, whose last relationship ended some months ago and who's been too busy with work since then to think about such things, finds her own legs tingling pleasurably in response to their handshake. "I'm at Wynn-Williamsport University," Jenna says. "Still doing my doctorate, I'm afraid. I'm giving a paper tomorrow."

Wynn-Williamsport's a recent foundation, Marcie recalls: until recently the sparsely-populated southern coast of the Hellas Ocean got by with sending its young people north to Harrisville or Saheki for their studies. Others go further afield: Marcie knew a few at Hecates Tholus. Hellanders have a reputation for dourness, talking mostly about the weather and fish – and for all she knows that's true of the ones who stay at home. The ones she's met, though, were twenty-four-hour-and-change party people.

She smiles involuntarily at the memory, and – recognising perhaps that this time it's genuine – Jenna smiles back. "Well," the younger woman says, "I'll let you get up to your room. I'm heading out soon, in any case. See you at the welcome session tomorrow morning?"

"See you then," Marcie smiles, and takes her key from the receptionist. With more reluctance than she expected, she takes the lift up to her room, where she spends a while wondering whether she might not want to socialise with certain of the other delegates after all.

Marcie remembers the first time she asked the question in a professional, or at least a semi-professional, context. It was perhaps five years ago now, when she was still at university, and just beginning to develop an interest in folklore.

She was hanging out at the youth hostel in Hecatapolis, chatting to the tourists, skiers and drifters, as well as the serious mountaineers who'd come to scale the picturesque yet trivial peak of Hecates Tholus as practice for the greater challenge of Elysium Mons. She hoped to gather some examples of backpackers' tales to take back to her supervisor, to persuade her that this would be a fruitful topic for her Master's.

The boy's name was Pieter, and he was – of course – trying to impress her. Marcie was leading him on a bit, she had to admit, but only in order to get him talking more freely.

He was a Hellander too, as it happens, one of the kind who extract themselves early on from the trawling, gutting and processing of fish which forms the area's chief economic activity, and never look back. In his case this involved climbing as often and as high above sea level as he could, and preferably above the breathable atmosphere altogether.

"The strangest thing I've seen, though," he was telling her, having run through the usual repertoire of urban myths about poisoned beer and stolen kidneys, "was up in the Maze. I was backpacking up there with this girl I'd met doing bar work in Oudemans. We took an oxygen tent and plenty of supplies, and stuck to the regular hiking trails – at first, at least. I wanted to show her the proper redlands, up beyond the vegetation limit. That's the real planet there, the way it was before the terraformers had their way with the place.

"You ever been up in the Maze, babe?" he asked her suddenly.

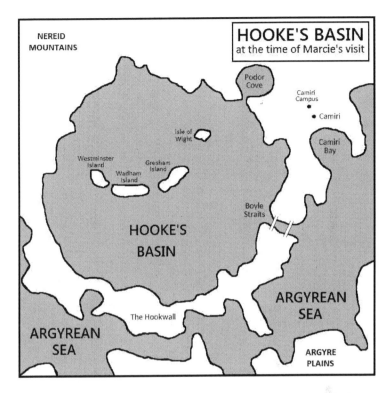

Marcie shook her head. The vast primeval spaces of the Noctis Labyrinthus held little to attract her. She was interested in *people*. She risked a quick glance at her phone, to check that it was recording Pieter's account.

"It's treacherous up there," the boy said, "all chasms and scree. The River Noctis is frozen most of the year, and it grinds away at those vallis-walls. If you're not crawling over a crevice you're just as likely to be dodging a landslide. It's always freezing up there, and there isn't even the air to start a fire, not that the Rangers would let you.

"All that means they've never mapped that region properly, not fully. Sure there are satellite pictures and drones and survey teams, but who's going to chart every single ravine and gulch up there, even on fly-past?

"On the third day we wanted to try something different. We stocked up on food, water and oxygen at one of the waystations, and hiked a long way off the track. I've got a good sense of direction, but in those narrow valles

231

with the rocks shifting around us and that weird sharp lenslight you get up in the redlands, we ended up turned around somehow.

"We came up on a razor ridge, and then we saw it – down in a deep chasma, with no way of getting down there. Hundreds of machines, rusting and falling apart in the thin air. Air they'd never been built to last in."

He'd told this story before, Marcie could tell. Taking care to look suitably awed, she asked, "What were they?"

"We could see they were vehicles," he says, relishing the big reveal, "but they'd been built to walk. Not all of them had all their legs left – some had collapsed, and one whole row had fallen like dominoes. But some of them were still standing, and those ones had three legs. And what do you call something that stands on three legs?"

"A tripod," Marcie supplied obediently.

(It was easier then, at the beginning of her career. Since then she's heard eighteen distinct variants of the Tripod Graveyard story, and in most of those the interviewee's claimed to have personally seen the resting-place of the mythical artefacts.)

"So right, babe," Pieter grinned. "And we're thinking, *No way, this is impossible, the Locals are a legend – aren't they?* And then we hear this noise. The air's so thin up there sound doesn't travel far, so although it was faint we knew it was close by. It was a voice – a high-pitched, eerie voice – and it was singing." He made his own voice go falsetto. "*Ulla, ulla, ulla...*"

Marcie laughed. "Nice one," she scoffed.

"Swear on my life," Pieter said, though he was laughing too. "We ran away from there so fast the Rangers came to check out our dust trail. We couldn't show them the way back to that ravine, though."

Marcie picked up her phone, and surreptitiously switched off the recording. She'd got what she needed from this one.

She had to ask, though. If he thought she was mad – well, so much the better for extricating herself from the situation. "Did you...," she began. "Did you see any other kinds of machine up there?"

Marcie reads the news as she waits for the monorail to campus the next morning. Arabian hauliers are boycotting Alban businesses over encroachment on their Northern Ocean fishing rights. An agriscientist at Newton thinks she's developed a way to improve soil nitrogen yields by up to four per cent, but she needs to check. Environmentalists want hiking permits near the poles restricted. The President's giving a minister who fiddled his expenses her full support as usual, and a man in Aonia owns a cat that looks like film star Adri Kremer.

Eventually the train arrives. As Marcie sits, she sees Jenna Farris getting on behind her. The tall woman's wearing slightly more professional attire today, a short-sleeved blouse and trousers which go all the way down to her ankles. She's still wearing the bangles, though, and hefting that huge holdall.

Marcie catches her eye and smiles, and Jenna comes to sit next to her.

"Sorry," the younger woman says. "I didn't want to disturb you at the stop. You seemed last night as if you didn't much like being disturbed."

"Sorry," Marcie says in turn. "I was tired from travelling. You know how it is."

"Tell me about it," Jenna says rhetorically. The feel of their hips and shoulders pressed together in the narrow seats is giving Marcie those tingles again. Close up, the postgrad student smells of some exotic perfume — patchouli oil, possibly. "You know, I was hoping we'd meet here," Jenna adds. "At the conference I mean. 'Legends of the Locals'. It seemed just your sort of thing. I mean, I'm kind of surprised you're not giving more than one session, to be honest." Her hand flies to her mouth. "Oh dear, I'm sorry, was that tactless of me?"

Marcie shakes her head. "Not at all. It came as a surprise to me, too. I was down for two, but then Desmond Blannik let it be known that he had something he might be willing to give them, and you don't pass up a name like Desmond Blannik's. Even if he's never shown any interest in your subject before, apparently." She briefly wonders whether anyone in Aonia has a weasel that looks like Desmond Blannik, before uncharitably deciding it's more unlikely that anyone has a weasel that doesn't look like him.

"I slept terribly last night," Jenna confides. "The beds in that place are so *short!* I'm going to ask whether they can find me somewhere last-minute on campus after all." She pats her luggage affectionately.

Marcie feels a pang of disappointment, but reflects that they'll both be there all day during the conference anyway. The monorail track's climbing the hill to the campus already, an impressive assemblage of steel-and-glass buildings encrusting the hilltop like diamonds.

She steals a surreptitious glance at Jenna's arms. Her bracelets are some reddish metal, bronze perhaps, and etched with intricate abstract designs.

"Have you hurt your arm?" she asks. There's a patch of redder skin near the sleeve of Jenna's blouse.

"Oh no," the postgrad smiles, "it's just a touch of eczema. I've got a cream for it. Nice of you to notice, though."

Marcie feels her own skin begin to flush, but as she turns to admire the vista, she could almost swear the younger woman winked at her. Rather too abruptly she asks, "What's your research topic?"

"Oh," says Jenna, flustered at the sudden professional interest. "Same as yours really. I mean, your work's a huge inspiration, except I've tried to specialise a bit more. I'm recording folk tales about Locals, but I've been looking at a subset – the ones where there's a Local passing for human, but something unexpected gives the game away. I'm calling them Changeling Variations."

"Interesting." Marcie means it. There's definitely a rich vein to be tapped there, and her own embarrassment falls away as she considers it. "Stories like the Coy Stripper, you mean, where they finally force her to go naked only to discover she hasn't got any genitals?"

"Exactly!" Jenna's obviously delighted to be discussing this with her role model. Her enthusiasm's flattering, though Marcie can't help feeling it's a little more than she deserves. "I've catalogued four variants of that one that are either new or... well, ones you missed before. In one of them she's an exotic dancer with a snake she performs with. Only it isn't a snake."

Marcie's intrigued. "What is it?"

"Well, the story implies it's her offspring. Some kind of larval form. And I've found lots more versions of the Fake Charlatan – the fraudulent psychic who it turns out actually can read minds – and a new one I haven't seen mentioned before, the Incompetent Ghost, where the Local imitates a dead person but make some subtle mistake which gives them away."

Their carriage pulls into the Camiri Campus terminus. With the seas' waters glinting like rumpled mirrors in the morning light from the solar lens, the view down past the sprawl of Camiri to the jagged ridge separating the twin coasts is, Marcie has to admit, authentically spectacular.

"Nice," she says, meaning Jenna's new urban legend. "I'll look forward to hearing your paper. Do you fancy getting breakfast before we face the other delegates?"

The book of Marcie's which Jenna so admires, *The Angels of Pavonis Mons: Evolution of a Wartime Legend*, started off as her doctoral thesis and made her name in the field.

The story's an old one, dating back more than eighty local years to the Tharsis War, and well-known in its general outlines, but Marcie was the first academic to trace systematically how it had evolved between contemporary accounts and modern folk-memory. She remembers when she first had the idea for the book, in another of those early data-gathering excursions, this time to an upmarket old people's home.

"It was my great-grandfather Frank who fought in the war, as a young man," the fifty-year-old retired actor told her. Marcie guessed the woman was a retired actor because of the many photos which covered the walls of her on stage with people she vaguely recognised, and she knew she was fifty because she'd shown Marcie her message of congratulation from the President when she first arrived. Tiny and frail she might be, but this was not a woman who was likely to be shy about telling stories.

"He told me about it when I was a young girl," the woman – whose name was Isabel – continued. "He actually saw them, you know, the angels."

"Tell me," Marcie suggested, switching on the recorder.

"He was terrified going into battle, you understand," Isabel said. "Nobody really knew about what had been going on in Acheron until after the war, but there were lots of stories about atrocities on the battlefield – some of them propaganda, of course, but not all. Frank and his fellow soldiers all put a brave face on it, but all of them hoped that if it came down to it, they'd be killed rather than captured.

"He was one of the soldiers who were defending Pavonis Chasma from the Acheron ground assault – I'm afraid I don't really understand the details of the battle, dear, you'd need to talk to a historian for that..."

Marcie assured her that she could always look it up afterwards, and that what she was really interested in was in what Isabel's great-grandfather had witnessed.

"Well, he was terrified, as I said, and between you and me I've always wondered whether that might have affected what he saw. He said his friends saw it too, though, as plain as day, although in fact it was night at the time. I'm sorry dear, I may get rather muddled telling this. I'm fifty years old, you know."

235

Again Marcie did her best to reassure the old woman.

"Well," said Isabel, "they'd been waiting in the chasma for three days, loaded down with all their breathing equipment of course, and really, anyone would have been overwrought. But as the Acheron infantry made their advance up from Pavonis Fossae that third evening, Frank thought that he saw something coming with them. Robot weapons, he thought at first, but the way they moved was like an animal, though not like any animal he'd seen. They looked as if they were *hopping*.

"His unit had lost their only set of binoculars in an early grenade attack, so they couldn't really make them out, but word spread along the lines that the Acherons had with them... and this is what he always swore, my dear, to his dying day – did I tell you he lived to be fifty too? We're a long-lived family, you know. Where was I?"

"The Acherons had with them..." Marcie prompted.

"Oh yes. Well, my great-grandfather saw them too, in the end. To his dying day he swore that there were... you know, Locals... fighting with the Acherons. Advancing with them up into the chasma, getting closer and closer to his position. Great leaping things like locusts, he said, with long antennae that could have been horns. As they came, they shrieked, a sound full of hate and rage. He'd never heard anything so dreadful in his life.

"The Acherons closed in on his position, and those terrible things with them, and soon he was entangled in the hand-to-hand fighting.

"Some early grenades from his side had destroyed some of the Acheron tanks, and they were burning, on their internal air I suppose, sending smoke up high into the sky above the fossae. He said it just built up there instead of dissipating, and it... took shape. A giant locust made out of smoke, framing Deimos in its horns as it stared down at them. Frank said the thing positively radiated malevolence.

"He said it was as if the Devil himself had come to help the Acherons, and sent his demons into battle with them. He was on the verge of throwing down his weapons and running away. And then..."

At this point, much to Marcie's frustration, one of the home's staff arrived to give Isabel a cup of tea and check that Marcie wasn't getting her overexcited. By now, though, Isabel was thoroughly enjoying herself, and sent the man impatiently away.

"Well," she went on, "at first the locusts had the upper hand, just like the Acherons – insects don't have hands, though, do they? – well anyway, the great malignant creature above them seemed to spur them and the Acherons on, until Frank thought that all was lost... but then, the angels came.

"They were hard to see, great-grandfather Frank said, like columns of light, or vortexes in the air. More like a change in the way you see the world than a *thing*, and moving as fast as thought. Just seeing them was a relief, he said, though – they brought a kind of comfort with them. They brought more Locals with them, too – he didn't get a good look at them, but there were very tall stick-figure people, and furry people like walking otters, and some hopping things as well, but more like frogs than the locusts.

"They moved down into the chasma from behind him, from the slopes of Mons Pavonis itself, and immediately, he and his comrades knew they were saved. The angels tore into the locust-creatures' ranks like a magnifying-glass ray through a column of ants, and where they passed the creatures burst into flames, although the humans fighting next to them weren't harmed. They swept across the battlefield like wildfire – then up into the sky, to whirl around that terrible shape until it dissolved into the cloud of smoke it was.

"Within a few minutes, the Acheron forces had been routed. And that, you may know, was the turning-point of the war.

"It was as if there were two battles on Pavonis Mons that day, Great-grandfather Frank said, happening in parallel, never touching, just... using the same battlefield.

"After that day he became very religious. He always said he'd seen angels save him from the Devil, and what were intellectual arguments next to *that*? They searched the battlefield thoroughly afterwards, of course, but all the remains they could find were human. The locust-things had faded away into that thinnest of thin air."

Marcie realised that she'd been holding her breath. She suspected that Isabel had been a rather good actor in her time.

It was difficult asking the question after that, but she worked her way around to it.

It's late – nearly the change, in fact. A bunch of delegates sit in the conference centre bar, all fairly drunk and talking too loudly. Conversation moved on early from academic issues, has ranged through current affairs and recent works of various popular media, before getting predictably lodged in the inescapable cleft of university politics.

When Marcie planned this trip, she resolved she'd get to bed each night well before the change – those 2,243 awkwardly liminal seconds between midnight and one-second-past-midnight, which mark the difference between a standard 84,600-second day and the time it actually takes the planet to rotate. The only reason she's still here is because of Jenna.

Jenna's paper on the Changeling Variations went down well, and she's celebrating in a way Marcie lost the knack of some time ago, with copious beer, flirtatious one-liners and occasional bouts of singing. Her conviviality and her devastating good looks have ensured that the party's accreted around her like a pearl in a Hookwall oyster, with Marcie hovering rather awkwardly on the edges. Jenna's making an effort to include her, though, with plentiful eye-contact and smiles, and in her present mood that's sufficient incentive for Marcie to stay – despite the unwelcome fact that Desmond Blannik's one of the party, and leering much more noticeably in Jenna's direction.

On this basis, Marcie has to admit that she is, by any reasonable standard, humiliatingly smitten. Jenna is quick, witty, intelligent and beautiful, and in her self-confident jubilation, quite the most gorgeous thing Marcie's seen in months. Marcie, wearing a sweaty blouse and last year's conference suit (which was slightly too dour even when she bought it, and has had some kind of pale stain on the shoulder since this morning), feels utterly frumpy by comparison.

On the other hand, Jenna might conceivably be... well, into her. She's younger, but even a three-year age difference isn't so disastrous, and she's made it clear how much she loves Marcie's work. Marcie's out of practice with reading signals, but it's obvious that Jenna's well-disposed towards her, and she's getting the sense it goes some way beyond simple friendliness.

Desmond Blannik makes some facetious remark about the faceless bureaucrats who allocate higher education funding, and the whole table erupts in sycophantic laughter. Jenna joins in dutifully, but when Blannik looks away she rolls her eyes at Marcie in mock despair.

*Well,* Marcie thinks to herself, *time will tell.* Specifically, the time when the party breaks up and everybody goes to bed. Either Marcie will end up on a night-bus into town, while Jenna retires, alone or otherwise, to her smart new room on campus, or...

Well, time will tell. Assuming Marcie, who's unused to both the late nights and the beer, doesn't fall over first.

As she stands up to visit the bathroom, she realises this could be a bigger danger than she thought. Her legs are more erratic than she's accustomed to, and she weaves her way quickly to the ladies, where she sits down again gratefully.

Emerging from her cubicle, she sees Jenna at the mirror, applying lipstick to those soft-looking lips. She smiles up at Marcie's reflection in the mirror, and this time Marcie's certain she winks.

"It's been a big day," Marcie says inanely. She feels she has to do something to test the waters. This suspense is getting unbearable. Being careful not to slur, she adds, "A long one, too. Way past my usual bedtime."

Jenna presses her lipsticked lips together, then grins. "Not mine. Although... it would depend on the reasons for going to bed."

And then, immediately it seems, their mouths are pressed together, hot and wet and, yes, soft. Sensations pop in Marcie's head like smoke-filled bubbles, each clouding her already-fuddled mind a little further as it bursts.

Then they're apart again. Marcie has no sense of the time it's taken, though that's at least partially the drink's fault. "I didn't –" she gasps. "I wasn't sure..."

"I know," says Jenna. "I got that. It's OK."

They pause and stare at each other for a few moments, Marcie in serious danger of becoming marooned in those sea-blue eyes. Then Jenna says, "I'd better just... The others. This week's a networking opportunity for me. I can't just vanish without saying goodnight."

"Sure," Marcie says. "I'll wait." If networking was of much interest to her, she'd be staying on campus. Her career would be in a better state, too, but what the hell.

"OK," says Jenna. "See you soon."

She makes to go, but Marcie says, "Wait."

She wants to make a gesture. Something to show her gratitude, and her appreciation. Some sign of the... well, tenderness and the... intimacy she's feeling.

There's something she's never asked another researcher. The question she's posed to all her interview subjects, in so many forms over the years, has never found its way into her publications. Unless one of the interviewees has let on, there's nobody in the field who knows about it other than her.

The time, she thinks, may have come to share it. "Jenna," she says. "Your work..."

Quickly, Jenna says, "We don't need to talk about that, Marcie. That isn't why I'm doing this."

Marcie flushes again, furious at herself. "I know, I know. For God's sake, I didn't mean *that*. I just wanted to ask... There's a story I've only got one source for, and it's one I've always been fascinated by. I've been trying to track it down for ages now. Have you... have you at any point in your data-gathering, come across any stories about Locals who travel in a large red bus?"

Jenna stares at her in shock, her face utterly aghast.

The Locals. If all the stories were true, they would be everywhere.

And in so many different forms.

"There's a whole tribe of them still, roaming free on the Arctic Continent. Eight feet tall and blue as ice – or green, I've heard both. You know something like two per cent of Arctic hikers never make it back? Those icy bastards are sacrificing them to some god of theirs up there..."

"Nah, they used to live in the canals, you hear me? Those fossae, those valles, those chasmata – they all used to be full of water, and that was where the Locals lived, great octopus things, or merpeople maybe. They like the water, is my point. Then what did the terraformers do, but go and cover a quarter of the planet in that stuff? I'm telling you, those Locals are thriving like never before..."

"They're watching over us, I really believe that. If we really believe in them and trust them, they protect us. I was crossing a road once in Curiosity, and an out-of-control haulage truck came hurtling right at me. There was no way it could have missed me, but suddenly I found myself across the street, watching it all happen, and out of the corner of my eye I caught a glimpse of blue, like lightning streaking away into the sky. The truck driver and a hitchhiker both died, but I really believe there was a Local watching out for me that day..."

"...and he comes at Christmas and he's got a beard and a shiny red suit and he's got a green face and he's got funny antennae but you can't actually tell whether they're bits of him or not, and he comes to your house at

Christmas and he gives you presents and, and, and Carla says he's just your mum or dad but your mum or dad haven't got any antennae, have they, and…"

"You sees his eyes down in the mines, like red lights flashin' in the dark. We leaves him gifts – things he can eat, like bars. Chocolate bars, iron bars, it don't matter to him. Honey, too, peanut butter – anything comes in jars. We don't feed him, he gets hungry, starts in on the mine-cars, and that won't do. They says the other Locals trapped him down there, for fear he'd get out and start eatin' up the stars…"

"Me auntie found a bunch on 'em once, lyin' up in one o' her fields. Makin' this peculiar electronic burblin' noise, they was, an' flappin' their tin mouths up an' down like lids. Seems they thought her potatoes was bloomin' hilarious, for some reason…"

Marcie's heard every story, catalogued every kind. The human-like, the robotic, the ethereal, the arachnid, the tentacled, the green.

And for every story she's heard, in some form or another, she's asked the question.

"Did you see any other kinds of machine up there?"

"But how does he *get* to your house every Christmas?"

"Is it… only cars he eats? No other vehicles?"

For years now, Marcie's been seeking corroboration for one story in particular – the only one she's never dared to catalogue. Because she only has one source for it, and that source is herself.

Towards the end of the change, shouts of alarm start to go up around the accommodation block. The night staff rouse the conference organisers, who emerge in panic from the rooms where they've been sleeping, working late or indulging in the usual extracurricular activities. It takes a while to establish what's been going on, but it quickly becomes clear that Desmond Blannik's had some terrible shock.

After fifteen minutes or so, during which the bar's unlocked and brandy's liberally applied to the eminent social scientist, it emerges that he went over to a join a student in her room during the change, after she gave him to understand that he'd be welcome there.

"And weren't you?" asks a member of the organising committee in alarm. Another leaves quickly but discreetly, to try to find the student in question. Over the years Blannik's acquired a bit of a reputation for this sort of occurrence.

"Well, she bloody well wasn't expecting me!" Blannik explodes. "She was... She'd been in the shower or something I think. She was naked..."

"Oh, Christ almighty," another committee member groans, and dashes after the one who's just left.

"But listen!" Blannik wails. "Her skin had changed colour! She was *red*, man!"

The organisers who remain exchange a baffled look. "Some kind of skin condition..." one of them begins.

"I know a skin condition when I see it!" Blannik snaps. "This woman was *red*, I tell you! Red all over. And she... she was... she was sitting... on an egg..."

The organisers find Jenna Farris' room empty, her clothes gone. The sludgy residue in the shower has a distinct skin-colour tone to it, and her bedclothes are rumpled by what does look a little like the impression of two wet feet and a giant egg. Surveillance footage shows her leaving on a night-bus with her enormous holdall, minutes after Blannik's shrieks raised the alarm. The colour resolution isn't good enough to see her skin properly.

It won't be until the afternoon of the next day, when Dr MV Thackrall's due to give her paper on "Grokking Vulthoom: The Role of Indigene Legends in Modern Cult Formation", that it will be discovered she's gone missing too.

Marcie's mummy and daddy were busy drinking coffee and talking to Fr Craig – probably one of those talks about Unifying Humanism which always ended up with someone saying something rude and having to say sorry afterwards – and the other children were playing a chasing game, so Marcie went to look at her Green Man again.

He had a funny face. It was bulbous, with big goggly eyes and a nose that was two deep grooves. Two little horns sat where a proper person's eyebrows might be. The mouth had funny sharp teeth, which two huge tusks sticking up from the jaw. This particular face had been carved as if it was peering over the top of a wall, and on either side the fingers of large, nailless hands were added as if they were gripping the top of it.

The lenslight was bright outside today, but a shadow suddenly fell across the window. It was too high up to be a person, so Marcie looked up to see what it could be.

Outside there was a Green Man, just like the one in the carving. He was peering into the window with his hands on the sill, just like Marcie's Green Man did, and the corners of his mouth beyond his tusks were curled up as if he was smiling at her. His skin was, indeed, a succulent pine-needle green.

Marcie didn't make a fuss. Her Green Man was friendly, she knew that, so it followed that this real green, toothy giant would be her friend too. But first she needed to get to him.

Her mummy and daddy were still arguing with Fr Craig, and Ms Bexley was trying to persuade the other children to stop haring around and sit down nicely for their squash and biscuits. Marcie sneaked round to the vestry and out that way, so that nobody would see her going through the big doors.

She saw the huge tall back of her Green Man disappearing through the trees. "Wait for me, Green Man!" she shouted, but all the leaves were rustling as he passed and he didn't hear her. She hurtled after him as fast as she could go, but his legs were so much longer than hers, she soon lost sight of him.

Still, he was leaving a trail through the woods, in broken twigs and branches and in the marks of his bare feet pressing into the mud. Marcie followed it, running through the wooded bowl of the crater until her legs ached and her breath came in little gasps.

Up to the wall of the crater she followed his trail, and there, over the open ground of the moor, she saw him disappearing into the ruined oxygen factory. With all her might, pushing all the energy she had into her pumping legs, stumbling and toppling on the rough ground, Marcie chased after him.

Eventually she burst through the gaping rusty hole where her Green Man had disappeared, and into a great cavernous, echoing space where corroding pipes dangled and hulks of long-abandoned machinery squatted in the gloom.

"Green Man, I'm here!" she cried, and ran around the nearest mass of collapsing tubing to the clearer area in the centre of the ruin.

And it was there, for just a few seconds before it grumbled and roared and faded away into complete nonexistence in front of her eyes, that she saw the red bus.

"Green Man!" she shouted again, but he was gone. He'd taken the bus – or rather, the bus had taken him, away from her.

When her parents found her up there, still sobbing bitterly half an hour later, everyone was far too cross with her to listen to her stories.

This time, Marcie was ready. There's no way she's letting this one get away.

When Jenna gave her that appalled stare, turned wordlessly and walked out of the ladies, she guessed the postgrad would be leaving imminently. The monorail's shut at this time of night, and Jenna doesn't have a car, so it was just a question of getting the next night-bus and loitering near the stop in town to see what she does next.

It takes her longer than Marcie thought, in fact – so long that she wonders whether she was quite wrong, whether she's lost Jenna already – but at last the young woman arrives, striding briskly onto the pavement, her bracelets jangling, that big bag slung across her shoulder.

What she does next is to get a taxi out to Camiri airport, the decidedly downmarket counterpart to the various private airfields and helipads out on the Hookwall. Marcie follows in another taxi, whose driver seems far less interested in this fact than she expected.

By four o'clock in the morning, they've touched down in Olympus.

Marcie's maxed out her credit-chip – the one she keeps for emergencies and never actually uses – first on the taxi, then on a rudimentary disguise of headscarf, dark glasses and a paperback to hide behind, then, most expensively of all, on the flight to Olympus Mons itself.

The peak of the shield volcano is twenty-four kilometres above sea-level, far higher than the viable altitude of a jet plane. A train from Camiri to the Gordii terminus, then the funicular up to the summit city, would have taken the best part of a day, and Jenna, it seems, is in something of a hurry. Marcie blanched at the price, but she shelled out for a seat on the same sub-orbital shuttle flight, taking care to sit where the younger woman wouldn't see her.

Marcie's only been to Olympus three times: once on holiday with her parents, twice since for conferences. As one of only two domed cities that survive from the pre-terraform era, still relatively untouched by the processes which brought wind and weather erosion to the lower reaches, the summit's the planet's primary tourist destination, and way beyond her usual price range.

Marcie works out quickly enough that Jenna's heading for the Arboretum, the giant park on the west side of the city that supplements the work of its oxygen plants. It makes sense, under the circumstances. The Arboretum's a popular tourist spot during the day, but at this time of night it'll be all but deserted. Just like the ruined factory on Sacrament Moor.

As she follows Jenna's distant figure along the well-worn woodchip tracks between the stands of beech and bay trees towards the Amazonis View Point, Marcie has a strong suspicion she knows what she'll find there.

The View Point is a semicircular clearing marked by redwoods which soar domewards. At this level the dome's a vertical wall, scarred in only a few places by meteorite impacts, and about nine hours ago it would have provided an astounding view of lens-set across the Amazonis Gulf. As it is, the roads and cities are still marked out with strings and clusters of lights, and the curve of the planet is quite visible against the too-bright, star-pricked sky.

The bus is parked by the picnic area. Two people are sitting next to it, drinking from a bottle of something blue that's set out with some glasses on one of the picnic-tables.

One is a woman, honey-blonde and wearing an extravagantly snug catsuit in some spangly silvery material. The other's a hugely burly man, surely a professional body-builder or something, who's naked to the waist and wearing an equally tight-fitting pair of leather trousers.

As Jenna kisses the woman on the cheek, Marcie runs out into the clearing, determined that this time nobody's going to vanish without talking to her first. When she pelts up to the bus, though, the three of them stare at her in silence and she realises that she has no idea of what to say.

Eventually the blonde woman opens the conversation. "Who the heck are you, then?" she asks.

"Iris!" says Jenna, obviously shocked by her rudeness. "It's Dr Marcie Thackrall. Don't you recognise her?"

"I see," says the woman called Iris sternly. "And what exactly is she doing here, young lady?"

"Well," Jenna says meekly, "we met at the conference. I suppose she must have followed me." She smiles hesitantly at Marcie, acknowledging the awkwardness of the situation.

"I see," Iris says again. "And why would she have done that, I wonder?"

Jenna gives Marcie an embarrassed look. "I'd better go and get out of these grubby things," she says, and lugs her holdall through the bus doors. For the first time, Marcie notices that all the windows are curtained.

That's hardly the most bizarre thing going on here, though.

Iris crosses her arms. "You've got some explaining to do, missy," she says.

"*I've* got some explaining to do?" Marcie's astonished at the effrontery of this, but Iris just keeps up her glare until she finds herself complying. "Jenna and I met at the conference, just like she said. We hit it off. When she left early, I followed her here."

"What, just because you *liked* her?"

The woman isn't buying that, clearly. Marcie decides that under the circumstances there's little point lying.

"No," she says. "I asked her about this bus. I saw it years ago. On Sacrament Moor, just above Remittance."

Iris unfolds her arms. "Ah," she says. "Yes, that would do it. My word, Ras Turkan will be furious to know he was followed by a four-year-old girl."

"I was two," Marcie says, puzzled. "But I've always remembered it. I've been trying to find anyone else who's seen it since. I could tell from how she reacted that Jenna knew more about it than just that."

*Also, I think I might be in love with her*, she doesn't add.

"Who is she really, though?" she asks, straining to see whether she can glimpse Jenna through the bus" curtains.

"Someone's a bit slow on the uptake," Iris says. "Obviously she's a Martian."

"Martian?" asks Marcie, puzzled. "I'm a Martian. Do you mean... a Local?"

"If that's what you call them, dearie. The ones who came from here in the first place. The ones who were here before you."

Marcie shakes her head. "No, there wasn't anyone. That's why I'm a folklorist, not an archaeologist. There aren't any Locals."

"Not here there aren't." Iris smiles infuriatingly.

"Not anywhere," Marcie insists. "Only us. On every planet, moon and asteroid we've visited, every body of any kind humanity's explored or sent probes to, in the solar system or elsewhere, the only life is what we've taken with us." It's such a fundamental truth she can't believe she's having to articulate it. "There are no such things as 'Martians'."

"Well, as I say – that's true *here*," Iris repeats smugly. "And that's the problem, lovey. You see, this Mars of yours is special. It's the... well, the dominant Mars. The ultimate Mars – or the first one, depending how you look at it. I'm not explaining it very well."

"You mean the platonic Mars," the huge man rumbles. His voice sounds like distant munitions going off. "Or archetypal?"

"He likes that word," Iris confides. "But no, that's not it either. This is the Mars that gets to tell the others what they can and can't be like. It's the... oh, it's on the tip of my tongue..."

"*Real*," a florid voice declaims behind her. "The word you're looking for is 'real', you hopeless ignoramus. This is the *real* Mars." A tiny black-and-white toy bear stumps out of the bus doors, on the face of it somewhat undercutting this claim.

Iris snaps her fingers. "That's it! I knew I knew it. We're all a long way from our usual stamping-ground here, Panda love. But what we're doing is important.

"You've turned your Mars into such a drab place, you see," she tells Marcie. "You've terraformed and humanised it until there's nothing left unexamined. It's all bioclines and atmospheric oxygen levels and endless conversations about soil ecology. All very practical and necessary, I'm sure, but where's the scope for speculation? All your technology's focussed on keeping yourselves comfortable and safe, and as for your fiction...

"The only books you lot set on modern Mars are about the bleak yet fulfilling lives of Helland fishermen, or bored Elysian agronomists having epiphanies and shagging farmhands. Or eminent authors on the Marineris Riviera struggling with writer's block, of course, because *those* never get old. Nobody reads the old books any more, either – why would you, when you know exactly what life on Mars is like? There's no room left here for imagination. And so..."

"So what?" asks Marcie. She's never had much interest in literature herself, academic works aside. Stories in books remind her of pinned butterflies.

"And so my world is dying," says Jenna, emerging now from the bus. "All the other Marses are."

She's removed her flesh-tone foundation, the stuff that Marcie found smudged on her suit yesterday morning, leaving her copper-red skin exposed. In fact, that's somewhat understating the case, as she's also dispensed with all her clothes. Naked except for those ornate metal arm-ornaments, her thick black hair pinned into a peculiar triple bun, she looks more magnificent than Marcie could ever have imagined.

"My name is Jenah Pharis," Jenna says, "and I am a princess of Mars."

Marcie feels it necessary to sit down heavily at one of the picnic-tables.

"You shouldn't have followed me here, Marcie," says Jenah Pharis, "but I'm glad you did. It's thanks to you my world might survive after all. I'm glad to be able to thank you for that."

At the third attempt, Marcie manages to speak. "Me? What did I do?"

"You're helping us keep the legends alive," says Iris. "Only just, mind. There's a lot more work to do. But all the while the stories you've collected of the Locals are still read and studied, the poor sods on all the other Marses get a bit more life."

"You mean..." Marcie thinks she's on the verge of working it out, but the panda creature doesn't have the patience for drawn-out revelations.

"She *means*," it sighs theatrically, "that we've been smuggling fictional Martians across into your world for ages now, so they can start the urban legends you've been studying. Jenah Pharis here –" Marcie could swear it leers at the princess "– is the latest of many. It's a brilliant scheme, though I do say so myself."

"Credit where it's due, Panda," Iris chides the tiny figure. "It was Ares' idea in the first place, remember? We just came along and pitched in. Despite having *certain misgivings* about helping him again after last time." She rolls a baleful eye at the enormous muscle-man.

"Him?" the panda scoffs. "Oh yes, leave the planning to the war-god. *His* idea of subtlety was sending armies from two entirely unrelated Martian civilisations to join a human battle. That and leaving piles of discarded war ordnance lying about the place."

"I still know how to smite, you know," the man called Ares – no, apparently the *god* Ares – grumbles.

"You mean..." Marcie says, standing up again. She quickly adds, before the panda can open its mouth, "You mean you sent the Green Man there that day to... what, inspire me? Get me interested in the legends of the Locals? I was two years old and you were *grooming* me?"

248

"She's got a point, Iris," the panda thing supplies. "It wasn't exactly fair on the child."

"She was supposed to dismiss it as a childhood daydream," Iris complains. "She wasn't supposed to see my bloody bus. Next time I see that Ras Turkan I'm giving him a piece of my mind."

"So what was Jenna all about?" Marcie finds herself furious suddenly: furious with this smug, ridiculous, mad witch and her utterly impossible friends. "What, did you think my commitment was wavering? What was she meant to be, a top-up?"

"Marcie, no!" Jenah Pharis says, distressed. "It wasn't like that at all! I had a specific mission here – to start a new story. The Oviparous Student, if you like. I followed it to the letter – I wish you could have seen Desmond Blannik's face!" She stifles a giggle. "It was never the plan for you and me to become... involved. I shouldn't have stayed in the hotel, that first night. But I wanted so much to meet you. I really do admire your work, you see."

"I see," says Marcie, coldly, then remembers what "oviparous' means. "You laid an *egg*?" she asks.

"Oh, it's not mine," the princess says, glancing back at the bus. "My sister lets me look after my nephew sometimes."

"OK," says Marcie, thinking she'll just accept that. "But now... what, you're going to vanish away, back to your own Mars? And I'm supposed to go back to *writing* about those stories? Going round asking whether anyone knows any good ones about the Locals? Always looking out for rumours of a red Martian woman, and knowing it could be you?" To her fury, she feels tears dripping down her cheeks.

Iris' voice is softer now. "You have to, Marcie love. Don't you see, Jenah Pharis' world depends on it? All of them do."

"The red Martians and the green," Ares intones. "The tripods and the octopods. The telepaths and the balls of light. The spindly men, the otters and the... froggy things. All of them are depending upon you, Martia Thackrall."

Jenah Pharis is in tears, too. "Oh, Marcie," she says, "I can't bear this." She reaches out and enfolds her in her arms, pressing Marcie's face against her terracotta breast. "I was never pretending, you know. When we kissed... that was completely real, I promise you."

"And that's all we get?" Marcie asks, her voice slightly muffled. "Now I just have to let you leave?"

"Yes," Ares says shortly.

"Yes," says Iris.

There's a long silence. Then Jenah Pharis says fiercely, "No."

Marcie looks up at her in astonishment. The Martian princess takes her hand in a tight grip, then steps away from her towards Iris. "Iris, we *owe* this woman," she says. "All of us. But you especially – you picked her out when she was two."

"Four," Iris says. "But if it wasn't her it would have been someone else." She cocks her head. "What are you getting at, your royal highness?"

"We need Marcie here," says Jenah Pharis, "in the long term. But there's no reason why she shouldn't come away with us for a bit, is there? Like it or not, she knows there's a battle now. That's bound to make a difference to how she fights. But she doesn't really know what she's fighting for.

"If she could see our other Marses – walk the red deserts beneath our orange skies, ride with our warriors on their fabulous beasts, sail our canals under the light of the silvery moons, share water with us in our gemstone cities – well, wouldn't she feel better able to defend them?"

Marcie's pulse is hammering, from tension and the sheer heady proximity of the Martian woman's flesh. Her breath won't leave her lungs as Iris considers the proposition.

"Well," the blonde woman says cautiously at last. "It's not the worst idea I've ever heard, I'll give you that."

"No," booms Panda. "That would be the time you bet Carl Sagan the Viking probe would find a face on Mars, and we had to nip to Cydonia and carve one with your nail-file."

"Yes, thank you Panda," Iris says, a little sharply. "I must say she looks like she could do with a holiday, too. You've been working too hard, Marcie love, you're positively peaky. Everybody needs a bit of rest and relaxation now and again."

"And there's the course of true love to consider," Panda says portentously. "You were always a stickler for the course of true love, Iris."

"Oh... all right then," Iris complains. "You've talked me into it. Go on then, princess, give your girlfriend the guided tour. We've still got an exotic dancer and an armoured reptile to wait for.

"No hanky-panky, mind!" she calls after them, as Jenah Pharis leads Marcie gently by the hand to the bus doors.

"I can't wait to show you my world," the princess whispers to her as they mount the steps. She pulls the doors shut gently behind them.

She still smells of patchouli oil.

# ALSO AVAILABLE

## *Wildthyme in Purple*
An Iris Wildthyme and Panda Short Story
Collection, edited by Cody Quijano-Schell and Stuart Douglas

ISBN: 9780956560551

pur·ple (pûrpl) n.

1. Any of a group of colours with a hue between that of violet and red.
2. Cloth of a colour between violet and red, formerly worn as a symbol of royalty or high office.
3. Imperial power; high rank: e.g *born to the purple*.
4. In the Roman Catholic Church, the rank or office of a cardinal or a bishop

And now 5. Those literary worlds visited by Iris Wildthyme where the prose is as sensual, convoluted and self-aggrandising as Iris herself...

*"my favorite of the Obverse Iris books so far... of a particularly high quality and consistency"*- JD Burton

*Available as hardback and ebook*

# ALSO AVAILABLE

## *The Ninnies*
A Young Adult Novel
By Paul Magrs

ISBN: 9781909031005

*Mum wouldn't believe me when I told her Dad had been taken away by the Ninnies.*

*She thought he'd left us of his own accord. She thought he'd taken his bucket, ladder and chamois leather on his window round that Monday and simply never came back because he'd gone off us. Or that he'd imagined a better life somewhere else. But I knew. I knew he'd never just up and leave us. I knew what had really happened.*

*He had been taken away by the Ninnies.*

'*If you imagine that the 'League of Gentlemen' had written an episode of the 'Sarah Jane Adventures', which had then been novelised by Roald Dahl, you might come close to capturing the atmosphere and quality of 'The Ninnies'.*'
– British Fantasy Society

### *Irish Times Top 30 Children's Novels of 2012*

*Limited Edition Hardback edition and ebook now available*

# ALSO AVAILABLE

## *Tales of the City*
A 'City of the Saved'
Collection Edited by Philip Purser-Hallard

ISBN: 9781909031012

*Beyond the end of the universe exists a city the size of a galaxy, packed with every human being that ever lived, from the first Australopithecus to the last posthuman, resurrected in a city in which nobody can die…or rather, that used to be the case.*

*"Tales from the City' may be the perfect gateway collection for anyone wanting to engage with this fictional universe but unsure where to start.'*
– Chris Limb, British Fantasy Society

*'an amazing collection of stories – not only with no duds, but nothing even "average".'*
– JD Burton, Gallifrey Base

*Available as paperback and ebook*

# ALSO AVAILABLE

## Burning with Optimism's Flames
A Faction Paradox Short Story
Collection edited by Jay Eales

ISBN: 9781909031050

*'He would clasp me around the shoulder and say that we were like stars. We had to use the energy within us to defeat the cold spaces, to turn away the dark things that dared to destroy life. We had to find our own calmness and serenity even when it was denied us.*

*I don't think I understood him then. I was too small, and my brother never spoke in the concrete terms that my brain could comprehend.*

*Looking back on it, though, I think that's when P.J. began to burn'*
— Intermediant Izzy Ring, The Heaven Facility

*'a very, very impressive collection'* – Andrew Hickey

*'a fine collection of tales with real scope and depth'* – Immaterial Blog

Featuring stories by Steven Marley, Sarah Hadley, Kelly Hale, Simon Bucher-Jones and many more!

*Available as hardback and ebook*